LETHAL LEGACY

PAULA WALSHE

FEHU PRESS

Copyright © 2024 by Paula Walshe and Fehu Press.

All rights reserved.

No part of this book may be reproduced in any form or by any electronic or mechanical means, including information storage and retrieval systems, without written permission from the author, except for the use of brief quotations in a book review.

*For the Happy Girls
And their spicy adventures.
Thankyou for your service, ladies.*

LUCIA
I've spent six years running from the Orlov bratva.
I might have left behind my real name and the Petrovsky
fortune, but my libido seems to have remained stubbornly
hardwired to Russian bad boy.
On paper, Roman Stevanovsky is the billionaire CEO of Hale
Property.
But that doesn't mean he isn't a killer in practice.

ROMAN
I know how it feels to have no choice but run.
To guard secrets that aren't mine to tell. To live with a revenge
I can never take.
I don't want to involve myself in whatever storm is chasing
Lucia.
But if the storm decides to come for her?
Well, I protect what is mine.
And I'm no storm.
*I'm the f***ing apocalypse.*

OTHER BOOKS BY THE SAME AUTHOR

Under the name Lucy Holden:
Paranormal Romance
The Nightgarden Saga:
Red Magnolia
Moonvine

Poison Berry
Bayou Rose
Dusky Dahlia
Blue Lilies
Night Shade
Fleur de Lis
A Sip of Sangre
Seam of Gold

Read a free prequel at www.lucyholden.com

Fantasy Romance
Woven in Darkness

<u>Under the name Paula Constant:</u>
Historical Fiction
The Visigoths of Spain
The Saharan Queen (free on Amazon)
The Votive Crown
The King's Coin
Spania

Travel Memoir
Slow Journey South
Sahara

Sign up to receive more free books and updates at www. fehupress.com.

LUCIA

"Stevanovsky at twelve o'clock."

Abby tilts her chin at the café door and gives me a sly wink. "And he looks pissed."

"So what else is new?" I bury my head in the coffee machine to avoid looking at the door. Roman Stevanovsky is the kind of danger I've spent the last six years running from. He's also been the object of my every fantasy from the moment Hale Property moved into their gleaming offices across the street.

I might have left my bratva upbringing back in Miami, along with my real name and the Petrovsky fortune, but my libido seems to have remained stubbornly hardwired to Russian bad boy.

"I don't know why he doesn't just send a minion for his coffee." Abby puts her tray down with an audible crash. "Going by the size of the Hale building, he can definitely afford to. Although I guess if he did, he'd miss his daily dose of 'let's make Lucia the hot barista blush,' which is clearly his favorite game."

I shoot her a warning look, but she just grins.

"I say you slip him your number with his coffee, Luce. Then he can slip you his—"

"Shut *up*." I try not to look at the powerful thighs moving into place right in front of me. Unfortunately that leaves me staring at a chest and shoulders that are definitely too hard to belong inside a suit, even an elegantly handmade one. At least he's got his suit jacket on today.

Small mercies.

I raise my eyes, bracing myself for the daily gut punch of desire.

"Café Americano." He growls the same black coffee order every day, usually while still speaking into his phone.

No *please*.

Just the order.

"*No pasa nada.*" Telling him it's no problem is a lie.

Roman Stevanovsky *is* a problem.

A six-foot, five-inch problem made of corded muscle, sinfully chiseled lips, and dark hawkish eyes that are currently watching me with a definite shit-stirring spark in them.

And how the fuck can a coffee order send a ripple of desire straight from my ears to my groin?

I adjust the dials slightly on the machine to avoid looking at him. Discovering the exact temperature at which he prefers his coffee was a big win in our daily battle of wills, as was setting the machine to a strength he can't fault.

He leans against the counter, hands slung casually in his pockets, watching my every move. Despite the bubble of tourist chatter in the café, or perhaps because of it, his silence seems pointedly obvious.

He never takes his coffee at one of the small round tables by the window.

He always stands at the counter to drink it—just inches from my station at the coffee machine.

That much hotness should be illegal.

Especially around twenty-seven-year-old women who haven't, as Abby kindly enjoys pointing out, been laid in . . . well, *so* long.

He takes his coffee in a slender glass, as is customary here in southern Spain. I put the glass on a small saucer and push it across the counter.

"*Gracias.*" Midnight eyes meet mine, as unreadable as ever, set into an unsmiling face I imagine strikes terror into his minions, but has quite the opposite effect on me. His strong fingers around the glass are almost as disturbing. His knuckles are scarred, like a boxer's. Given how brutally he deals with his poor subordinates, I can only imagine the damage he does to a punching bag.

That thought leads in dangerous directions.

CEO Man bare chested in the ring, dripping with sweat . . .

I realize he's still staring at me, awaiting a response to his *gracias.*

"*De nada.*" My voice is slightly husky, but at least I don't stammer. And so far, he hasn't made me blush, which is how I measure who wins and loses each of these little encounters.

I blush, he wins.

I surprise him, I win.

So far we're running about even.

I stick my head back in the coffee machine and focus on not flushing. It's ridiculous, the effect Roman has on me. Going by the dark salon car that whisks him to and from the glass-plated office building opposite, not to mention the minions usually running after him, he's definitely the boss at Hale Property. But I know he's a lot more than that, even if

I've never seen the star tattoos on his shoulders. I looked up Roman Stevanovsky the first day I heard him bark orders in Russian. Intriguingly, he's buried his trail almost as effectively as I have mine.

On paper, Roman Stevanovsky is CEO of Hale, a property development company with varied investments.

But that doesn't mean he isn't a killer in practice.

I don't need to see the ink under his shirt, or touch the gun under his jacket, to know he has *bratva* written all over every muscled inch of his body.

Roman Stevanovsky might use the facade of a boardroom, but I'd lay every one of his lavish tips that his real work involves blood and steel.

Which is probably why I can't take my eyes off him.

Roman's phone vibrates on the counter. He picks it up, scowling with annoyance.

"*Da*," he barks.

He catches my eye and points at his coffee, not pausing for a moment in his constant stream of abuse at some poor soul who hasn't, I gather, delivered the furniture for his new apartment on time. I stand in front of him with a jug of hot milk in one hand, hot water in the other, eyebrows raised in question. He frowns and shakes his head, then nods at the sugar bowl, which is only inches out of his reach.

I don't bother to hide my eye roll. Without moving either foot I stretch sideways, pick the sugar up with exaggerated care, and place it directly in front of him. Then I fold my arms and raise my eyebrows again.

Anything else I can do for you, my lord and master?

Holding my eyes, ridiculously perfect lips curled in an insolent grin that makes me want to simultaneously throw him through a window and onto the floor naked, Roman slowly drips a teaspoon of sugar into his glass.

Well, asshole, you haven't made me blush yet, so the game is anyone's.

I think he worked out early that the longer he stares, the more inclined I am to blush. It's gotten worse since the weather warmed up.

Revolting Pete, as Abby and I call our sleaze of a boss, changed our uniform to shorts that barely cover our butts and white T-shirts cut so low that I spend half the day scared I'll show up on an Instagram post for #freethenipple.

Pointedly ignoring the midnight eyes watching my every move, I turn back to making the terrible milky tea that English tourists insist on drinking despite the brilliant Mediterranean sun blazing down on the pavement outside the café. Malaga is full of Brits at any time of year. Right now, in the weeks leading up to Easter, or Holy Week as the Spanish call it, they're everywhere. Our café stocks newspapers in multiple languages and is a favorite among the expat community.

Roman pulls a Russian newspaper across the counter and glances through the pages as he talks.

He finds the completed crossword and frowns at me. I suppress my smile.

One of my finer moves in our little war is to complete the crossword in his favorite Russian newspaper every morning before he arrives, just to piss him off.

Roman Stevanovsky might be hot enough to melt tarmac, but he's also a grade A asshole. And not even a subtle one.

Hell is what he creates, and as Abby enjoys pointing out, he's as seductive and dangerous as the devil that rules it.

In the five months since he's been coming in, I've watched him reduce several assistants and at least two grown men to tears. I've seen at least half a dozen semifamous models throw everything from drinks to diamond necklaces at him. And not once have I seen any of it make even the slightest dent in his impeccably handmade, far too well-fitting suit.

You'd think that a lifetime of danger, not to mention six years of running from the Orlov bratva, would be enough to make me run the first time I heard Roman bark *da* into his phone.

The fact that I'm still here in Malaga, Spain, serving coffee every day to a man who is clearly from the same world I've run halfway around the globe to escape, is the kind of issue that could pay a psychologist's mortgage.

One last *da* barked down his phone, and he's done with what I imagine is his first savaging of the day. Which means that it's time to go to battle with me instead.

"Miss Lopez."

"Mr. Stevanovsky."

I wait to see which language he will decide to throw at me. It's another part of our daily game. So far he's tried French, Spanish, German, Russian, and English. He still hasn't worked out which one is my native tongue.

Nor will he. Keeping my accent neutral is key to maintaining my identity as Lucia Lopez. So is choosing to live in a city renowned for being run by various clans of Russian bratva.

Hiding in plain sight is a real thing.

"Would I be presuming too much," he says, using the upper-crust English accent that is my personal favorite in his arsenal and that also, to be honest, completely undoes me every time, "if I asked for some water to accompany my coffee?"

"Well," I say lightly, as if I'm considering it, "you can ask."

"Ah." The insolent smile grows slightly. "Then I'm asking."

"Now would that be a cold glass of water? A room temperature one? Or would you prefer lukewarm? Oh, wait." I look skyward. "Is it an actual bottle you require? And if so, would you like that cold, at room temperature, or . . ." I turn a questioning hand upward with an innocent look.

"Surprise me." The sardonic twist of his mouth is disturbing. "Although I would prefer to take it without the added flavor of snark that's on offer."

I reach into the fridge for a bottle of Novoterskaya still water. I began stocking it after I overheard Roman complaining loudly to his assistant that he didn't understand what, exactly, was so difficult about obtaining that particular brand. It took me several long hours on the phone, heated arguments with various suppliers, and a decent bribe to a Madrid truck driver, but the following day, I served Roman a bottle of Novoterskaya with his coffee.

Slightly chilled, just as he had reduced his assistant to a quivering wreck for failing to anticipate.

His face that day was one of my most satisfying victories in our little war.

He picks up the bottle and puts down his coffee glass. "Next time," he says in that low growl that does dangerous things to my entire body, "make sure the sugar is close by."

"Next time," I retort, "go to any other of the thousand cafés in Malaga. Like I've been telling you to do from the day you walked in."

"And miss running the gauntlet of discovering whether my coffee has been laced with acid? Never."

He leans across the counter, his dark eyes pinning me in place.

"A life without danger," he says in a low growl that sends lethal heat licking through my body, "is like sex without passion: not really worth having. Wouldn't you agree, Miss Lopez?"

He stares just long enough to see the flush I've been fighting all morning rise up my neck.

Then he strides out.

Not, however, before I've seen the satisfied smirk on his stupidly perfect face.

Game, Stevanovsky.

THE CAFÉ REMAINS busy all day. The retail shops around us close for siesta between one and five in the afternoon, but restaurants in Spain never stop. Abby and I run nonstop until the late-afternoon pause between the lunch and tapas crowds.

I wasn't raised to work like this. I wasn't raised to work at all.

Darya Petrovsky grew up in a Miami compound. She attended boarding schools in France and England, and later, finishing school in Switzerland.

Yes, finishing schools still exist. These days they just tend to be stocked with the daughters of oligarchs, cartels, and oil sheikhs, rather than with royalty.

Darya Petrovsky was raised to sit in beautiful rooms and wear beautiful dresses, all in preparation for the time when I would give birth to beautiful children.

Boys, preferably. Bratva men need sons to wield the guns that run our world.

Sons are raised to manage crews of *vor*, the warriors who enforce the hard rules of that world.

Daughters are an afterthought. Cherished, certainly. But incapable of running anything more serious than a dinner party.

Gender equality hasn't really penetrated the hard world of Russian men in general, let alone the bratva clans who run the world of organized crime.

The Petrovsky bratva clan once ran the largest, most powerful organized crime network in Miami. And Miami is a city that knows crime.

Now the Orlov clan live in my family compound. My brother Alexei is their hostage. The Orlovs killed my mother, and they'd dearly love to kill my father. Not to mention me.

They just have to find us first.

I take a quick break and look at my phone. It has four missed calls, all from Papa's carer. The familiar dread steals through my heart.

It's been eight years since my father's first stroke, and six since I ran from Miami in the middle of the night with nothing more than a lone bag and an old man in a wheelchair. Part of me never thought either of us would live this long. But expecting death doesn't lessen my fear of it.

Particularly his.

Sergei Petrovsky was once a giant of a man. To me, he still is.

I stop Abby as she passes. "Can you cover for me until seven?"

"Is it Juan?" She shoots me a sympathetic look.

I nod. I don't tell anyone Papa's real name, or even that he is my father. Here, he's simply Juan Ortega, a fellow illegal immigrant whom I befriended on my way to Spain.

"He's so lucky to have you." Abby squeezes my hand. "Of course I can cover for you. Revolting Pete won't be in until nine. So long as you're back by then, it should be fine." She gets a rather fierce look on her face. "And I'm going to tackle him about these *fucking* uniforms again. If I get slapped on the ass one more time by a drunk tourist, I won't be held account-able for what I might do."

"Good luck with that." I roll my eyes. "Pete tried to tell me last week that these uniforms are the reason we make so many tips. I pointed out that if he paid us properly, we wouldn't need them."

"Let me guess. He told you that you're an illegal immi-grant, so if you don't like his rate of pay, you can take your chances lining up for the fruit-picking trucks every morning?"

"Spot on."

Abby sighs. "He's *such* a douche." She turns me around so we both face the mirror lining the back of the bar, resting her chin on my shoulder. Her blonde hair clings to my black plait, her round blue eyes a direct contrast to my sloping almond ones. Abby is an Australian who bought a ticket to England five years ago and hasn't stopped traveling since. We bonded over fifteen-hour days and sore feet. Now I can't imagine my life without her.

Among the many things we share is a history of associating with bad boys.

But those I grew up with were mainly good men, who did bad things when necessary.

Abby's men tend to do unnecessarily bad things to her.

She came to Spain on the promise of a social media influencer who swore he'd marry her so she could have a visa. He didn't deliver, and now Abs has been here illegally for over a year. Lately she's been dating an equally sleazy footballer who, in my opinion at least, cares far more about his own paparazzi shots than he does about Abby.

"It's a good thing we're such hotties." She kisses my cheek. "Imagine the terrible jobs we'd have to do if we weren't." We laugh at that, which is all you can do, really, when a slimeball like Revolting Pete holds your fate in his hands. Despite Pete's chronic neglect, or maybe because of it, the café does make seriously good tips. Especially since Hale moved in over the street, despite my ongoing war with its incredibly arrogant CEO. Hale turns over so many billions every year that I'm surprised CEO Man doesn't take his coffee gold-plated.

Since Pete has a terrible reputation for mistreating his staff, Abby and I have as many shifts as we can take. And we take every single one.

Abby is living high while saving for her next adventure. I'm paying for Papa's care while saving for new fake passports.

Soul sisters with different histories.

"Luce!" One of the chefs sticks his head through the window, loading a pile of food-delivery cartons on the ledge. "Can you take this order to the Stevanovsky place when you go? It's on your way."

I inwardly groan, but I can hardly say no when Abby is covering for me. I take the address and load myself up with the boxes of food, which tower over my head, blocking my vision.

I swear that evil, sexy bastard did this to me on purpose.

"Just be careful." Abby frowns out the window. "Some pap photographer who keeps following Miguel and me is standing on the other side of the road. Don't give him any quotes, okay? That prick has been trying to get my photo all week."

"No chance." The boxes hide my face completely anyway. There's a certain irony in Abby worrying about me providing a quote. I'm literally the last person who will ever cultivate publicity.

Fortunately, I don't notice anyone when I walk out of the café. I stagger through the streets to the beachfront address, a grand historic building with a soaring dome. It used to be crumbling stone and faded grandeur, a beautiful remnant of Spain's ancient history lost amid the newer developments. According to a gushing lifestyle article in one of the expat papers, Roman bought the entire thing for an eye-watering price when it was about to be turned into a tourist hotel. He gutted it, then rebuilt it to his specifications, while restoring the original architecture.

I'm not proud of the fact that I read the entire article.

Several times.

Roman Stevanovsky has begun to take up a dangerous amount of my headspace over the past few months.

Going by the fresh paint in the lobby, and the flustered-looking doorman who lets me into the private elevator, he's only just moved in. I'm a little surprised at the lack of security. Roman Stevanovsky strikes me as a man who'd protect his home with a veritable arsenal.

Then again, one glare from those eyes is probably more than enough to make his enemies burst into flames.

That thought leads to a vision of him barking orders at his minions, which in turn leads to him barking far dirtier orders at me.

Bend over the desk, Miss Lopez.

Spread your legs, Miss Lopez.

I'm going to fuck you now, Miss Lopez . . .

The elevator slides to a stop before I can slide too dangerously into fantasy land. My mind has a seemingly endless capacity to envisage the different ways Roman Stevanovsky might choose to savage my body.

Bracing myself for a scathing put-down about the grease stains on my T-shirt or the tardiness of my delivery, I'm relieved when I step out of the elevator and hear no signs of life. It seems that CEO Man and whatever army he's feeding are yet to arrive.

I stack the food cartons in the gleaming kitchen and pad down a dim marble corridor that is clearly made for Louboutins rather than my ratty trainers. It opens into a vast living room with a domed ceiling, beneath which stands a long formal dining table. Plate glass windows look out over the sea on one side and the ancient part of the city on the other. A fully stocked bar lines one wall, beneath hanging lights. At the other end, rich leather couches surround a low carved table, upon which sits an ornate Russian samovar.

It's been so long since I've seen a samovar, especially one that is clearly used. The musky scent of the boxed tea beside it is achingly familiar, twisting my heart with memories of the life I've lost.

Despite the penthouse's undeniable opulence, it looks like nobody has so much as sat on any of the furniture. The restoration is stunning, though. A seamless blend of the ancient and modern. I can just imagine Roman standing up here like an emperor of old, surveying his empire and planning what he will conquer next. I close my eyes and savor both the silence and the nostalgic scent of Russian tea. It mixes with something newer, a crisp, smoky scent that is both familiar and oddly disturbing.

Oh, fuck.

It's the smell of hellfire.

"What are you doing here?" There's nothing lighthearted about Roman Stevanovsky's snarl, or his lethal bulk filling the entrance to the corridor.

Clearly whatever game we normally play doesn't apply in his inner sanctum.

"I delivered your food."

I wince. I sound as pathetic as Baby from *Dirty Dancing*: "*I carried a watermelon . . .*"

"I told my assistant to deliver it herself." He steps barefooted into the living room. His dark hair is tousled, the top of his starched shirt unbuttoned, sleeves rolled to the forearms. Having clearly just woken up from siesta, his appearance is a highly dangerous cross between angry bear and serious thirst trap.

By the look on his face, yet another Hale assistant is clearly about to be fired, if not actually shot, for mistakenly sending me instead of bringing his food herself. And it looks a bit like he might take me out when he's done with her.

"I was told to bring your food. I brought it." I'm surprised my voice is still functional. I try not to stare at the corded forearms or narrow V of bare chest. Both are going to be keeping me up tonight. "Now I'm leaving."

I head toward the elevator doors, which unfortunately means I have to pass right by him.

"Not so fast." One muscled arm shoots out, blocking my path. There's no trace of his customary *Miss Lopez* or his twisted smile.

Roman Stevanovsky isn't just pissed.

He's dangerous.

That should terrify me.

Unfortunately, danger is kind of my body's default setting.

Heat burns straight through the thin material of my T-shirt and directly down my shorts. I fight the urge to touch the taut muscle blocking my way.

Not to mention the urge to touch myself.

"Nobody comes into this apartment without a security check." Roman's curt voice sends a second wave of thrill through me. "Give me your ID and phone number."

Oh, shit.

The thrill halts instantly.

Just like that, I'm back to reality.

Don't forget who you are. Or where you are. Be smart, Darya Petrovsky.

"I don't make a habit of carrying my passport around." It sounds plausible enough. "Besides, you have the café's number. You don't need mine."

He rubs an impatient hand over his half-day stubble. "I don't have time for this."

So much for being smart. My logical brain always seems to short-circuit when CEO Man is anywhere nearby.

And right now, he's close. *Very* close.

Oh, that stubble scraping up the soft skin of my inner thighs . . .

I'm clearly deeply disturbed.

. . . Not to mention what that lethal tongue would do when he reached the tops of them.

He thrusts his hands into his pockets, pinning me with an arctic stare. "This is my home. And I don't appreciate you invading my privacy without prior warning."

The sexy stubble fantasy gives way to a decent dose of indignation.

"Invading your privacy?"

I just carried a mountain of food through the heat for you, asshole.

"Whatever mistakes your assistant made aren't my problem. Your doorman let me in without question."

He's still giving me the Stevanovsky death stare, and my indignation swells into anger.

I'm not one of your Hale minions, to have my ass handed to me at your convenience.

"I had no idea you were here," I say frostily, "let alone that delivering food that *you* ordered would be considered *invading your privacy.* But now that I do know, it certainly won't happen again."

Ever. Like, until hell freezes over.

Roman's jaw is hard as a razor's edge. "Your phone number, Miss Lopez."

I fold my arms angrily and rattle off Abby's digits, which I know by heart. He punches them into the keypad, then hits the call button.

Of course he's going to check it.

Bugger, as Abby would say. She doesn't answer, of course, since she's probably knee-deep in customers. But before Roman can start tearing into me for lying, his phone vibrates with a text message. He holds it up so I can see the screen.

Da fuck is this?

The text message is a fine example of Abby's native Australian diplomacy.

Rather absurdly, given the seriousness of the situation, my lips twitch with the urge to laugh. But not at CEO Man. He can go straight back to whatever hell he came from.

"Shall we try this again, Miss Lopez?" Roman says dryly.

Reluctantly, I give him the right number. He hits the buttons, and my phone vibrates in my hip pocket. I pointedly ignore it.

"Are we done here?"

"Except for your tip." His insolent smile is back.

I ignore that, too. Or at least my brain does.

My body is ready to lie down on the vast dining table and invite CEO Man to eat whichever part of me he likes.

"Keep it." I march into the elevator with as much dignity as my arousal, not to mention my grease-stained clothes, will allow.

I wish I could say that I'm done taking either his tips or his shit.

But the truth is, Roman Stevanovsky had me hooked from day one. And whatever I might like to tell myself, five months of enduring his savage asides have only made me more addicted than ever.

2

LUCIA

A half-hour hike up narrow alleyways, followed by three flights of stairs, do little to improve either my mood or my aching feet. The stairs are a bitch, but our Moroccan carer's family lives in the apartment below us, which is convenient for both her and us. There's also a small terracotta-tiled terrace outside that catches the sun and offers a glimpse of the Mediterranean Sea. It's a nice place for Papa to sit, even if it's a far cry from the fountains and courtyards of my childhood.

To my relief, Mariam is smiling when she opens the door. A smile means that Papa isn't dead or in the hospital.

She bursts into a torrent of heavily Arabic-accented French, from which I discern that although Papa is sleeping now, he's been very agitated all afternoon. Mariam can't make out why.

"It started after our walk," she explains. "But he speaks in the Russian, and I don't understand." Like all our acquaintances, Mariam believes Papa to be my friend rather than my father.

"That's fine. I'll find out what it is when he wakes up." I hug her, and despite my protestations, she insists on feeding me a plate of the heavenly tagine sitting in a conical terracotta pot on the stovetop. One of the best parts of having Mariam care for Papa, other than her truly gorgeous heart, is her utterly amazing cooking.

"You are too thin," she says, eyeing me critically. "You are working too much. How do you ever sleep?"

With one eye open, most of the time.

"That's why I'm so lucky to have you." I smile at her, but instead of returning it, she glances sideways, chewing her lip nervously.

Oh, shit.

"What's going on, Mariam? Is there something you need to tell me?"

Please don't say it, please don't say it . . .

"My son got an engineering job in Madrid. We will be moving next month."

Yep. She said it.

I plaster a smile on my face like I mean it. "That's wonderful news, Mariam. You must be so proud."

I'm genuinely happy for her. From a selfish perspective, however, it's a massive crisis.

It took me six months to find this apartment, and Mariam. The thought of trying to manage Papa alone for that long again, plus working fifteen hours minimum a day, seven days a week, is daunting, to say the least.

"You don't worry," she says, covering my hand with her own hennaed one. "I will help you find someone."

But they won't live downstairs, nor will they be Mariam.

I smile and tell her not to worry at all, but the truth is, I'm exhausted even thinking about returning to the merry-go-round of agencies and temporary staff.

After she leaves I enter the plain, whitewashed bedroom where Papa's long frame is stretched out under the covers. Despite his age and frailty, there's still a certain breadth to his shoulders, a nobility in his long nose and deep-set eyes, that is a reminder of the feared *pakhan* he once was. Founder and boss of the mighty Petrovsky clan—until Vilnus Orlov, a man Papa considered an ally, staged a coup while Papa was lying in a hospital bed recovering from his first stroke.

Vilnus would have killed Papa the same day. Along with my brother Alexei, my mother Maria, and me. Except for one problem: he couldn't access the vault beneath our Miami compound.

The vault is the reason the Orlovs came for our family in the first place. And without its contents, Vilnus will never truly rule my father's empire, no matter if he now calls the Petrovsky interests his.

Vilnus spent four years torturing my parents, my brother, and me, in his bid to open the vault. When his efforts managed to actually kill our mother, Alexei and I knew we had to get Papa out.

In the end, though, it was only Papa and I who managed to escape.

I feel the familiar pang of guilt. It kills me every day that my little brother is still trapped with the Orlovs. I would happily have stood between Alexei and those bastards until my last breath. Papa had certainly intended to do just that. But he was sick, Alexei was barely sixteen—and neither of them would even consider running without me.

In the end it was only my fear of what the Orlovs would do to Papa that convinced me to leave Alexei behind.

Not a day goes by that I don't question that decision.

Papa stirs on the bed. I sit on the mattress beside him,

covering his hand with my own. His pale blue eyes flicker open. His hand grips mine suddenly, with surprising strength.

"I'm here, Papa," I whisper in Russian. "It's okay. I'm safe."

But his hand grips mine even harder, with an urgency that makes me raise my head and frown as he tries to mouth a word. He shakes his head angrily as I try one, then two, suggestions. Finally, with an effort that strains his entire body, he gets the word out.

"*Ko-rob-ka*," he says.

Box.

I freeze, my heart slowing to a dull thud. I go to the cupboard where I keep the lockbox containing our money and fake passports.

It's gone.

I slump to the floor, my head in my hands.

Nothing else is missing, but then again, there's nothing else in the tiny apartment worth taking.

Any opportunist would have taken the lockbox.

I can't be sure that the thief was the Orlovs.

And you can't be sure that it wasn't.

Either way, we certainly can't stay here.

But we can't run, either, no matter how much I know we should.

I barely have enough cash in my bag to pay for a room for the night. I think of the tip I told Roman to keep and actually laugh, a choked, strangled sound that I immediately stifle so Papa won't hear.

What I really need is the kind of power CEO Man represents, the hellfire needed to regain the world that was stolen from my family. But I'm about as close to possessing either power or hellfire as I am of making my crazy fantasies about Roman himself come true.

It takes another two hours for me to gather our few possessions, get Papa and his wheelchair down the three flights of stairs, and check in to a cheap motel down the hill. I leave a note for Mariam, wishing her luck. I can't ask her to come with us. I won't put her in that kind of danger.

I get Papa settled as comfortably as is possible, given his wounds, and buy some soup, which he insists on feeding to himself.

Then I kiss his forehead and go back to work.

If we plan to eat tomorrow, I don't have a choice.

BY THE TIME I finally stack the last of the chairs on the tables, it's after two a.m.

I'm exhausted in a way that goes beyond the physical. I've spent all night with a knife slipped under the register, scanning every face that walks in. Anyone could have been watching where I took Papa, even though I made the taxi double back a dozen times, costing me even more money I can't afford. For all I know, right now, Orlov men could be torturing my father.

As if in response to my thoughts, the sparrow tattoo on my upper left shoulder tingles as if it was a real bird.

Suddenly I'm back in Miami, strapped face down on a table, my skin bare under the tattooist's needle.

"Do you know what happens to little Russian blyats who think they can fly away? Do you?"

Vilnus's scarred, brutal face is only inches from mine. He hits my cheek, hard, with his open palm. "They have their wings cut off."

"Leave her alone!" Fifteen-year-old Alexei struggles with his bonds in the chair opposite, his eyes glowing with rage despite the blood running down his face.

"Tell me how to get into the vault and I will."

"He doesn't know," I gasp, trying to breathe through the dual pain on my face and back. "If we knew, we'd tell you."

"*Pizdozh!* Don't lie to me."

Alexei strains against his bonds. "She doesn't know. I don't know. None of us do. How many times do we need to say it?"

Crack! A fist smashes into Alexei's nose.

"No!" I scream. "Don't hurt him, please. It's true. We don't know how to open the vault."

"Then we should just kill you all now and blow the damn thing up." Vilnus fingers the long blade that is his favorite tool of torture.

"You can't." This comes from a man I assume must be another Orlov. He's an older man, his forearm inked with the tattoo of a rose entwined in barbed wire that signifies a long time spent in a Russian prison. He rarely comes to the compound, but when he does, he terrifies me.

"Their fingerprints are part of the vault's security system, that much we do know." His eyes are as cold and dead as if he were already a corpse.

"Fingerprints can be copied." The tip of Vilnus's blade presses into my back, right above where the tattooist is working. I know what the needle is marking me with: the red sparrow of the Orlovs. All his men carry that tattoo on their hands, the mark that warns them against either speaking to outsiders or, more specifically in my case, of ever trying to leave.

"And we can't ever be sure a copy will work," snaps the older man. "What we need is the man who built that vault, but you've already killed him, Vilnus, haven't you? So now we have to find someone who knows what he does."

"Or"—Vilnus drags the knife down my back in two short, brutal strokes that makes me scream and Alexei struggle in vain against his ropes—"we cause enough pain for these two spoiled little brats to start talking. Until then . . ." He draws the knife across my skin again, this time horizontally. ". . . let this serve as a reminder: if you *try to run away again, little sparrow, I will find you. And then, fingerprints or not, I will kill you."*

I REACH OVER MY SHOULDER, touching the raised scars still there. Vilnus drew the knife deep enough down my back that the tattooist worked around the wounds while they were still bleeding.

A red sparrow, with its wings and head cut off by the scars Vilnus made.

When we escaped six years ago, the first thing I did after we'd reached the relative safety of Argentina was get ink over those scars. Now they are drawn over to look like a cage with an open door.

Because Vilnus's little sparrow did fly away, despite his threats. And I'm never going back.

Not alive, at least.

I RETURN to the motel after my shift, bone achingly tired and terrified of what I might find when I open the door. I'm almost catatonic with relief to find Papa awake, sitting stiffly upright in a motel chair. His gnarled old fingers grip the kitchen knife I took from the flat when we left.

My heart cracks a little more.

Papa should be safe in his own bed, with an army of servants looking after him, not trying to protect himself from possible killers.

"Papa." I ease the knife from his hand, speaking in soft Russian. "You should be sleeping."

He tugs gently at my hand.

"Docha," he says, more clearly than I've heard him speak in

weeks. Touched, I fold down to rest at his feet. Papa isn't given to endearments. And it's been a long time since he's called me *docha*, which is a little like "sweet daughter" in English.

He puts a hand on my head, and for a moment I savor it, the touch that for my earlier life meant safety and security.

Until it didn't.

"*Docha*—shouldn't—work," Papa says, laboring over the words.

"I'm okay, Papa." I squeeze his hand. "I'm happy to work."

"Petrovsky." He thumps the side of his chair as he says the word, a dangerous spark in the pale, washed-out eyes.

Danger. The life force of our family.

He thumps the chair again. "Petrovsky—work—enough."

My heart twists so hard it hurts. I know what he means.

Sergei Petrovsky is almost ninety years old. He has worked from the time he was born in a Russian gulag until his first stroke at eighty-four. Along the way he's lost two wives to violence and hardship, and all but two of his children. Through it all, never once did my father lose faith.

And never once did he stop working.

He worked tirelessly his entire life, to ensure that the next generation of Petrovskys wouldn't have to.

Yet now he's here, the strongest man I know stuck in a squalid hotel I can barely afford, being babysat by illegal workers I have to bribe. We have hardly enough money to buy breakfast, let alone new identities.

In all the six years I have been running, this moment feels pretty close to being the lowest.

Roman Stevanovsky's words pop unexpectedly into my mind, even though this morning seems like a lifetime ago: "*A life without danger is like sex without passion—not really worth having. Wouldn't you agree, Miss Lopez?*"

In some strange way, those words give me comfort.

Danger is lifeblood.

It keeps me alive, and Papa alert.

The life that was stolen from us still exists out there. I have to believe that everything we are enduring now is just another step on the way to building it back.

"Papa." I cover his hands with my own, speaking in the Russian of my childhood. "Do you remember what you used to tell me, when I asked you to let us see inside the vault?"

He shakes his head impatiently, but I go on anyway. "You always said the same words: *that is a story for another day, myshka.* Then you would tell me that loyalty, honor, and integrity are treasures far greater than any behind that locked door. You said that a future built on those qualities cannot be bought or inherited, only earned. Well—now is my time, and Alexei's time, to earn our own futures." I grip his hands, and he tightens his own around them, his eyes boring fiercely into mine.

"But I promise you this, Papa: one day, Alexei and I will take back everything Vilnus stole from us.

"All of it.

"And on the day we open that vault, we will have earned the right to call ourselves Petrovskys again. We will have earned the right to call ourselves Sergei Petrovsky's children."

3

LUCIA

At 7:30 the next morning, I'm woken by a text from Roman Stevanovsky.

You're late, Miss Lopez. Coffee. In my office. As soon as you arrive.

I stare at my phone in astonishment.

You have got to be fucking kidding me.

My uniform is still damp, and there's no time to braid my hair. Even at a run, it's almost nine a.m. by the time I've ridden the elevator to the top floor of Hale Corp, where a tearstained assistant is clearing out her desk. Before I've finished explaining why I'm here, the intercom on her desk buzzes.

"Send her in," Roman barks.

Balancing the tray precariously on one hand, I open the heavy door and step into an office big enough to rival his penthouse. Roman Stevanovsky is standing by the plate glass windows with his back to me, hands thrust deep into his pockets, which makes it almost impossible for me not to look at his entirely too perfect ass. I can smell the faint hint of citrus and leather that always clings to him, fresh and somehow smoky.

Hellfire.

"You left without a tip when you delivered my food yesterday."

Oh, that voice. Low, gravelly, and enough to make my body go from exhausted to quivering arousal in all of six words.

"I understand the issue with delivery was my assistant's error, not yours," he continues. "There's an envelope on the desk with your name on it. Hopefully the amount inside is enough to ensure my coffee remains arsenic free."

I'm so stunned I almost drop the tray.

Roman Stevanovsky, apologizing?

Either hell really has frozen over or I'm still asleep and this is just a fever dream. Both possibilities seem far more likely than the current scenario.

I put the tray down and stare at the indecently thick envelope, my name scrawled across it in a bold hand that could only belong to him.

"I would have given it to you in person at the café." His voice is coming closer, the sardonic edge to it signaling the end of his apology and the beginning of his daily bid to disturb my body's peace. "But it appears you have yet to master the alarm app on your phone. You're slipping, Miss Lopez."

Oh, game on, CEO Man.

Or it would be. Except that the word *slipping* combines dangerously with the fact that I'm currently bent over his desk. Not to mention the fact that my shorts have ridden up the crack of my ass during my tray-carrying journey, which means I am at present treating him to an eyeful of bared butt cheek.

A treacherous rush of heat between my legs tells me he's just won the first point.

Hastily I straighten up, willing my nipples to stop their determined swelling beneath the damp sheath of my T-shirt.

I turn to find him regarding me with politely raised eyebrows and an insolent smile that suggests he knows exactly what I was just thinking.

The smile lasts about as long as it takes for him to notice my disheveled appearance.

Then his eyes narrow, and all trace of amusement disappears from his face.

"Well, well, Miss Lopez." His eyes travel slowly over my body, from the messy topknot to the damp shirt clinging to me like a second skin. "Clearly I interrupted more than just your sleep this morning."

Wait. I struggle to wrestle my overstimulated body into submission and kick my caffeine-deprived mind into action. *Is he trying to imply what I think he is?*

His next words remove any doubt. "Doing the walk of shame, more than an hour late, in yesterday's uniform?" His light tone is completely at odds with the dangerous gleam in his eyes. "Your employer is clearly more tolerant than I am, Miss Lopez."

I stare at him in astonishment. I don't know whether to laugh, slap him like some maiden out of an eighteenth-century novel, or put my head in my hands in despair. In the end, all I manage is a strangled "Seriously?"

"Your personal life really isn't any of my concern."

There's no trace of snark, no insolent smile.

Just curt dismissal.

He picks up the envelope from the desk. "I think we're done here."

Oh no we're not, CEO Man. Not even close.

Not least because I have a sneaking suspicion that if I take that envelope and walk out right now, it will be the last time I ever see Roman Stevanovsky. And despite yesterday's exchange, and the fact that he is currently being a world-class asshole, that thought fills me with a strange sense of loneliness.

Maybe it's the stolen lockbox. Maybe I'm just so overtired I can't think straight. Or maybe it's the fact that his face has haunted my dreams, or more aptly, my fantasies, for months now. Whatever the reason, I don't like the idea of not seeing CEO Man every day.

I don't like it at all.

Right now, I need all the escapist fantasies I can get. I need to hold on to them for my own sanity, against the dark night that is my life.

So I decide to give Roman Stevanovsky a dose of his own medicine.

"Do you honestly think," I snap, "that I spent last night rolling around in some man's bed?"

He gives me his death stare, sending a thrill straight to my groin. "I'd say that much is perfectly obvious."

"And I'd say you're perfectly deluded." I send the death stare straight back to sender. "It's been less than seven hours since I finished my last shift, and I have at least fifteen hours to go until the end of this one. I don't have time for a *personal life*, as you call it. And I certainly don't have time to be delivering your food, answering your messages—or doing whatever this is."

I'm doing my best to ignore the effect that his close proximity and even closer scrutiny is having on my body. But it seems that with every word of my tongue lashing, CEO Man's eyes become darker and more penetrating. And the truth is, the more he stares at me, the more I think about his tongue lashing *me*. Preferably right here. Right now.

"You can keep your guilt money." I'm going to regret that

particular decision, but man, it feels good. "And for the record, I don't appreciate being woken up and summoned to your office. Your daily cup of coffee is already a twisted form of punishment."

Oh, damn.

The way that last comment came out was just a little too close to the truth. And by the sudden narrowing of his eyes, Roman Stevanovsky sees right through it.

For a moment we stare at each other, my breath coming short, his eyes examining mine with the intensity of an x-ray machine. Then he throws the envelope onto the desk and closes the space between us, his eyes gleaming with something dark and dangerous that makes every nerve in my body thrum.

"Believe me, Miss Lopez." His eyes rake me from head to toe, leaving a trail of hellfire on every inch they touch. "My methods of punishment are far more twisted than you can possibly imagine—and take a lot longer than a cup of coffee to administer."

He did not just say that.

But he did. And by the way he's staring at my chest, he knows exactly the effect he's having on my body. The familiar prickle of heat starts to spread up from the twin points that currently have his attention, turning my skin a deep crimson.

Damn it.

Reaching out with one finger, he touches the bare strip of skin between the edge of my T-shirt and the top of my shorts. I freeze, willing myself not to react, and his mouth curls slightly. "It's a pity," he murmurs, trailing his fingertip from one side of my navel to the other, never taking his eyes from mine, "that you don't have time to find out." Finishing his leisurely exploration, he takes a step back, out of reach.

I have to bite my lip to stop myself crying out in protest. Somewhere between my tirade and his filthy response, I've tipped right past the point of no return. My nipples are hard as bullets, and my T-shirt is definitely not the only part of me that's wet right now. The pulse between my legs has grown to a throbbing, swollen ache that is threatening to rob me of the power of speech entirely.

"I could make you wait, for example." His mouth curls evilly. "The way you look right now, making you wait would be a game I'd enjoy very much. Do you want me to make you wait, Miss Lopez?"

I bite my lip to stifle a gasp. I'm so hot that if he touches me, I'll explode.

"I'm sorry." He raises his eyebrows innocently. "You'll need to speak up. Did you want me to make you wait?" His eyes drop to my nipples again, which flare in response. "Although," he murmurs, "I don't really need to ask. Somehow I doubt you'll make it down the elevator. There are cameras in there, you know. I could always watch."

My legs spread high and wide on the elevator walls, one hand down my pants, the other on my nipples—and CEO Man watching me from his office, cock in hand.

I'm so far gone I can only stare at him.

"Your habit of blushing is very useful, Lucia." His arm snakes out, lightning fast, spinning me around and pulling me in so my back is hard up against him. The corded forearm I've been aching to touch sears across my bare belly, locking me in place. "It's an easy way to know when you're telling me the truth. For example." His mouth is close to my ear, his hard length pressed against my ass, and I'm pretty sure I stopped breathing a while ago. One calloused hand strokes slowly up my outer thigh. "How long has it been since somebody touched you, Miss Lopez?"

I can't answer. All I can think of is the hand roaming ever higher.

"No blush. I think it's been a while." I have no idea how he can tell. I'm pretty sure my entire body is flaming red at this point.

"What about here?" The long fingers slide over my hip and waist to cup my right breast through my T-shirt. I make a small, incoherent noise, straining toward it.

"Hm." His fingers slip either side of the nipple virtually poking a hole through the material. "A long while, then," he murmurs, pressing his palm down and manipulating my nipple until I'm squirming against him. "In that case, I should go slowly."

Fuck, no. Don't go slowly.

If I could force Roman Stevanovsky to throw me face down on his desk right now, I would. As it is, I have as much hope of breaking his iron grip as I do of stopping my nipples from swelling and growing impossibly hard under his slow touch.

"But I'm a busy man. And I don't think you want slow. Do you, Miss Lopez?" His hand stops moving and lifts away. My breast tries to follow it, and he gives a low chuckle. "Fast it is, then." Dipping his hands into the front of my T-shirt, he scoops my breasts out of my bra and free from the T-shirt they've been threatening to escape for weeks now. His hands cover them, the calloused palms grazing my nipples. I groan, my head dropping back against his shoulder. His tongue trails up the curve of my neck. He palms my breasts and I push into his hands, trying to force his fingers onto my nipples.

Then his mouth is hot and wild on my neck, his fingers rolling my nipples until I'm writhing beneath them and ready to scream.

"I don't think it's just your nipples that are desperate to be touched." His lips touch my ear, sending a shudder of pure lust straight through me.

Oh, God, yes.

He chuckles again, and I realize the breathy, hoarse words weren't only in my head.

I'm way past caring.

His hand is cupping me through my shorts, covering the swollen heat of me entirely. I push down shamelessly, squirming against his palm.

"You're so wet I can feel it." There's a faint catch in his voice, a crack in the perfect composure. I feel a dark rush of satisfaction. I start to undulate my hips on his hand, riding it as hard as he'll let me, thrusting my nipple between his fingers.

He allows this for a few moments. My undulations become a bucking urgency, and I feel the slow, delicious creep start spiraling in my belly.

Then he takes his hand away—and I actually do scream.

He whips his hand over my mouth to muffle it. "Stay silent," he growls.

I make a noise against his mouth.

"If you scream," he says against my ear, "I can't give you want you want. What you need, Miss Lopez. And you *do* need it, don't you?"

I nod frantically against his hand, helpless to deny it. Even if I wanted to, my body would make a fool of me. My breasts are spilled lewdly over my T-shirt and bra, swollen nipples thrusting toward Roman's tantalizingly out-of-reach mouth, and I'm so wet and aching even the seam of my shorts is about to make me come.

"Remember," he murmurs, drawing my zipper down frustratingly slowly. "Don't scream, or I'll stop." He slips his hand inside my underwear.

Fuuuuuuuuuuuuck.

His warning was useless. If he hadn't clamped his hand over my mouth again, I'd have howled the building down. It means my breasts are left without his fingers, but given the way he's now manipulating my swollen pussy, it doesn't matter.

"I did warn you I'd stop if you screamed. Should I stop, Miss Lopez?" His low voice against my ear is as ruthless as the steady stroking of his fingers, driving me relentlessly toward the place I need to get to, more urgently than I can ever remember before.

Nooooooo! I scream into his hand.

He slips one finger inside me, then two. "Christ, you're wet," he mutters. The huge, swollen length of him twitches against my ass. His fingers hit the spot inside me that needs them, and I start bucking in earnest against his palm.

"Touch your nipples," he murmurs in my ear. "You know you need to."

As if compelled by his voice, my hands rise to my breasts. "Show me," he murmurs, and so I do.

He makes a rough sound low in his throat, and that's the moment I can feel it starting, the slow tidal wave of the most intense, all-consuming, body-shaking orgasm of my life.

As the first ripples hit, he turns my head and captures my mouth with his own, drowning my scream with his perfect lips.

4

ROMAN

"A porn site?"

I glare around the table, trying to ignore the fact that even the word *porn* conjures up images of Lucia Lopez, wet and aching under my hand. Three days after our encounter in my office, the slightest thought of her still makes me hard as an iron bar.

I push the dangerous images aside and channel my energy into glaring at the faces around the table in front of me.

"It's not a big deal," Pavel says, "just something the kid used to run a test. We'll make sure he hasn't left any trace." My head of software development rattles away on his laptop screen with one hand while turning one of those fidget spinner things in the other. Calling someone else *kid* is ironic, given that Pavel is only a few years out of his teens himself. He has thick glasses, a dark beard decorated with pizza crumbs of several varieties, and an ever-present giant cup of soda on the table next to him. He spends fifteen hours a day wired into the lab, which is what we call the operations room of our server center, surrounded by acres of blinking lights and low-humming machines that have cost the economy of a small country to set up. He heads up a handpicked army of hackers and tech heads drawn from across the globe.

The tech heads are all brilliant. They also piss me right off.

"Pavel." I spin his chair around and whip the fidget spinner out of his hand. "Amuse me. What, exactly, is Mercura?"

The man looks around nervously at his fellow geeks, all of whom are busy staring at the ceiling, and pushes his glasses up his nose. Pavel has worked on my flagship concept since he was a teenager. If anyone understands Mercura, it's him. He just doesn't understand what I'm trying to get him to say right now.

"Mercura is, um, an untraceable cryptocurrency. Faster than the Flash." He smiles weakly at whatever comic book reference I've just missed.

"Funny, Pavel." I'm not laughing, and his smile fades. "Why don't you explain what cryptocurrency is?"

Given that the people sitting at this table virtually invented it, Pavel looks around to see who I expect him to explain it to. When I don't move, he begins to stammer. "It's a digital form of currency."

"Glad you've read the manual. And why is Mercura untraceable?"

Pavel swallows. Despite the arctic air conditioning down here, he's starting to sweat. "Because it can only be used on our platform, and only by invitation. Mercura is designed to be so invisible that no government agency in the world can find or monitor it."

"Amazing." I fold my arms. "Does it seem smart to you to test the world's most secret currency by using it to watch *Candy does Cunnilingus* on the world's busiest porn site?"

"No, sir."

"No shit." I point a remote to a wall-mounted screen, and up comes the offending video, in which one girl is at work tonguing the swollen pussy of another, in eye-watering detail.

Lucia Lopez, open under my mouth. I'll have to try that next time.

I catch myself.

Not going to be a next time.

My only consolation is watching Pavel, face bright red, glancing sideways at his tech army, who are all shifting uncomfortably in their seats. I doubt most of them have ever actually seen a naked woman in the flesh. I leave the writhing women onscreen just to add to their discomfort.

"Mercura has been exposed." I don't hide my fury, and I take a savage satisfaction in watching the table recoil. "Now we're facing the risk of it being identified, and traced, before we've finished building a digital vault around it. It's not only a *big deal*, Pavel. It's a potential fucking disaster. I want to know if we can still avoid that disaster."

Pavel clears his throat and launches into a convoluted technical explanation that loses me within seconds. I hold up my hand, pinning him with the death stare I perfected as a teenager in the back alleys of Miami, and which has reduced much harder men than this one to piss-soaked wrecks. "I asked *if* we can avoid the disaster, Pavel, not how. Yes or no."

He gulps. "Yes, sir."

"Then get it done, and fast. I want a full risk analysis on my desk by tomorrow morning." I glare at him. "The CliffsNotes version, Pavel. Not the entire fucking textbook."

The geeks might be the ones building Mercura, but none of them truly understand its scope. In fact, I've made certain they don't.

Mercura isn't just another crypto coin. It's built for a far darker world, the criminal one that always has, and always will, exist. It's been built in so much secrecy that most of those working on it don't even understand exactly what the end goal looks like.

From acquiring the land under which the server is built, to the construction companies who dug out the vast bunker it's housed in, to the state-of-the-art equipment humming all around us, Mercura has taken thousands of man hours, secret meetings, international visas, and government bribes, not to mention billions of dollars, to develop.

Mercura is the safest, most sophisticated money laundering operation in the world.

And the Stevanovsky bratva will harvest a percentage of every single coin washed through it.

Mercura is our future. It takes us off the streets and into the big game.

It means my three godchildren won't be lost in a car bomb like their father, or jailed for the rest of their lives like their grandfather.

Mercura is what I owe Yuri Stevanovsky for taking me off the streets and adopting me. It's what I owe Mikhail, his son, who was my closest friend as well as my adopted brother. After he was jailed, Yuri made Mikhail *pakhan*. When Mikhail was blown to pieces in a car bomb two years ago, Yuri named me *pakhan* in his place.

Mercura is our legacy.

At least it will be, if that fucking kid hasn't already destroyed it.

As if to prove my point, the kid in question walks toward us between the lines of machines, head down. Unlike the rest of the tech kids, who all wear baggy pants and T-shirts, he's sporting pressed chinos, a button-down shirt, and a neat haircut.

Ambitious, clearly.

He has headphones on, nodding to some beat only he can hear. He's barely a foot from the op center's fishbowl window when it penetrates the faulty wiring of his brain that we're here. It takes another long moment for him to realize that *I'm* here.

It never ceases to astonish me that people can be so fast on a keyboard and so fucking slow in real life.

"Everyone out onto the floor."

I don't want to get blood all over the op center.

The tech kids move out onto the polished concrete floor of the server center with alacrity. I nod at a round table near a vending machine, and they obediently take their seats.

The guilty kid doesn't bother removing his headphones before he pulls out a chair. I kick it to the wall before his ass even gets close. He stares at it, then up at the porn playing on the op center screen, with a sullen expression.

"Good of you to join us, Leo."

Pavel glances at me, then scoots his chair out of the line of fire. He knows this isn't going to go well.

The little prick finally removes his headphones, which are almost bigger than him. "My name is Teo."

Oh, I'm going to enjoy this.

"Tell me, *Leo*. What is your job title?"

"System test engineer." He mutters the title as if it's beneath him.

"And do you like your job?"

The rat-faced little *mudak* shrugs. Actually shrugs.

From the corner of my eye I see Dimitry, my second-in-command, move off from where he's leaning on one of the machines, balancing evenly on his feet.

He knows what's coming.

The tech heads who have been with me for a while do, too. They go pale and eye the floor nervously.

Headphones doesn't, though. He slouches against the

machine bank, moving from one foot to another as if it's hard work holding himself upright.

"You look bored, Leo," I say softly. "Are you bored?"

He tilts his head as if he's actually considering the question. "I think we should be more aggressive in our testing." He nods at the screen. "Mercura should be able to slip in and out of sites like this unseen. I thought our job was to test its resilience."

It takes a certain level of either stupidity or balls to keep bluffing when death is standing in front of you. I almost admire the idiot.

Almost.

I crack my knuckles slowly. "So you decided to get creative with your job, instead of just fucking doing it?"

The kid glances around properly for the first time, taking in the muscle lounging against the walls and the terrified faces of his coworkers, finally beginning to realize that our little gathering doesn't quite pass the vibe check. He licks his lips nervously.

"Your job is to run the resilience tests we give you." I get up nice and close, and the kid's nostrils flare. "Not go ahead and decide what tests need to be run." He tries to step back, but there are only machines behind him. I get even closer and he steps sideways, standing in the middle of the corridor between machine banks.

That's better. I'd rather not get blood on the machines.

"You especially don't get to decide to run a test on a website made by our biggest competitors. One they set up specifically so they could watch every new digital coin that hits the market. But I think you already knew that, Leo, didn't you?"

There's an audible gasp from the table behind me, followed by a very tense silence. All of them know, or at least suspect, the price for selling me out.

And the kid definitely isn't shrugging anymore. His eyes move from side to side as he tries to think up a good story, but it's way too late for that. It was too late before he ever walked in the room.

"I hope they paid you more than the amount I found in your account." I pull out my gun slowly and watch his eyes go from defensive to terrified. "Because if not, *Leo*, your life is worth about as much as those shitty chinos you're wearing."

I shoot him straight between the eyes.

He lands just where I planned, away from the machines, although he still manages to spread his brains all over the glass screens covering them. The tech heads hit the floor the moment I fired and are currently cowering under any available surface. Funny how they can all play Call of Duty without batting an eye, but the moment the real thing is in their face, they're losing their guts all over my lab-clean floors.

"Chill, little dudes." Dimitry's calm drawl cuts through the chaos. "None of you have suspicious zeros in your accounts. So long as you keep it that way, you'll keep your brains, too." He nudges Leo/Teo's limp body. "This dickhead lost his long before they wound up on the floor."

"I-I'm sorry, sir." Pavel stares at me, stuttering with shock and terror. "I had no idea—"

The others chime in from various positions behind machines and under tables. "I had nothing to do with it—"

"I didn't know—"

I hold up my hand. "I know you didn't. Our security team picked it up."

That gets their collective attention.

I raise my eyebrows. "What?" I say lightly. "Did you lot think you were the only tech heads on my staff? If you think I don't know every last thing about every one of you, from what you ate for breakfast to the brand of porn you favor, then think again."

I lean forward on the table, eyeing each of them in turn.

"I pay you fucking well. And you all own a piece of Mercura, so you'll be paid even more when we launch. I like ideas, and I love ambition. I encourage both, and I reward them. I also don't mind if you want to leave because it isn't for you. Sign your NDA and go, and good luck to you.

"But take a good long look at your buddy there on the floor, and hardwire it into your brain. Because that's what happens if you ever betray me."

I let them all take a long look, and I let the silence draw out for a while. Sometimes, demonstrations are necessary.

None of them will be selling information anytime soon.

I nod at two of my men by the machines. "Get this cleaned up. Pavel, your team can get back to work, but I need a word with you."

Pavel goes from pale to green. I know he thinks he's next. I let him sweat a little before I take him into his own office. "We're only months away from launch, Pavel. You've been on this from the start, so you know what it's taken to get to where we are."

He nods vigorously.

"Hale Property was purposely built to mask Mercura. It's taken close on six years to convince the authorities the Stevanovsky bratva are now a legitimate realty corporation, especially after its former CEO went up in a car bomb two years ago."

Pavel winces. He liked Mikhail. Everyone did. Mikhail was the front man, the smiling CEO who made the front page of *GQ* when Hale made its first billion. I was the dark muscle behind that billion, and happy to stay in the background. Mikhail and I were a team, closer than any brothers could be. He killed at press conferences; I killed anyone who got in our way. I tried to argue with Yuri when he made me *pakhan* in his son's place. I never asked for the spotlight, and I still hate the bullshit that goes with it. But the truth is that Mercura was always mine, just as Hale was, even if it was Mikhail who pressed the flesh.

After the initial grief of losing my adopted brother, followed by the ruthless bloodletting when I murdered every single one of the bastards responsible for leaving three children without their father, I've found that I don't mind leading.

But in moments like this, I think grimly, looking at Pavel's terrified face, *I could do with Mikhail's charm.*

"If the authorities discover we're developing an invisible currency, it's not just me who's fucked. It's also fifteen-year-old Ofelia, fourteen-year-old Mickey, and five-year-old Masha. You've met Mikhail's children, Pavel. Mercura is Mikhail's legacy, and his children's future. I need to know you're going to help me keep it safe."

"Yes, boss." The color is back in Pavel's face, along with the determination that made me hire him in the first place. "I dropped the ball." He sounds almost as pissed off as I was when I discovered Teo's betrayal. "It won't happen again."

I grip his shoulder firmly. "I know it won't."

It better not.

"Are we putting bullets in the people who paid that kid?" Dimitry glances sideways at me as we walk away from the gleaming software development facility we built to conceal what we're actually doing in the server room lab below it. There are real software experts in the facility, doing real work —including the security team who discovered Teo's little side hustle of selling information.

"No." I shake my head. "Despite what I said back there, the breach is already plugged, hopefully with no harm done. A body trail will only make them think there's something to hide."

"Damn." Dimitry grins. "We're so woke these days, brother."

I roll my eyes. "Tell me about it."

"Not to mention getting a bit of a hipster vibe happening."

"What are you talking about?" We get in the back seat, and the driver points the car down the winding road toward Malaga.

"Apparently a brand-new coffee machine just arrived at your office." He shoots me a sly smile. "Something wrong with what the lovely Miss Lopez has been serving up?"

I give him the same glare I treated Pavel to earlier. Unfortunately, Dimitry has been watching me pin men with that stare since we were prepubescent kids, so it has rather less impact.

"Dimitry?"

"Yes, boss?"

"Fuck off."

He shuts it, but he remains grinning the entire way back to Malaga. I toy with the idea of taking him to the boxing ring and reminding him of exactly how *woke* I am not, but I don't have time. I don't have time for anything—and particularly not for the unholy distraction that is Miss Lucia Lopez.

I rub a hand over my face and stare out the window. Hearing Dimitry mention her by name annoys me. The fact that he's noticed her at all annoys me, particularly long enough to call her lovely. It's the wrong word for her, anyway.

Snarky? *Yes.*

Feisty? *Definitely.*

Tempting, intriguing, and insanely sexy? *Tick.*

Fucking dangerous?

Absolutely.

Watching her delicious curves in that ridiculous uniform sashay up to serve my coffee, not to mention the daily battle to make her blush, has become the hottest ten minutes of my day. The smoky sideways glance of topaz eyes as she decides what insult to hit me with. Scraping her teeth over that absurdly full lower lip as she thinks of a comeback, a habit I'm almost certain she's unaware of. Watching her shorts ride up that delectable ass when she bends down to the fridge. She might have ordered in Russian water just to score a point in our game, but I hit the jackpot every day when she has to bend over and get a bottle of it out of the fridge. I've been fighting the urge to bend her lush, tantalizing curves over any available surface for months. And now that I've had my hands all over her, my dick is obsessed with finishing the job.

Multiple times. On *every* available surface.

I need to get under some model ASAP.

I don't do relationships. I do mutually beneficial situations that satisfy my cock and leave my head alone. I don't date, and I certainly don't take advantage of those less fortunate than myself. I know how it feels to be the person washing dishes out back or serving coffee to rich pricks who don't remember your name. It's the reason I tip properly, and the reason I felt like a class A bastard after I handed Miss Lopez her ass for a mistake that wasn't hers.

Then she'd run from my office without a word—and without taking the tip.

If she'd just taken the goddamn envelope, I could have walked away with a clear conscience, I tell myself, even though the way my cock throbs at the mere memory of her bending over my desk makes a total liar out of me. And after implying that she'd spent the night *rolling around in some man's bed*, as she put it, sending an envelope full of money over to the café with my assistant would definitely send the wrong message.

Not that it matters, if I'm never seeing her again. And it's none of my business if, or indeed who, Lucia Lopez is, now or at any point in the future, rolling around in a bed with.

I grind my teeth.

Keep telling yourself that.

I'm a possessive prick, always have been. I keep what

belongs to me close. Safe. I don't allow anyone to take what is mine.

The thought of some other man putting his hands anywhere near the sweet curve of Lucia's ass, or the bee-stung lips my dick has some seriously filthy ideas about, kicks something primal inside me into gear. Which is the only excuse I have, poor as it is, for almost losing myself entirely with her the other day in my office. It took every ounce of self-control I possess not to tear her shorts off and get balls deep inside her hot, wet, and insanely tight pussy.

Pizdozh.

Not a chance my hard-on is going down after that thought.

But Lucia Lopez isn't mine. Even if I wanted to change that, there's no room for her in the clusterfuck that is my personal life.

As if in confirmation, my phone lights up with a call from *nanny agency be nice.* I grind my teeth even harder.

"Mrs. Laidlaw," I say as politely as I can manage, glaring at Dimitry, who is smirking in the passenger seat. "What an unexpected pleasure." I put the call on speakerphone. If I have to listen to this bullshit, Dimitry can fucking well suffer with me.

"I'm not calling with good news, I'm afraid."

When do you ever?

I stifle the retort with an effort. "What seems to be the problem?"

"I'm sorry to inform you," Mrs. Laidlaw begins, in a tone that suggests she isn't sorry at all, "that Stefania has terminated her employment as your children's nanny."

"What?" Aghast, I grip the phone hard enough that I'm going to need a new one. "The Holy Week school holidays are coming up. The children will be off school for at least a week—"

"And perhaps you should have considered that."

Mrs. Laidlaw launches into a tirade of complaints, the broad thrust of which are that my godchildren are the spawn of the devil, and that I am Satan himself.

I tune her out and stare through the windshield at the city lights, trying to work out what the fuck to do about this particular disaster.

We're almost at the Hale offices, and Lucia's café is coming up on my left. She wasn't lying about her hours. Since our encounter I've been discreetly watching Lucia Lopez. She works more hours than even I do.

What I don't understand is why.

What drives a beautiful young woman to work every available hour in a job she's clearly far too intelligent for?

It's just one of the mysteries about Lucia Lopez I'd very much like to solve.

Preferably while she's naked and impaled on my cock.

Christ.

I drag my thoughts back to the problem at hand with no small effort.

"Mrs. Laidlaw." I start again, this time in the icy tone that has reduced countless criminals to shaking wrecks. "Stefania was contracted to stay for the next school term and the entire summer holidays. Your agency has been paid a three-month advance. All the security checks have been completed. And now you tell me that after less than a week, she's quit? What, exactly, do you expect me to do on such short notice?"

"Cope, Mr. Stevanovsky," she says, in a tone even more arctic than my own. "People do, you know. You could try spending more time at home, perhaps."

I stare at the phone in astonishment. Across the car, Dimitry is shaking with silent laughter. I send him a death stare, which only makes him laugh harder.

"If you are unable to fulfill my requirements," I say coldly in an attempt to regain ascendancy, "then perhaps your agency doesn't deserve its reputation."

"And if you insist on completely ignoring your three children, not to mention setting impossible standards for their nanny," snaps back the haughty English voice through my car speakers, "then I suggest you find yourself a new agency. Although given that you've gone through five in as many months, Mr. Stevanovsky, I don't like your chances. Good day—and good luck."

The line turns into a series of long beeps.

"I think," Dimitry says, barely containing his laughter, "that the good Mrs. Laidlaw hung up on you."

5

ROMAN

Following a much needed and exceedingly satisfying session in the boxing ring with Dimitry, I head back to my penthouse. It's been strangely quiet the past two days, which has, to my surprise, felt a bit odd. As much as I've done everything humanly possible to resist having Mikhail's three children thrust into my life, during the five months they've been living here permanently, I've become strangely accustomed to hearing their chatter drift up from the floor below.

I don't allow them into my penthouse, of course. And beyond taking down delivery cartons on the nights the chef is off, I rarely visit their apartment on the floor below.

No matter the instructions in Mikhail's will, bequeathing care of his children to me, their godfather, this situation is definitely temporary. I'm not cut out for parenthood any more than I am for relationships. Besides, children need a mother.

And just as soon as Mikhail's nightmare of an ex-wife finishes her modeling contract in the USA, I'll be forcibly impressing that fact on her.

I push away the unwelcome knowledge that Inger is hardly perfect mother material. She's going to have to change. Or at least find enough nannies to do her job for her. I can't raise three children, particularly when one of them is a very angry fifteen-year-old girl who hates my guts.

What the fuck do I know about teenage girls? Or five-year-old ones, for that matter, like the youngest. Let alone thirteen-year-old Mickey, who doesn't play sports and has more in common with my tech geeks than the bratva he was born into.

I could kill that damn nanny.

How am I supposed to find a replacement by tomorrow? Bitter experience has taught me not to try using my assistants in the interim.

I throw my bag down in the corridor, trying not to think about Lucia Lopez standing right here, only days ago. Part of the reason I lost it so badly that day was because for once, I was expecting the children for a late meal before driving them to the airport for their flight to London, where they're currently staying with Yuri's wife, Vera, their paternal grandmother.

Thank God the kids weren't in the apartment when Lucia turned up. The thought of Ofelia's sharp teenage eyes watching me with Lucia Lopez doesn't appeal at all.

Which brings me neatly back to the other problem I'm currently facing: Miss Lopez's undelivered tip.

Oh, sure. It's the tip that's bothering you.

I shower and sit down at the wide dining table with my laptop. I have cameras in my office, of course. I'm the only person with access to them.

For the past three days, I've been resisting the urge to watch the footage they captured that morning in my office.

I know I should delete it. I know it's beyond wrong to possess it, let alone even think about watching it. Probably illegal, too, not that I could give a shit about the law.

I hit play anyway.

I get hard the minute I watch Miss Lopez sashay into my office. She pauses, staring at my back, and her nipples suddenly become visible outlines under her shirt.

Christ. This was a bad idea.

And there's no way in hell I'm turning it off.

I put my hands behind my head to resist the urge to jack off. I might allow myself to watch the damn thing, but I'm not going full creep.

The view of her luscious ass bending over my desk is even better from the overhead camera than it was from behind, since I can also watch her gorgeous tits nearly fall right out of her top on their own and her nipples swell as I make the comment about her slipping.

That word wasn't an accident.

After months of imagining Lucia bent over my desk, the reality made me even harder than I am right now. Clearly, going by the suddenly glazed look in her eyes and the way she's scraping that delicious lower lip, I'm not the only one who's been imagining that particular scenario.

She turns around. I watch my furious reaction to her disheveled appearance and feel a not-insignificant amount of self contempt.

I called her a whore in every way but the actual word. Which, given my own ability to fuck around, is some level of hypocrisy.

Subtle, asshole. Real subtle.

Then I watch her rip straight back into me, with a ridiculous lack of fear for someone who knows exactly what level of savagery I'm capable of. Eyes flashing, chest heaving—even tearing me apart, she's the sexiest fucking thing I've ever seen.

By the time she gets to the line about twisted punishment, tying her to my bed is all I can think about.

It doesn't get any easier after that.

Every moan. Every hitched breath. The way her eyes flutter closed and her head goes back on my shoulder, like she can't even hold herself up anymore. That delicious peach of an ass pushing back against my dick. The way her breasts thrust toward my hands, even before I've released them from that joke of a T-shirt.

God, I thought my imagination might have exaggerated just how perfect her tits are, but the truth is even my wildest fantasies didn't come close to doing them justice. I'd give Hale's entire yearly income to get my mouth around the two swollen scarlet buds thrusting up from the ripe flesh beneath.

And that pussy . . .

When I slipped my finger inside her, she was so wet I could have come just from touching her.

Watching her orgasm a second time tests my self-control to the limit.

By the time I've watched her scream and buck under my hand, shaking with the intensity of her orgasm, I'm painfully fucking hard.

I know there's no chance in hell of me walking away from Miss Lucia Lopez, or at least, not until I've fucked every last one of those delicious moans out of her.

I pause the screen on the frame of her at the moment of orgasm, her fingers clutching the swollen orbs on her chest, the bee-stung lips wet and open against my palm, her ass thrust back against both my shaft and my fingers, and walk over to the plate glass windows.

It's going to take an ice bath to get my cock down.

Meanwhile, I have an idea.

Potentially an extremely dangerous one, but then, I've never been one to walk away from danger.

And it does fall under the category of mutually beneficial.

I call my lawyer, explain the contract I want drawn up, and tell him I'll take care of the background check. Pavel is the most discreet and loyal of my employees; I'll give the job to him. I don't like the idea of outsiders knowing things about Miss Lopez until I do.

Then I find Lucia's number on my phone and start punching out a message.

My office, ten am tomorrow. If you miss our appointment, my offer will be taken permanently off the table.

I did warn her that my methods of punishment were twisted.

Lucia Lopez is about to find out just how true that is.

6

LUCIA

"I cannot go up there."

The sun is gleaming down outside, but I'm as oblivious to the glorious spring weather as I am to the throng of tourists already clamoring for breakfast. All I can think about is the text message I received from Roman last night.

"And he didn't give you any idea about what this offer is?" Abby takes the coffees I've just made. "Nothing like, *Make sure you wear a hot bra and no panties so I can get my hands into your tiny shorts again, Miss Lopez? Or maybe I have a severe case of blue balls that only you can relieve, Miss Lopez?*"

My glare only makes Abby laugh.

The truth is, I haven't got a clue what he wants.

I'm not certain what I thought might happen when I fled Roman's office, fixing my clothes as I went, to the low sound of his amused chuckle behind me. But three days of deafening silence and Roman's notable absence from my coffee machine had sent what I thought was a pretty clear message of disinterest. Until I received his message last night.

"I have no idea what he wants, or what his so-called offer is." I get more milk as an excuse to bury my flaming head in the fridge.

It doesn't help.

I feel like my entire body has been on fire for days.

"But after what happened last time, going up to his office is definitely not a good idea."

"And like I told you the day it happened: it's about time you got off, Luce. You know I'd never put up with you being pressured into anything, but you two have been eye fucking from the day he walked in. And you have to be missing the size of his . . . tips."

For all Abby's sarcasm, the last comment is, sadly, true. I'm so broke I almost wish I'd taken that damn envelope when I fled Roman's office.

Almost.

"I hate to break it to you, chica, but it's not just you who's missing those tips. The kitchen boys have been literally paying their rent from delivering to the Stevanovsky apartment. And besides." Abby shoots me a lascivious wink. "CEO Man's bodyguard is my favorite piece of eye candy on the daily. Hot. I mean *super* hot. And you can't tell me," she says, pausing to push coffees across the counter and ring them up, "that you aren't into whatever kinky fuckery CEO Man pulled in his office. I saw you when you got back here." She wags a finger at my crimson face. "You were barely able to stand up, let alone speak. Is there really any harm in going back for an encore?" She eyes the clock. "You've got fifteen minutes to make your mind up."

Gah. Fifteen minutes.

No matter how many times Abby tells me there's nothing wrong with what happened between Roman and me, I feel absolutely terrified to face him again. What am I supposed to do, just walk into his office and say, "I know the last time I saw you I screamed into your hand and all but begged you to fuck me senseless—but, hey. How *you* doin'?"

I'm never getting those images out of my head. I'm pretty sure the entire experience will be seared on my brain forever.

And Abby knows me too well. Despite my absolute certainty that I should stay the hell away from CEO Man's office for my own sanity, I spent the entirety of last night wondering if his offer might just involve some kind of repeat performance.

Surely not, if he's avoided the café for days on end.

But what if it does?

I admit that I prepared for work today with a little more care than usual. There's not much I can do about the uniform. But I've put my hair up properly. Added mascara, lip gloss, and nice earrings.

Oh, and I might also have spent a few euros I don't officially have on an underwear set I definitely can't afford.

Just in case.

"Earth to Lopez." Abby clicks her fingers under my nose with a sly smile. "Clock's ticking, chica."

"I can't face him, Abby." But even I can hear the wavering tone in my voice.

"Be selfless. Think of your friend, who hasn't been laid in almost a week and hasn't even had her daily dose of bodyguard thirst trap." She gives me lewd wink. "Unless Stevanovsky is chaining you up and using a whip, go and get our Hale business back."

Chains and whips.

I shiver, hearing Roman's husky voice: *"My methods of punishment are far more twisted than you can possibly imagine . . ."*

"Eleven minutes." Abby gives me a Cheshire cat grin. "You better hurry. Fifty floors is a long elevator ride."

"Oh, for goodness' sake." I untie my apron, throw it on the counter, and run for the building opposite.

I ONLY JUST MAKE IT, and in only a slightly less flustered state than last time. A new assistant, male this time, buzzes me in at exactly ten o'clock. The light in Roman's office is almost blinding, sunlight streaming in through the floor-to-ceiling windows. It gleams on sleek black couches and glitters off the long oval glass conference table. At the end of the room Roman is sitting in a tall leather chair behind a midnight steel desk the same iron color of his eyes, speaking in low Russian to someone on his cell. He looks up as I enter and nods at a chair in front of him.

If we were playing our old game, I'd have lost already.

I was blushing before I even got here.

Now, staring at the desk and remembering what happened last time I was close to it, my face is on fire. Roman, by contrast, is coolly impersonal and focused on his call.

"*Nyet*," he says curtly, staring at something on his laptop screen. "*Segodnya.*" *Today.* Some poor minion has just been given an impossible deadline. It's almost a relief to find CEO Man behaving so true to form, like a return to our weird normal.

Then he hangs up and stares at me, so long that my toes begin to curl and the color mount on my face. He waits until every inch of me is siren red before he finally speaks.

"You cut it fine this morning, Miss Lopez." His expression is as unreadable as ever, his steel gaze pinning me to the seat. "Another minute and you would have been too late." The ice-burn eyes run over my still-heaving chest and red face with the same narrow scrutiny they did days ago. "Last-minute decision, I gather."

I can think of a dozen things to say, but they all sound incoherent even in my head, so in the end I just gulp and stay silent.

Roman steeples his fingers on the desk. "Your recent departure from my office left me with something of a dilemma, Miss Lopez," he says finally.

I can't imagine what kind of dilemma he means.

Whether to come back for coffee again? Whether to have me deliver it every day?

"First, you left your tip behind."

Every part of me is burning red. "I told you that I don't need your money. And it seemed inappropriate—"

"I think we both know the first part of that statement is untrue." He cuts me off brusquely. "And given that you came on my hand the last time we met, I think we are long past *inappropriate.*"

I almost choke on air.

"Tell me, Miss Lopez. In my shoes, how would you approach this dilemma?" Sitting back in his chair, he regards me with polite interest.

Completely unnerved, I open my mouth and let whatever is in it fall right on out. "Just forget what happened and let things go back to normal?"

"Oh, I don't think that's an option, Miss Lopez." He stretches and cracks his knuckles, then interlaces his hands behind his head. It's hard to look at those hands without remembering what they were doing to me last time we met, and by the faint smirk on his face, Roman is well aware of my discomfort. "Here are the two options I am putting on the table. You can take either offer or neither. It's entirely up to you."

He opens the drawer and pushes two envelopes across the desk toward me. "One of these contains the tip you left behind. Given my previous assurance that I wouldn't call you back to my office, I've doubled the amount inside it.

"The other"—he taps it with one forefinger, his eyes holding mine—"contains a contract of employment."

Employment?

"Take the tip, and you have my word you won't hear from me again. Take the contract, and for the next several months, you will belong, exclusively, to me."

There's an odd ringing in my ears, and the air around me dances with strange lights that make me think I'm about to actually faint for the first time in my life.

"*Belong to you*," I echo hollowly. "You mean . . . wait." I swallow, catching myself before I say something I can't come back from. "What *do* you mean, exactly?"

He nods at the larger of the two envelopes. "Open it."

I do, withdrawing the sheaf of papers inside and glancing at the opening page.

Then I glance at it again.

At first I think I must be misunderstanding what I'm reading. Then I feel a passionate rush of relief that I didn't embarrass myself by finishing my initial interpretation of his words. Then, finally, I read it again and suspect this is some kind of weird joke.

"A nanny." I stare at him in complete astonishment. "You want to hire me as a *nanny*?"

I don't even attempt to hide my disbelief.

"You have children?" I shake my head. "*You.* Children?"

I can't reconcile it. It's like my entire universe has just juddered off course. Roman Stevanovsky—father figure?

The same grade A asshole who reduces grown men to tears on a daily basis? Seducer of models and beloved by paparazzi? *That* Roman Stevanovsky has *children*?

"Godchildren." Roman's insolent smile says he's clearly enjoying my incoherent shock. "Three of them. They are temporarily in my care, hence this contract being for a matter of months only."

I check the contract again. There it is. Three godchildren. Aged fifteen, fourteen, and just turned five.

Who the hell was insane enough to make the devil himself the guardian of their children's spiritual and moral well-being? Let alone leave them in his so-called care?

More to the point, why would Roman want me to look after them?

It makes not one lick of sense. Given Hale's resources, he could hire anyone he wants. His local waitress, especially one he recently brought to an earth-shattering orgasm in this very office, hardly seems the most sensible choice.

"There must be a thousand nanny agencies in Spain. Why—?"

Oh, no. Unless . . .

"Page two, Miss Lopez."

I flip hastily to the next page. Roman just sits there, hands behind his head, legs stretched out in front of him, watching me with a dark gleam in his eyes that does nothing to reduce the tension racing around my system.

Tension that gets worse with every word I read. Oddly enough, this one I don't have to read twice. It's blatant enough to leave no room for misunderstanding.

"I'd be living in your building." I read over the lines without looking at him.

"That is a requirement, yes."

"But not just to care for the children."

"Your apartment is on the same floor as theirs. But no, that isn't the only reason I require you to live in the build-ing." I finally meet his eyes. He's lounging in his chair, entirely unperturbed by the extremely disturbing proposi-tion he's just put in my hands. "You said it yourself, Miss Lopez. You don't have time for a personal life. Neither, as it happens, do I. I believe this arrangement meets both of our needs."

"You want me to be your . . . au pair, with benefits."

"Do you know what the literal definition of the term 'au pair' is, Miss Lopez?"

"Amaze me," I mutter, still staring at the pages.

"It comes from the French term meaning 'at par,' or 'equal to.' The term is meant to indicate that the relationship is one of equals, rather than the position of a traditional domestic worker." He watches me with still, dark eyes. "That is what I am proposing, Miss Lopez. A five-month contract between equals. One for which you will be extremely well compensated."

Roman seems to have blithely skipped over the outrageous part of his proposal, as if it were nothing more than a meaningless subclause. I'm not sure entirely what I expected to be on offer. My new underwear is evidence enough that I was prepared for *something*. But not this. This is right out of the park.

"Just to be clear," I say slowly, surprised I can actually talk at all. "You're proposing that for the next five months I will live in your building. In addition to providing nanny duties for three children, I will also be providing naked duties for *you*." I glance at the wording. "*As and when required, to be exact*."

"Naked duties." The sudden narrowing of his eyes sends a savage rush of heat between my legs. "Not the term I would have used, although the idea of you naked and dutifully on your knees does have a certain appeal, Miss Lopez."

Oh, save me.

"But essentially, yes. During the designated hours, you will be a nanny. And outside those hours, you will be mine. Exclusively." Something dangerous flares in his eyes, there and then gone. "That part is nonnegotiable. No dates, no boyfriends. I don't share, Miss Lopez."

There's a certain ruthless edge to his words that makes absolutely clear the kind of savagery that will be unleashed if this particular clause is broken.

It should horrify me.

It doesn't.

Going by the intense pulsing between my legs, savagery is my own personal brand of aphrodisiac.

"There are other conditions, too."

The dark gleam is still in his eyes, suggesting he can at least sense how aroused I am.

Will he do something about it? I'm ashamed of how much I want him to.

"You might want to take the contract away and read through them. But do it quickly. I need an answer by this afternoon. Your start date, if you agree, is tomorrow." He lifts the screen on his laptop, a move I've seen him make a thousand times in the café when he wants to get rid of one of his minions.

So, no naked duties today, then.

I'm not sure whether it's my frustrated body or my indignation at being treated like a subordinate that triggers the sudden return of my snark setting.

"This exclusivity clause." I fold my arms and regard him as steadily as I can. "Is that mutual, too?"

He's silent for a considerable amount of time, his blank expression giving nothing away. Finally he nods curtly. "For the duration of the contract, yes, I will agree to that."

Roman Stevanovsky. Exclusively mine.

I'm not going to deny how tempting that sounds, even for a short time. Nor can I deny the amount of zeros in the salary he's offering.

Enough to move Papa into a new apartment.

To get him proper care.

Enough to buy us new identities.

Even, perhaps, to start rebuilding the Petrovsky bratva.

In short, life-changing money. Not for me, but for my father, and possibly my brother.

It's the only reason I haven't told Roman to go to hell, just on principle.

Or at least that's what I tell myself.

"You have until five this afternoon." Roman glances at his phone. "Six and a half hours should be more than enough time to read through the contract." He nods curtly in dismissal and starts typing.

I'm not sure what I was expecting. A trial run of some kind? A naked session on the oval table? Bent over the desk, an ever-winning fantasy?

Certainly not to be dismissed without even the chance of parading my fancy knickers.

I walk to the door slightly unsteadily.

"Miss Lopez." I halt, heart thudding, half hoping and half dreading what he will say next. But if I thought some kind of indecent proposition was forthcoming, I'm sadly disappointed.

"There is one condition I must insist on before you leave." I turn to find him pinning me with an uncompromisingly ruthless stare. "While your position as au pair in my household will be public, the rest of our agreement will remain strictly confidential. Do I make myself clear?"

I give a strangled laugh. "If you think that asking me to formally become your live-in sex slave is a fact I want widely advertised, then you're even more delusional than I thought."

Then, for the second time in a week, I flee.

LUCIA

I work through lunch, barely noticing the customers I speak to. Fortunately we're so busy that beyond Abby's initial shock, she doesn't get a chance to question me too closely, although she also doesn't miss any opportunity to slip in dry comments.

"Au pair," she mutters sarcastically on her way to the serving hatch to pick up plates toward the end of the lunch hour.

I roll my eyes at her. Abby's been giving me hell about Roman's offer all day. I dread to think what she'd be saying if she knew the full nature of his proposal.

A moment later, Roman's bodyguard walks in, and Abby licks her lips and grins at me. "Speaking of au pairing, you can definitely ohhhhhh-pair me up with *that*."

She proceeds to flirt shamelessly with the bodyguard, who, I notice, doesn't seem to mind at all.

He waits until Abby is distracted, then beckons me over and hands me the fat envelope I saw on Roman's desk earlier today.

"Mr. Stevanovsky asked me to give you this as an advance on your first paycheck."

I bite down on a retort about CEO Man having next-level arrogance by assuming I'm going to say yes to his job.

It doesn't escape me that Roman found a neat solution to his little dilemma of how to diplomatically give me my tip. Making it a pay advance is kind of hard to argue with.

If I take the job, that is.

Which I'm by no means sure I will.

On the other hand, the envelope could not come at a better time. At least I have enough to pay for a week in the motel and look around for a new apartment. A privately let one, of course. It's pretty hard to get a lease with only our Spanish medical cards as ID. And having no official lease is one less trail for the faceless men to follow.

Fortunately, southern Spain is plenty used to housing illegal immigrants.

"CEO Man is back, at least, along with those juicy Hale tips." Abby looks extremely pleased with herself. "The bodyguard's name is Dimitry, by the way."

I'm not entirely certain if it's correct to refer to the huge, tattooed Dimitry as Roman's bodyguard. Going on the silent understanding I've observed between the two, I've no doubt that in bratva terms, Dimitry is Roman's closest *vor*. There's absolutely no way he's anything but bratva. He came in wearing a T-shirt one day after a workout that left Abby starry-eyed with lust, and I noticed a tattoo of a rose entwined in barbed wire on his forearm.

Papa has a similar one.

It's given to Russians who are incarcerated when they are

still teenagers, usually in a juvenile facility. Of course, in Papa's case, it was a Russian gulag, not a juvenile facility.

Because I was expecting to move motels again today, I've given away my afternoon shift to a backpacker friend of Abby's, something I'm very grateful for right now. I need time to think.

Our current motel is only a block from the café. The day nurse has taken Papa out for a walk when I return. I pay for the week in advance, ignoring the manager's comments about Papa's wheelchair damaging the walls, and his even more pointed comments that a motel isn't an aged care facility.

I pull out the contract and study it properly.

Half an hour later I've read it through three times, and I still have no idea what to do.

I'm not going to pretend the money isn't important.

Papa and I have been living on air for too long for me to lie to myself about how desperate our circumstances are. Without some kind of miracle, things are unlikely to get better anytime soon. Seen in that light, Roman's contract is a gift only a fool would turn down.

A fool with principles.

Desperate circumstances aside, I can't pretend this contract is anything other than money for sex.

I'd be selling Roman Stevanovsky my body, to use however he wished, whenever it pleased him to do so.

And I wish that idea didn't turn me on quite so much as it does.

I throw the contract down and stand up, moving restlessly around the room.

What the fuck is wrong with me, that I would even consider such an offer? Let alone find it actually arousing?

My bad-boy hardwired libido is one thing. But selling myself for money is quite another.

And if Papa should find out . . .

I shudder. Old and infirm my father might be, but something tells me that wouldn't stop him finding a way to put a bullet between Roman Stevanovsky's eyes.

Roman can never know who Papa is.

Even the thought of a meeting between the two men sends a cold trickle of fear down my spine. They would recognize each other as bratva in an instant. And from there, it would be a very short leap for Roman to discover who Papa and I truly are.

On the other hand, Papa and I are not safe out in the open, staying in motels where we are noticed. Somebody has already stolen our money and passports. Regardless of whether the thief was actually looking for us or just an opportunist, if anyone starts looking into the names on those passports, they'll get suspicious fast. Our fake identities won't stand up to any real scrutiny.

What better place to disappear than into Roman's fortress? With the money he's offering, I can easily find a discreet apartment and excellent care for Papa.

That contract offers me time—and invisibility.

And God knows we are in desperate need of both.

I stare at the contract again, feeling both the seductive attraction of it and the moral compromise it represents.

Then, with a physical effort, I put it to one side.

No matter what Lucia Lopez has had to do to survive, somewhere within me, I am still Darya Petrovsky. Heiress not just to the legendary contents of the Petrovsky vault, but to my father's legacy, the life he built from freezing cold poverty with nothing but his bare hands and ruthless determination. I can't dishonor that legacy now, no matter how dire the situation we face. To do so would be to betray everything he worked for.

I stuff the contract back into the pocket of my work bag, next to the fat envelope with my name on it, trying not to think of the fact that the money inside it is the last I will ever receive from Roman Stevanovsky.

I know that declining his offer means I'll never see him again. CEO Man isn't one to waste his time.

I lie down on the sagging bed and turn to the wall, closing my eyes and trying not to think of my aching feet, the men hunting us, or the eight-hour shift still ahead of me.

8

ROMAN

I t's been four hours since Lucia left my office.

Two hundred and forty minutes.

And despite my phone's incessant buzzing, the only message I'm waiting on remains noticeably absent.

Will she sign it?

With every passing moment that Lucia doesn't answer, my tension ratchets up a notch.

It's just because you want to fuck her.

There are a million other women out there who'd leap at what that contract offers. Damn, I wouldn't even need to throw in the offer of money. And despite what I told Lucia, au pairs are hardly a rare breed. One phone call and a decent salary package would have another one on my doorstep within the hour, even if I had to fly them in from overseas.

Lucia Lopez is no more than a passing urge, the contract just a means to an end.

But no matter what I tell myself, her final words as she left my office have left me with a distinctly uneasy feeling. *"If you think that asking me to formally become your live-in sex slave is a fact I want widely advertised, then you're even more delusional than I thought."*

I stare out the car window to avoid Dimitry's eyes and press my fingers to my temples to alleviate an increasingly uncomfortable headache. It's been a long time since my sex life has caused me any kind of concern.

Actually, I've *never* allowed it to cause me concern.

I don't do love. I do mutually convenient sex.

Frequently, and with willing partners whose names I rarely recall after the momentary lust has passed.

Love leaves only wreckage in its wake.

I learned that lesson as a child. It's not one I intend to repeat.

It's a measure of how unsettled I am that it's almost a relief when we pull up outside Alhaurin prison. The relicf lasts as long as it takes for me to exit the vehicle and notice the license plates on the black SUV parked nearby.

"What the fuck is that *mudak* doing here?" I slam the car door with enough force to shake the whole vehicle. "Nikolai should know better than to turn up on my day."

Dimitry rolls his eyes. "Since when has Nikolai known anything?"

Good point. I stalk through security, seething. Mikhail's younger brother has been a gigantic pain in my ass for over a decade. In my current mood, seeing him seated opposite Yuri, clad in his customary shiny track pants and designer T-shirt, blond hair greasy with product and slicked back from his narrow little face, has me grinding my teeth. Where Mikhail always favored his mother's darker coloring, Nikolai is the spitting image of his father, which only annoys me more today.

"*Otets.*" I greet Yuri with the respectful title of father, completely ignoring Nikolai. At seventy, and after six years in prison, Yuri is no longer the feared *pakhan* who once ran Malaga with an iron fist. Without the benefit of a well-tailored suit, his sagging paunch stands out against the thin frame, and his features are slack, the once bright blue eyes sunken and nervously darting this way and that.

"Don't be angry, *moy syn.*" Yuri licks his lips and glances around, leaning in as if to speak in confidence. "I have good reason for inviting both of my sons to meet with me today."

I swallow my annoyance for the second time. It's bad enough that Yuri insists on these weekly updates of "his" business. There are always eyes watching our movements. Such regular visits to a convicted felon don't help the rumors that continue to swirl around my name and Hale's reputation.

Including Nikolai in the meeting increases the risk tenfold.

"I paid the guards so we could both visit." Nikolai shoots me a rather triumphant glance, as if this accomplishment shows some kind of genius.

"And now they're all watching us have this little meeting. Way to stay under the radar, Nikolai." I don't attempt to soften my tone. He scowls and lights another of his ever-present cigarettes. Clearly his payment to the guards also includes the right to smoke.

"Nikolai tells me you haven't been to visit Pillars since it reopened." Yuri takes one of his son's cigarettes and lights it, leaning back in his chair as he blows a long plume of smoke directly into my face. "You are *pakhan* in my place, Roman. Your bratva need you."

It's an effort to keep my expression blank. This is an old argument, one Mikhail and I carefully navigated for years.

I miss you, my brother.

For an instant I feel Mikhail's absence so much it takes my breath away.

Yuri so adored his eldest son that he would bow to Mikhail's judgment without question. But I am not Yuri's natural-born son, and adopted or not, I won't ever have the same standing Mikhail did.

"I have told you before that I do not interfere in Nikolai's business interests, *Otets*." It's a struggle to maintain the facade of respect with Nikolai's smug face in punching distance. "Pillars nightclub, and the associated interests, are entirely his responsibility. Nikolai has his own *vor*. He doesn't need me looking over his shoulder."

And I've worked night and day so that your grandchildren can grow up with clean hands, far away from your dirty legacy of girls, drugs, and gambling that occupies Nikolai's time.

But I don't say any of that. Yuri comes from another time, a different mindset. He and Mikhail fought bitterly over the establishment of Hale, but by then Yuri was in prison and Mikhail was *pakhan*. By mutual agreement, Mikhail and I never told Yuri about Mercura. Both of us instinctively knew that Yuri would never understand it. As far as Yuri knows, Hale Property is just our legitimate front, while Nikolai runs what Yuri considers to be the "real" end of the Stevanovsky bratva.

Nikolai's business is the old way of doing business, and the one Yuri understands. For the past two years, since Mikhail's death, I've walked a delicate line between pretending to respect Nikolai's independence and keeping him and his sordid business well away from Hale. More importantly, away from Mercura, about which Nikolai knows absolutely nothing.

It hasn't been easy, and I don't like lying to Yuri, who is the reason I'm not still on the streets, and to whom I know I owe everything.

But in the end I had to choose between protecting Mikhail's legacy and making his father happy. And loyal though I am, Mikhail's children are my priority. Yuri will spend the rest of his days in jail, whereas the children have their whole lives in front of them.

As for Nikolai—if it wasn't for what I owe Yuri, I'd have put a bullet between his eyes long ago. The little prick is as nasty as he is incompetent. It's almost a full-time job keeping his bumbling ineptitude from sinking Hale altogether.

"I understand what you and Mikhail had to do, after the raids." Yuri nods sagely, as if Mikhail and I built Hale at his command, rather than despite it. "I made you *pakhan* over my second son because it was Mikhail's wish, and because I thought you had the balls for the job."

I stiffen, and Dimitry shifts uneasily in the seat behind me.

"Am I to understand you are reconsidering that decision, *Otets*?" My tone is still even and respectful, but by the way Nikolai shifts his chair subtly away from me, my cold fury is clear enough.

"No, no." Yuri waves me away, but the light of petty triumph in his eyes makes me grit my teeth. "Sixteen years ago you stepped between Mikhail and a bullet. That is not something I will ever forget, Roman. You were poor, an orphan surviving on the streets. There was no reason for you to come to the defense of a rich college kid on spring break, and yet you did." He smiles ingratiatingly at me, but the petty light remains in his eyes.

I've learned over the years that Yuri only ever tells this story when he wants something. It's his subtle way of reminding me of where I came from and what he has done for me.

I also know there's no point in interrupting him once he starts telling the story.

I force my face into a neutral expression and distract myself by remembering the juicy heat of Lucia Lopez's open mouth as she screamed against my palm.

Khuy.

I'm immediately hard, and this is no place for that.

I drag my attention back to Yuri.

"You saved Mikhail from the consequences of a stupid mistake with no thought for your own safety." Yuri smiles fondly in reminiscence, and despite the fact that I loathe the occasions when he drags this story out, I feel my heart soften a little. If there is one thing that Yuri and I unquestionably share, it is our love for Mikhail.

Yuri's eldest son was reckless, there was no doubt. But even as a teenager, he was also incredibly generous, with the biggest heart I've ever known.

The week I met Mikhail in Miami, he was drinking every night in the restaurant where I was busing tables. He lit up the place night after night, with laughter and enormous tips. One night he even took me with him and his friends after the restaurant closed, insisting I drink tequila with them until we were both rolling drunk. Unfortunately, his generosity put a target on his back.

The following night I noticed two of the more notorious thieves in our district eyeing up Mikhail and his friends. When I saw them follow the college kids on their way to a beach party, I knew it meant trouble. It might not have, if Mikhail was the kind of person to just hand over his wallet when they pulled a gun.

But of course he wasn't. He was Yuri Stevanovsky's son, after all.

"You saved my son's life when you stepped between him and that bullet. Then he saved yours by bringing you out to my yacht, where we found a discreet doctor and managed to keep you out of jail." Yuri gives me his serious look. "That is why you became brothers, and why I brought you into my family. When a man saves a life, that life belongs to him. You and Mikhail belonged to each other. I always respected that."

Nikolai has stayed silent throughout this little recital, though he has chain-smoked the entire time, his face wearing a petulant expression that is all too familiar. Nikolai was barely ten when Mikhail and I met at the age of seventeen. He's only twenty-five now. And he hates this story almost as much as I do. Nikolai was still a teenager when Mikhail and I lived the blood-soaked days of the bratva wars that followed Yuri's incarceration. Unfortunately, while we were fighting, Nikolai was visiting his father in prison and absorbing Yuri's business views. Back then it had seemed harmless enough. Now, I fervently wish we'd taken him in hand.

"Nicky has a proposition for you," Yuri says now.

Pizdozh. Here it comes.

"Oh?" I say politely, still not looking at Nikolai.

"Cádiz Football Club." Yuri announces this with the same pomposity Nikolai used when he boasted about bribing the prison guards. "The manager has approached Nicky, looking for sponsorship."

"You want us to launder Nicky's income through Cádiz FC?" I keep a straight face with no small effort. "You don't think that might be, er, a *red flag*, if you'll excuse the football pun?"

Dimitry's snort of laughter is discernible enough that I hastily speak again to cover it. "I mean no disrespect, *Otets*. But using a football club to launder profits is how you ended up in jail the first time. I just think it might be . . . risky, to repeat that pattern."

"Not if it's Hale, rather than Pillars, who is the official sponsor." Nikolai speaks up for the first time, glancing resentfully in my direction. "Nobody would see anything wrong with that."

Nobody except the hundreds of federal officers currently watching our every move.

God, Nikolai is stupid.

"If you want to work with Cádiz, Nikolai, you have my permission to do so." I've heard enough, and I don't have time for this shit. It's time to remind them both that no matter how I got here, I am now *pakhan*. What I say goes, and they both know it. "When I gave you Pillars, you asked for complete autonomy in running it. I gave you that, with my respect and trust. I don't interfere with Pillars, or any of the businesses you operate from it. I don't even ask," I say pointedly, "for you to pay tribute on those businesses, as is my right. I have given you free rein, Nikolai. Helped when you've asked for it and stayed away when you haven't." I glance between Yuri and his son to make sure my next point drives home. "But nor will I risk Hale to wash your income any more than I already do. I've set up an entire branch of the company to manage your earnings, at no small cost to the organization as a whole. If you want more than I can offer, then you are free to pursue Cádiz independently." I pin Nikolai with a look hard enough to remind him of who I am. "You will also take whatever consequences might come from that decision. Am I understood?"

For a moment it looks like he might argue.

Oh, please do, you little fuck.

Between my state of semi-arousal and waiting for Lucia Lopez to say yes to that goddamn contract, I'd like nothing better than to connect my fist with Nicky's face.

But in the end, he just nods sulkily and lights another cigarette.

Good choice.

I spend another twenty minutes giving Yuri a bullshit update and listening to Nikolai boast about the celebrities that are patronizing Pillars and all the money he's making. I even pretend to be interested, for Yuri's sake.

I'm about to make my excuses when Yuri pipes up again, this time in a wheedling tone that makes my skin crawl.

"When will you bring the children to visit their grandpapa? And what about darling Inger?"

Never is the answer to the first question.

And "darling Inger" is a walking nightmare.

Yuri, however, has always believed Mikhail's ex-wife to be the epitome of what a Russian wife should be, and Mikhail never had the heart to take her down from the pedestal Yuri put her on.

"The children are in London with Vera." Vera is Yuri's dragon of a wife. To my vast relief, after her husband's incarceration, Vera chose to live in London rather than Spain. Personally, I think she's just happy to be far away from Yuri. "And Inger is currently on a modeling contract in the US."

"Ah." Yuri nods, yet again as if all of this is by his decree. "Inger is so beautiful. Such a beauty needs a good husband, Roman. And it would be Mikhail's dream, I think, for you to raise his children together." The pale blue eyes turn a little misty, his Russian accent growing harsher. "A man needs a wife, Roman. You could do a great deal worse than Inger." He gives me a sly smile. "As I recall, it was you she favored in the beginning, was it not?"

You just stepped over the line, old man.

"I told you I don't plan to marry." The cold finality in my voice wipes the sentiment right off Yuri's face. "Mikhail's son will inherit Hale, and I will raise him to run it, as his father would have wanted. I have no need of either wife nor heir since, as you no doubt understand, I am *pakhan* only until little Mickey comes of age."

I barely manage not to add that even if I were to marry, Inger would be the very last damned person on this planet I would choose.

"Inger was Mikhail's wife. I would thank you not to disrespect your son's memory, or dishonor her, by bringing up a past that is long forgotten by us all." I glare at him across the pockmarked table. "Do I make myself clear?"

When Yuri finally drops his eyes, it's with the same sullen resentment his son showed moments earlier.

I spend the next ten minutes pretending to give a shit about Nikolai's business and to take Yuri's advice. It's never smart to piss off a man who has nothing but time in which to dwell on his grudges. Nor do I fancy making an open enemy of Nikolai, no matter how useless the little prick is. By the time I take my leave, we're back on amicable terms, which is just how I like it.

I've got bigger things to worry about than dealing with those two.

Like whether or not Lucia Lopez is going to surrender to me.

9

ROMAN

"**Y**ou want to talk about it?" Dimitry glances at me as we turn onto the highway.

"Nope." I stare at my phone, which is still silent. It's been five and a half hours since I gave her the contract.

Three hundred and thirty minutes.

And only thirty minutes remain until the deadline is up.

I keep seeing Lucia as she was when she came to my office this morning: eyes wide, lips glistening, and hair piled up in a way I haven't seen before. I have an almost irresistible urge to tug it free of whatever pin is holding it precariously in place and watch it tumble down. Preferably over my hands, while her mouth is full of my dick.

By the way her luscious chest was heaving when she arrived in my office, she'd clearly left it until the last minute to decide to actually show up. And now here I am, for the second time today, watching my phone and counting the goddamn minutes.

I don't like being strung along, any more than I'd liked her referring to her proposed role as my *"live-in sex slave."*

Not that the term doesn't raise a mass of delicious fantasies, many of which involve those glistening, bee-stung lips.

Moaning my name.

Devouring my cock.

Screaming as she loses it.

I want to make her come undone, bring her to the edge over and again until those lips beg me for release. I can already imagine them against my ear, whispering every filthy fantasy she's been harboring in the months since we met.

"Lick me . . . please . . . I need your tongue. I need you inside me, Roman."

I shift restlessly. The lingering state of arousal I've been in ever since I watched that video playback is turning into full-blown fantasy. The slightest recollection of her trembling under my hands is enough to make me iron hard.

Which, I tell myself, is the exact reason I put this proposal to her in the first place.

I need to get Miss Lopez underneath me as soon as possible. Get into her, then get the fuck out of the weird state of crippling lust her mouth-watering body has put me into.

"Hey." Dimitry snaps his fingers in my direction. "I said, answer your phone. Pavel's trying to get hold of you. Something about a background check?"

I answer the eternally vibrating phone without meeting Dimitry's curious eyes. "You got what I asked for?" I snap.

"Well—yes and no." Even down the phone line, I can tell the tech head is quaking in his ridiculous trainers.

"What the fuck does that mean?" I drum my fingers on the leather seat impatiently. "You can hack the damn Pentagon.

Surely a simple background check is within your capabilities?"

"It is if I have enough to go on." Pavel's indignation is palpable. "You gave me a name. Nothing else. No birth date, no address, no passport number. Do you have any idea how many Lucia Lopezs there are in Spain?"

"I gave you her workplace."

"Which is notorious for hiring illegal immigrants and paying them in cash. Despite that, I did manage to narrow the options down based on approximate age and location."

"Then stop fucking around and give me what you've found."

"Sending it through now, sir." Pavel's injured tone makes it very clear that he doesn't appreciate his skills being used for such mundane tasks as running background checks. I don't give a fuck. I pay him to do whatever is needed. And Pavel is the only person I trust to sift through Lucia's past.

"Background check, huh?" Dimitry has a shit-eating grin that tells me he knows exactly who I'm looking into.

"I need an au pair." I open the file Pavel has sent through.

"And you think the delectable Miss Lopez possesses the appropriate . . . erm . . . *skills*, for that particular role?"

I give him a look that's left hundreds shaking in their boots, but seems to have no discernible effect at all on Dimitry, the prick.

"She speaks several languages. She's clearly a hard worker. And she needs a job." Despite my harsh rejoinder, he's still grinning in a way that thoroughly pisses me off.

I flick through the pages Pavel has sent. He's right; there's fuck all here, and what there is comes from the application she made for a medical card, and its subsequent use.

Lucia is listed as Argentinian. She may or may not have come from Morocco by boat. It seems she's currently living in cheap motels, shifting every other day. The medical card has been used far more than I would have expected, and the current motel manager, Pavel reports, is very annoyed about the wheelchair used by the "old man" who is her companion.

I put my phone down and frown out the window.

Old man?

If he's in a wheelchair, it's unlikely to be a boyfriend.

Which is good, considering that even the thought of Lucia Lopez having a boyfriend is enough to make me want to punch something again.

But if it's an ailing relative, then that can only work in my favor. It means Miss Lopez has responsibilities. Someone she has to care for.

A reason to say yes to my contract.

I stare at my phone.

There's fifteen minutes to go.

10

LUCIA

The buzzing of my phone alarm jolts me out of siesta at four forty in the afternoon.

The contract stares at me from the table by my bed. I fell asleep reading it over again.

Twenty minutes to go before time is up.

I scramble off the bed and into the shower. I normally wake up long before the alarm goes off, setting it just as a precaution.

Maybe I just didn't want to wake before the deadline was up.

Not that it matters, I tell myself as I hastily dress. *I'm making the right decision. The only decision.*

I push Roman's face determinedly out of my mind. I can't afford to think about him again.

If I do, all I see are the minutes ticking down to the moment when I say goodbye to him forever.

A muffled thump comes from next door, and I freeze. Then I hear a muted grunt and spring into action.

"Papa!" Heart racing, I tear open my door and then, key shaking in my hands, unlock Papa's.

There's no sign of the nurse. The first thing I see is Papa's wheelchair, upended on the floor, one wheel spinning in the air. Then, to my utter relief, I see Papa.

He's lying on the floor, pushing himself grimly upright with his one working arm, trying to drag himself back to the chair. He shakes his head angrily when he sees me. "Sleep," he grunts, waving me away impatiently. He thumps his chest. "Stupid," he says in Russian, his face twisted with frustration.

Then I see the shattered teacup and toppled electric kettle beside him on the floor, the boiling water from it still steaming where it's spread across the tiles.

The cord from the kettle crosses the floor at ankle height.

Just the wrong height for Papa's wheelchair.

For the sake of his beloved afternoon cup of tea, my father is sprawled on a hard tiled floor.

He narrowly missed being scalded by an entire kettle of boiling water.

What if I hadn't been here? What if he'd knocked himself unconscious and lain here all night, possibly badly injured and burned?

My blood runs cold at what I might have come home to. It's also unlike Papa to be so careless.

"How did this happen?" I gently help him upright, ignoring his muted protestations that he's fine. Papa will be telling me he's fine on his deathbed.

He gestures to the window, frowning, trying to form words. Through a combination of garbled speech and hand movements, I understand that he wasn't watching what he was doing, because he thought he saw someone out of the window. My chest hitches with the familiar, dragging fear.

"Someone like who, Papa?"

His hands mimic a camera. I close my eyes briefly, willing my pounding heart to calm down.

It could be a coincidence. You don't know for certain that it was someone looking for you.

But I see the same grim caution in Papa's eyes that I feel, the ever-present edge of danger that haunts our every moment. "Are you sure they were trying to photograph you?"

He makes an impatient gesture, an inarticulate noise of frustration. I understand the thrust: *does it matter?*

I don't need Papa to point out the obvious. First the robbery, and now this? When you're running, you don't wait for coincidences to be disproved. You assume that a coincidence means you've been found. It's how we've survived this long.

That means I have to assume that someone has become suspicious about us. I don't know who or why, but I do know that I have no choice but to work on the assumption that we are no longer safe.

Combined with the loss of our passports, our current poverty, and my father's weak state, the thought that anyone might have noticed us is beyond terrifying. I've never felt more vulnerable, less able to find a way out. I'm swamped by an overwhelming wave of exhaustion and defeat.

Where the hell are we supposed to run to now?

And how will I take care of Papa?

The second question gives me an outlet for my fear.

"What about the nurse?" I ask angrily. "Where the hell was she when this was going on?"

Papa shakes his head, frowning, and pats my hand. Through his shortened words and gestures, I understand that the nurse had a family emergency. He insisted she go home early. "*Ne—nuzhno,*" he chokes out. *Don't need.*

I purse my lips, but don't bother trying to argue that he

most certainly *does* need help. More than I have been able to give him. Much more.

My father does not deserve to live this way, and I'm riddled with guilt every time I confront the circumstances to which he has been reduced.

Never once in our chaotic journey has he ever complained, no matter how arduous the conditions. Not during our terrifying midnight escape from the Miami compound, when we raced through the dark waters of Biscayne Bay in a tiny tin fishing boat. Not in the weeks that followed when we lived in squalor, disguising ourselves among the other lost and downtrodden while the Orlovs combed the city for us. Not during the long sea journey that followed, as we reversed the path taken by so many South American migrants, traveling first to Cuba and then across to Cancún. Not for all the months it took us, by boat, bus, truck, and sometimes just on foot, to finally reach Argentina and the contact of my father's who helped us with passports.

Papa didn't complain years later, when we made another, far more dangerous crossing by sea from Morocco to Spain, in a hazardous inflated raft that we all believed would sink at any moment.

During all those journeys, Papa had cradled other peoples' babies when they cried. Before the strokes got worse and claimed his voice, he'd sung songs in Russian. He'd gripped the arms of men who feared death, staring the fear right out of them.

Sergei Petrovsky had seen worse and survived it. And somehow those around him sensed that and took strength from him, even without knowing from where that strength came.

My father was always careful about what he told my brother and me about his past. As an adult, I realized the tales he did tell when we were young, and after he'd drunk a little too much vodka, were carefully crafted to amuse and entertain children rather than to give any real picture of the truth.

All Papa would ever say about the two thousand miles he walked to escape Russia, across frozen tundra and multiple borders, all the way to Switzerland, was that the terrible journey through starvation and below-zero temperatures had been worth it, just so that one day he might give my brother and me life.

All of this I think of as I tidy Papa and help him to bed, ignoring the fierce look in his piercing blue eyes and his insistence that he is entirely capable of looking after himself.

Papa has faced death a thousand times and more. Never once has he lost his will and determination to survive, to transcend his circumstances.

And now, when we are facing possible exposure and the hideous prospect of being recaptured by the Orlovs, Papa is too weak to save himself or anyone else—and I am hesitating to do the one thing that could save us both.

Roman's contract offers me the means to not only hide from anyone who might be searching for us, but also to set about regaining everything we have lost. I'm being offered a chance to ensure Papa is safe and well cared for until I've had time to organize what we both need.

I'm being offered all this not through hardship, but by sleeping with Roman Stevanovsky.

A man who, let's face it, has literally owned my every sexual fantasy for the past five months. A man whose single glance makes my heart pound and my body liquid with desire.

A man who is undoubtedly a killer.

Which, given the life I lead, isn't a bad thing.

I am Darya Petrovsky, daughter of bratva legend Sergei Petrovsky. Any man involved with me needs to be a killer. A damn good one.

And something tells me that Roman Stevanovsky is the most ruthless killer I've seen in a long time.

Does that mean you plan to be . . . involved, with Roman Stevanovsky?

I close the door to Papa's room and glance at my phone.

4:57.

I pull the contract out of my bag. Holding it up against the motel wall, I scrawl my fake signature on it. Then I snap a photo of the signed paper.

4:59.

I take a deep breath and open up my messages.

I send Roman the photograph just as the numbers click over to five p.m.

AT ONE MINUTE PAST, Roman answers my message with a simple command: *My office, 6pm. Dress for dinner.*

My heart lurches to a stop, then starts racing like a horse in the Grand National.

It's the first time I will meet Roman wearing something other than my hated hot pants uniform. I tear the damn thing off without an ounce of regret and leave it lying in a discarded ball on the floor of my motel room.

What the hell does one wear to meet the man who wants me to be both a nanny and his sex slave?

It's not like the two roles are exactly complementary. And I've hardly accumulated a wardrobe full of options, given that I've spent most of the past couple of years in a work uniform. Nor am I sure if I'm dressing to get laid out on Roman's desk or to meet three children.

Laid out on his desk . . .

Oh, the filthy thoughts I've had about that smooth steel-gray surface.

I text Abby as I try on my limited wardrobe, explaining briefly that I'm resigning to take CEO Man's offer of being au pair to his godchildren.

OMG!! she messages as I'm standing in front of the mirror in my best lingerie. Then, a moment later: *SOOOO HOT.*

A third message pops up as I stare at the contents of my suitcase, desperately wishing that something appropriate will magically appear. *I hate you for abandoning me. But super stoked for you, too. Love you, Luce. Put in a good word for me with the hot bodyguard?*

A series of eggplant, fire, and laughing face emojis follow, with one last message: *I want to know EVERYTHING.*

Since there's absolutely no chance of that ever happening, I just reply with a laughing face and a love heart. My own is still thudding erratically.

After half an hour, and the entire contents of my suitcase being strewn haphazardly over every available surface, I finally settle on a strappy turquoise slip dress—*sin dress?*—that is both demure enough for children and . . . well . . . easily removed.

Oh, dear lord.

I bury my flaming face in my hands. Is this going to be my life now? Dressing with the expectation of sex at any given moment?

And *why* doesn't that horrify me quite as much as it definitely should?

I apply light makeup, not wanting to overdo it, and pile my hair up in a loose top bun. Then I open the small box I've carried with me ever since the day we fled Miami. Inside it is a pair of earrings, the only jewelry I took when Papa and I ran. They once belonged to my mother, who told me they're one of the rare treasures my father carried with him on his long journey from Russia to the West. They're turquoise teardrops encased in filigree white gold and studded with tiny diamonds.

They would also fetch over a million dollars in an auction house.

Which would solve all our problems, except that putting them up for sale would be painting a House of Fabergé–sized target on our backs.

While nobody knows exactly what lies in our Miami vault, for as long as I can remember, whispers have swirled about my family's rumored association with Peter Carl Fabergé, the legendary goldsmith who made jeweled eggs for the Russian imperial family before the 1917 revolution.

This much I know is true: Papa's father, my grandfather, did indeed help Fabergé escape Russia. It's the reason he and his entire family were locked up in the gulag, where my father was born.

I don't even remember how I first learned that part of our family story was true. What I do know is that our history was a fact that hid in the shadows, a past I inhaled with my first breath, but that was never spoken of.

Ironically, since we left Miami, not even knowledgeable jewelers have given my earrings a second look. I guess that nobody imagines an illegal immigrant will be walking around wearing over a million dollars on their ears.

And I usually don't wear them. My mother's earrings have a value to me that goes far beyond money. But some old vestige of pride inside me wants to wear them tonight. Wants Roman Stevanovsky to catch a glimpse of Darya Petrovsky, the woman I've had to hide for so long.

It's dangerous, I know. But given that I'm about to visit the office of a man who has just bought my body for the foreseeable future, I figure I've well and truly crossed the danger line.

11

LUCIA

By the time I'm checking my reflection in the Hale elevator, it's two minutes to six. I step out to find the reception desk empty and the entire floor seemingly deserted. Heart thudding, I knock tentatively on the heavy door.

"Come in."

Roman's low growl sends a thrill straight from ear to groin.

The lights are low when I enter the vast office. Beyond the plate glass windows, the dying sun is setting fire to the sea, painting a brilliant backdrop to the pinprick city lights below. Roman is standing behind his desk, unsmiling and unreadable as ever.

"You do enjoy living dangerously, Miss Lopez."

I almost laugh aloud at how closely his words mirror my own recent thoughts.

"Your message came right at five p.m. Now you make it to my office right at six. Let us both hope your precision timing is an indication that you take punctuality seriously." The sardonic tone in his voice suggests his meaning is quite different than his words. It also gets my inner sassy coffee bitch going.

"You could always try giving me a little notice of your intentions."

His eyes gleam. "I give the orders, Miss Lopez. I don't take them."

The thought of Roman Stevanovsky giving me orders opens a realm of possibilities that make my mouth suddenly dry.

Take your dress off, Miss Lopez.

Wrap your mouth around my cock, Miss Lopez.

I'm going to fuck you hard against the plate glass windows until you scream, Miss Lopez . . .

The mere thought of any of those options has me swollen and ready for every one of them. Suddenly I'm impatient as hell to get on with this. Ever since I screamed into his hand, my body has been screaming out for him to take it, any which way he pleases, as hard and often as he can. And right now I'm so damned hot I just want him to—

"The children arrive tomorrow morning."

Uh . . . what?

"Sit down, Miss Lopez." His dark eyes are hooded and unsettlingly disinterested. He waits until I'm seated, then takes his own chair. "Luis is the children's driver. He will pick you up at eight thirty tomorrow morning and take you to the airport to meet their flight, which arrives at ten." He sounds like he's giving orders to one of his minions.

Then I remember that I *am* one of his minions.

"Luis will take you straight from the airport to the children's apartments, where your rooms are. You will have your belongings ready when he collects you in the morning, since you will be living in my building from tomorrow."

I swallow, my throat suddenly dry. Of course, I knew the contract began tomorrow. But that gives me only tonight to organize accommodation and care for Papa, not to mention concoct a story that he won't see through.

"Is there a problem, Miss Lopez?"

For a man who has recently signed me up to be his sexual plaything, CEO Man appears to be anything but interested in ravishing me. Which, after the tension of the last few days, I find oddly disappointing.

Oh, girl, I hear Abby's voice chiding me in my head, *you have got it baaaaad.*

"I just have—a few things to organize."

He frowns. "Then I suggest you organize them, Miss Lopez." He glances at his laptop screen. "I notice you haven't provided us with bank account details for your salary, nor your passport number, as stated on the form."

Oh, crap. I should have seen this coming. Actually, I *did* see it coming.

I just hadn't wanted to.

"I also need an address for Luis to collect you from." He pins me with a penetrating stare that sets my danger radar to sky-high. "Or should I assume you will be in the same motel in which you passed last night?"

I swallow again, barely trusting myself to speak. "You spied on me?" But if I hoped to sound challenging, I fail dismally. My voice is a faint rasp, and even I can hear the trembling fear beneath it.

Damn it.

I can't control the sudden wash of terror that leaves me breathless. If Roman can find me, then others can. And if he knows where I live, does he know about Papa?

How much does he know, exactly?

Mentally I calculate the distance from desk to door, but part of me already knows it's futile. The pounding of my heart is like the roar of the ocean in my ears, and I'm blazing hot then freezing cold at the realization of my own stupidity.

How did I ever think I'd get away with this?

"Relax, Miss Lopez." Roman is watching me through narrowed eyes, but I don't see humor in his expression. I can't read it at all, if I'm honest. Not to mention that I'm still reeling with shock and fear. "I run a background check on all my employees."

And no background should exist. None.

"I ran yours privately." He's still watching me. I get the feeling he is aware of every terrified heartbeat, every hitched breath as I try to calculate what damage has been done, what has been exposed and to whom.

"I thought it was wise, given that most of the employees at that café are here without visas. My security man is very discreet, and his online activities well hidden. Then again"—he leans back, clasping his hands behind his neck—"so are yours. My search turned up very little indeed. You are something of the enigma, Miss Lopez. And given the skills of my security team, that is saying something."

I stay silent. I have no idea what to say. I'm still cursing my own naivety in thinking he wouldn't check into me. Of course he would. What self-respecting criminal risks hiring another one?

"I will require your passport, Miss Lopez."

"I don't have one." That answer is easy enough. And honest. I meet his eyes when I say it.

"Your date and place of birth, then."

He watches me hesitate. Finally I give him the Lucia Lopez date of birth from my fake passport. It shouldn't lead anywhere or raise any red flags. But that doesn't mean I like taking the risk.

"I take it that your lack of a bank account is due to your illegal status?"

He nods curtly when I confirm this. "I will give you access to one of our business accounts. It won't be in your name, but you have my word it will be exclusively yours. It will also be entirely untraceable. I take it that will be acceptable?"

Acceptable? Who the hell can organize an untraceable account under a fake name at a moment's notice?

Bratva, that's who.

But given the circumstances, it's also an incredibly generous offer. If I'm honest, such sensitivity isn't something I'd have expected from CEO Man. He hasn't particularly struck me as the caring type.

Except when his hands were taking care of every inch of you . . .

I wrench myself out of that line of thought, deeply disturbed that when faced with the possibility of my carefully disguised identity being uncovered, all I can think about is getting naked with the very person threatening my exposure.

"Yes." I gulp. "That will be acceptable."

"This doesn't mean my security man will cease his background search, Miss Lopez." Is it my imagination, or is there the faint hint of a question in that comment? Either way, it doesn't matter. I'm not saying anything that will make this situation more perilous than it already is.

And besides, his security man won't find a damn thing, no matter how clever he is. Beyond one long-ago flight from Argentina to Morocco, Lucia Lopez barely exists. Nor is there any connection between her and Juan Ortega, an old Argentinian man who made the same flight several days after her and never returned. There's no record of either of us ever arriving in Spain.

There is no trail to find. Which, I remind myself, inhaling deeply, is why I *did* feel confident to take this job. No, I didn't have time to play this exact scenario out in my mind, and despite all I've been through in the past few years, this moment is probably the first time I've genuinely feared someone looking closely into my false identity. *But you're* not *a naive fool, Darya,* I tell myself sternly. I've covered our tracks at every step. Nor am I a criminal. Or not in any way that poses a threat to Roman's household. As far as he will ever know, I'm just an illegal immigrant who needs to catch a break.

And this is that break.

Now all I have to do is keep my mouth shut for a few months—then run. As far, and as fast, as I possibly can.

Roman stands up, and my heart starts that slow thudding again.

Is this the moment?

His hands grip the edge of his desk, and all I can think of is how those long fingers stroked me until I was wet and wanting, before plunging into me and sending me rocketing into oblivion.

"Miss Lopez." Roman is looking at me with slightly raised eyebrows. "I said that we have a table waiting."

He stands, gesturing to the door. I stumble to my feet, almost knocking the chair over in my haste.

That's it?

No ravishing on the desk? No clever fingers right where I'm aching for them?

Maybe he wants dinner first.

I wasn't expecting seduction. But so far, this is all far more businesslike than I *was* expecting.

ROMAN DRIVES us to the restaurant himself, in a gleaming black Mercedes-Maybach sedan that whispers through the streets in the silent luxury only custom-made leather and steel can deliver. He drives with the same ruthless precision he runs Hale. I try not to imagine the dexterous hands on the wheel caressing my body.

We don't speak for the duration of the journey, not least because I'm trying to work out how the hell I'm supposed to organize the shitstorm that is my life by tomorrow morning. Especially if I'll be spending tonight spread out across Roman Stevanovsky's bed.

I cross my legs and look away from those hands. My almost unbearable state of sexual tension is extremely unhelpful in my efforts to think analytically.

Roman parks at the rear of a restaurant I've never heard of, and we're met by a maître d' who is clearly expecting us. He shows us to a private terrace overlooking a small cove just beyond the main beaches. Night has fallen, and we're far enough from the city lights for the stars to glisten on the sea below.

Champagne arrives in tulip glasses, along with morsels of tapas I have absolutely no appetite for.

"Lucia."

Oh, the way he says my name.

"Mr. Stevanovsky." I sip the champagne, which is, predictably, divine.

"Outside the office, please use Roman." His mouth quirks at my visible surprise. "It's less confusing for the children if you address me as they do."

"Roman, then." The name feels like sin on my lips.

Sin and danger.

"I invited you here tonight because there are some matters that are better said in a less formal setting than the office."

"Oh." I swallow more champagne to hide my nerves. I'm not certain if this is my signal to leap into seductress mode, nor do I have any idea of how I would go about that anyway.

"In the children's presence, I will be your employer,

nothing more. Our private arrangement will, under no circumstances, be disclosed to them in any way."

"I'm pretty sure I got that message loud and clear in your office." I don't know what it is about him that triggers my snark setting. I just can't seem to help it, just like I can't help holding his eyes as I take another sip.

His eyes darken. "I don't generally tolerate sass in my employees, Miss Lopez."

"And I think it will be *less confusing* for the children if you call me Lucia."

"Touché." His lips almost tug at the corners. "And agreed."

"Look at us," I say, sitting back in my chair. "Agreeing already." I'm pushing it, and I know why. What I really want to do is to reach across the table for his strong hands and put them on me. I want to close the door on the restaurant and beg him to take me on this terrace, or anywhere else he chooses.

Now that I've signed his damned contract, I want what I signed up for. Only I can't ask for it. I'm more than aware that no matter the intimacy of this setting, Roman Stevanovsky will explore the details of our contract entirely on his own terms, and not a moment earlier.

Which does nothing to alleviate the strung-out tension in my body.

"Our agreement is a financial one, Miss Lopez. Nothing more." His curt use of the formal address is enough to confirm my suspicions. "I will provide you with enough money to take care of whatever personal and financial commitments may make demands on your time."

My hand stops halfway to bringing the glass to my lips, hovering uncertainly in midair. What, exactly, does he know? I'm thrust back into the same anxiety I felt in his office. I force the glass to continue to my lips, trying not to let it shake.

"In exchange," he goes on, "you will make yourself entirely

available to meet whatever demands *I* make on your time." He turns the tulip glass slowly on the table, never taking his eyes from my face. "But I don't date, Miss Lopez, and I don't have either the time or interest to meet anyone's emotional needs. Do not mistake our agreement for anything other than a business one."

His meaning is cold, loud, and crystal clear. But contrary to the grim warning he surely intends, his words almost make me laugh aloud with relief.

As far as I'm concerned, the less interest he takes in my life, the better.

"You mean you're going to try not to fall in love with me? I'm shocked, Mr. Stevanovsky." I raise my glass in his direction. "And good luck with that, by the way. I make a hell of a good cup of coffee."

This time I get the sardonic smirk that always makes my flesh quiver. "I've been drinking your particular brew for several months now, Lucia. Trust me when I say there's no chance of any unexpected side effects."

"No chance, huh?" I shake my head in mock disappointment and give him my best Scarlett O'Hara impersonation. "You, Mr. Stevanovsky, are no gentleman."

"And you, Miss Lopez, are no lady." He throws Rhett Butler's line right back at me. "Or you wouldn't have signed that contract."

Ouch.

"I think we can both agree we've crossed a moral line, Lucia." He leans across the table and fixes me with the stare that always leaves me breathless. "But I've always liked the danger zone. It's where the most exquisite pleasures are found. And the delivery of exquisite pleasure is a skill I enjoy practicing. At every available opportunity." His eyes linger just long enough to set my nerves afire. Then he lounges back in his chair with a return of the sardonic smirk, toying idly with his glass. "Our private contract will be played out only in my penthouse. I will ensure you always return to your own apartment before the children wake."

"No pajama parties, then?"

The dark eyes gleam. "Pajamas play no part whatsoever in any of my plans, I assure you."

I asked for that one.

"There is some personal time built into your schedule." His tone is crisp and businesslike once more. "Rest assured I will respect it."

I tense slightly. "Can I trust that *personal time* means I won't be followed?"

He scowls. "I have better things to do with my time than trail every one of my employees, Lucia."

Well, that's something, I guess.

If he means it, of course. I try not to think of how much I'm going to need to organize in whatever sliver of *personal time* he allows. It's a moment before I realize Roman is watching me closely.

And he doesn't look happy.

His hand has stilled on the table, his jaw hardening as his eyes bore into mine. "If you're contemplating any illicit liaisons, Miss Lopez, I advise you to reconsider."

I'm not contemplating anything of the kind, obviously. But that doesn't stop his death stare from sending a shiver down my spine.

"For the sake of absolute clarity," he snarls, "let me reiterate the exclusivity aspect of the contract. You're mine now, Lucia. To touch. To fuck. To take whichever way I choose. Mine, and nobody else's. Do I make myself clear?"

I'm not laughing now.

In fact, I can barely breathe.

I should be appalled by him claiming me as his possession. Instead, it's a measure of how far over the line I really am that my body is so hot and ready I'm almost squirming in my seat.

"Perfectly, Mr. Stevanovsky." My mouth is dry. "And just as we agreed, that exclusivity goes both ways?"

His eyes flatten with boredom.

"I don't make a habit of repeating myself, Miss Lopez." His tone is clipped and dismissive. He glances at his phone. "We should eat. As you mentioned, you have a lot to organize before tomorrow morning." He nods at the window, and the maître d' appears with a selection of exquisitely arranged tasting plates, which, unfortunately, I barely appreciate.

I can only think of what will come after this meal.

Will he fuck me right here? Take me back to that sinfully decadent penthouse? On the leather sofa? Or maybe up against the windows, so the whole city can watch him take me from behind . . .

I push the food around on my plate, my body heavy with anticipation.

"Let me make one thing very clear." Roman's harsh tone snaps me right out of the fantasies that have me wet and wanting and quite abruptly back to the present. "Please do not misinterpret my agreeing to the exclusivity clause as anything other than good business. Don't for an instant imagine this contract will lead to anything other than financial and sexual satisfaction. Our agreement lasts until the end of the school year. Five months. There won't be any extensions."

I'm mortified. My eyes have always given me away, and if they're a window into what the rest of me feels right now, Roman probably thinks he's contracted some dewy eyed desperado. I gather myself with an effort.

"Ah, you say that now." I return to snark setting with no small effort. "But they tell me coffee withdrawal is a bitch. I predict it will be you begging for the extension, not me."

He clasps my wrist, his grip loose but undeniably strong, dark eyes boring into mine. "The only person begging will be you, Miss Lopez. Begging me not to stop. Or to do it again. Harder. Faster. Deeper." His words send my body into a hot tailspin, his fingers searing straight through my skin. "Five months, Miss Lopez," he growls. "No extensions. No withdrawals. I will take you, Lucia. I will have you." His eyes reach into my soul, setting the flames inside me licking higher and higher. "And then," he says, letting my wrist drop limply to the table, "I will let you go."

I suck in a breath. I've never felt more unhinged in my life.

"Understood." I'm astonished my voice sounds so even.

"Good." He sits back and nods at the food. "Then perhaps now we can eat."

I have no idea how I get through the meal. The food is divine, of course. The setting is stunning.

I barely notice any of it.

I do, however, make certain to keep my attention on what Roman is saying, rather than what will come next. I might have just signed my body away to him, but I'm going to try to keep at least some of my mind to myself.

Try.

"Luis will pick you up at the motel," he's saying now, "unless you change addresses before morning, in which case you can text him. You will find his number in the file I've sent to your phone. It includes details about the children, as well as their schedules and all the relevant telephone numbers. Obviously, I expect you to study it tonight in preparation for their arrival tomorrow."

"Obviously."

Before or after you fuck me senseless? Sleep is clearly not going to be on my agenda tonight.

The rest of the meal is taken up with various logistics pertaining to the apartment block security, codes, etc. Then Roman picks up his phone and gives an order. He stands up as the last of the plates are cleared away and walks me down-stairs, where a black SUV is parked by his own.

"Luis will take you where you need to go." He opens the rear door.

"You mean that I'm not—that we won't be—" *Oh wow, Lucia. Subtle.*

"Since you're clearly a *Gone with the Wind* fan, let me give you another quote, Miss Lopez." His mouth settles back into his customary sardonic smirk. *"Some day, I will kiss you and you will like it."* The smirk deepens. *"But not now."*

I stare at him, torn between indignation and crippling desire.

He grins. "Tomorrow is another day, Miss Lopez."

Then he shuts the door.

I settle back into the leather seat, every part of me unsettled and restless.

That's the second damn time I've wasted my best lingerie.

12

ROMAN

I have three missed calls from Pavel, but I wait until I'm
back in the penthouse to call him. After spending my
evening battling a serious desire to tear Lucia's dress off
and fuck her senseless, I'm going to need something stronger
than champagne. And part of me is dreading whatever information he might have found. Not for the first time since I had
the bright idea of making Lucia Lopez my personal beck-and-
call girl, I wonder what the fuck I'm doing. Or more importantly, why.

Forget that. I know exactly why.

It took every ounce of self-restraint I possess not to make
her mine the second she walked into my office this evening.
But she's going to have a busy night, and I've made a life out of
practicing self-restraint. When I do take that body and make it
my own, I want to be certain I have Lucia's undivided atten-

tion. And I'm not going to deny that there's a certain dark satisfaction in knowing I've left her wanting.

It's a good thing I deleted the video of her in my office. Otherwise, I'm not certain I'd be able to resist the temptation of watching her again.

I pull my jacket off and pick up my phone. I need a distraction, fast.

"I don't know who the old man is, boss." Pavel's voice on speakerphone echoes off the empty walls. "I don't even have a name for him, other than Juan, which I learned from the day nurses she's been hiring lately."

I frown out the penthouse window at the city lights. "So it's a recent thing, her caring for him?"

"I don't think so. Her medical card has been used on his behalf several times over the past two years. His name isn't registered anywhere, even on a medical card."

"I thought that was illegal?" I shake my head. "Scrap that." The irony of me concerning myself with what is or isn't illegal doesn't escape me. But there's something about Lucia Lopez's situation that feels odd.

And I don't like odd.

Even if it waltzes into my office with siren-red lipstick and wearing a "tear it the fuck off me" dress that still has me hard.

"Boss?" Pavel asks tentatively.

"What?" I bark, trying not to think of how those siren red-lips would look wrapped around my cock. I keep imagining her dressed in silk and lace, dripping in quality jewelry instead of knockoff Fabergé earrings, no matter how good the fake replicas might be. There's something about the idea of seeing Lucia dressed in clothes I've bought her, wearing diamonds I've chosen, that gives me an almost savage rush of pleasure. Although, not nearly as much pleasure as does the idea of stripping that silk and lace slowly away from her body, leaving just the diamonds around her neck as I fuck her, slowly and thoroughly, in every part of this penthouse.

Christ. I grip the window divider hard enough to turn my knuckles white. I need to get that little *vedma* out of my head. I was so damn terrified she wasn't going to sign that contract I wound up handing my new secretary her ass this afternoon, meaning I've just added yet another crisis to a day that's tested me more than any I can recall in recent times.

All because for some reason I cannot understand, I want Lucia Lopez in my bed more than I can remember ever having wanted anything in my life.

But not if she's trouble. And so far, everything about her screams exactly that.

If I hoped Pavel's next words would set my mind at ease, I'm sadly disappointed.

"If you will permit me to say so—"

"Just fucking say it," I snarl. "I don't need the preamble."

"Yes, boss." The injured tone is back. I ignore it. "There's something strange about this girl."

No shit. I tear my tie loose, pour a drink, and brace for the worst.

"Most illegals leave a paperwork trail a mile wide. The only evidence of this girl's existence is her medical card."

I take a mouthful of Scotch. It's my preferred drink, but tonight the smoky taste feels wrong. I empty the glass and frown out at the midnight-black sea beyond the city lights. It's the same color as Lucia's hair.

"She's Argentinian," I say. "Surely there's a record of her in that country."

"If there was, you'd be holding it in your hands." Pavel's indignation is palpable. "Her passport was issued in Buenos Aires just over two years ago. The home address given was an apartment block that has since been demolished. She took a flight to Morocco the same day she got the passport and was given a tourist visa on arrival, after which she simply disappeared. Soon after that, she showed up working in the café here in Malaga."

Which means she's trouble with a capital T, and the last person I should be exposing Mikhail's children to.

I certainly shouldn't have her anywhere near either Hale or Mercura. My internal alarm ratchets to high alert.

"And she's never even made an application for refugee status?"

"She's never set a toe inside an official building, according to—"

"What you can find." I cut him off brutally. "Which seems to be fuck all, so far."

"If there was anything to find," Pavel says with a long-suffering air, "I would find it. That's why it's strange. Everyone leaves a trace, boss. Everyone. But not this girl. She uses burner phones and replaces them on a regular basis. She doesn't make close friends. She avoids crowds and cameras, pays only cash, and never uses her real name if she can avoid doing so." He pauses. "I'm sorry to say this, boss, but—"

"What?" I snap, but I already know what he's going to say. It's obvious enough, even to a non-tech head like me.

I just don't want to hear it.

"The girl is using a cover identity. A good one. Without fingerprints or DNA, what I've given you is all the information you're likely to find. This is a girl who doesn't want to be found. And one who's used to running. I'd say the only thing you can know for certain about Lucia Lopez, boss, is that it's only a matter of time until she runs again."

His words slice through the years and walls I've built between myself and the past with ice-cold brutality.

"Your mother is gone, Roman." My father's voice echoes down the pathways of memory, accompanied by the fierce, sudden pain that has never, not even after more than twenty years,

disappeared. *"She had no choice but to run. It isn't your fault, Roman . . ."*

I thrust the memories down with the discipline of long practice.

"Pavel." My voice is rough. I swallow hard, and the next time I speak, it's back to my usual curt delivery. "Don't leave the office for now. I might need you later." I end the call before I betray myself, or before the little shit can start arguing. I pay him more than enough to soak up a little overtime every now and then.

I need time to think all of this through.

For all I know, Lucia could be an intelligence plant from the government, custom-made to exactly suit my preferences.

Except that she doesn't.

Lucia is nothing like the women I usually date. She has more curves than any of the rail-thin models I take to public events, and none of their practiced seduction. She works more hours than any human ever should. And when I touched her naked body, she melted against me like I was shelter from the storm.

Not to mention the fact that she was working in that damn café long before I even bought the Hale building.

I twist away from the window and walk down the dimly lit corridor. It's vodka I need tonight, not Scotch. I slip a card into the locked door I rarely open, then go to the safe. I keep only one item in the safe: a bottle of Graf vodka. It was my father's favorite. I keep only one bottle at a time, and I save the drinking of it for rare occasions.

Even before Pavel's report, there was no doubt in my mind that Lucia is hiding something.

I knew it the moment I saw the panic in her eyes when I mentioned the motel she slept in last night. The blood drained entirely from her face, the lush bottom lip sucked savagely inwards beneath her teeth, hard enough I feared she'd bite right through. Her eyes darted to the door, and for a moment I genuinely thought she'd make a run for it.

You can't fake that kind of fear. The fear of being hunted by death itself.

I should know. After my mother's disappearance and my father's murder, I ran with that fear for six years. And no matter how hardened I became during that time, I've never forgotten how it felt to look over my shoulder, or the tension of keeping my identity a secret. Ten-year-old Roman Borovsky disappeared the night his father died in Miami. Six years later an orphan with no surname stood in front of a bullet intended for Mikhail and became Roman Stevanovsky.

I found a way out. And nobody, not even Mikhail, has ever known who I truly am.

I toss off the glass of vodka and refill it, gripping the edges of the vast dining table, staring at the clear liquid in the glass. *None of this solves the problem of what to do about Lucia Lopez.*

Except that for some reason, it does.

I know how it feels to have no choice but run. To guard secrets that aren't mine to tell. To live with a revenge I can never take.

I don't want to involve myself in whatever storm is chasing Lucia. But I can certainly give her a way out, or at least the resources to outrun it.

And if the storm decides to come for her?

Well, like I said, I protect what is mine.

And I'm no storm.

I'm the fucking apocalypse.

I put the stopper into the vodka bottle and walk back to the safe, which is the only piece of furniture behind the locked door. The safe cost me a small fortune at auction a few years ago. I anonymously outbid hardened thieves and Russian oligarchs, who were all drawn by the irresistible challenge of cracking a Borovsky safe. Not that any of them would have succeeded. They'd have wound up blasting it open, and even then, they'd have had trouble.

It took less than three minutes for me to crack it open.

After all, I'd watched my father build it.

I run my fingers over the brass plate bearing my family name. Opening the heavy door, I place the vodka bottle gently on the shelf inside.

"*Za Zdorov'ye*, Papasha," I say softly. "Have a drink on me. It's your favorite."

This is the room where I keep my father's memory locked away, a private place only I visit. The safe is the last one he ever made. I keep it empty, except for the lone bottle of Graf vodka.

I close my eyes briefly, remembering my father's strong, lined face. He was already an old man on that long-ago day when he knew they were coming for him.

"*You must run, Roman,*" he'd said, gripping my shoulder. "*Do you understand me? The men coming for me know I have a son. I will not see you die beside me, or forced to live the same life I've given everything to escape. Do not try to help me. Promise me, now.*"

His Russian accent was thicker than normal, as it always was when he was emotional. "*Run, my boy, and do not look back. No matter what you see or hear. Go to the compound I showed you, and ask for Sergei Petrovsky. He will help you. And remember what I taught you. Live a good life. Make me proud.*"

He'd waited until I gave my promise before thrusting me out the back door, moments before the Russian men crashed through the front one.

He never knew that I stayed, watching through the window, until the last breath was stolen from his body.

I did run to the compound. But when I got there, a car arrived at the gate. I saw the driver through the windshield.

His hands on the steering wheel had the same sparrow tattoo as the hands that tortured Papasha to death.

I kept running, and I never looked back.

"I ran just like you told me to," I say now, my voice harsh in the empty room. "But I didn't escape your life, Papasha. I became the king of it instead."

It hasn't been the life he wanted for me, I know that. And I doubt my father would approve of many of the things I've had to do to survive it.

But I know that he would approve of helping Lucia.

There was nobody to help my mother when she ran. Nobody to save my father after she left, or when those gutless fucks came for him. And there sure as hell wasn't anyone to help me the night I fled the sight of my father's lifeless eyes, nor during the hard years of street survival that followed.

But it doesn't have to be that way for Lucia.

I want to shelter her from whatever storm she's fleeing. To stand in between her and whoever put that fear into her eyes. Preferably with a gun in my hand. In fact, the idea of coming face-to-face with whatever caused the fear I saw in Lucia's eyes gives me the kind of killing lust I haven't felt in a very long time.

Mind made up, I dial Pavel back. "I want the beach villa set up for accommodating a wheelchair," I snap. "Hire whatever medical help and equipment is needed to take care of that old man. And I need a bank account set up, along with a line of credit." I give the long list of orders swiftly, then ask him to read them back in case I've missed anything. "And Pavel?" I say at the end.

"Yes, boss?"

"This stays between us. Entirely between us. Nobody knows about that girl's presence in this house, nor one single detail of what you've learned, either about her or the old man in her company. If I ever hear the name Lucia Lopez leave your lips, or see it on a computer screen, my gun will be the last thing you ever see. Do I make myself clear?"

"Crystal, sir."

"Good."

I end the call, then place another one, this time to London. It takes less than five minutes and the offer of carte blanche with my black credit card to convince Vera to delay the children's return by one day.

That dinner left me with an appetite that nothing but Lucia's naked body is going to satiate. And selfishly, I want one night alone with her before there are any other demands on her time. One night to make her scream aloud, over and over. One night to tongue-fuck every bit of lipstick off her luscious mouth. One night when she is thinking about nothing more than my hands on her body and my mouth devouring her flesh, inch by inch.

One more day until she's mine.

I shift restlessly. It's almost unsettling, how much I want her. Setting up an anonymous account with a great deal of money in it for Lucia's exclusive access is just good business, I tell myself. As is placing the old man she cares for into luxury medical care. It frees Lucia up to focus exclusively on my needs. All of this is simply the most efficient way to ensure that those needs are met.

And besides, five months is long enough to tire of any woman.

Hell, I'll probably be paying her off within the week.

Except that I can't help imagining the relief she will feel when she knows she is finally safe. And knowing it is me who has provided her with that safety gives me a deep-seated, primal sense of satisfaction. Which is nothing compared to what I'm going to feel tomorrow night, when I finally have Lucia Lopez naked and moaning under my hands.

I strip off my clothes and head for a very cold shower. It's going to be a long damn night.

13

ROMAN

"I thought the kids were coming in this morning?" Dimitry casts me a curious glance the following day in my office.

"Change of plans," I say curtly. "And I need you to head to the address I'm texting you. Pick Miss Lopez up and bring her here. She'll be expecting you."

"Will she, now." Dimitry lounges by my desk, smirking.

"After you've brought her here, I want you to go back to her motel room. Discreetly, Dimitry." I glare at him. "Very discreetly. That means not a single motherfucker knows you're there, including the old man in the room next door to her."

"What am I looking for?" He lifts a quizzical eyebrow. "I thought the geek squad was doing the background."

"Lucia is using a fake name."

Dimitry's smirk fades.

"And she's running from something."

He starts to frown.

"I don't know from who or what. But we have to assume they're searching for her. That means we do nothing that might alert whoever it is to her whereabouts."

I might use Pavel to do a digital search, but when it comes to keeping a confidence, Dimitry is the only person I truly trust. Briefly I give him a rundown on what little we know. "I want to know who Lucia is, and for that I need DNA. She's been in that motel room for two nights, and she definitely uses a hairbrush. Get in and get out without being seen."

"Got it, boss."

There's no trace of a smirk now. Dimitry knows when I mean business, just like I know nothing will stop him carrying out my orders.

Except that instead of jumping to them, for some reason he's still standing in my office.

"You should probably fuck off, if you want to beat the traffic."

Dimitry doesn't move. I frown. "Something you want to say, brother?"

"The children." He folds his arms and gives me something close to a glare. "After everything they've been through, do you really think it's wise to give them a nanny who poses that kind of flight risk?"

I scowl, not least because I know damn well he's right. Under normal circumstances, there's not a chance in hell I'd let anyone near those kids without a high security check.

But Lucia Lopez isn't normal. And whatever else she might be, my gut tells me she's not a threat. At least, not in the way Dimitry means.

"Do you honestly think," I snarl, "that I'd do anything at all that might put Mikhail's children in danger?"

"I don't doubt you can keep them safe." His glare doesn't diminish in the least. "But I also think that it's about damn time you did something more than just keep them safe. They need more than just a nanny, Roman. Especially one who might leave at any minute. They need a father. And a mother. One who actually gives a shit about them."

I'm torn between punching him out and giving him the mother of all roardowns. Not least because his remarks about Lucia being a flight risk hit home far more than I find comfortable. But the truth is that Dimitry, the stubborn prick, is the only person I know who has the balls to face off with me.

Most of the time I like it.

Right now it pisses me off.

And Dimitry clearly knows it.

"Fine." He holds his hands up in mock surrender. "I'm going. But those kids deserve better than what you're giving them, and you know it."

He closes the door, leaving me furiously pacing the floor of my office.

The worst of it is, I know he's right. I also know that I'm not the person he wants me to be.

Dimitry has some romantic notion that being tasked with the care of Ofelia, Mickey, and Masha will somehow magically transform me into a soft-hearted family man.

I know there's zero chance of that happening.

That was Mikhail, not me.

I won't ever understand why Mikhail gave me the care of his children. How he ever thought I could be anything more than the cold-hearted bastard I have been for the past two decades.

And if anyone should know exactly how ruthless I am, it's Dimitry, who has known me for almost all of that time. The fact that he seems to expect more of me pisses me off.

I'm still fuming when Lucia walks in.

Holy. Fucking. Shit.

The floaty sun dress itself is demure enough. But the way the thin cotton clings to the curve of her ass and dips to reveal the swell of that fucking delicious cleavage is pure sin.

The combination of lust and fury makes my voice harsher than I intend as I hand her a document folder.

"I've set up a company account for your exclusive use, as we discussed. Inside that envelope is the access card. There is also an opening balance, the amount of which is also on the paperwork inside the envelope."

But she doesn't open the envelope.

"I thought," she says, frowning at me, "that I was supposed to be at the airport this morning, meeting your children."

"Godchildren," I correct her. "And I've delayed their return until tomorrow, by which time you will have had time to shop for an appropriate wardrobe and move into my building." I nod at the envelope. "Why don't you open that?"

Frowning with confusion, she opens the envelope and pulls out the paper inside. Her eyes widen as she reads, and the color drains slowly from her face. When she finally puts the paper down on my desk, her hands are shaking.

"This is more money than we discussed," she breathes. "This is—it's a fortune, Roman." The breathless way she says my name, the hint of brilliance in her topaz eyes, makes me feel ten feet tall.

That's right, I think savagely. *I did that. Nobody else. And more, besides.*

"Take out the other paper in the envelope." I watch as she pulls out the single sheet that shows photographs of the beachside villa conversion I've had an entire crew working on since late last night.

"A medical team will arrive at your motel in an hour." I speak curtly to disguise the fierce rush of pride. "They will move the old man from the room next to yours into the villa you're looking at. It's within easy walking distance of your own and is fully equipped to manage his needs."

"Juan." I barely hear the small whisper, because her face is turned to the floor. "His name is Juan."

"Juan, then."

I'm quite certain that isn't his name at all, but that's fine. I'll have his DNA soon enough.

"Any specialist care Juan requires will be arranged after he's been properly assessed. You can help him settle in and meet the team yourself to make sure you're satisfied. They've been hired by Hale," I add. "Your name hasn't been used. And they will call you, and your friend, by whatever name you tell them to. Hale people also handle the security there, so nobody enters or leaves without express permission. The medical team will be fully background checked."

"Why—" Her voice cracks, and she lifts a trembling hand to her face. "Why are you doing all this?" She raises her face, and I realize, in horror, that she's actually crying.

Oh, fuck no.

"Pull yourself together, Miss Lopez."

I don't do tears.

"This is a business arrangement. It's my experience that people perform at their best when their time is free of distractions."

"But this money." She swipes her hand across her eyes and takes a shuddering breath, then another one. It's actually pretty impressive, watching her regain control of herself. "The villa. You didn't have to do any of this. Or take care of . . . Juan. I could have done it all with what you were already paying me."

"And you would have been stressed out trying to take care of it all. This way my godchildren will have your undivided attention during the day—and I will have it at night." I shrug. "It's just good business, Miss Lopez."

She's still deathly pale, but now two hectic spots of red glow on her cheeks. "You cannot know what this means to me." Her voice is shaking slightly, her body taut with inner tension. "I'm more grateful than I can ever tell you for what you have done. What you are doing," she says quietly. "But I do wish you'd left . . . particular issues, for me to sort out alone."

That pisses me off.

"I would imagine," I snap, "that signing a lease would be difficult when you're trying to stay under the radar."

She stiffens. Her eyes narrow. "I thought you said you had no interest in my personal circumstances."

"I didn't. I don't. But I do have a vested interest in ensuring that nothing interferes with the children's schedule—or mine." I don't like the suspicion I can see in her eyes. They aren't darting this way and that anymore. Instead, they're watching me as if I'm a serpent about to strike. There's no trace of the vulnerability of a moment ago. And even if I did intend to put her in her place, it still upsets me to see her retreat, to pull down that shield. More than anything, I want to break that wall down, see her entirely bared to me.

And I will.

But for now, I need to reset the power dynamic between us. At the same time, something tells me that unless I lay some truth down, Miss Lopez might just be gone before I ever get to see the body hiding under that dress.

And that is not an option.

"Look, Miss Lopez." It's time to cut the bullshit. "I know you're living under an assumed name."

She freezes to the spot, staring at me like I'm about to thrust a dagger into her. But we're doing this now. She needs to know who exactly she's dealing with. A bit of mystery might be intriguing, but I'm a busy man. I'm not dancing around whatever game she's playing, and it's time she understood that.

"I know you're running from something or someone," I say curtly. "And since you won't give me the information I require to do a proper security check, I intend to stay informed of every detail of your life for the duration of our agreement. If you can't accept that, then I suggest we take that contract back out of my drawer and tear it up on the spot. Because while I might not give a single fuck about your *particular issues*, I take my own very seriously. For the next five months, my issues will be your entire world. And in my world, you play by my rules."

The topaz eyes have remained glued on me the entire time I've been talking, their depths slowly shifting from cold fear to hot defiance. The transformation infuriates me. It intrigues me.

It turns me on more than anything ever has.

She chews her lower lip slowly, in a way that makes me want to throw her up against the window right now, before she can change her mind.

For a long, very tense moment, I think she might actually call my bluff.

And in a way, she does.

"Mr. Stevanovsky." Her eyes glitter, not with tears, but with a strange kind of fire that sets my blood racing and makes me instantly hard. "I speak Russian," she says in a deceptively calm tone. "Enough to read the same expat newspaper you do every morning. I know who you are. Not this," she adds, gesturing around at my office. "Not Hale. I know *what* you are. And just so you know, I've met worse monsters than you. I've also outsmarted them."

I'm stunned into silence. Actual silence. Not even Dimitry and his fucking nagging floored me quite this much.

And I do *not* like the feeling.

Lucia takes a step closer to me. I can smell her sweet vanilla perfume, the faint hint of coconut in her hair.

"I truly am deeply grateful for all you've done. I'll play by your rules, because that's what I signed up to do. But there's no amount of money, no contract, and no threat, that will stop me breaking them if I have to. As you said last night, we've both already crossed a moral line. You say that you know I'm living under an assumed name. Well—I know you're bratva."

She throws the word onto the table like a high roller placing a dangerous bid.

But if she thinks I'm going to react, she has no idea who she sat down to play cards with. I stare straight back at her.

"So how's this for a verbal addition to our agreement?" She's so close I can almost taste her, topaz eyes staring straight into mine. "You don't go looking into my background. In return, I'll abide to your contract by the letter, and pretend I don't know what hides behind the Hale facade."

I'm at a level of tension that isn't just dangerous. It's deadly. My fingers are itching to take hold of her and fuck every last ounce of resistance from her body.

Tonight, Miss Lopez, you're going to find out exactly how high stakes our game really is.

For now, however, it's my turn to call her bluff.

"This isn't some kind of negotiation, Miss Lopez. You've already signed a contract." I tear myself away from her with an effort and walk around the other side of my desk, eyeing her coldly. "There are no additions to be made to that, verbal or otherwise. Take it or leave it. Frankly, I don't give a fuck which option you choose. But if you intend to honor it, you'd better get moving." I look at my watch. "I'll be back in the penthouse at seven this evening. I expect you to have made whatever arrangements you need to by then."

She stares me down for a long moment, the color slowly mounting on her cheeks. An extremely tense silence is broken by Dimitry strolling in.

"Boss." He stops dead in his tracks when he sees the look

on my face, the envelope on my desk, and Miss Lopez's stiff spine.

"I'll come back," he says, backing toward the door.

"No need," I say icily. "Miss Lopez was just leaving."

I take my seat and open my laptop, forcing myself not to look at the envelope. From my peripheral vision, I see a small hand reach out and pick it up. My flood of relief only makes me more furious.

"Seven p.m., you said."

I don't look up from the screen. "I'm not in the habit of repeating myself."

"So you said last night. And yet here we are." My head jerks up in surprise. Her eyes are still glittering. "I'll be there, Mr. Stevanovsky." There's just enough subtle emphasis on my name to remove any respect from the formality at all. "Let's hope you've learned some manners by then." Turning around, she stalks out of the room, perfect ass swaying that dress in a way that makes me grit my teeth.

Dimitry gives a low whistle as the door shuts behind her. "Holy shit," he says, eyeing me with even more curiosity than he did earlier. "And you let her get away with that?"

"She's just signed her life away," I say brusquely, ignoring the rapid thudding in my chest. "She's not getting away with a damn thing." *And after tonight, she'll be walking differently, that much I can promise you.*

I'm throbbing hard at the thought of it.

"You get what I asked for?"

"Got it." Dimitry hands me a screwed tube with a long black strand inside it. "But that old man is sharp, Roman. It wasn't easy dodging him. He watches everything from the window."

And I have a funny feeling I know why.

So Miss Lopez knows I'm bratva, huh? That thought should horrify me. Instead, it intrigues me.

The pieces are coming together. I'm another step closer to knowing exactly who, and what, Miss Lopez really is.

And she's about to discover *exactly* what kind of monster I am.

I look at my phone.

Seven hours to go.

14

LUCIA

"He rented an entire *apartment?*" Abby stares at me over the belongings strewn across the motel bed. "And medical staff for Juan?"

I nod, color creeping up my neck. I had to tell someone, even if I can't disclose the entire truth. "Wow." She lifts a skeptical eyebrow. "CEO Man must *really* need an au pair."

"I got the impression he's run out of agencies, and it's short notice." I bury myself in the task of packing to avoid her scrutiny.

"Hm." Abby looks entirely unconvinced. "And the kids? Have you even met them yet?"

"Not until tomorrow. But he sent me a file half a mile long to study before they arrive." In fact, I spent most of last night reading over it, trying to pick up everything I can. I'm desperately relieved I also have today to read more. The medical team came for Papa when I got back from that hellish meeting in Roman's office. I lied to Papa, of course, though keeping the story as close to the truth as possible. I told him I gained a job with a wealthy English family who need a multilingual live-in au pair on short notice. Papa became very agitated when he realized my new employers know of the connection between him and me, but I smoothed it over by reassuring him they don't know he is my father. I said they had an empty villa previously used for their own elderly relatives, and that it was no trouble for me to rent it. I also said I hired the medical staff.

I didn't make any mention of my new employer being a single man.

Or Russian.

I definitely didn't mention him being bratva.

In short, I lied like hell.

Even so, I think the only reason Papa eventually agreed was because he saw someone lurking around the motel today when I was in Roman's office. Going by the description he gave, I'm fairly certain the person he saw was Dimitry, which is all the proof I need, after our encounter this morning, that Roman is intent on digging up my past.

I know that calling him out as being bratva was probably the most foolish, reckless thing I could ever have done.

But if he plans on looking into my past, and clearly he does, it's also a calculated risk. My identity won't withstand a Hale security check. Roman might not be able to work out who I am, but if he's determined to look, then sooner or later, he'll find enough to make him concerned about what danger I might pose, either to the children or his business. Given his incredible generosity, or perhaps despite it, the thought of him suspecting me of being some kind of spy or danger to his family makes me deeply unhappy. I might have spent only one night reading that file, but I already feel a strange bond with the story I read in between the cold lines of fact.

"Earth to Lucia." Abby clicks her fingers as she folds Papa's clothes. She took the morning off to help me, even before I insisted on paying her double what she'd normally earn at the café. Although, to my private amusement, I suspect her eagerness might also have something to do with Dimitry being my driver for today. "The children," she prompts me. "Tell me what you've gotten yourself into."

"Right." After studying their files all night, I can see their faces in my mind as if they were standing in front of me. "So Ofelia is the eldest. She's a few months away from her sixteenth birthday. Apparently her mother is a model, and it shows, because this girl is stunning. And I do mean *stunning*."

No wonder Roman is stressed out about keeping an eye on his eldest goddaughter. Ofelia is a vivid example of classic Russian beauty, with a sheet of white-blonde hair, arctic blue eyes, high cheekbones, and perfectly shaped legs that go on forever. Physically, she looks like she stepped straight off the catwalk. Emotionally, however, one look into those wary, shuttered eyes was enough to convince me she's a trainwreck. "She lost her father when she was thirteen," I tell Abby. "And her parents had been engaged in a vicious divorce long before that. From what I can gather, her mother spends more time on magazine covers than tucking her children under bedcovers. And given that Ofelia has just been expelled from her third school in as many years, I'd say that Roman's parenting skills leave a little to be desired."

"Roman, huh?" Abby shoots me a sly gaze. "Dropping the formalities already?"

I flame red. "Mikhail," I go on, mustering as much dignity as I can, "is called Mickey for short. He's just turned fourteen."

If his sister looks more guarded than the Kremlin, Mickey looks awkward and withdrawn, hiding behind a pair of thick glasses and floppy dark hair that conceals much of his face. Neither of the elder two Stevanovsky children are smiling in their respective photographs. "He's academically off the charts, apparently, particularly math and science. He wrote an actual software program for a school project."

Abby snorts. "Can't imagine CEO Man relating to a computer nerd."

"Hm," I say noncommittally, though inwardly I wince, since I had exactly the same thought.

"Masha is the youngest. She turned five a few months ago." I can't help but smile. I imagine it would be hard for anyone not to, looking at Masha's picture. She has a riot of dark curls, the same bright blue eyes as her siblings, and a gap-toothed smile that could light up a room. In the photographs of all three children together, the elder two stand on either side of their little sister, both turned inward as if to shield her from any perceived threat. Masha is the only one smiling in any of these shots, always clutching the hands of her brother and sister as if they were a lifeline. "Masha was born during the marriage breakup, from what I can make out." There's not a lot more to know. While Ofelia's file is pages long, with one tirade after another from a series of teachers and head mistresses, Masha's is more or less a blank slate, with nothing more than a few childish drawings as examples of her interests. In all of them, there are no adults shown, just her two siblings, standing on either side of her as they do in the photos.

"Well, you're going to have your hands full." Abby gives me another sly smile. "With more than just the children, I'm guessing?"

I give her another noncommittal "hmm" and bury myself in packing our meager possessions. Close friend or not, and even if Roman hadn't made his orders more than explicit, there isn't a chance of me admitting to Abby, or anyone for that matter, the exact nature of my new employment status.

Dimitry drives us both to Papa's new apartment, but

thankfully, doesn't enter. Abby and he bicker for the entire duration of the journey, which makes me smile. Bratva or not, I'd rather see her flirting with Dimitry than the idiot footballer Miguel, who seems to give her little more than red eyes and a defeated look.

Abby helps me upstairs with the bags, but doesn't come in. It's one of the unspoken boundaries I've always been grateful that she doesn't overstep. Generally, I keep Papa well hidden. I'm not at all at ease with the heavy-handed way Roman has simply rehomed him without even consulting me. Even if I can't deny the sheer relief I feel at knowing Papa will finally get the help he needs, the thought of him coming face-to-face with Roman or Dimitry terrifies me. There's no chance they wouldn't all instantly know each other for what they are. I can only hope that the medical staff aren't quite so astute.

The villa itself is luxurious beyond even my wildest imaginings. An elevator whisks me straight up from the basement garage to the middle level, where I wander through the sunlit rooms, all tiled for easy wheelchair maneuvering. There's a gleaming modern kitchen on the same level as Papa's bedroom, with the fridge set up for disabled access and low benches that will offer him some independence in getting his own food, if he wants to. An entire room is equipped as a rehabilitation studio, another set up as a hospital room. His actual bedroom is a wide, pleasant studio with an enormous bed, comfortable furniture, and a window that looks over the garden below. From the central salon, doors open out onto a large central terrace overlooking the sea. Grape vines and wisteria twist overhead, and a chess board is set up on one table. Tears prick my eyes as I take in the peaceful vista and gentle scent of growing plants all around. I can't imagine anywhere more suited to Papa's personality than the villa's rustic yet modern elegance. It's simple, calm, and luxurious.

The staff are just as reassuring. They all speak both

Spanish and fluent English, which means Papa will be fine, as he speaks both. The majority are male, except for the house-keeper, Anna, who is similar in her welcoming manner to Mariam.

I find Papa in the central salon, eating a delicious-looking fresh salad at a wide wooden table that, for once, is spacious enough to easily accommodate him.

"This." He lifts his fork and gestures around at the villa. "Expensive," he manages, his brows lowered in a frown.

"We can afford it, Papa." I sit down opposite him and smile reassuringly. "My salary is more than enough to cover all of this, and more besides."

But his frown only deepens. "Who—pay—so much?"

He might be handicapped, but his brain is as sharp as ever.

"I think they have family money, Papa. And the Holy Week school holidays are coming soon. They couldn't find anyone on short notice. Like I said, they've previously used this when their own parents come to stay." I cross my fingers under the table and mentally apologize for the lies. "It would have just been empty if you weren't in it. And besides, it's only for a few months." I cover his hand with my own and lower my voice. "We'll move on after that. And this place is secure. Nobody can get in or out without the codes." This is probably my biggest relief. At least here, Papa will be safe from whoever might be looking for us.

If locked up in a bratva-owned villa is considered safe, of course.

But then again, that's the kind of safety I understand. And which, at the moment, we both need.

I just have to make sure Papa doesn't learn who, exactly, is offering us that safety.

He looks only marginally relieved. "Need—to—move," he grunts. "Not—safe."

"I know." I squeeze his hand. "We will, Papa. But we need

this money, too. And you need medical care. You'll have physical and speech therapy while you're here, which means that
when we move next time, you will be even fitter than you are
now." This at least gets a grunt of approval.

"As soon as school holidays finish I can come and see you
every morning, after the children are off to school. But this
week, I will be caring for them full-time, so I might not come
often. I will call every day, though, so you know I'm safe." He
nods, but the frown is settling in again.

"Shouldn't—be—working," he says, and I suppress a sigh. I
know how humiliating it is for him to think of me, who was
raised with my own au pair, caring for somebody else's children. But this is our life now.

And at least he doesn't know all of it.

"It's a much better job than the café, Papa." He grunts again,
this time slightly less begrudgingly. I know how much he
hated watching me work those hours. "But I do have to go." I
stand up. "I need to get settled in before the children arrive
from London."

One of the male nurses appears at the door, a smiling,
strong-looking man who has a gentle manner and, clearly, the
strength to move Papa about. By the time I leave, they are
engaged in a game of chess on the terrace, and Papa actually
manages a smile.

I LIED about getting settled in.

What I actually need to do is shop.

Roman's contract did, in fact, give quite explicit instructions about the dress code required—for both aspects of my
job. And Dimitry has clearly been given equally explicit
instructions about where to take me to purchase what I need.

Over the next few rather bewildering hours, I'm dropped

off at one boutique store after another, where I'm met by staff who greet me by name and with an assortment of clothes that all carry price tags I would have balked at even back in the days when I had access to a black credit card of my own.

For daytime there is a selection of casual but elegant outfits, from designer jeans and knit tops to dainty summer dresses. Everything from beachwear to yachting has been considered, as well as multiple options for entertaining the children at home. It's divine to feel quality fabric against my skin again, to wear clothing that looks and feels like *me*. The more formal daywear of pantsuits, neat skirts, and blouses will cover any meetings with teachers or other parents. But it's when we get to the boutique catering to the other part of my contract that things get really interesting.

Dimitry, thankfully, drops me at the door, which has innocent-enough evening gowns in the window, and diplomatically offers to collect me a little later. After being fitted out for gowns for everything from a cocktail gallery opening to a royal visit, the assistant opens a door into another room, and I almost choke on my complimentary glass of champagne.

No wonder Dimitry made himself scarce.

The room is gilded as any palace—and full of a vast lingerie selection that makes Victoria Secret look like a bargain basement.

"We have our own designers," explains Nina, the French woman outfitting me. "But we also have pieces from Italy, and France, of course. Now, we start with the basics."

The basics are matching sets of lingerie in a variety of luxury fabrics and sexy, if reasonably demure, cuts. They're actually surprisingly low-key, though still sensual enough against my skin to send a thrill through me.

Daywear, I'm guessing.

These are followed by nightwear I imagine is for the children's benefit, silk lounging pajamas and cami sets with matching robes.

Then, however, come Roman's choices.

"So now we think of the nights, yes? We think of the man."

Oh, yes, we do. Much more than we should.

I shiver slightly as the businesslike assistant maneuvers me into a series of increasingly risqué scraps of silk and lace, all of which reveal far more than they cover. All of the pieces are tasteful and of exceptional quality—but all of them scream to be torn off or peeled away, inch by silken inch.

I've never owned anything like the bewildering array of lingerie piling up in boxes on the counter. Never had anyone to buy things like this *for*.

I was too highly protected before I left my family's compound, and in the years following, whatever encounters I've had with men have been largely unplanned and, by necessity, fleeting. Up until a couple of recent purchases, both of which Roman hasn't even seen, I've never bought lingerie explicitly intended to be taken off my body. There's a deeply erotic thrill in choosing pieces while also imagining, in disturbing detail, exactly how Roman might remove them.

Will he fuck me while I'm still wearing this? I think, staring at a balcony bra that pushes my breasts up so high half my nipples are visible. Then, picking up a thong with a strategic part missing, *Will he want me to wear these while we're out somewhere, so he can touch me?* The thought of him slipping a finger onto my clit under a restaurant table has me wet and quivering.

There are corsets and suspenders, lacy stockings and camisoles that can be easily slipped off. Bras that have my nipples obscenely exposed and corsets that take a full five minutes to lace up. The thought of Roman slowly unwrapping me almost brings me to orgasm in the dressing room.

By the time we're done, I'm in a heady state of arousal, my

head spinning with a thousand dark fantasies. Every piece of lingerie sets another scenario racing through my mind, especially those chosen specifically by Roman himself.

Then a terrible thought occurs to me. "Mr. Stevanovsky," I say to Nina. "Does he—do this often?" She looks confused. "I mean," I say, stammering slightly and turning fire red for the fiftieth time today, "does he send many women to you for fittings?"

"Oh!" Her face clears, and she gives me an understanding smile. "*Non, ma petite*, this you do not worry for. It was Mr. Stevanovsky's brother, Mikhail, who was our biggest customer." She leans in and winks. "And he was a *prolific* customer, if you take my meaning. Mr. Stevanovsky used to bring his brother's mistresses here to shop, back when we were just a small boutique. But Mr. Roman, he knows the good business, yes? So a few years ago now, he give me some funding to expand, *et voila!*" She gestures around her. "Now, we are not so small, I think!"

I'm desperately curious. "Mikhail's mistresses," I repeat. "What about his wife? Inger, I think her name is?"

Nina's face screws up with distaste. "This one! Pah!" she says scathingly. "This one I do not allow in my store. It is no wonder Mr. Mikhail, he had the mistresses. Inger, all she want is money." She leans in close. "I am not sorry when the divorce is happening. But those poor children!" She shakes her head sorrowfully. "I remember little Ofelia when she was just a baby. So beautiful. But her mother . . . no taste. And the way she dressed that child! Making her look like a movie star, when she was just a baby."

She *tsks* disapprovingly. Then, catching my eye in the mirror, immediately returns to professionalism. "Of course this is none of my business," she says hastily. "But no, to answer your question, Mr. Roman does not bring anyone to visit me before now." She assesses me critically in the mirror. "But I think I see why, *non*?"

Embarrassed by that, I hurry out soon after, even more embarrassed at the mountain of boxes the boutique staff load into Dimitry's car. He makes no comment other than when we arrive at the apartment building and he murmurs instructions to the doorman to have the obscenely large amount of purchases taken upstairs and unpacked.

"There's a maid who will take care of it," he says before I can argue. He gets into the elevator with me, explaining the security codes as we rise to the floor I will share with the children.

"This is your apartment." He punches in a code to open the door. "I'll show you how to reset the door code, so only you will have access. The children have their own security, obviously, so the entire floor will be attended at all times."

Obviously.

He holds the door open for me and then turns to leave.

"Wait."

Dimitry turns back, eyebrows lifted in polite inquiry.

"I wondered—that is," I say, rather nervously, "do you know the children very well?"

His hard face softens. "I've known them all from the day they were born."

"Can you—is there anything I should know, before I meet them tomorrow?" Seeing his rather reluctant expression, I hurry on. "I don't mean to put you in a difficult position. I just wondered if you might have any advice. I'd like to do the best job I can."

"Well." Dimitry gives me a rather hard look. "What I can say is that you won't have an easy time of it. Those kids have had more disruption in their lives than most people ever face. They don't like outsiders, and they don't trust anyone, with good reason. They need stability, Miss Lopez, and they need a lot of care. My advice?" He fixes me with a distinctly grim eye. "If you plan on leaving, then go sooner rather than later. Those kids deserve better than to get attached to someone else who doesn't plan on sticking around."

He nods curtly, leaving me feel uncomfortably like I've just been given a warning rather than advice.

I SPEND the remaining part of the afternoon meeting the staff and getting settled into my new home.

My apartment is spacious without being overwhelming, two bedrooms and an enormous bathroom with a deep tub I can't wait to sink into. There's a small but functional kitchen. The maid tells me most of the children's meals are prepared in the separate chef's kitchen on the floor below and that I will usually eat with them. There's a central salon with a deep, plump sofa and a bigger flat screen than I know what to do with. Wooden doors with glass insets open onto a large balcony terrace. The salon alone is bigger than the old apartment Papa and I shared.

The maid, a sweet-faced woman called Maria who, to my surprise, seems to absolutely worship Roman, shows me into the children's quarters. These cover the rest of the floor and are almost as lavish as Roman's penthouse. Each bedroom has its own en suite. There are a number of smaller rooms, one with sophisticated-looking computer equipment I imagine belongs to Mickey and another containing numerous musical instruments, including a huge grand piano. Despite the luxury and amount of money that's clearly been spent, I can't help but notice the sterility of the environment. It looks more like a hotel suite than somebody's home. The toys in Masha's room are all neatly put away, the clothes on hangers neatly dry-cleaned, the bedspreads neutral colors and tucked in with hard hospital corners. The only photographs are formal portraits from the children's earlier years, in which their father beams and their mother poses with ice-cold elegance. I walk through the empty rooms feeling a strange sense of loneliness. It's like a museum, in which the central display is yet to arrive.

I try to reassure myself that the building is only newly finished, that the children have had little time to make it their home. But somehow, I suspect that the soulless feel has little to do with time and everything to do with the absence of any real affection. When I look in the pantry, there are no indications that children even live here, no cookie jar or stash of lollipops. Going by the menu on the fridge and the gleaming, immaculate dining table, meal times are as rigid and formal as a hotel as well.

I remember back to my own childhood, before everything went wrong. I think of my mother dancing in the kitchen as she cooked up a wild storm of sweet South American treats, my father shaking his head and laughing at the chaos of flour and butter in which my brother and I inevitably wound up covered during these explosions. I think of corn kernels popping on the stove and eating around the kitchen counter or snuggled up on the sofa watching a movie. Sure, we had formal dinners. But those were for show or special occasions. Most days we just ate around the long wooden kitchen table, often joined by many of Papa's men, who were as much family to us as our own.

And none of whom are alive now, I think with a sudden pang of sadness. Papa's *vor* meant almost as much to me as my own blood. Knowing they all lost their lives trying to save ours still breaks my heart. They had families, too. Children who are orphans now, all thanks to the Orlovs' savagery.

I push the memories aside determinedly.

Of course I'm thinking of my past. Given what Roman is, it's only natural. It's also not remotely surprising that the children have known tragedy. As I know all too well, for the children of bratva, tragedy is almost inevitable. At least that much I can understand. After Dimitry's warning, I just hope I don't cause them any more.

I close the door on their apartments and go back to my own.

My phone buzzes with a message from Roman.

Come upstairs in one hour, Miss Lopez, it says. Then a photo comes through, and my heart skips a beat.

It's one of the lingerie sets from today's shopping. One that Roman had picked out.

I go into the bathroom and run water into the tub, every nerve ending on fire with anticipation.

ROMAN

The elevator dings right at seven p.m. I hear the doors open and then the light tap of stilettos on marble.

Even the sound has my dick swelling.

"Dining room, Miss Lopez." The heels tap hesitantly toward me, accompanied by a soft scent that reaches the room before she does, sending my senses into overdrive. It's been a long goddamn day of waiting.

Lucia rounds the corner, and I almost choke on my Scotch.

She's wearing a scarlet wraparound dress, fixed at the waist. One tug of the silken sash and the entire thing will be undone. The dress plunges deep into her cleavage, showing a hint of the black lace I instructed her to wear. Every time she takes a step, the dress rises to show a glimpse of tanned, toned thigh as she walks slowly toward me. Her hair is piled up, and she's wearing subtle makeup that makes her eyes smoky as hell. Her lips match the scarlet dress.

I've never wanted to fuck anyone more in my life.

For a hot minute, I seriously considering pushing restraint aside, and Lucia Lopez down on the dining room table.

But after so much anticipation, I don't plan to make this a simple fuck fest.

No.

Tonight is my revenge for the past five months of temptation Lucia has subjected me to and a down payment on the next five months of sin I plan to enjoy.

"Drink this." I hand her a vodka martini.

She sips it. The hand holding the martini glass shakes slightly. The other is curled into a tight ball. Miss Lopez might look like sin custom-made for my delectation, but she's nervous as hell.

The speed with which she knocks off the martini only confirms that diagnosis. I mix another and refill her glass. "Slowly, this time, Miss Lopez." I hold her eyes. "All good things should be savored."

That gets the first blush of the evening, a slow crimson burn that starts right between the luscious divide of her breasts and travels gradually upward. I let my eyes linger where the color is. By the time I raise my eyes to hers, her pupils are wide, her breath slightly hitched.

She wants this as much as I do.

"Did you know there are cameras in my office?"

I feel a savage sense of satisfaction as the color mounts in her cheeks.

"You needn't worry, Lucia. I deleted the footage of our little encounter. But not before I watched it through."

Her breath comes in a short gasp that makes my cock surge.

"More than once, actually. Watching your face when you came on my hand was particularly fascinating. Even better was watching you put your hands on yourself."

Her pupils dilate a little more with every comment, her breath coming shorter. Seeing her color deepen when I know I'm minutes away from seeing her naked is far more satisfying than making her blush over my morning coffee. I take a step closer, and she sucks her lower lip in, slowly drawing it through her teeth. I doubt she has any idea how fucking insane that drives me.

"By the time I finished watching it, I knew that you and I were far from done, Lucia." I pour myself another Scotch. "Do you know what else I discovered?"

She shakes her head wordlessly, just watching me.

"I discovered that you like taking orders. So I'm going to ask you a question. Are you ready to take orders from me, Miss Lopez?"

She nods. Her sharp intake of breath, and the swollen nipples beneath the silk, tell me just how ready she is, but this is my game.

"I need an answer, Miss Lopez. Not a nod."

"Y-yes," she says hesitantly.

"Yes what, Lucia?"

"Yes, I'm ready to take orders from you, Mr. Stevanovsky."

"Excellent." I don't move, though the sound of those damn words coming out of her mouth has my cock straining for release. "Then I want you to walk down the corridor ahead of me. I think you know where my bedroom is. After all, you saw me coming out of it on your last visit, didn't you?"

She nods. "Yes, Mr. Stevanovsky."

"Roman," I growl.

"Roman," she repeats in a whisper. She gulps and turns around, walking ahead of me so I have an eyeful of the globes of her ass shifting under the silk.

She pushes open the door, and we step inside. I don't have curtains. There are steel shutters outside I can lower if needed, but the glass is tinted so nobody can see inside, and I like looking out at the sea when I wake. Reaching around her, I pluck the martini glass from her hand and place it down on a side table, then lounge back in the wide leather armchair.

"Turn around."

She obeys. The ceiling lights are dim, but not low enough that I won't be able to see every curve of her body. I turn my Scotch slowly in my hand. "Come closer."

She walks hesitantly toward me, until she's standing just in front of my splayed legs. Her own are slightly parted, inviting my hand to slide between them. I force myself not to accept that particular temptation, or this will all be over in minutes.

Instead, I give the silken sash one tug, and the entire dress falls open.

Holy hell.

I've been watching Lucia sashay about in hot pants and tight T-shirts for months now. I've seen her breasts bared and had my fingers inside her.

But nothing, not even the video recording in my office, prepared me for the lush ripeness of Lucia's body, naked but for the sheer black scraps of silk and lace.

And I don't plan to have her wearing those for long.

"Turn around," I order her. "Slowly."

She bites her lip again, then does a slow turn, her legs endless and smooth above the stilettos. The sheer cutaway underwear accentuates the round, perfect ass that makes me ache to bite it, then to bury my face in the dimples just above it. The long lines of her waist dip inward then flare out at the hips. High above them is a tattoo I can't really see clearly; I make a note to study that at close range, preferably while my dick is sunk deep between the cheeks of that ass. By the time she turns back to face me, leaving me face-to-face with the curved navel and the mound outlined beneath it, I'm dry mouthed enough that I need another sip of Scotch. And going by the smoky-eyed stare she's giving me, Lucia is in a very similar state.

"Take the bra off."

"Yes, Roman." Her voice is low, huskier than before. She reaches behind and unclips the material, freeing the gorgeous breasts and swollen crimson nipples.

Then she throws the bra right at me.

It hits my shoulder, dropping straight down to where my cock is pounding with need. I can actually feel the warmth of her body still on the scant material. But that isn't what has every nerve in my body on high alert.

It's the look in her eyes. They glow richly topaz, and despite the faint trembling of her body, I can see the edge of defiance in them, the wildness hiding just behind that composed exterior.

"You like the dangerous side, don't you, little *vedma*?" I say softly.

Her lips part slightly, and the noise that comes out of her mouth makes me throb.

"What was that?" I tilt my head toward her. "Is there something you want to say?"

"Yes." Her voice is strangled, and I can visibly see her nipples swelling.

"What is it, Lucia?"

"I'm not a *vedma*, a witch." Her hands are tightly clenched, her legs actually shaking. The sheer triangle between them is dark with moisture that slicks the inside of her thighs.

I laugh softly. "Oh no?" I shake my head, my eyes drinking in the sight of her arousal. My cock twitches angrily. I'm almost beyond arguing with it at this point. "Fuck, Lucia. I've never seen sexier curves. Your body has been bewitching me for months. And naked?" I raise my glass to her, intrigued at the way her eyes drop at the compliment, her face flushing anew. "A *vedma* is exactly what you are." I nod at the remaining black triangle. "Off."

She bends down to slide the offending garment off, and the scent of her is like crack cocaine to an addict.

I'm not going to be able to hold out for long. Not with her this close, her musky scent taunting my senses, her body just begging for me to touch it, her lips open and eyes glazed with need. I can sense her desire to make this a darker game, and also her absolute reluctance to ask for what she wants.

Lucia Lopez might have a body made for fucking sin, but when it comes to these games, her uncertainty is obvious in every shaking limb and hesitant word that comes from her mouth.

She might know danger. But by the way her eyes ducked away at my compliment, nobody's ever told her how hot she truly is.

Which is a very good thing.

Because the mere thought of any man seeing her like she is now makes me want to tear the fucking walls down.

"Take out your hair," I growl.

Fuck. Does she have *any* idea how hot she looks, reaching up to pull the pin out of that coiled mass? Or how devastating it is to watch it fall down her body, all the way to the top of her ass?

By the way she's biting her lip, I'm guessing she doesn't have a damn clue. Which is the hottest thing about it.

"Lie down on the bed," I say hoarsely. I'm long past hiding how much this is getting to me.

"Yes, Roman." She slips the stilettos off, then slides onto the bed with her back to me, one knee at a time, her peach-shaped ass high in the air and slightly parted legs affording me a glimpse of her smooth pink cleft, already swollen and glistening.

Oh, fuck me.

"Turn over," I order, and she does. "Now open your legs."

She isn't just glistening. She's dewy wet, her knees far enough apart that it's a mute plea. I clench the glass to resist the urge to slide either my fingers, or even better, my cock, right inside her.

Not yet.

"Touch your nipples."

I know it isn't her nipples that need attention. I know it by the way her knees sway from side to side, trying to stimulate herself where she needs it as she rolls her nipples, giving a soft moan that drives me insane. Her hips are moving in slow circles, arching toward me, begging for relief.

"What do you want, Miss Lopez? Tell me."

"Oh," she moans softly.

"Tell me."

"I want—between my legs—"

"What do you want there, Miss Lopez?"

"You," she gasps, her legs splaying wide so she's laid open and wanting for my eyes to feast on. "Your hands."

I laugh softly. "Not yet. First, I want to watch *your* hands. You can touch yourself now, Lucia."

Her breasts arch up as her hand slips between her legs. Her soft gasp as one finger begins slow, intense circles on her clit makes my cock surge beyond any last shred of comfort. She's still rolling one nipple with her other hand, and the way she's writhing on the bed has me gnashing my fucking teeth.

"You look so fucking hot, Lucia."

She gasps, a breathy, throaty sound that makes me lose it.

"I've been hard for days, imagining you like this."

She moans, her finger increasing its pace.

"Stop," I command. "You're not allowed to come yet." Her finger reluctantly stops.

"Good girl. Do you want to see what you do to me, Lucia?"

"Yes!" she gasps.

I stand, and she raises herself on one elbow. Her mouth is swollen, her eyes wide and smoky, and she stares as I pull my shirt over my head, her eyes drinking in the ink and scars on my shoulders and chest, the marks of my past. When I open my pants, setting my raging cock free, she groans aloud, her tongue running along her lower lip like she can already taste it. I step clear of my clothing and stand at the end of the bed, right between her open legs. Wrapping one fist around my shaft, I pump it slowly as I stare down at her.

Her hair is a tangled mess on the pillow above, her nipples thrusting up toward me, and her pussy is a hot, swollen mess.

"Tell me what you want, Lucia. Before I fill your mouth so you can't speak."

She gives a strangled scream. "Your cock." There's no hesitancy in the throaty words now, just raw, naked need. "I want your cock."

"The last time I made you come it was only my fingers inside you. But my cock is a lot bigger than my fingers, Lucia. Do you think you can take it?" I'm fisting myself slowly, my cock impossibly hard. Her eyes don't move from it, her hips moving in time with my own movements, as if I'm already inside her. She nods mutely, her eyes wide.

"Tell me." I'm barely holding on to the last of my discipline.

"I can take it." Her voice is low and urgent, her hands gripping the sheets.

"Tell me where you can take it," I growl. "Where do you want my cock, Lucia?"

She's writhing on the bed, her hands clutching at the sheets, her legs spread obscenely wide as she thrusts upward toward me. "I want it in my mouth," she gasps. Her hips move faster, her eyes locked on my cock. "I want your cock—*ah*—inside me."

"And what about *my* mouth, Lucia? Where do you want that?"

Her hips jerk, and she groans. It's too good, teasing her like this, watching my words drive her wild.

"I want your mouth everywhere." Her breasts thrust upward. "On my nipples. On my clit. I want your tongue inside me."

My mouth is watering.

"You can touch yourself again now, Lucia."

"Ahhh!" She falls back, writhing on the bed, her hands slipping straight between her legs. The sound her fingers make as they plunder her wet, swollen folds makes my balls tighten, and I force my orgasm away with sheer will. Her hips are lifting upward, begging me to thrust inside her, and her eyes flutter closed as she works her clit faster.

Eating that amazing pussy is going to have to wait. If I don't get inside her soon, I'll go fucking mad.

"Who do you want inside you, Lucia?" There's no way I can hold back much longer.

"You," she gasps, her breath coming shorter. "I want you, Roman. I want you to—*uhhh*—fuck me until I scream." She raises her head slightly, staring unashamedly at my cock. "I need it," she says, and the naked pleading in her voice almost breaks me.

"Tell me what you want."

The way her body jerks at the command makes my shaft leap.

"Your cock." Her hips lift and writhe as her fingers go into overdrive. "I want you to fuck me, Roman. I want—ohhh."

Her voice fades as her fingers pick up pace on her beautiful clit, her eyes fluttering closed.

"Open your eyes." I'm fisting myself to the edge, pulling back every time.

Her eyes fly open, locking onto my shaft leaping in my hand, and her whole body shudders.

She's close.

"Tell me how you want it." Her eyes move with my hand, her breath coming in short pants. "And then I want you to come for me, Lucia."

"Ah!" She sucks in her breath, trying to hang on, to get the words out, her hands moving faster and faster.

"I want your cock so fucking deep inside me I can't breathe . . ."

Fuck me.

"Good girl. Now you can come for me, *milaia*."

Her fingers slide deep inside her wet, stunning cunt, her palm bearing down on her swollen clit. At the last minute she raises her head and stares directly at my cock.

"I want you to fill me up and—*Fuuuuuuck!*"

Her body almost levitates with the spasms, and I've never seen anything so sexy in my entire fucking life as Lucia Lopez, screaming her orgasm all over my bed.

Finally, when the aftershocks recede, and her body is limp as a rag doll on the sheets, she opens her eyes. They almost roll back in her head when she sees me, hard and needing, standing right over her.

"You said you wanted this," I growl. "And that's why you're here, Miss Lopez. To cater to my every need. Remember?"

She licks her lips. "Uh-huh," she says, and the sultry note in her voice kills me. "I remember."

"Good. Because that's twice I've made you come now—and I'm still waiting. You're going to pay for making me wait, Miss Lopez."

Her eyes flash topaz fire, and her breath sucks inward. "What—how do you want me, Mr. Stevanovsky?"

Oh, you did not just say my name like that. With your eyes slightly downcast and your mouth as swollen as if my cock has already been inside it. You did not just ask me exactly which of the million fucking filthy fantasies that have been playing on loop in my mind I would like to play out first.

Because the answer is that right now, the only thing I care about is sinking myself balls deep inside her sweet, succulent pussy, so far I forget my own goddamn name. Her mouth will have to wait. Eating her will have to wait.

The only thing that matters now is getting inside her.

"You're mine now, *milaia*." I flip her over and hoist the ass I've been watching for months high into the air. Her head goes back and she moans, the vibration thrilling against my skin. She twists her head around, and I see the hunger in her eyes, the thrill of danger.

It fucking undoes me. I lean into her, shutting my eyes briefly as my thumb slips inside first, savoring the hot wetness, this last moment before I plunder her. "You're mine," I murmur into her ear, "and I'm going to do exactly what the fuck I want with you."

She makes a strangled noise that makes me smile darkly. I pull back and settle myself behind her ass, my dick swollen beyond reason and straining toward her gleaming, wet lips. She pushes back toward me, spreading herself, and I stroke the head of my shaft down the dripping slit to her clit and slowly back again, until she's moaning and pushing back against me. I repeat the same action several times, holding myself in iron control. She whimpers, pressing her clit against me, trying to ground down on the swollen, hard head of my cock.

I can't take another second of waiting. My discipline is all gone, shattered by my own teasing.

I withdraw, and she gives a frustrated growl. Then I take hold of her hips, spread her wide open, and thrust deep inside her.

She screams, but I don't muffle her. I want to hear her scream. I don't give a fuck who hears her. I *want* people to hear her. I want them to know I've marked her, inside and out, as *mine*.

The world disappears, taking with it the ever-present tension and worry. The stress slides away, as does my past, and all the darkness. There's nothing but the deep sweetness of Lucia's body, the animal desire of thrusting further and harder inside her, until I'm sheathed completely inside the sanctuary of her body and finally fucking *home*.

Her body is divine.

It takes me like I belong in it, holding me, bucking back against me, fitting so goddamn perfectly I never want to leave it. I'm deep inside, rocking against her, my balls against her clit so she moans every stroke, her coming spasms already tensing about my dick so my own orgasm starts building at the base of my spine with mind-blowing intensity.

My fingers slip underneath her. She screams as I touch her clit.

This is everything I need.

Her open and wet under my hand. Me filling her so completely I can feel every ribbed edge contracting around me. The two of us moving together like a fucking symphony.

I pull her upward and hold her hips deep onto me, my fingers stroking her as I do, marveling at how insanely swollen and wet she is. Then I feel her tighten, and before she can let go completely, I flip her over, spreading her wide so I can get between her legs and get my mouth on her nipples.

Then I fold her beneath me and bury myself to the hilt.

She comes as I drive home, her hands on my ass pulling me deeper, screaming the fucking house down.

Her wild, gripping spasms are fiercer than anything I've ever known. It's as if there's an abyss inside her, tugging me over the edge, into a wild oblivion in which I can abandon myself completely, and yet also find utter peace. I can't devour enough of her flesh, my tongue tasting her neck, her breasts, the valley between them that has called to me for months. And all the while she's bucking against me, wracked by an orgasm that seizes my cock like the ocean tide and holds me there, like a wave about to break, an ecstasy I both want and yet want to hold off.

I take her mouth, swallowing her scream. She tastes of sweet desire, hot and restless. I want to plunder her mouth, to sink my cock into it, own it like I have her pussy. We're a tangled mass of limbs, and yet I still can't seem to get close enough. I feel an almost desperate need to stave off my own release, to savor this, to try to stay in this moment forever.

But then I remember that I have months to explore her body, her mouth.

I have a fucking *contract* that says she's mine.

And that's when I abandon myself to the abyss, roaring like a bastard as I pulse my release deep into her, feeling her own intense spasms milking every last searing drop from me.

She shudders around me, her arms and legs gripping me close. My arms are lifting her off the bed, holding her so hard against me I can't tell where she ends and I begin, and nothing has ever felt so fucking good.

When I watched that video, I knew I needed to make Lucia Lopez mine.

I thought that would mean a night or two, possibly even a week, of dedicated fucking. Skillful, calculated, technical sex, designed to bring about mutually satisfied endings.

But that isn't what this is.

This is intoxicating. All-consuming. Addictive. It's the storm, and it's the peace that follows it. It fires my blood beyond recognition, and then turns to a warm hearth.

Sex with Lucia reminds me of who I am and why I'm here.

And I have no idea how I'm ever going to give it up.

16

ROMAN

Dimitry calls while I'm still contemplating a second round with Miss Lopez. She's currently sprawled across my bed, her ass temptingly close to my hand. It's unsettling how much I want to touch her.

"*Da.*" I remember a moment after answering in Russian that Lucia speaks it just as fluently as I do, meaning my normal method of disguising business conversations is gone.

"I'm at Pillars." I can hear the club noise in the background.

"What the fuck are you doing there?" I frown at the phone screen. Something is off if he's calling this late. Dimitry dislikes Nikolai as much as I do. And he knows better than being seen anywhere near the kind of side business Nikolai runs out of his club.

"You know Abby, who works in the café? Lucia's friend."

"I guess." I can see the dark dip where Lucia's thighs meet beneath her ass. I trace one finger under a butt cheek, and she moans sleepily, shifting her thighs slightly, inviting my fingers to explore her lush crimson folds. The view makes me salivate. My dick hardens instantly.

"Yeah, well, Abby's been dating the Cádiz striker. He told her to meet him here tonight. I came to . . . er . . . make sure she was safe."

"So?" I'm only half listening now. My hand cups Lucia's ass, and her hips tilt a little more. *Is she already wet again?* I'm ready as hell, despite our very recent and intense session.

"Wait." Dimitry's voice holds an edge of amusement. "Am I interrupting something?"

"Fuck off."

My hand roams over one rounded globe of her delectable ass. He better get to the point fast.

"So the striker is in a VIP room. With the Cádiz manager, a couple of very shady-looking investors, and Nikolai. And, Roman, there's something else."

"What?"

Lucia shifts on the mattress and moans softly, pushing her ass against my hand, clearly wanting more. My cock jerks again.

"There's a journalist in there with them. I wouldn't have known who he was, but Abby recognized him. Apparently he's photographed her a bunch of times. She says he's a real creep, a freelancer who sells to the tabloids."

"So he's probably stuck to that footballer she's dating." My fingers stroke closer to Lucia's creamy opening. "I don't see why this is so important that you had to—"

"He's been asking questions about Lucia, Roman."

My hand stills. Dimitry suddenly has my full attention.

"Speak," I snap.

"Apparently this guy has been lurking outside the café for a few weeks now. Abby thought he was waiting for her, but then he asked one of the kitchen boys what happened to the 'other waitress.' Abby thinks it might be Lucia the guy was snapping, not her. She didn't want to scare Lucia by saying anything."

Something fierce rips through my chest, sending a lightning bolt of anger into the pit of my gut. I stand up and carry the phone into the bathroom, out of earshot.

"And he's in Pillars now?"

"Yup."

"Don't move. And make sure he doesn't leave. I'll be there in twenty minutes." I'm already stepping into the shower by the time I end the call. I turn the water on ice-cold to make my throbbing cock subside, already regretting the interruption to what was about to be a magnificent act two.

It's probably for the best. I don't want Lucia getting too comfortable in my bed. That isn't part of our arrangement, after all.

My resolve almost weakens when I walk back into the room to find her propped up on an elbow, one rosy nipple poking through the curtain of soft curls falling over her shoulder, staring at me with wide topaz eyes and lips still swollen from my mouth. The way her eyes go smoky when I look at her doesn't do anything to make the decision easier.

Frustrated, and more than a little pissed off that my one night alone with Lucia has just been rudely interrupted, I turn my back on her. "I have to work. And you need to go back to your own apartment. Get some sleep. You have an early start tomorrow."

When she doesn't answer, I turn to find her chewing that full lower lip and frowning. The fact that she's still naked is really getting to me. "What?" I snap.

"I just . . ." Her voice trails off, and she drops her eyes. "Never mind," she mutters, reaching for her dress.

I feel like an asshole. And I don't have time for any of this.

"What?" I ask again as I pull on my shirt, eyeing her down-turned eyes. "I warned you there was no emotional entanglement, Lucia."

"I know that." Her quiet dignity makes me feel even worse. "I just—if it wasn't good, then you need to tell me what to do, so I make you happy next time."

I'm momentarily stunned into silence.

She's worried she wasn't good enough?

I could almost laugh, except that it's not remotely funny. I'm still slightly shaken by the intensity of being inside her.

There isn't any comparison between sex with Lucia and . . . well, anything else, ever. It's like comparing flying to space with taking the bus.

But there's no way in hell I'm saying that to her. And again, there's no time.

"I don't give out scorecards, Lucia. And I don't have time for this." I nod at the elevator. "I'll see you back to your apartment."

She dresses without any further comment, but she doesn't look at me, even when we're standing in the elevator. Her hair is still down, the scarlet dress only loosely wrapped around her naked body, underwear balled up in her hand. I stand opposite her with my back to the wall. The knowledge that she's only feet away, still wet and swollen from my cock, is a temptation that's taking every ounce of control to deny myself.

The elevator stops at her floor, and she exits first. I walk at a safe distance behind her, trying not to stare at her ass, and wait while she opens her door. "Did you reset the code?"

She nods, still not looking at me.

"Don't share that code with anyone." She frowns, looks like she's about to speak, but I cut her off. "I have security posted on this floor, so if you hear movement, that's who it will be. Luis will pick you up in the morning. He'll send the doorman up to your apartment to collect you. Don't leave the apartment tonight, and don't open the door for anyone other than the doorman or me, do you understand?"

Her frown deepens. "I didn't realize I would be your prisoner."

Oh, for fuck's sake.

"You're not." I don't try to soften my voice. "We've just had a mild security breach, and I don't need my team distracted by searching for you. Are we clear?" I barely wait for her nod before I turn away, ignoring the uncomfortable feeling that's something like guilt as the door clicks shut behind me.

I stalk to the elevator and thrust her from my mind with effort.

I need to focus. And I need to work out what the *fuck* is going on.

———

Pillars nightclub might be Nikolai's domain these days, but despite the bullshit he runs from here, he has enough sense at least not to fuck with the original setup. Set in an old basement by the commercial port, Pillars was one of Mikhail's and my first joint ventures, back in the days before the raids, when we were still dreaming up what would become Hale. It's named for the art deco pillars that are its central feature, beneath a vaulted ceiling that dates back centuries. I still take pleasure from the sophisticated-lounge feel of the low couches and carved stonework. Giving it to Nikolai after Mikhail's death was a gesture of friendship and trust, a relatively harmless way of easing him into responsibility. I gave him more than one chance to show me he was ready to step up, to become part of the new Stevanovsky clan.

But Nikolai never took that outstretched hand, any more than he took my advice.

In the end, cutting him loose was a matter of survival.

Sadly, I doubt it will be long before Nikolai finds himself in a cell close to his father.

I wish it were different.

But ours is a hard world. You end up smart, or you end up dead. Sometimes, jail is the place in between where you learn how to be smart, so you can escape death. I hope that's how it will go for Nicky, but somehow I fucking doubt it. That little prick has been writing checks his balls can't cash for a while now. And he doesn't show any signs of wising up.

He wouldn't have lasted a goddamn day on the streets where Dimitry and I came up, nor in the halfway house where we truly became brothers.

"Brother." I don't need to turn around to know Dimitry's at my shoulder. "They're still in the VIP room."

I nod, scanning the crowd for any familiar faces, nodding at the few of Nikolai's crew that I know. They visibly stiffen, but none of them are game enough to do anything other than approach me and pay their respects. Dumb fucks know who runs our clan, even if they sold their souls to Nikolai's bullshit long ago.

"Gregor." I address the one I find the least offensive, nodding at the others, who take the hint and fuck off. "What do you know about the pap who's in the room with Nicky?"

"He came with Miguel, the Cádiz striker." He shrugs.

"Name, Gregor," I snarl. "I need a fucking name." He has the grace to look embarrassed. He's probably the hardest of Nikolai's pathetic crew. "Lance Ryder. He's an English guy."

Lance Ryder? Jesus, even the fucker's name annoys me.

"He's not a new face," Gregor goes on. "Nicky usually gives him access to the celebs who come in here. In return, Pillars gets good press coverage."

It's a normal enough setup. But Lucia is no celebrity, and bratva don't make a habit of inviting paparazzi to their business meetings.

Something is off.

Still, I'm not about to bust down the door and make a dirty situation into a stinking pile of shit that will end up in a tabloid.

"Take me to the security room."

Gregor takes us upstairs. The security room is a wall of screens. Cameras cover every angle of Pillars, a precaution I'm relieved to discover Nikolai hasn't disposed of. A pack of his muscle monkeys lounge in front of the screens, exchanging nervous glances when I open the door. For a second, I actually think the dumb fucks might be about to refuse me entry.

Luckily for them, they think better of that idea.

I order the monkeys out, then close the door behind them and zoom in on the VIP room.

"That's the Cádiz FC manager, Carlos Perez, with two of the Cádiz investors." Dimitry indicates a small, stocky man whose face I vaguely recognize from news stories, flanked by two mugs in bad suits and too much gold jewelry. "His son, Miguel, is sitting next to him. He's the Cádiz striker." Miguel is as stocky as his father, but with the athletic build that comes from hard training. He's got slicked-back hair, a face made for B-list status, and an arrogant posture that tells me he thinks he's definitely A-list. But I'm not interested in the footballers. I already know that particular story, and I'm not overly happy about being anywhere near the place Nicky is doing his idiotic deals.

"Which one's the pap?"

"Him." Dimitry points, and I wonder how I didn't immediately see it.

In a room full of footballers and criminals, Lance Ryder stands out like a lily growing in a sewer. He's an all-English-private-school boy straight out of a Lacoste advertisement. With tousled hair and blinding white teeth, he's wearing a check shirt rolled to the elbow and chinos, and has a nice

Malaga tan. I bet he fucks as many C-listers as he photographs.

So what's he doing slumming it here?

I frown. "Is that friend of Lucia's still here?"

"Abby?" Dimitry's face takes on a rather stubborn expression. "No," he says shortly. "I sent her home."

I glance sideways at him. "Oh, you did, did you?"

Prick deserves some payback for his earlier swipe about Lucia being in my room.

"She doesn't know anything, anyway. Apart from what I told you." Other than a slight hint of color, Dimitry resolutely ignores my jibe. "And I've already questioned the kitchen boy. Apparently Ryder bought him a drink after work one night. The kid thought Ryder was going to pump him for info about Abby. Then Ryder asked what the kid knew about Lucia, like did he know where she was living now, that kind of thing."

"Where she's living *now*?" I jump on that like a rat up the sewer. "When was this?"

"The night before last, Abby said."

The same day Lucia quit her job and started working for me.

I'm liking this less and less.

I stare at the screens, studying the faces in the room. There's no doubt Nicky is making some kind of deal. "Where's the audio on this fucking thing?"

Dimitry sticks his head out the door, and Gregor sidles warily in. "Nicky doesn't like people listening when he's doing business. He had it disabled."

"Then fucking enable it."

"I can't." Gregor gives us both a nervous look. "Only Nicky has the codes."

Despite my sincere dislike of my adoptive brother, I can reluctantly concede that at least he's security conscious, which is more than I gave him credit for. Not that I appreciate Nicky suddenly growing a brain when it's least useful to me.

I make a snap decision.

"Dimitry came here for a drink." I glare at Gregor. "He saw the Cádiz FC crew turn up for a meet and thought I should know. Which, for the record, I fucking should have. He called me, I came down. We saw, we left." I get up close. "We didn't ask about any paparazzi. We didn't even notice one here. That's what happened, and that's what you will tell my brother when he comes out of that room. Are we clear?"

Gregor gulps. "Clear."

"And the rest of the monkeys outside the door?"

He swallows. "None of them heard our conversation. I didn't say anything to them."

"You better not have," I snarl. "Because if I find out that you did . . ." I let my voice trail off menacingly enough for him to get the message. I stare long enough until I'm sure he has. Then I go in for the sweetener. "You weren't a bad kid once, Gregor. Before you threw your lot in with Nikolai."

It's true, actually. Gregor got lost in the nightmare of the raids. When the dust cleared, Nikolai owned him. I've always felt a bit bad about that.

"If you see anything, hear anything, about that meeting or the reason the pap was in that room, then you come to me. Nobody else. I reward loyalty." I hold his eyes. "Do this, and there might be a place for you at Hale."

To his credit, the kid doesn't do a happy dance. Just nods once, takes the offer like a man. "I'll come to you, boss," he says quietly. "You have my word."

"Good."

We get the fuck out of there before anybody else notices us.

"So?" Dimitry says as we drive back to the city. He left his motorbike at Pillars and is driving my Mercedes. "What do you make of it?"

"I don't know yet." I'm frowning out the window, trying

not to think of whether it's too late to wake Miss Lopez up for another round. It is, of course. And even if it wasn't, I'm not going to give her that kind of power this early on. Best to keep her waiting.

I shift uneasily. *Best for fucking who?*

I turn my mind back to the problem at hand. "Obviously, I want people on Lance Ryder. And I want Pavel to know what the rat-faced bastard ate for breakfast for the past twenty fucking years."

"Done," says Dimitry immediately.

"I want Lucia's name kept out of it." I glance at him. "Entirely out of it. But feel free to ask your little friend what she knows."

His face shuts down. "I think she's told me all she knows."

"Still." I take a slightly sadistic pleasure in making him squirm. "Ask her anyway."

"Boss," says Dimitry stolidly, but I don't miss his white knuckles on the steering wheel. It seems my second in charge has got quite the thing for Lucia's friend. Not that I give a fuck. I've got bigger things to worry about.

Much bigger.

"I didn't want to mention it in the club, where we might be overheard," I say slowly. "But there's a chance it isn't Lucia that pap is chasing. Or should I say, he might be chasing her in the hope of a bigger story."

Dimitry frowns. "What do you mean?"

"Mercura."

His head spins toward me as he does the math. He whistles hollowly. "Oh, shit."

I nod. "Exactly. If Nicky has got wind of Mercura, and has a pet journalist at his disposal, he might be trying to find out more."

And what better way to find out more than by befriending the broke waitress who's suddenly been elevated to au pair status inside my home?

It seems unlikely. But then again, Mercura is a game changer. A megaproject that will change everything.

It's also something that Nicky has been completely shut out of.

I know that keeping Nikolai out of Mercura was the right thing to do, and I've made damn sure my security is tighter than MI6. But that doesn't mean Nikolai hasn't taken it upon himself to do some digging of his own. And for all that Lance Ryder is a pap, he's got the kind of look that suggests he might have contacts that go beyond the sewer in which the paparazzi usually swim.

"I sent Nikolai's lawyers an email advising him that I hired a new au pair," I tell Dimitry. "It's standard practice—I keep all the family updated on what measures I've taken in relation to the children. I didn't mention Lucia's name, only that it was a private arrangement rather than agency organized."

"And you think Nikolai bothered to check?" Dimitry sounds skeptical. "He's never shown that kind of interest in the kids before."

"Maybe. Maybe not. Maybe it was Inger who checked."

His derisive snort indicates his opinion on the likelihood of Inger taking any more than a cursory interest in her children.

"Either way, with barely six months to release, I'm not risking Mercura. We need to know what this Ryder wants, and why. And then if he requires a bullet between the eyes, we need to take care of it." I glance sideways at Dimitry, who nods. That isn't an order that needs any further elaboration.

We drive in silence for a while, and I'm just starting to slip back into filthy fantasies about what I plan to do with Miss Lopez tomorrow night when Dimitry speaks up again.

"Boss?" There's a certain edge to his voice that makes me

fairly certain I'm about to get the benefit of his advice, whether I like it or not.

"What," I say resignedly, mentally kissing Lucia's curves a reluctant goodbye.

"First we couldn't get a background check on Lucia. Now we find out there's a pap following her." He shakes his head. "I don't mean to question your decisions—"

"Then fucking don't," I snarl. "I've got more security than the Kremlin, and a DNA test on the way. Meanwhile the children arrive in less than twelve hours, and they need a nanny. Until and unless I say otherwise, Lucia Lopez is that nanny. Got it?"

"Loud and clear."

"Good."

We make the rest of the trip in silence. The grim line of Dimitry's mouth, however, says I haven't heard the last of his views on Miss Lopez.

The worst of it is, I know he's fucking right.

And despite what I just told him, there isn't a DNA test on the way. I did think about it. I even called Pavel and asked some questions about running it.

The problem is that DNA searching involves a whole lot of dangers we aren't set up to handle. Once a test has been run, and matched against others, it leaves a trace. It's one of the reasons I'm almost pathological about never having my own run.

What if running her DNA leads whoever is hunting Lucia straight to her door?

I have that strand of hair. Hell, after last night, I've got Lucia's DNA whenever I goddamn want it. But that's just the problem. If she's never had a test done, then she's not on any database. But if she has . . .

There'll be people watching for it.

And that means putting not only Lucia, but my godchildren, at risk. Not to mention possibly exposing Mercura.

There are other ways to find out what I need to know. Safer ways.

The easiest way of all is to gain her trust. Convince her that she can tell me her secrets. Seduce her until she has no thought of hiding anything from me.

And I like that idea a whole lot more.

It means I can stop pushing her away. Means I don't have to exert self-discipline in taking her whenever I like.

I'll make Lucia mine. Make her feel safer than she ever has, more relaxed and happy than she knew she could be. And then, when she's utterly at ease, I'll ask her the hard questions. In the meantime, I've got enough security to stave off any threat that might come our way, as well as a technological powerhouse that can see digital searches coming long before the seeker even knows they're being watched.

I settle back into the seat, feeling an almost exhilarating calm spread through my body despite the stresses of the night.

In fact, I feel calmer than I have in years. More centered. More . . . certain.

And if sex with Lucia is the secret sauce that gets me there, then I can't see any downside to my current plan. Because I intend to have a whole lot more of it.

Soon.

In fact, I intend to fuck Lucia Lopez until she forgets her past entirely—and I become her only future.

17

LUCIA

The children's flight is late. Luis takes the sedan to the underground parking garage, and I go upstairs into the lounge and order a coffee. I'm grateful for a moment to myself. Luis is less conspicuous than Dimitry, lean and wiry with a ready smile and easy manner that I imagine makes him the perfect driver for the kids. He is watchful, nonetheless, and this morning I don't feel like being scrutinized.

I barely slept after being unceremoniously thrown out of Roman's bed. Partly because I was, and still am, attempting to process the utterly mind-blowing sex we had. Partly because I'm worried that it wasn't quite so mind-blowing for Roman, given how abruptly he kicked me out. And finally, which possibly should be the top reason, because I'm concerned about the security breach he mentioned.

I've been trying to tell myself it can't possibly have

anything to do with me. But I can't know that, any more than I can ask Roman directly, without giving myself away more than I already have. And now I'm about to pick up his godchildren, and there's a possibility that I'm putting them at risk just by being close to them.

I try to suppress the sick feeling that gives me. It isn't like I haven't considered the risks already, from the day that Roman offered me the job. I've countered my fears about the children with the argument that even if the Orlovs somehow manage to track me down, there's no advantage at all to them in harming Roman's family. They want Papa and me. If they found us, they'd simply take us. There's no reason for them to start a war with another clan, particularly one as powerful as Roman's clearly is. I wouldn't have taken the job if I genuinely thought my presence in Roman's household would pose a risk.

But my internal argument doesn't make me feel any better about what is, essentially, deception. Nor does it lessen my worry that I'm putting Roman, and his godchildren, in danger.

And those are just the first of my worries today.

"Miss Lopez." I look up, startled, to find Dimitry's rugged bulk looming over the table. He pulls out a seat, which looks comically small when he settles into it. "Roman wanted me to join you this morning, make sure everything goes smoothly."

That means the security breach is a real thing. Or does it mean he just doesn't trust me?

I can hardly ask him either of those questions.

"Is everything okay?" I ask cautiously.

"Sure." But he doesn't quite meet my eye, and there's a certain grim set to his mouth that makes me deeply uneasy. Dimitry, I sense, doesn't entirely trust me. And even though I shouldn't care less for the opinion of Roman's second in charge, I don't like the idea of anyone close to Roman thinking ill of me. Especially given how easily he kicked me out of his room last night.

"I warned you there was no emotional entanglement, Lucia."

"I don't give out scorecards, Lucia."

I knew not to expect too much. I just hadn't expected to *feel* so much.

I've *never* let myself go in the bedroom like that. I've never experienced anything even remotely close to how it felt to have Roman Stevanovsky inside me, dominating me, controlling my every movement, down to when I actually orgasm.

God, even the memory of it has me biting my lip and rubbing my thighs together.

It clearly didn't affect him the same way, if he could leave so abruptly.

If it wasn't for the rules of his damned contract, I'd already be in the elevator, knocking at his door and begging for a second chance to prove to him that I can do more than simply obey orders.

Feeling Dimitry's eyes on me, I thrust the thoughts from my mind. I can't afford to think about having sex with Roman when his children are arriving any minute now.

The flight number shows on the arrivals board as having landed. I stand up. "Dimitry. Can I ask you a favor?"

"You can ask." His eyes continue to scan the room.

Wow. Dimitry is a tough nut to crack.

"I know you have to keep an eye on everything. But I'd like to meet the children the first time without too much . . . fuss." I remember all too well what it was like as a child to walk out of customs and into a huddle of security men. No matter how casually they were dressed, how unobtrusive they tried to be, still I felt as if I was walking out with *Russian oligarch's daughter* tattooed on my head.

"They don't know who you are." Dimitry still hasn't looked at me.

"Actually, they do."

That gets his attention.

"I asked Luis to message Ofelia, Mikhail, and their security detail in London to ask if I could contact them directly. I set up a group chat with them and sent a photograph of me wearing these clothes this morning, so they'd know what to look for. Luis verified it with their security team, so everyone is on the same page."

Dimitry frowns. "Can I see the messages?"

"Sure." I hand him my phone. The plane is still taxiing down the runway. I watch the screen and Dimitry's face as he scrolls through the messages, trying and failing to read his reaction.

MARY POPPINS: *Hey, humans. Figured you'd rather avoid any fuss, so if it's ok with you, I'll get Luis to meet us with the car. My name is Lucia by the way. Here's a pic so you know what I look like. In case you can't tell, I'm really not good with selfies.*

The photo is a full-length one of me in the light pink sundress I'm wearing now, pulling a rather droll face.

Ofelia: *K*

Mickey: *Who's Mary Poppins*

Mary Poppins: *Man, I'm clearly old. See link.*

The link connects to a YouTube clip from one of the Poppins movies.

Mickey:

Ofelia: *Lose the umbrella*

Mary Poppins: *I always do. I lose stuff all the time.*

Ofelia: *Thought you were supposed to be the responsible adult*

Mary Poppins: *Been working on that for a while, clearly still a long way to go*

Ofelia: *If you're that useless why did Roman hire you*

Mary Poppins: *I'm an excellent liar.*

Ofelia:

Mickey: 😂

Ofelia: *This is us just in case you get lost.*

She has attached a photo of the three kids on the plane, all pulling weird faces. Masha has her face screwed up and her tongue poking out.

Mary Poppins: 😬 *Now I'm scared.*

I've attached a photo of me, wide-eyed and clutching my face.

Hey it's definitely today you turn up, right?

Ofelia: *OMG you need adult supervision*

Mary Poppins: *Obviously (said in a Snape voice). See you soon.*

Mickey: *GIF of Severus Snape from Harry Potter saying "Obviously"*

Mary Poppins: 🧳😀☂️

Ofelia: 😂

DIMITRY HANDS the phone back with raised eyebrows. "You don't exactly sound like the voice of authority."

I shrug. "I doubt they need any more voices of authority in their lives."

He gives a rather surprised laugh. "True enough. Well, I can respect that. I'll stay out of the way." He almost grins. "Unless you're going to get lost between here and the gate?"

I return his smile. "I'll do my best." I start to walk away, then halt and turn to him. "But you'll still be watching?"

He nods, but this time there's nothing curt about it. "Of course. I'll stay close."

I walk over to stand at the very end of the banner railings, a few steps behind the first line of waiting people.

The kids are among the first to emerge, which makes sense, given that they've traveled first-class. They come out of the doors, trailed at a discreet distance by their security detail, holding hands in the same formation as their photos: Ofelia and Mickey walking on either side of Masha, her little hands clutching theirs for dear life. A sparkly pink wand dangles between the fingers holding Ofelia's.

Mickey, his hair almost covering the top of his glasses, is taller than I expected. He's wearing jeans and a T-shirt that reads *Try turning it on and off again*. Both are too big for his thin frame. He walks with his head down, carrying both his own day pack and a pink rainbow one I assume belongs to Masha.

Ofelia has designer sunglasses perched atop her white-blonde ponytail and a Prada backpack slung over one shoulder. She stares straight ahead, icily ignoring the interested glances of every man in the airport. Even in studiedly casual crushed linen trousers, low mules, and a tight-fitting spaghetti-strap top, she's difficult to look away from. Standing nearly as tall as my own five feet ten inches, slender, and with endlessly long legs, she appears much older than her fifteen years.

Masha's wearing pink leggings and a unicorn T-shirt that has clearly had something spilled on it. Her little face lights up under the mop of dark curls, and she points her wand at me. *Poppins*, she mouths with a gap-toothed smile.

Ofelia turns her arctic gaze my way, raking me up and down as she approaches with a critical eye so like Roman's it's slightly unnerving. Clearly she's picked up some habits from her godfather. Mikhail glances at me, then quickly back down again, stuffing his spare hand into his jeans pocket.

"Umbrella?" Masha says hopefully as they reach me.

I make a face. "I lost it."

"She made us download the movie before we got on the flight," Ofelia says in a bored voice. "She thinks you can fly now."

"I wish." I fall into step with them so they don't have to

pause amid the crowd, and nod toward the door. "Luis is going to meet us outside with the car."

"Sure that's the right exit?" Mickey shoots me a shy glance from under his floppy fringe.

"Nope." I smile back at him. "Guess we're about to find out."

"Oh my God." Ofelia rolls her eyes theatrically. "You really are shit at directions." The other two kids immediately look sharply at me, clearly waiting to see what my response will be to her language choice.

"Well, you're the frequent fliers." I shrug. "I figured I was in safe hands."

Ofelia shakes her head. "Yes, it's the right exit. See if you can manage not to get lost between here and the car."

"I'll do my best."

Masha drops her wand on the ground and stops to pick it up. "Hurry *up*, Masha," says Ofelia impatiently, looking around with a wariness that makes my heart catch. I bend down and pick the wand up, meeting Masha's eyes. She pulls back, eyeing me carefully. I wave the wand in the air. "Open," I say, just as Ofelia reaches the doors. They slide open and Masha's eyes widen. I lean in. "Want to fly, sweetheart?" I whisper. She nods, her eyes widening even further. I pick her up, hand her the wand, and face her little body toward the doors. "What's the magic word?"

"Super-cala-frocious," she says, and I swoop her through the exit. She giggles, waving her wand in the air and trying to say the word.

"I told you, it's *supercalifragilisticexpialidocious*," says Mickey, shaking his head with the weary air of someone who has clearly spent a lot of the flight explaining this particular point.

"Stop being so embarrassing," hisses Ofelia. She points to the sedan. "There's Luis." Her eyes narrow. "Why's Dimitry here, too?"

"Because he's a sucker for punishment," Dimitry answers cheerfully, taking Mickey's bags as we approach the car. "And because Mary Poppins here is a serious flight risk." He gives me the ghost of a wink.

"I *tol'* you she can fly," Masha says triumphantly to Mickey.

"Well, I hope she can cook." Ofelia gives me a rather challenging look as she climbs into the front passenger seat. "I'm starving."

"Sit wiv me and Mickey." Masha tugs me into the back, where I settle in between the two of them. A grinning Dimitry shuts the door and gets into the car behind us. The security guys are in the one in front.

"At least he didn't send the limo," mutters Ofelia. "It's *so* embarrassing getting picked up in that thing."

"Lucia said the same thing," says Luis as he pulls out into the traffic.

Ofelia twists around in the seat and pins me with another x-ray stare. "You argued with Roman?"

"Not *argue*, exactly." I pull a slight face. "Maybe just . . . didn't ask?"

"Woah." Mickey speaks up for the first time, exchanging a glance with Ofelia. "Dude, you're crazy."

I lift a shoulder. "That has been said before, yes."

"What are we supposed to call you?" Ofelia is still staring at me narrowly. "Poppins? Miss Poppins? Mary?"

"Poppins," says Masha happily. "Poppins, Poppins, Poppins."

"Up to you, really." I cast my eyes up and to the side as if I'm considering it. "Although it's probably safer for us all if you keep any obscene versions to yourself. It could get a bit awkward if we're in your principal's office and you're calling me *shitface swizzle sticks*."

Luis snorts, and Mickey gives a rather shocked laugh that

he quickly muffles with his own hand. Ofelia stares at me for a long moment, then tilts her head. "Lucia, then."

The small matter of my name out of the way, I give Luis directions to take us to the supermarket. "There's almost nothing in the fridge," I explain. "And I've no idea what you like eating. Probably easier if we do a shop together, if that's okay?"

Mikhail exchanges another curious glance with his sister. "You want us to come *food* shopping?"

"Only if you want to. Otherwise you can just eat whatever Chef has made for—"

"No" comes an immediate chorus of certainty.

"Definitely shopping," says Ofelia, sounding slightly less icy. "There's never any decent stuff to juice with. I'm doing a juice cleanse," she says loftily. "It's good for my skin." She gives me a rather disdainful look. "You should try it."

"Oh, I'm more of a *baking is therapy* kind of girl, to be honest," I say cheerfully. "Then again, that's possibly why you can wear spaghetti-strap tops and I need a loose dress."

Ofelia gives me a considering look in the mirror. "It's not a *bad* dress," she says quietly.

"So. Stuff for juicing." I turn to Mickey. "What culinary delights do you require, Mickey?"

"*Culinary delights.*" Ofelia snorts. "You talk so weird."

Luis is openly laughing in the driver's seat.

"I believe we have already firmly established that I'm weird. Mickey?"

He pushes his hair aside and actually meets my eyes. "Snacks for when I'm gaming. There are never *any* snacks in that house."

"Snacks. Got it. I may need specifics on your preferred options." I look at Ofelia and Mickey over Masha's head. *"Do I ask?"* I mouth silently.

Ofelia shakes her head violently, her eyes widening,

shooting a warning look at Mickey, who turns hastily back to the window so Masha doesn't see him trying not to laugh.

"Masha loves cut-up fruit," Ofelia says loudly. "Don't you, Masha?"

Masha frowns, as if this is news to her, and Mickey jumps in. "Yes, you do, Mash. You like watermelon cut into star shapes, remember?"

"Water stars." Masha's face lights up.

"Ah." I nod sagely. "Then water stars it is." We drive down the highway, the kids bickering amongst themselves about what they do, and don't, consider vital staples for the kitchen cupboard.

Catching my eye in the mirror, Luis gives me a conspiratorial grin.

———

WITH MASHA PERCHED inside the shopping cart, and Mickey and Ofelia arguing loudly over what to buy, we descend on the supermarket, the grinning security guys unobtrusively behind us.

"We have a crisis," I say sotto voce to Mickey and Ofelia as we near the end of the fruit section. I nod at the confectionary aisle then at the back of Masha's head. "Something tells me that's the danger zone."

They nod vigorously. "She's *terrible*," Ofelia whispers back. "If you let her loose in there it will be tears for sure."

"What do you guys suggest, then?"

Ofelia and Mickey exchange a look. "Maybe we decide on, like, one thing we all like? And get Bryce to get it for us?" Ofelia indicates one of the security guys.

"Smart." I nod. "So what's it going to be?" After a brief,

hushed conference, the two decide on a particular type of chocolate, and Bryce is sent off to procure it. We make our way down the aisles, Mickey whizzing Masha in circles that make her giggle and the other shoppers smile indulgently.

I put vegetable chips into the cart. "These are my snacks, by the way," I say warningly. "Keep your grubby hands off them."

Mickey grabs a packet and throws them on top of mine. "What if I do this?"

I grab another packet, then dried fruit and mixed nuts. "I'm going to label them."

Mickey gets the same things, his grin getting cheekier. "Good luck with that."

I put some flour, condensed milk, butter, and sugar in the cart, and Ofelia eyes them disdainfully. "That stuff is *so* fattening."

"But it makes amazing *alfajores*," I counter. Ofelia raises her eyebrows questioningly. "Argentinian cookies," I explain. "They're *lush*."

She shakes her head. "I'm going to have my work cut out getting you into a smaller dress size." She glances sideways at me. "Argentinian, huh? *Entonces, ¿hablas español correctamente?*" So, you speak Spanish properly, then?

"*Por supuesto*." Of course.

"*Je parle français aussi*," she says challengingly.

I grin. "*Peut-être, mais ton accent est horrible.*"

"Miss Harrison said my accent was perfect!" She gives me an indignant look.

Mickey snorts. "Miss Harrison was a total kiss-ass."

"I'll just pretend I didn't hear that," I say primly.

Mickey grins. "Because you're *so* worried about language, Miss *Shitface Swizzle Sticks*." All three kids giggle like they've said something incredibly naughty.

I cast my eyes skyward. "I should have known that one

would come back to bite me on my . . . ear." That makes them laugh even harder.

"Anyway," Ofelia whispers in Russian to Mickey, "they never know when we're swearing about them in Russian."

I halt the shopping cart. *"Pover'te, ya znayu Russkiye mater-nyye slova gorazdo khuzhe, chem vy." Believe me, I know far worse Russian swear words than you.*

Mickey gapes at me, turning slowly red. Ofelia is staring at me like I've just stepped off a spaceship. "You speak *Russian?*"

"Yup." I grin at her. "As well as German, Swiss, and a bit of Arabic." I wink at them. "So good luck with *that.*"

"Even Roman doesn't speak that many languages." Ofelia looks at me consideringly. And then, suddenly, like the sun coming out from behind winter clouds, she smiles. "Can you teach me to swear in Arabic?"

"Oh, Lord." I sigh dramatically and they all giggle. "Somehow I don't think your godfather would approve of that."

Mickey snorts. "Since when does he approve of *anything* we do," he mutters. Ofelia and he exchange knowing glances.

I pretend I didn't hear.

It's patently obvious that Roman is even more remote from the children's day-to-day lives than I previously suspected. It's equally obvious that their security detail are immensely protective of them, beyond simply a professional capacity. Dimitry, in particular, seems to have an easy familiarity with them that I wouldn't have predicted. It's somewhat incongruous to watch his tattooed bulk piggybacking little Masha to the car, the careful courtesy he shows Ofelia, or the gruff humor he shares with Mickey. All of the security men are polite and young enough to be reasonably inconspicuous, although, just as I did when I was younger, the children treat them with a wary tolerance. I used to hate being followed everywhere I went by Papa's henchmen, even if I understood why it was necessary.

By the time we're home, the shops are shutting for siesta, and the kids are hungry enough to have no objections when we sit down to a traditional three-course Spanish lunch prepared by Chef. There's still no sign of Roman.

The kids are yawning by the time they've finished lunch, and all head off happily to have a siesta which, Ofelia loftily informs me, "English people just don't understand."

"I'll be across the corridor," I say. "But you can message me if you wake up before I do."

"Will you wait till I wake up to make the cookies?" Masha says sleepily as I tuck her in.

"Sure I will." I close her door and find Ofelia and Mikhail already crashed out, clearly exhausted from their early start.

Luis stretches out on the sofa, yawning. "Go." He waves me away. "I've got this." I'm glad to see the security detail outside the apartment are alert and clearly still on English time.

I message one of Papa's nurses. He answers with a photograph of Papa and him playing chess on the terrace, a wry-smile emoji, and the message: *he's beating me.*

Content that all the humans in my world are, for now, either occupied or at peace, I open my own door.

In my apartment I strip off and stand under the shower. It might be only early spring, but the Malaga air already feels like soup by midday. And I need to clear my head. It's the first time since reaching the airport that I've had time to really think through what happened last night.

I haven't heard a word from Roman, though I suppose his security team alerted him that the airport pickup went off without any difficulty, so there's no real need for him to call. And it isn't like he hasn't made it abundantly clear that this isn't a romantic situation.

I almost snort with laughter at that. Given how fast he got rid of me, *romantic* is the last word I'd use.

But still.

My body doesn't seem to notice the difference. Or care that it's being exchanged for money. I showered this morning, of course, but the faintest trace of his scent has still clung to my skin until now. I wash slowly, my hands traveling the same places his did hours earlier, catching the occasional smoky hint of his aftershave as I scrub every inch of myself. I called it hellfire the first time I was in his penthouse. But if hell is a place for sinners, then it's me who's most definitely there now. As my own vanilla-and-coconut body wash gradually replaces the dusky notes of his scent, I find myself wanting to cling to it, to hold it to my skin like a secret. Without his actual presence, last night feels almost like I imagined it. If it wasn't for the faint soreness between my legs and the strange sensation of loose-limbed satiation throughout my body, I'd seriously wonder if fantasy had overtaken reality in my mind.

Was it really me who lay bare in front of Roman last night, touching myself while begging him to take me?

I shiver as the needles of water hit my bare skin, awakening my body to the state of semiarousal that seems a permanent affliction these days. I find myself wondering when he will text me. *If* he will text me.

Oh, for goodness' sake. He's not your boyfriend, Darya Petrovsky. I use my own name to jolt me out of my dangerous state of limerence. *It's a business deal. He's your employer. And of course he'll booty-call you—he's already paid for your ass, girl.*

That should make me feel ashamed, or at the very least, extremely aware of my place.

Only it doesn't.

I dry myself slowly with the plush, thick towel and take my time rubbing moisturizer into my skin. After all, if I'm being paid to be his beck-and-call sex slave, then I have standards to keep up.

I just wish I wasn't watching my phone with a pulse throbbing between my legs, half hoping he'll slip home during siesta.

I have to wrap my head around my new role. Stop looking for reassurance. Do my job and lower my expectations.

I slip in between the crisp sheets and sigh with pleasure at the bliss of sleeping on a cloudy mattress. My enjoyment of it is made even better knowing that Papa is safe and that I'm not facing the prospect of a backbreaking eight-hour shift and Pete's roving hands. Instead I'm looking forward to an evening of banter and baking with the kids, followed, if I'm lucky, by round two in Roman Stevanovsky's apartment.

Don't get invested. He might not even bother.

After all, the contract only states that I have to be available *in case* he wants me. Nowhere does it say he *will* want me, or specify how often.

I set an alarm and pummel the pillow, trying to ignore the dull pulse between my legs. I need to get my head in the game, and the rules of it very straight.

I'm Roman Stevanovsky's fuck toy, nothing more. And if I hope to stay sane for the duration of this insane contract, I need to remember that.

ROMAN

Somewhat uncharacteristically, I work through siesta. Given the late hours I keep, I usually embrace the Spanish rhythm of a long lunch and some downtime, followed by a workout and the second part of my business day.

But the thought of spending siesta in my penthouse, all the while knowing that Lucia is probably sprawled out naked on a bed one floor below me, isn't a temptation I need right now.

Fuck. I rub my temples and try to focus on the figures in front of me. Part of me is desperate to fuck her again. And after all, I've decided that seducing her is the best strategy to get the answers I need from her. But another part of me is already questioning the entire arrangement.

I get hard the second I think of her writhing underneath me. During strategy meetings all I can think of is her naked body, and the way the rose silk slipped to the floor. I keep envisaging the lingerie options I chose and wondering which set I should tell her to wear next—and then, the myriad of ways I might remove said underwear from her body.

I need to get myself under control. And seduction or not, I need to make sure there's no confusion about boundaries. Which means I need to go home early today and spend time with the children while she is there. Make sure everyone knows their place.

Even if the only place I want Lucia to be right now is on my bed with her legs spread wide and my cock deep inside her.

I reach for my phone, smiling darkly. I might be all about boundaries, but nothing in the contract says I can't torment her a little. Unfortunately, my phone rings before I've even started typing. The number on it kills my hard-on more effectively than any ice bath ever could.

"Inger." I attempt to maintain a courteous tone.

"Why is Nicky telling me about a new nanny I haven't heard of?" Her tone is so shrill I hold the phone away from my ear, wincing.

How did I ever find her attractive?

"I sent you the same email Nicky got, Inger."

Maybe you should take enough interest in your own children to read it.

"I'm on a modeling job, Roman. I don't have time to check emails."

I roll my eyes. *But you have no problem making time to be seen at every nightclub in Miami and be photographed daily for the tabloids.* "Would you prefer me to call you next time?"

I know perfectly well she won't prefer that at all.

Inger's idea of parenting involves complete detachment, followed by a brief flurry of temper, like now, when she feigns concern and indignation, followed by an even briefer stage of wounded victimhood, during which the children are bombarded with sickeningly sweet declarations of love.

Then comes the detachment again.

And with it, inevitably, Ofelia's expulsion from another boarding house and Mickey's withdrawal into his computer den.

"No," she says, after a long pause in which she's clearly weighed up the burden of having to take calls from the children against her desire to pursue an active night life. "But at the very least, tell me about this girl, Roman. I don't have time to read the background brief."

Which, for once, is a good thing.

"Not much to tell," I lie. "Miss Lopez is Argentinian. Came with excellent recommendations." I'd cross my fingers, if I believed in that shit. "She speaks several languages fluently, including English and French. She picked the children up from the airport today, and as far as I can tell, it's gone smoothly so far."

"Ha." Inger gives a smug laugh. "I give her a week."

I swallow a very sharp response. Despite ignoring her children almost entirely, Inger is insecure enough to be extremely threatened by anyone she suspects of gaining their affection. As a result, she has actively encouraged the worst of Ofelia's behavior toward the au pairs I've hired. "You're probably right," I say dismissively. "It doesn't really matter anyway. The Lopez girl is just a temporary solution until I find another agency."

Inger is also pathologically jealous. And despite the fact that our brief affair took place back when I was sixteen, just before I took a bullet for Mikhail, she still considers me her property.

"Well that's a relief," she sniffs now. "We can't have you sleeping with the help, Romie. It sets a bad example for the children. And besides." Her voice drops to a husky note I'm sure she thinks is seductive but which for me grates like nails on a chalkboard. "I might be in Malaga for a short visit soon. The Russian Cultural Society want me to attend their annual benefit. Which means we can get together, Romie."

Oh, fuck no. Then again, thankfully, Inger's promises are notoriously fickle. "We'll see," I lie again. I listen to her rabbit on about her modeling career, which, despite her boasts, is very much on the downturn, and hang up as soon as I can.

The truth is that the minute Inger met Mikhail and realized it was he, not I, who was heir to Yuri's fortune, she dropped me like a hot pan and never looked back. Which, even at seventeen, I didn't see as any loss at all. Mikhail enjoyed a brief fling with Inger that should never have become any more, except that Yuri had taken a liking to her. First because she looked and spoke like a perfect Russian princess, and later because Inger knew exactly how to flatter him. Mikhail then found himself coerced into meeting her parents, who were not only first-generation Ukrainian immigrants, but quite poor. They thought all their *Rozhdestvas* had come at once when Mikhail, with his college education and Yuri's inheritance behind him, walked through their door. When Inger managed to fall pregnant, Yuri wouldn't hear of Mikhail doing anything but putting a ring on it. And Mikhail, with his happy-go-lucky nature, just shrugged and said cheerfully that he figured he'd have to get married some time or other. My affair with Inger was diplomatically not referred to by either of us again.

Inger handed Ofelia off to a series of nannies weeks after the child's birth. When little Mickey was born, she considered her wifely duties entirely done and turned her full attention to her always middling career. She and Mikhail had long been living separate lives when Masha came along, the result of a final drunken night when Inger attempted to seduce Mikhail in exchange for a better divorce settlement.

In the years since I rose to take Mikhail's place, Inger has renewed her efforts to seduce me. I take her out exactly as often as it takes to keep the peace. I've become extremely adept at dodging her advances without offending her. If it weren't for the children, I would have cut her loose entirely years ago. But she's their mother, and the only parent they have left. Cutting her off isn't, sadly, an option.

And at least her lack of interest means she won't inspect Lucia too closely.

I, on the other hand, want to inspect Lucia extremely closely, as soon as possible. Fortunately, the phone call with Inger has dampened my libido enough to make me hold off from contacting Miss Lopez until after I see her at home this evening.

Anyway, I tell myself, keeping Lucia guessing is a good seduction tactic. By the way her body reacted when I touched her before Dimitry called, she was more than ready for another round. And that means the longer I string her out, the more she'll be thinking about it.

I imagine her in bed now, thinking about our last encounter, and swear softly. The torture is supposed to be on her end, not mine. She's here to take care of the children, and for me to fuck her out of my system. Not necessarily in that order. She's here to make my life easier, not send my head into a goddamn tailspin and my body into chaos.

I refocus on the screen, counting the hours until I can go home and set my plan in motion.

I AM NOT REMOTELY prepared for the scene that greets me.

It starts with heady scents that hit me right out of the elevator: sweet, buttery, and almost unbearably familiar. The door to the children's apartment is open. Both security guards are leaning around it, laughing. They straighten up smartly enough when they see me, but they clearly didn't hear me, since the music coming from inside is only mildly quieter than the squeals of laughter.

"Boss," says Bryce, composing himself. Dimitry, however, doesn't even bother acknowledging me.

"I could have been anyone," I snap. "Do better." It's not entirely true; there's good security downstairs, and nobody rides the elevator without a personal code, but still. Dimitry should know better. The fact that he doesn't actually need to be here at all, and has clearly just stuck around purely for entertainment value, annoys me more than it should.

"Boss." He nods politely, but he's still grinning more than he should be.

I walk in to absolute chaos.

The apartment itself is clean enough. It's the kitchen where the action is clearly happening. From the doorway, I can see Mickey perched at the counter, laughing at something. It's been so long since I've seen him laugh that I pause for a moment, just taking that little miracle in by itself. He's drumming two wooden spoons on the counter in time with the fast Argentinian salsa playing, and as I watch, he points the spoon at someone I can't see. "No, Masha, it's Luce's pick next," he says, then reaches forward and dips his spoon into something. When it comes back it's covered in caramel, which he promptly licks off.

Masha, out of eyesight, is squealing something that sounds like "Poppins" over and over.

"No way," I hear Ofelia say, and to my shock, it sounds like she's laughing too. "I will not listen to 'A Spoonful of Sugar' one more time, Masha. Put another one on, Luce."

"Fine. But you have to dance too, then."

"I can't!" Ofelia protests, laughing helplessly. "I don't know how."

"It's easy." I hear Lucia's voice. "And you can't make *alfa-jores* without dancing. It's illegal in Argentina."

Alfajores. No wonder the scent is so familiar. Two melt-in-your-mouth cookies stuffed with a luscious dollop of creamy dulce de leche caramel. My mother made them every Friday, when the school week was ended. We used to call them Mary cookies, though I can't remember why. I don't think I've eaten them since the day she left. I shrink back against the wall, sliding just beyond eyesight, until the kitchen comes into view.

The benches are all covered with flour, caramel, and trays of the butter cookies ready to be made into caramel sandwiches. Most of the caramel, however, seems to be either on the counter or on the children themselves. Masha, her face absolutely covered in a sticky mass of caramel and baking goods, spoon in hand, is propped up on a stool, jiggling her little body in wild movements that would topple her if Ofelia didn't keep hauling her upright. Ofelia, flour all over her tank top, is mixing more caramel in a bowl, hauling Masha up with the other hand, and watching Lucia with shining eyes and a smile. An actual *smile*.

Lucia is dancing. Only *dancing* doesn't begin to describe the bewitching sight before me.

Her hair is up in a messy bun, stray curls dripping down the nape of her neck. Her hips are fluid as any professional dancer's, rotating in a way that makes her dress flip enticingly high up her thighs, while her feet move so rapidly they're almost a blur. She's wearing some cute little floral number that skims her hips and flares out to just above her knees. Under normal circumstances, the dress would probably be perfectly innocent.

Except that Lucia's curves make it a sultry invitation. Especially dancing salsa, solo, in the middle of the kitchen.

I pull back behind the dividing wall and stare shamelessly

at the vision in front of me. She's laughing aloud, one hand extended in invitation to Ofelia, a half-mixed bowl on the counter in front of her.

I've never come home to such chaos. And I've never felt a bigger gut punch of desire, along with something else that aches deep inside, in a part of my soul I thought long forgotten to me in this life.

Lucia takes Ofelia's hand and spins her around, then spins herself beneath Ofelia's arm. They both emerge breathless and laughing, caramel streaked down the swell of Lucia's cleavage and smudges of flour on her face.

Then she catches sight of me and comes to a dead halt, mouth open in a perfect O of surprise.

"I gather you weren't expecting me," I say dryly.

The children freeze. Mickey's smile fades. He puts down his wooden spoons, placing them carefully to one side. Ofelia taps her phone, and the music stops. Her face falls back into its customary haughty lines. Only Masha keeps jiggling on her stool, pleading aloud for Ofelia to "play Poppins again."

"Well, no. Clearly we weren't expecting you." Lucia gathers herself with admirable alacrity, but I can see the glitter in her eyes, the nervous tension in her body. "But since you're here, you can test our second batch of *alfajores*." She picks up a tray sitting on the stovetop and carries it over to the counter. "Masha was just about to dust them with icing sugar for me."

"It's my job," Masha tells me solemnly.

"Shhh, Masha," Ofelia hisses, casting me a wary look that makes me feel oddly ashamed.

When did I change from being "Uncle Roman" to someone the children fear?

Fair enough, I was never exactly the superfun uncle. But I threw a ball with Mickey. Tossed Ofelia in the air. Turned up with presents on birthdays.

I don't remember the last time, though, that I saw any of

them laugh. And that suddenly strikes me as a profound failing on my part.

"Don't stop for me." Taking off my jacket and tie, I throw both over the back of the couch and walk into the kitchen, rolling my sleeves up. "Show me how to dust those cookies, Masha." I remember just in time that the apartment door is still open and turn around, glaring at the grinning guards, both of whom immediately exit and close it behind them.

"We promised Dimitry he could try the second batch," says Mickey quietly, staring at the counter.

"Dimitry has been our official tester," Lucia explains.

I feel a stab of something uncomfortably like jealousy. Which makes no fucking sense. Why the hell would I feel jealous of Dimitry, taste-testing cookies for a six-year-old? Except that they all looked so damn *happy*—before they caught sight of me. Not to mention that he also got to watch Lucia dancing, which is close to the hottest thing I've ever seen. I don't like the thought of him, or anyone else for that matter, watching her.

I don't like the idea of Dimitry replacing me in my own household. Even if it is just as professional cookie taster.

"Well, I used to eat a *lot* of *alfajores*." I look at the three little faces staring warily back at me and feel another unwelcome pang of something like guilt. "Can I try one first?"

Mickey glances at Ofelia, who gives a faint shrug of one shoulder. Masha looks between her elder siblings, then breaks into a gap-toothed grin. "Here," she says, holding out a rather misshapen cookie. "Ofelia done them."

"Did them," Lucia corrects mildly.

"You put caramel in 'tween two," Masha says importantly, pushing so hard on her example that she completely crushes the soft cookie and sends caramel oozing out the sides. "Oops," she says, not looking remotely sorry.

"I think I understand how the kitchen wound up looking so . . . colorful," I say.

Lucia grimaces. "Yup. Sorry about that."

I bite into the cookie and close my eyes briefly. It tastes exactly like those of my childhood: meltingly soft, intoxicatingly sweet, and immeasurably comforting. It's like biting into the happiest time of my life.

"Well?" Ofelia demands. Three expectant faces turn to me.

I swallow. "The last time I ate *alfajores*," I say musingly, "was in a world-famous restaurant." Their faces begin to fall. "And do you know," I go on, "I think these are actually better?"

Mickey frowns. "Yeah, *right*," he says heavily.

"Um, excuse me!" Lucia raps his arm with a caramel-covered wooden spoon that leaves a significant smear. "Oops," she says, making Masha giggle. "But I did tell you I make the best *alfajores* you will ever taste." She shakes her spoon at them in a way that makes even me smile. "Don't you be doubting me, or you'll hurt my feelings."

"God forbid." I roll my eyes theatrically, which seems to mildly thaw the children's faces. I put a handful of cookies onto a plate and hold it out to Masha to dust, which she solemnly does, before handing them to Mickey. "You should probably put Dimitry out of his misery," I say, grinning.

Mickey actually meets my eyes. They're the same deep cobalt as his father's, I realize with a pang. I wonder why I never really saw that before. But where Mikhail's were always sparkling with laughter, Mickey's are usually shadowed and wary. Right now, though, there's a faint hint of his father's fun in them, and it makes me want to see more of it. "Dimitry ate the entire last batch almost by himself," he says, with something akin to awe.

"Good. That should slow him down in the boxing ring," I say with a slightly vicious smile.

"Wow." Ofelia gives me a look that's almost admiring. "You're seriously mean."

"I do my best," I say cheerfully. "So." I look around at the disaster that is the kitchen. "Are you guys going to help me clean this up?"

"You?" Ofelia looks at me incredulously. "*You're* going to help clean up?"

"Well, Lucia spent all afternoon teaching you to make cookies, which I now plan to enjoy eating. I think it's the least we can do to say thank you, don't you? And just for your information"—I wag a spoon in her direction—"I'll have you know I was once a professional dishwasher."

Ofelia's mouth drops open. "Shut the front door," she says flatly.

"Ofelia!" Lucia reprimands her. I have to turn away to stop myself bursting out laughing.

"It's true," I say, gathering up plates. "I spent more than two years elbow-deep in a restaurant kitchen when I was the age you are now."

"No way." Ofelia is staring at me as if she's never quite seen me before. "Why weren't you in school?"

"Oh, that's a story for another day." Suddenly rather uncomfortable, I look around for the dishwasher. I catch Lucia watching me with an expression not unlike Ofelia's and get even more rattled.

"Oh my goodness." Ofelia impatiently pushes me aside. "You seriously don't even know where to start."

Mickey comes back in, waving the plate triumphantly. "Dimitry says they're perfect!"

"Well," I mutter. "If *Dimitry* says so . . ."

Lucia elbows me. "We told you so," she says sweetly to Mickey. "Now, never let me hear you question my cookie-making skills again, or we just won't be friends."

"I'm your friend," says Masha solemnly, taking one of Lucia's hands.

"Me, too," says Mickey, taking the other.

I drop a pot, and Ofelia cocks an eyebrow at me. "I thought you were a professional?"

I should never have told them about my past. "It's been a while." I'm unsettled enough that my voice sounds rather curt. This is all way too cozy.

"Luce!" Masha waves a wooden spoon covered in caramel under her nose. "Is your turn to make it clean!"

"No!" Lucia protests, laughing. "I can't eat any more caramel."

"Your turn!" Masha shouts, clapping her hands. Ofelia and Mickey join in the chorus. Shaking her head, Lucia brings the wooden spoon up to her mouth, and just like that, I'm glued to the spot.

The sticky mess slides through those bee-stung lips, and I catch a glimpse of pink tongue swirling around it. She closes her eyes briefly. "Mm."

Oh. Holy. Fuck.

Her eyes open, widening when they meet mine. For a moment we stare at each other as the children cavort around the kitchen, and the heat in hers is enough to bake a thousand fucking cookies.

"Well, you've clearly got the cleaning up under control." Even I can hear the hoarse note in my voice. "I'll leave you to it. Goodnight, everyone."

Ofelia whispers something that sounds like *swizzle sticks*, and all three children burst into a fit of giggles.

Feeling severely jolted by the entire thing, I beat a hasty retreat, ignoring Dimitry's sly fucking smirk at the door.

I DON'T CALL Lucia upstairs, despite an almost desperate desire to do so. I almost wish I hadn't soundproofed the penthouse during the renovations. I have an intrusive desire to know where she is. Whether she's returned to her own apartment yet or not. Whether she's showering all that caramel off her body . . .

That leads to very dangerous images of licking the caramel off, inch by luscious inch. I'm terrified of how much I want to.

All this, and you've only fucked her once? I'm more thoroughly unsettled than I can ever remember being. Worse, it isn't just the mind-blowing sex. It's seeing the children smile again. Feeling, even just for a short time, as if that apartment was actually some kind of home, instead of a beige fucking hotel suite, which, no matter what I do, it has always seemed to be.

Except it isn't your home. Or the children's. And it definitely *isn't Lucia Lopez's.*

I need to shut this train of thought down.

Right now.

Yes, it's great that I've finally found an au pair that the kids seem, miraculously, to like. The fact that Lucia also happens to be mind-blowing in bed is a definite bonus. But it's barely been a day. All this could come to an end at any minute. Not to mention the small issue of Miss Lopez's fake identity.

That pulls me up short.

Pulling on sweats, I head for the basement gym. I need to punch the hell out of something, and I'm fairly sure Dimitry, damn him, has already left.

I set about methodically pummeling the bag.

I keep thinking about the way Lucia looked, salsa dancing in the kitchen. I want to take her to my holiday villa in the mountains outside Malaga and watch her dance just like that on the terracotta terrace as the sun sinks over the Mediterranean Sea in the distance. I want to walk into a house filled with the scents that make it a home. I never knew how much

I'd missed that until I stepped out of the elevator tonight. I want to sit on stools at a kitchen counter, instead of at a formal table with silver cutlery and chef-made food.

I want to see Lucia's belly swollen with my child.

I freeze with my fist in midair.

What the fuck?

Where the hell did that thought come from?

Children aren't on the agenda for me. I'm a criminal, raised and honed on hard streets. No matter the perfect facade of Hale, or the hidden machine of Mercura, my life will always be one of danger and violence. It's a world that destroyed my life once, but which I could never quite escape. It's the world that has taken everyone from me, including the adopted brother I loved more than anyone. I'm doing everything I can to raise Mikhail's children far from that world. Shielded from it. I want them at college, doing degrees. Choosing careers that don't involve nightclubs or guns or running from home in the middle of the night. By the time Mickey inherits Hale, it will be clean as any normal company.

I can run Mercura in the background. Keep the darkness well away from him.

It's too late for me to choose a different life. I'm bratva, in the mud as deep as anyone could possibly be. That's why I can't get attached to my godchildren. It's better that they look at me with the fear-edged wariness I'm accustomed to, rather than the spark of warmth I saw tonight. I can't be what they need from a parent. It's why I put up with Inger, encourage her to spend time with them. They need a mother. Not a godfather who has no idea where to start parenting and an au pair who could run off at any moment, without warning.

And yet.

I can't rid my mind of the image of Lucia as she was in the kitchen tonight. Only in my fantasies, her belly is swelling softly under the dress. The vision is like a seed that has taken root somewhere in my chest and simply refuses to leave.

I'm going fucking mad.

This is a business arrangement, I tell myself sternly as I punch my way around the bag. It isn't a goddamn future. Besides, she checked the box on the contract saying she takes the pill, and she has no reason to lie.

But for some reason, that doesn't shift the image out of my head.

Alongside the jarring thoughts of Lucia carrying my child comes the infinitely more terrifying thought of her alone somewhere, running for her life, in that state. Deep down, I know she's going to flee again. If I'm honest, that fact is maybe part of the reason I suggested the contract in the first place. It's safe. Has a finite end date. I use her for what I want, with the knowledge that she doesn't want to stick around any more than I want her to.

Has it really taken only one night inside her body for those plans to go so profoundly out the window? It makes no sense. I've had countless women, in more ways than I can even remember. And never once have I wanted any of them to stay in my bed beyond the moment I've taken what I wanted from them.

Now I can barely think straight for planning when I'm going to have Lucia right back there again.

I think back to my earlier resolution of seducing her in order to get answers. It's a good plan, a logical one. I noticed the way her eyes softened tonight when she saw me with the children. But seducing her was supposed to be an entirely physical exercise. The slow, deliberate breaking down of Lucia's defenses as I make her body mine in every way a man can. A strictly compartmentalized seduction that belongs on my king-sized bed.

Not in the kitchen of the children's apartment.

Never, in all my thoughts, have I imagined domesticity as part of that seduction. And I'm wholly unprepared for how it makes me feel now.

I think of the shadows lurking in Mickey's eyes that, for just a moment tonight, cleared. I don't know if I've ever looked behind the thick glasses and seen the quiet intelligence and gentle strength in the cobalt depths. Just as I'm not sure I've ever realized that Ofelia's arctic glare is just a mask, or that Masha looks at her siblings as if they're her entire world.

I'm not sure that I ever *wanted* to see any of that. Maybe I knew that the moment I did, I'd feel exactly this disquieting sense of guilt. But now that Pandora's box is open, I can't suddenly put the knowledge away again. I can't just walk away from my brother's children knowing that I've failed them, and him, so profoundly.

And no matter how close I am to Dimitry, I cannot stand the thought of him being the one the children take their cookies to, the one lounging in *my* kitchen, lazily watching Lucia dance.

Fuck, no. My fist thuds viciously into the bag.

I might not have asked for this family. I may not even want it. But it's *mine*, goddammit. And I take care of what's mine.

It looks like my seduction of Lucia Lopez just became a full-time fucking job.

Given how overburdened my current work life is, that should annoy the hell out of me. Instead, it gives me a caveman-like sense of deep satisfaction that is as unfamiliar as it is fucking disturbing.

But it doesn't mean I can't reestablish some control. In fact, the thought of exerting control over Miss Lopez has a definite appeal.

I settle in to the punching bag with renewed vigor, trying not to think of how that spoon looked sliding between her bee-stung lips.

19

LUCIA

I stand under the shower, my skin so sensitive even the water feels erotic. My phone is propped up on the shower wall. I try not to stare it.

Call me, you bastard.

It's almost eleven. The children and I walked the entire length of the waterfront, stopping for evening tapas in a mosaicked piazza where twinkling fairy lights glittered off the night sea, but I'm still strung tight as a high wire. It's a miracle I managed to get the kitchen cleaned and the children into bed with anything even remotely resembling calm.

All I can see is his dark eyes watching me across the kitchen. Even the recollection of the savagery in their depths makes me shiver. He looked like he wanted to fuck me and kill me at the same time.

My body has been thrumming like a tuned instrument ever since, waiting on tenterhooks for his summons.

No. Not waiting.

Hoping.

But so far, nothing.

And what does that mean, anyway? It was just a look.

I turn the water off and step out of the shower. Even the touch of the towel on my overly sensitive flesh feels like foreplay.

Damn you for waking my body up. Now I seem to be existing in a permanent state of suspended desire, just marking time until Roman touches me again. I crave his touch as much as I resent him for making me want it.

But I also need to face facts.

Roman clearly doesn't feel the same way. And although I can't pretend that doesn't hurt, it isn't as if he's made me any kind of promise beyond that contract. I know I have no right at all to expect more from him than what we agreed on.

That doesn't stop me feeling thoroughly shaken up, and more confused than I've ever been.

If I'm honest with myself, it isn't just Roman who has rattled me. Being with the children has thrown me off-balance. Or rather, how I feel when I'm with them has taken me by surprise. As if some hole within me that I didn't know existed has been filled.

And that is just as dangerous as waiting for Roman to call.

More, maybe.

Being with the children, even for one day, has been deeply, profoundly satisfying. Watching Masha, tongue poked out and face screwed up in concentration, determinedly trying to mix a bowl almost bigger than she is. Finding the first cracks in Ofelia's haughty armor and watching her gradually relax into normal teenage banter. Seeing Mickey's shyness drop and his natural intelligence emerge.

In only a day, I've learned so much about them all—and even more about myself.

There was only Alexei and me when I grew up. We were a close family, it's true, but we were also incredibly isolated. We didn't have cousins or grandparents. My mother was an illegal immigrant from Colombia, an orphan when she met my father. I've never known anything about Papa's family except that they are all dead. Mine wasn't a house where other children came to play. At school, I was quiet and withdrawn. Even then, I knew my family was different than everyone else's. Knew that other children didn't have security guards who drove them to school in a limousine or live in a vast compound in the wealthy suburb of Coconut Grove, with a private jetty and armed men at every corner.

And after Papa's stroke and Mama's death, after everything went wrong, I knew the burden of being the eldest of two children, responsible for my little brother and the only one capable of saving Papa.

That's why I understand the stiffness in Ofelia's posture, her constant watchfulness. The way she's attuned to every emotional undercurrent and has a light in her eyes that looks far too old for her years. It's all horribly familiar.

The way she clams up whenever her mother is mentioned, however, is not. That worries me, tugs at my heartstrings.

I walk naked into the darkened kitchen of my apartment, looking for the baby monitor. I installed it myself, not to spy on the kids, but because I'm terrified something will happen and I won't be there to help them.

Damn. I've left the receiver in the other apartment. I pull on one of the lace-edged cami sets, then, on second thought, take it off and pull on a long silk robe. Somehow I don't think Roman would be overly happy at his guards ogling me in my pajamas.

"So, no pajama parties, then?"

"Pajamas play no part whatsoever in any of my plans, I assure you . . ."

Shivering at the memory of the dark gleam in his eyes, I wonder if everything I do from now on is going to remind me of Roman.

Slipping through the door, I give a surprised-looking Bryce a quick wave, then go into the children's apartment. It still smells of sweet caramel, warm and comforting. I pad down the corridor. Masha's bedroom door is open. She's sprawled face down like a starfish, a low bedside light casting soft waves across the ceiling. I leave her door open and move down to Ofelia's. No light shows through the crack in her door. I push it open gently. Her long figure is curled into a tight ball, the covers clutched hard in one fist. Even in sleep, she looks tense. The light from the corridor falls on the blonde strands of hair wrapped around her face. I cross the floor and gently brush them back, touching a kiss to her temple, then draw the door back as I found it.

Mickey has fallen asleep with his laptop open on the bed. I take it, careful not to disturb him, and put it on the desk. Brown curls flop over his face, and in the strange half-light, I can see the hard planes of the man he will become lurking under the boyish softness. Mickey might not know it yet, but he's going to be every bit as handsome as the picture of his father he has by his bedside.

I find the monitor where I left it, tucked in a cupboard above the stove. On impulse, I pick up the pot of leftover caramel from the stovetop, still liquid in the warm spring night.

I'm not going to sleep anytime soon. I may as well make something.

I tiptoe out of the apartment and close the door softly behind me.

To my left, the elevator dings, the sound echoing off the marble floor. I freeze like a deer caught in the headlights as the doors slide open.

Roman steps out, his head turned away from me as he murmurs to Bryce and the other security guard, clearly checking that the children are down for the night. They hold out the tablet that shows the security feed from inside the apartment.

Not that I'm paying any attention. I can't look away from Roman's bared torso, rising like a wall of muscle above a pair of gray sweatpants.

He's clearly just come from the basement gym.

Correction: from the shower in the basement gym.

Water trails rivulets down the scarred, tattooed breadth of his back, disappearing beneath the band of his sweats. The muscles on his shoulders and the backs of his arms are raised and corded, the skin slightly flushed from what must have been a vigorous workout.

And by the way the sweats are clinging to the taut lines of his ass, he's butt naked under the sweats.

Desire hits me between the legs with the force of a freight train.

Oh, God. I'm suddenly extremely aware of how naked I am beneath my robe. *I need to get back inside my apartment.*

Pressing the door code means audible beeps. On the other hand, if I stay where I am, it's only a matter of time until Roman turns around and sees me.

Roman spins around at the first electronic bleep.

The steel eyes narrow, then darken dangerously. Flicker to where the guards are still looking at the tablet.

His head inclines briefly to the elevator, a silent order I have no thought of refusing. He's holding the doors open with one massive arm, his body blocking mine from view of the guards.

When the doors slide closed, I'm standing with my back to the side wall, holding the pot of caramel protectively in front of me, the monitor balanced on top.

Roman watches me from the opposite side of the elevator, silent and deadly. From the front, his body is even more devastating.

The cords in his neck are raised from his workout, the veins in his shoulders and biceps visible under skin the same warm gold as rich olive oil. Every muscle is clearly delineated, his abdomen a ripped landscape still glistening with water. The sweatpants hang low on his hips. I watch, mesmerized, as a lone rivulet tracks down the narrow V that leads into the waistband.

The bulge just below the waistband is huge and unmistakable.

I draw a shuddering breath.

"Trouble sleeping, Miss Lopez?" One hand reaches out and plucks the pot from my hands. He frowns at the monitor atop it, but makes no comment, though he does turn it off. The elevator slows, but he doesn't move. "Perhaps I should have added a clause into our contract regarding dress code."

With one swift tug, he undoes the sash of my robe and lays my naked body bare.

He inhales sharply, his massive shaft visibly twitching beneath his sweats.

"Nobody," he says roughly, "sees you like this but me. Do you understand?"

I nod mutely. Even the slightest movement is unbearably erotic. The touch of the air on my body, the friction between my thighs when I shift. I've been high on memories since I left his bed last night, but none of them came close to the reality of his raw, sensual power standing half naked within touching distance.

The elevator doors slide open, but neither of us move. I'm not sure that I can.

"You started a dangerous game this afternoon, Miss Lopez." When I raise my eyes, his face is a solid mask of control that sends shivers down my spine. "One I intend to see through."

"Oh?" I meant it to be a challenge, but the husk of desire in my voice is obvious even to me.

"Drop the robe." Roman's voice is low and commanding as he tilts his head toward the corridor. I step out onto the cool marble and let the robe fall to the floor. The blunt head of his cock leaps above the waistband, swelling as I watch.

The pulse between my legs turns into an incessant pounding.

"Look at me."

I drag my eyes back up the wall of his chest. His eyes hold mine, dark and entirely unreadable.

"Turn around."

I do, the molten heat between my legs slicking down my inner thighs.

"Walk."

I move down the corridor. I can feel his eyes on my ass, sense him like a predator behind me. I come into the salon, lit only by the soft pools of downlight over the bar.

"Stop."

Roman moves past me to the long leather sofa. He stands before it, powerful thighs spread wide, the top half of his shaft now hard up against the carved musculature of his abdomen. The pot and monitor clatter to the coffee table beside me. He throws a cushion onto the marble tiles.

"On your knees."

"*Ah.*" I can't help the slight gasp as I drop, my knees splayed wide, eyes glued to the swollen girth thrusting above the narrow band.

He reaches past me and dips his fingers into the pot, twining caramel around them. "Open your mouth."

I part my lips and his fingers slide in, caressing the inside of my mouth with smooth, sweet dexterity. My tongue swirls around them, and I feel a dark satisfaction when he sucks in his breath, his fingers tracing the ribbed arch of my mouth. I want those fingers inside me. I want his cock in my mouth.

I squirm in frustration, my eyes barely inches from the swollen head I'm longing to taste.

"Eyes on me."

Reluctantly I raise my eyes. His are midnight black, narrow and focused as his fingers slide in and out of my mouth. His cock rears out of the sweats as if my mouth is already on it. His fingers probe my mouth more deeply, and I open wide to take them.

"Take them off." The harsh rasp in his voice betrays his own desire, sending liquid heat straight to my core.

He wants this as much as I do.

My knees splay even wider, my back arching as I place my palms tentatively on his thighs, the muscles there tensing under my touch.

I pull down his sweats, and he kicks them away. His cock surges free, slapping up against his abdomen. I saw it the other night, felt him inside me. But this close I can see the ridged vein running down it, the perfection of the blunt, broad head, the almost impossibly wide girth.

He's fucking huge.

I groan softly around his fingers. His shaft twitches, a bead of moisture gathering at the head. I lap at the calloused digits in my mouth, my hips thrusting slowly in a desperate bid to stimulate myself. I'm wet and open, hungry for his fingers, his mouth, his cock.

He traces my lower lip with his thumb, his eyes boring into mine as his fingers stroke my mouth as if they're inside my pussy. "Your lips are made to be fucked, Miss Lopez."

My body jerks convulsively, moisture trickling down my thighs.

His fingers leave my mouth and slide across my face into

my hair. "Keep your eyes on me," he rasps. Taking his cock in his other hand, he slowly feeds it to me, inch by throbbing inch.

He smells of the citrus soap he uses, sharp and fresh, undercut by the rich, oaky scent that seems to emanate from his being. I flatten my tongue as his dick stretches my lips wide, slowly but surely filling my mouth. The blunt head touches the back of my throat, and he pauses until I relax, then feeds me even more.

His large hands tangle in my hair, guiding the slant of my mouth, his eyes locked on mine. I draw my tongue up the vein on the underside and he grits his teeth, his fingers tightening in my hair, but still he doesn't break eye contact or stop the slow, steady movement of his hands on my head. I swirl my tongue around the swollen tip and his cock jerks, his thumbs tracing my jawline with exquisite delicacy.

I let him guide me where he wants me, loving the sudden surge of his shaft when the ridge under the head of his cock rubs over the edge of my soft palate. There's no way I can take all of him, and I reach out with one hand to grasp the base, but he captures it and holds it away.

"Mouth only," he growls.

I'm writhing on the cushion, desperate for his touch. I push my hips backward rhythmically as I suck him. I'm edging toward an orgasm of my own as I increase the movement of my tongue and hollow my cheeks, working on instinct. His hips jerk beneath me, but he's still holding on, his eyes boring into mine.

"Stop moving. You're not coming until I say so."

I groan around his shaft, and it jerks savagely under the vibration. My body is throbbing with the need to be filled. It's torture to hold still when all I want is him inside me. My mouth doubles down out of frustration, and I hear the hiss of his inward breath.

His thrusts become fiercer, fucking my mouth until my eyes are watering and I'm gasping for breath. He swells to an impossible size, pounding until he's right on the edge. I'm moving with him, aching for his own release as much as my own.

Then suddenly he pulls out of my mouth and steps away from me, his eyes dark pits of molten heat, every muscle corded with the effort of restraint.

I gasp at the loss. My knees are splayed on the cushion, my pussy dripping and my lips still coated with saliva. I stare up at the wall of muscle and the hot, hard shaft pounding against it, helpless to disguise my naked need.

"*Vedma.*" He says the word once, hoarsely, staring at my lips. "That mouth . . ."

He bends down suddenly, slipping his hands under my ass, lifting me with no discernible effort at all. My legs wrap around his waist, and his cock pounds against my slick heat.

"Oh!" My head goes back with the delicious shock of it, and I grind helplessly against him.

"I told you not to move." But not even the harsh growl can disguise the way his dick leaps against me, pressing directly on my clit as he walks me down the corridor toward his bedroom. His large hands spread my ass cheeks as he walks, his thumbs slicking through the moisture at the creases of my thighs, probing my dripping opening. He grunts sexily as he kicks the door open. "I need this pussy."

"*Yes.*"

His mouth captures the word as I breathe it, devouring my own. His tongue finds mine, and I'm lost in the heat of his kiss, the delicious friction of my breasts crushed against him. The base of his cock is right under my clit, driving me closer to orgasm with every step he takes, his hands under my ass grinding me against him despite his own orders.

He lowers me onto the bed without breaking the kiss,

folding my legs high around him as he goes. His fingers slip inside me on a liberal coating of my own juices, and he groans. I buck against his hand in protest, trying to reach for his dick. Fingers aren't enough. I was ready for him before I ever took that robe off.

I put my mouth against his ear, any last shred of self-control long gone. "I've been thinking about this all day."

"Tell me, *vedma*." His voice is raw with the last of his own control. "Tell me what you thought about."

"Your cock in my mouth." His thick shaft jerks against my ass. "Sucking you." My tongue swipes the shell of his ear. "I need you inside me," I whisper.

"Fuck, Lucia."

He pulls back, eyes midnight black, then fills me in one savage thrust.

"Ahhhh!" My scream hits the ceiling.

I clutch his ass, trying to draw him in harder, faster, deeper. He grunts in response, driving us both onwards.

"So fucking tight." He angles me to the perfect position and drives home, his dick hitting every nerve ending inside me. "So goddamn hot."

The intensity of my coming orgasm is an exquisite torture at the base of my spine, almost unbearable in the moments before it hits. He thrusts so far inside me that I gasp, then stops, his head rearing back so he can look at me. My legs are folded so high his pelvis is laid against every swollen fold. He rocks slowly, each small movement bringing me right to the edge, but not over.

"Give me your mouth, Lucia."

He takes it with unbearable sweetness, barely moving, holding us both in the unbearable moment before release as his tongue fucks my mouth with mind-blowing skill.

His lips leave mine, and I gasp. His large hands raise my ass impossibly high, and he stares down at me.

"Come for me, *milaia*."

He lifts his hips then plunges home, and my world fucking explodes.

———

It's almost dawn when I wake. Roman is sprawled across me, owning my body even in sleep. I ease myself out from his sleeping bulk and stand by the bed, staring down at his body like a criminal intruder. I feel like I want to imprint him on my mind, commit him to memory against the inevitable moment this thing between us ends. I've been running too long not to know how cold the nights feel when I am frightened and alone. I want to remember every mark, every scar, burn them into my mind so that when those nights come again, I can recreate him, hold his memory close for comfort.

The gray predawn does nothing to lessen the hard marks that scar his body. I stand by the bed, mentally committing every one to memory. The sheet covers only his ass, the rest of his powerful body splayed like a canvas before me. There is barely any part of him that doesn't show evidence of the life he's lived, the wars he's fought. From the puckered white scars left by bullet and knife to the ink, both old and more recent, Roman's body tells a story of violence and hardship that goes back much further than the years I can trace him as part of the Stevanovsky bratva. One tattoo, under the broad pad of his heel, catches my eye. It's a series of numbers, so tiny they're barely discernible and so faded they look to have been there since childhood. But there is something about the precision with which they are drawn that gives them an air of significance. I wonder what the numbers mean to Roman, what person or place they commemorate. I shiver when I think of how young he must have been when he had that work done, what kind of life he was leading. It's a reminder that while I may know Roman's body, I know less than nothing about the man himself.

Part of me wants to crawl back into the bed and curl into him. Try to know the man he is now, even if I can't ever meet the one he keeps hidden.

But I learned my lesson the first night. I'm not going to wait for him to order me gone. No matter how intense the sex, nor how seductive it would be to turn into his embrace and remain there until he wakes, I have to remember what my place is here.

Forgetting is a dangerous temptation. One that I'm increasingly afraid will break me, if I let it.

20

LUCIA

I walk to the café beneath a blazing early afternoon sun, hoping to catch Abby when she goes for break. The children have had a disrupted school term, having started in Spain then gone back to London for some time while the building renovations were finished. They've been back and forth between London and Malaga ever since, but have remained connected enough to their lives here that they are all involved in the upcoming Holy Week celebrations held by the Russian Orthodox Church. After a busy morning shopping for school supplies, Luis drove the children an hour out of town to the church, where the rehearsals are held, leaving me with a few spare hours.

It's not even been two days, and I'm horribly aware that I'm in far deeper than I ever imagined I could be—and not just with Roman.

Early this morning, not long after I returned to my apartment, I heard Ofelia talking to Masha on the baby monitor, which I took with me when I crept out of Roman's penthouse. I almost turned it off out of respect for their privacy, until I heard what Masha was saying.

"Is Luce gonna be our new mama?"

I froze, my heart thudding, completely shaken out of my half-awake daze.

"No, Mash." Ofelia slipped into Russian, as I notice all the kids do when they're talking privately. "We have a mama. Remember? Her name is Inger. She's really pretty." The pain lurking beneath that cheerful tone cut me to the core. I might not have had a mother for a long time, and ours might have been a strange household, but I know what it is to be loved completely by both parents. The thought of a child as young as Masha not knowing that feeling is heartbreaking.

"Oh." Masha's voice was small and uncertain. "Inger in 'Merica?"

"Yes, *myshka*." Ofelia's voice was quiet and pained. "Inger in America is our mama. Remember when we visited her? Remember how pretty she looked? She was having her photo taken."

"I 'member." Masha paused. "But if she's our mama, why do we call her Inger?"

"Because it's safer for her if people don't know who we are."

I almost leaped out of bed and ran across the corridor when I heard that. I also wanted to take this Inger woman and strangle her until she couldn't breathe.

"You want to keep Mama safe, Masha, don't you?"

"*Da*." I could almost see Masha's little head bobbing fiercely.

"Then we have to be careful, Masha. We always have to be careful, do you understand?"

"But why?" The fear in Masha's voice made me want to kill something. Or someone.

"You don't have to worry, *myshka*." I heard the rustle of the covers as Ofelia cuddled her little sister. "Mickey and I will always be here to protect you. We'll keep you safe." She began singing then, the Mary Poppins song Masha was playing yesterday afternoon.

I lay awake until long after they'd both fallen back to sleep, my heart aching and mind racing.

It feels like I've walked into far more than even that contract suggested. I already knew Mikhail Stevanovsky died in a car bomb. News like that makes the papers, and I've researched Roman and his business enough to get a rough idea of who the players are. I know, for example, that the children's grandfather, Yuri, is in jail, and that their other uncle, Nikolai, runs a nightclub that's frequented by celebrities. Abby's horrible footballer is a regular there.

But it feels like there's a whole lot more to this story that I *don't* know.

Like the fact that Roman worked in a restaurant kitchen as a teenager. I saw the flash of interest in Ofelia's eyes at that particular piece of information. I'm clearly not the only one curious about who Roman really is, where he's come from.

For some reason, I imagined that Roman had been raised to the bratva. As Mikhail's younger brother, perhaps he might not have been born to be *pakhan*, but certainly born to play a leading role. An honored family member born to the brotherhood. Born to violence.

I don't doubt that last part. I've been around dangerous men long enough to know a lethal killer when I see one. And bratva don't wear the kind of ink Roman does unless they've earned it, the hard way. The scars on his body alone are enough to tell me the violence he's lived.

But boys born high up in the bratva don't wash dishes in

restaurants at fourteen years old. Or if they do, it's some kind of punishment, over quickly. They certainly don't work in such a lowly position for two years. And the way Roman shut down after letting that piece of information slip has every instinct inside me on high alert.

I spent hours googling him while the children slept in this morning, but just like my earlier searches, I turned up nothing. Zip. Nada. Roman is as much a mystery to me as I am to him.

At first, I thought the deliberate shield over his identity was just an attempt to distance himself from the raids that broke up the Malaga bratva several years ago, and which local newspapers still love speculating about. But now I'm beginning to wonder if there might not be more to the story, and to Roman, than the sparse information available online.

I don't want to care about that story. I don't have room in my life for more bratva secrets than those I already live with. Roman's life seemed like a familiar fortress. I justified walking into it by telling myself that there was no better place to hide than the last place the Orlovs would think to look.

But now that I'm here, living in his home, my body thrilling to his touch, my heart being melted by the children in his care, I can feel the carefully constructed boundaries of my life falling away. I can feel myself starting to care about the children far more than is wise.

Most of all, I can feel myself reaching for a home that can never be mine. A home that is probably just as dangerous as the one I fled, and seemingly full of just as many secrets.

With every minute he spent in the kitchen yesterday, I felt myself becoming part of that delicate web. Wanting to build a bridge between Roman's gruff exterior and the children who so clearly are longing for his love. Even more dangerously, I can feel myself wanting to *be* that bridge. To be the one who makes Ofelia feel safe again. Who cuddles Masha when she can't sleep and makes her know, without ever having to question it, that she is deeply loved. I want to see Mickey's caution fall away and his confidence grow so he can become the man I sense inside him.

The children all need Roman to be a father to them if they are going to truly grow into themselves. And for some reason, he won't allow himself to take that role in their lives.

I should be worrying about where I'm going to find new fake passports. How I plan to hide the money I have now.

Not how to make three children feel loved and safe, or how to open the heart of a man who clearly has no desire for any such thing.

Even if he can take my body apart with devastating skill.

I need to put some distance between myself and Roman's home. I need to get some perspective.

I shiver despite the heat of the Spanish afternoon, picking up my pace as I near the café.

Thank God for Abby. She always makes me laugh.

I'm almost at the door when I hear my name.

"Hey, Lucia." I spin around, my heart racing. Even after six years, I still panic when a stranger calls my name.

A tall blond man with a gleaming smile and designer clothes is walking toward me, hand outstretched. I ignore it.

"I don't know you."

"Sure you do." He's English, with the posh kind of accent that suggests private schools and a lot of money. "I'm Lance Ryder, a friend of Abby's."

"Abby's never mentioned you." I keep walking toward the café.

"I just wanted to talk for a minute."

I speed up, ignoring him.

"I saw Abby in Pillars nightclub recently. Interesting company your friend keeps."

"Go away." I'm nearly at the café door.

"Do you know who runs Pillars, *Lucia*?" His faint emphasis on my name sends a cold trickle of fear down my spine. And I don't like where his questions are heading. Suddenly I recall Abby's warning about the pap photographer who's been stalking her for a quote.

"Look." I turn around, intending to tell him to go to hell and leave my friend alone.

Instead I find myself facing an enormous camera.

Idiot, Darya.

I hold my hands up in front of my face, too late to prevent him clicking a quick rapid-fire of pictures. I spin around and run the last few steps into the café, my heart racing.

I hide by the door for a moment, peering out onto the street, but Lance Ryder seems to have disappeared as fast as he turned up. I press against the wall, waiting for my pounding pulse to calm down. By the curious looks of the customers who saw me come in, I look as flustered as I feel.

I don't want Abby to see me like this. It will only lead to more questions I can't answer. Not without endangering her, and that's one thing I won't ever do.

I wipe my face with a shaking hand and take a deep breath. *I'm so tired of being afraid.*

When my heart has stilled and the perspiration dried on my forehead, I walk through the crowd to the counter.

Abs looks up and grins. "Luce! Where you been, *loca*?"

I roll my eyes, feigning normal despite my still-rapid pulse. "You really need to get over your *Twilight* addiction, Abs."

"Never." She sighs dramatically. "Team Edward forever, baby. I'm even thinking of getting a TITSOAK tattoo."

"A *what*?"

"TITSOAK. It's an acronym. As in, 'this is the skin of a killer, Bella.'"

"Oh, dear lord." But I'm laughing, which is a hell of a lot better than a moment ago. "That's the saddest thing I've ever heard. You're the *loca* around here." I glance over my shoulder and lower my voice. "But you should know—I think that journalist you told me about is outside. Is he a tall dude with blond hair? He just kind of accosted me in the street."

Abby's smile fades, her eyes scanning the street. "You mean he's here now?"

"He was." I glance over my shoulder again, but I can't see him. "It looks like he's gone."

Her face tightens. I frown. "Are you okay, Abs? Has this guy been harassing you?"

"Y-yes," Abby says uncertainly. "A bit. But you should stay away from him, Luce. Actually, it's probably better if you don't come in here again. He's been hanging around a lot lately."

Despite the fact that the café is still bustling, Abby takes her apron off.

"I've covered for the new girl every day so far, and trust me, she's no picnic. She owes me one. I'm taking you for a drink, no arguments." She nods toward the kitchen. "Let's go out the back door, in case that douche is still hanging around."

I'm still uneasy as we walk out of the restaurant, but there's no sign of Lance Ryder.

"So tell me." Abby links her arm through mine and steers me toward our favorite haunt, a little tapas place tucked away in a side alley off the beach. "How's it going with CEO Man?" She gives me a lewd wink.

Despite my best intentions, I blush. Badly.

She pulls back and stares at me. "Well, well." Her face stretches into an evil grin. "If my little Luce hasn't gone and done the horizontal tango with the devil himself."

"*Abby!*" I look around, horrified, but nobody's watching us.

"Don't you *Abby* me. I want every. Single. Filthy. Detail." She steers me into the bar, and we get a table at the back, well away from the window and any prying eyes.

Or camera lenses.

I shudder, scanning every face in the room while Abby gives her order, until I'm certain we're safe.

"Leave the bottle," she tells the waiter when he pours her a glass.

I cover mine. "I can't. On child duty."

"Suit yourself." Abby winks at the waiter. "Leave the bottle anyway. So." She gulps a mouthful, her eyes gleaming. "How'd it happen? Dinner? Drinks? Legs up in the back of the limo?"

"Oh my goodness." I bury my flaming face in my hands. "Abby, you can't tell anyone about this. I mean it." I look at her between my fingers. "Seriously. It's not just secret. It's like . . . CIA-level classified."

"Okay, okay." She puts her hands up in mock surrender. "I've got it. Don't mention the fuckpad."

"The *fuckpad*?" I shake my head, but I'm laughing. "You're the worst."

"I'm the best, and you know it." Abby covers my hand with hers. "Now spill."

"I don't even know where to start." I sit back, taking a deep breath. I really don't know where to start. I can't tell her about the contract. I can't, really, tell her about much at all. And right now the need for secrecy has never bothered me more.

"I guess I knew what I was getting into," I say slowly. "I mean, he isn't a commitment kind of guy, you know? He's made that clear enough from the start."

"But?" Abby prompts.

"But he's got these three kids. Godchildren. The ones I'm caring for?"

She nods sagely. "His excuse for getting you under his roof, you mean."

"Ha." I flush again. "But they're *so* sweet, Abby. You should see them. Their dad is dead, and their mother . . ." I explain the essence of the conversation I overheard between Masha and Ofelia without going into too much detail. "They're seriously damaged," I say quietly. "But they're also just kids. And they clearly idolize Roman. I just don't understand why he won't let them in."

Abby regards me for so long that I get uncomfortable. "What?" I ask finally.

"Okay." Putting her wineglass down, she folds her hands on the table and pins me with her *I'm serious* look. "You've told me all about the children and what they need. You seem very concerned about their relationship with Roman and about his interactions with them. But you haven't said a single thing about how *you* feel. And as for him not letting people in? Well, I have to say it, Luce—doesn't that remind you of someone?"

The heat fades from my face, and I take a mouthful of water to try to calm my suddenly jumping pulse.

"Look," Abby says quietly. "I know there's stuff you can't tell me. I've always respected that, and I always will. But at some point, you're going to have to trust someone. I'm not saying CEO Man is perfect." She rolls her eyes, making me smile. "But I do think he can look after you, Lucia. And I think that you need to be looked after. At least for a while." She covers my hand with her own. "Maybe this isn't about Roman, and who he will and won't let in. Maybe it's about *you* being scared to let anyone in. The kids, who you've clearly fallen in love with already, or CEO Man. Who, for the record, you are clearly head over heels for."

Unwelcome tears are prickling behind my eyes. I dash them away, embarrassed that Abby should see through me so clearly.

"I don't think he feels the same way," I mumble. "Like I said, this isn't about emotion for him."

"Bullshit."

I look up in surprise to find her staring at me without even a hint of mischief in her face. "Lucia, that man has been obsessed with you from the minute he walked into the café.

He never even learned my name, but within a week, he knew everything about you there is to know." Her mouth purses. "What little you *let* people know. Anyway." She waves an impatient hand. "What I mean to say is that first he got you alone in his penthouse. Then he ravished you in his office under the pretext of giving you his big . . . tip. Then," she goes on, and I laugh despite myself, "he hired you to live in his house and care for his *children*. Not to mention what other services were included in that little contract he made you sign."

She shakes a finger at me when I start to protest. "You know I don't give a shit about the details, Luce. You're speaking to the girl who screwed a dumb social media influencer for a visa, remember? Not that it worked, but that's beside the point.

"My point is that Roman Stevanovsky isn't some flake trying to get laid, or a skeezy footballer looking for a paparazzi shot. He's the real deal, Luce. He can have any woman in this city. Hell, probably any damn city in the world —but he wants *you*. So much that he's prepared to pay what I can only imagine is a king's ransom to have you. And not only that—" She cuts abruptly short, biting her lip, then takes a very large drink. Unusually, she's colored up slightly.

"Not only that what, Abs?" I study her, trying to work out what she isn't saying. "Do you know something about Roman that I don't?"

She pulls a face. "Well, I might have been doing a little horizontal research of my own. With the hot bodyguard."

"Dimitry?" My eyes almost pop out of my head, even though I did get a bit of a vibe about those two when I heard them bickering in the car. "Woah! Hey, I'm really happy for you, Abby. Dimitry's a great guy. He's so good with the children—"

"Yup," she cuts me off. "Whatever. It's not going anywhere.

What I wanted to say is that from what I can gather, CEO Man is *very* protective about you. As in, put you in his tower, throw away the key, and probably kill anyone who gets anywhere near you without his permission kind of protective. And I don't even think I'm joking about that last part."

Me either.

That should scare me. All of this should.

But it doesn't.

It makes me feel safer than I have in a long time. I don't know how to feel about that.

"I know you're running from something, Lucia." Abby says it quietly, without fuss. "I think I've always known it." She squeezes my hand, and I feel the tears threatening again. "All I'm saying is that everyone's got to stop running sometime. And for what it's worth, I think Roman would be a good place to stop."

"But what if I—what if it's dangerous? Not just for him. For the children. How could I do that to them, after all they've been through? And what if he doesn't—"

"What if he doesn't feel the same way?"

I nod.

"How will you ever know, Luce, unless you trust him? And as for putting him in danger—ha." She snorts. "If anyone was ever able to take care of business, it's Roman Stevanovsky. I wouldn't worry about putting that hard bastard at risk." She gives a huff of rather cynical laughter. "I'd worry about who gets in his way."

I look at her narrowly. "Do you know something about Roman that I don't, Abby?"

"Let's just say that I've been around." She upturns a third of the bottle into her glass. "More than you might think. And I know men. Especially dangerous men." She raises her glass to me in an ironic salute. "You'd think I'd know enough by now to know how to stay away from them, but clearly my body missed that particular memo." She rolls her eyes, but I don't laugh. "Fine," she says, eyeing me warily. "Then I guess you should know that Dimitry and Roman met in a halfway house, when Dimitry was ten and Roman was barely two years older."

"Wait." Every muscle in my body is on high alert. "*Dimitry* told you this?"

She nods.

I frown, a little uncomfortable that Dimitry would betray Roman's secrets so easily. "I'm surprised he opened up about Roman's past to you."

"Ah." Abby winces, her face coloring slightly. "I may have dosed his vodka a little last night. What?" she protests when I put my head in my hands. "I might like bad boys, Luce. But when my best friend is living with one of them, and I'm about to sleep with his friend, I reserve the right to get whatever answers I think necessary."

I shake my head in my hands. "You're *terrible*, Muriel."

"And you're welcome. By the way, you pick on me for my *Twilight* obsession, and then quote *Muriel's Wedding* to me? Who's tragic now? We both seriously need to stop watching old movies."

She grins, pulling my hands away from my face. "Anyway, now it's my turn to tell *you* something classified." She leans forward and looks around, like I did earlier. "Roman wasn't born a Stevanovsky, Lucia. He was adopted by Yuri when he was sixteen. Before that, he was an orphan living on the streets of Miami."

Miami?

I freeze. My blood runs completely cold.

"Roman is from *Miami*?" I can barely whisper.

"Yes, but listen up. That isn't the point of this story."

Fortunately, Abby doesn't seem to register my shock. I swallow hard and try to make my heart start beating again.

"They met after Dimitry had just been released from a juvenile detention facility," she says. "He was only a kid, got booked running drugs for some asshole who let him take the fall. When he got out, there was no family to take him, or at least none who wanted to. He was placed in one of those halfway homes kids stay in until they get fostered. Which, obviously, was never going to happen for Dimitry, not after being in prison. He was young enough, and small enough, to become a target for every abuser in the place. Not that he said that specifically but . . . well." She lifts a shoulder. "I know cigarette burn scars when I see them.

"Anyway.

"Apparently Roman used to run favors for the kids in there. You know, find things they wanted, trade it for something else. A knife, a gun, cigarettes, stuff like that. One day he came in with a knife one of the older kids had asked for. Roman found that same older kid holding Dimitry up against the wall, beating the shit out of him."

"What happened?" I'm hanging on her every word. I can't imagine hulking, burly Dimitry as a ten-year-old child being beat up any more than I can Roman as a kid running errands.

In fucking Miami.

"Roman used the knife on the same kid who'd paid for it," Abby says quietly. "Stuck him straight through and left him bleeding out on the floor. Then he grabbed Dimitry, and they ran."

I stare at her, too stunned to speak.

"After that they became a team. They dropped off the radar and stayed out of the system. Had each other's backs. From what Dimitry told me, they lived pretty rough, too. Right up until the day Mikhail Stevanovsky came into the restaurant where Roman was working and took a liking to him. According to Dimitry, they hit it off from the start, drinking on Mikhail's daddy's yacht like they'd been born brothers.

Unfortunately Mikhail was a dumb rich kid back then and flashed his cash at the wrong time and place. He got jumped. Roman got in between Mikhail and the bullet meant for him. And after that . . . well." Abby shrugs. "Yuri was forever grateful that Roman saved his son, yada yada, although my guess is that Yuri saw Roman as a useful soldier in his little organization. However it went down, when the Stevanovskys left Miami, Roman and Dimitry went with them, on Yuri's payroll. Dimitry said Yuri went so far as to formally adopt Roman, which is why he shares the same name as the children."

I try to digest all of this. "So . . . wait. What was Roman's name before Stevanovsky?"

"No idea." Abby sits back and drinks her wine. "I don't know what Dimitry's was, either. I just know they were both abandoned, or orphans or whatever. Dimitry wasn't exactly specific." She grimaces. "He might also have been *extremely* out of it at the time. Which he definitely hasn't forgiven me for."

"Did you two have a fight, then?" Not that I'm overly surprised, given that it appears Abby got him drunk *and* drugged him, by the sounds of it. From what I know of Dimitry, it's a wonder she's still walking around alive.

"I needed to know what I was getting into. Now I do. Or at least, I did." She lifts one shoulder half-heartedly. "I just can't do any more assholes, Luce," she says quietly.

"I'm not sure Dimitry *is* an asshole." I frown. "Maybe you should hear him out, Abs—"

"Hey." Abby leans forward and jabs a finger at me. "This is about you, not me, remember? Forget about Dimitry. I know I have." She pokes her tongue out to make me laugh, but that doesn't hide the shadow I can see in her eyes. "Anyway." She drains a good deal of the contents of her glass. "All of this is to say that I think you should let CEO Man in." She winks at me. "In more ways than one."

"I'm not so sure." I turn my water glass on the table, trying to make sense of all she's said. "I think that maybe I need to just stick to the terms of our . . . arrangement."

"Your *arrangement*, huh?" She winks at me. "Not that I need every detail," she says, holding a finger up, "but I do think it's very mean that you won't make my day by telling me *exactly* how many positions he ravished you in. Because, girl, I gotta say it." She leans back and grins at me as she swallows more wine. "You are looking *good*. And I mean taken apart at the seams, thrown up against every available surface kind of good."

The color rushes back into my face.

"Oh, wow." Abby's grin turns into a smirk. "You really do have him bad. Come on. At least throw me some crumbs. Tell me how hot it is."

I blush again. Harder than before. "It's . . ."

Roman ordering me to undress in front of him.

Roman's dick filling my mouth.

Roman so far inside me I can't even remember my own name.

"Mind-blowing," I mumble eventually. "Heat-wise, right off the charts."

"I *knew* it!" Abby crows. "And if it's that good, there's no way he's going anywhere, no matter what crazy opinions you have about the matter." Her smile fades back into serious. "Even if you can't tell him everything, maybe you should just relax a bit, Luce. Enjoy this for what it is. See where it goes. So long as you think you can, that is." She looks closely at me. "But that's the question, really, isn't it? You're clearly extremely into CEO Man. Do you honestly think you can live in his house, care for his children, and have mind-blowing sex on a regular basis *without* getting your heart involved?"

I laugh rather hollowly. "It's the only option, really."

"Hmm." Abby looks at me doubtfully. "You've never really

been a body-count kinda girl, Luce, and that's coming from the queen of slutdom."

That makes me laugh and change the subject.

I'm deeply unsettled. About how I feel. Where this is all leading.

But most of all, I'm shaken to hell about Roman being from Miami.

ROMAN

"Bit early for the boxing ring, isn't it?" Dimitry smacks one glove into the other and dances in front of me. "Not that I'm complaining. I've been looking for a good reason to knock you out for at least a week."

"You can fucking try." I need this more than I need to stare at figures on a goddamn computer screen for one more minute. Putting a ring in at the Mercura bunker was a smart move. You never know when you're going to need to clear your head. And nothing clears mine like knocking the hell out of someone else's.

After waking to discover Miss Lopez had done an early morning runner, I have a burning desire to hit something. I'm not sure whether I'm pissed off that she left without asking or if I'm pissed off that I care.

Either way, I'm going to take a certain satisfaction from

knocking Dimitry onto his ass. Fucker deserves it. For looking at Lucia. For the way he's looking at me now.

Thwack.

I get the first in, a bracing uppercut on his right jaw. Dimitry bounces back from it, still grinning. Prick. He's always grinned when people hit him, even as a ten-year-old.

"That the best you got?" He dances around me. "You're getting soft, old man." He bounces off the ropes then comes back in for more.

"Fuck you." I duck beneath the fist aimed straight for my face. "And you can talk." I land another one in his ribs. "How much did you drink last night, anyway? I can still smell it on your breath."

"None of your"—he lands a particularly sharp one in my gut—"fucking business."

I swing around and give his ribs a solid few strikes. "Sloppy. Same as your women." I get another one in. "Who was it last night? Some cheap bit from Pillars?"

His right hook comes too fast for me to duck. He follows it up with a couple more for good measure, snapping my head sideways enough to actually hurt. I grin through the blood from my cut lip. "Hit a nerve, did I?"

I manage to dodge the next one and catch him with an uppercut of my own. Dimitry's expression is rather grimmer than usual. I punch him again anyway. Unfortunately, it takes a lot more than a few fists to put Dimitry down.

"You can talk." He slams a fist into my gut. "You're the one playing happy families with the nanny."

I catch him a glancing blow on the shoulder that throws him off-balance. "She's there for the kids, asshole."

"Sure." Dimitry ducks away from my fists and lies back against the ropes, giving me that shit-eating grin again. "She's got hella salsa moves for a nanny."

"Mother fu—" I go in hard, landing them everywhere the

fucker has left himself open, until he's bleeding at the eyebrow and one eye looks set to be closed for a while.

Prick still doesn't go down.

"Looks like I've hit a soft spot." He spits blood onto the ring, still fucking grinning. "Or is that a hard spot?" He ducks and weaves, staying well out of range.

Smart.

I'm starting to get seriously pissed off.

"What the fuck's into you?" I land one on his shoulder, but it's not enough to slow him down. "Too drunk to get it up last night?"

His grin fades. "Fuck you." He throws a punch hard enough to leave a proper bruise on my ribs.

I spin away from his next one. "Looks like it's you who's got the soft spot." I bounce off the ropes and cross the ring, grinning as I wipe the blood from my face. "Let me guess. The other waitress. Annie? Abby?"

"Keep that fucking name out of your mouth," he snarls. He comes in hot, landing a series of blows to my gut that knock the breath out of me and almost put me on my ass.

Almost.

I take a breather on the ropes and eye him up. Dimitry is grinning again, little prick. "Even hungover, I can still take you." He cocks an eyebrow at me from a safe distance. "Especially now the nanny's got you whipped."

I growl and charge in, pummeling his ribs.

"Tell me," he grunts between blows. "What comes after that bullshit nanny contract? Marriage certificate and a baby shower?"

I roar and smash my fist into his face, and then we're in it, locked together as we grapple for ascendancy. "There's nothing there," I snarl, getting in a double jab that fucks his nose right up. "You're right off base, brother."

"Talking of bases." Blood is streaming from Dimitry's nose,

but the fucker's grin is bigger than ever. "Did she scream when you hit the home run, *brother*? It's always the quiet ones who—"

Oh, no you fucking didn't.

That's it.

I unleash the fury that made me a legend on the Miami streets a long time ago and that still lives in me when it fucking counts. I let him have everything I've got—in the ribs, the face, anywhere I can reach, landing every blow with gunshot precision.

Finally, Dimitry hits the mat like the great hunk of meat he is.

Bastard is still smiling.

"Stay down, asshole," I snarl.

He lies flat on his back, wiping blood from his face, still grinning. "Oh, I was planning to. And there's the added bonus of scaring the shit out of the geek squad, of course." He tilts his chin toward the ropes.

Clearly word of our bout must have gone around, because the room is full of every tech head in the building, all staring at us with an almost comical look of horror and awe. My own men are grinning ear to ear. They've all tested themselves against Dimitry before. None of them ever got up off the mat.

"They'll be talking about that one for a while," Dimitry says, wincing as he stretches his arms over his head. "Not a bad thing, them seeing you knock me down. They'll remember that if ever they get the urge to betray you."

I grunt in response, but he's right. Every now and then it's good to remind them of why I'm *pakhan*. Nice suits and slick cars can give people the wrong impression. Sometimes they need to remember how all of that was won—and fists is what it all comes down to. Who has the balls for the fight, when it counts. Who is prepared to face death and fight their fucking way out of it.

I might have put Dimitry on his ass, but I've always known he's the one I want by my side when death comes for me. Mikhail was my brother, and I loved him. But Dimitry is my blood. He's the one who lay curled beside me on the nights when we had only concrete for a bed and only our fists to protect us. I've watched Dimitry face down men three times his size before he was even in his teens, all with that shit-eating grin, like he was daring them to hurt him. And I've watched him get up from punches that would have killed a kid twice his size.

I could have left him behind when Yuri took me off the streets.

Instead I refused to go anywhere without him.

Dimitry and I are a package deal.

I'd have stayed in Miami if it meant keeping Dimitry safe. And he knows that, just like I know he'd die before he let anyone harm what's mine.

"What did get into you?" I cast him a curious glance as I pull him to his feet. "Haven't seen you hit like that in a while."

"Nothing important." His face shuts down in a way that tells me he isn't ready to talk about whatever it is.

I shrug and let it go, heading for the showers. You can't push Dimitry, and fuck knows, I don't like it when he pushes me.

I especially didn't like him talking about marriage.

Or babies.

It's uncomfortably fucking close to my own recent thoughts, and that is not a road I want to go down any more than my overactive imagination already takes me there.

Which reminds me of my resolution to spend more time at home. A glance at my phone says I can still make it in time for lunch, if I hurry.

To my own surprise, I'm actually looking forward to it. My shower will have to wait.

That thought leads immediately to more treacherous ones, of Lucia naked in my shower, her legs wrapped around me while I fuck her senseless. No amount of time under Dimitry's fists is going to drive away the memory of her luscious lips wrapped around my dick last night, the sweet heat of her whispered words in my ear.

For fuck's sake.

I need to get my feelings for that little *vedma* under control, before I find myself in serious trouble.

LUCIA

I walk through streets bustling with people returning to their homes for lunch, turning Abby's words over in my head: *"Maybe this isn't about Roman, and who he will and won't let in. Maybe it's about you being scared to let anyone in . . ."*

It's hard for me to separate my emotional defenses from the secrets I keep. They're entwined, my inability to disclose the truth about my past preventing me from developing intimate relationships. The first, by definition, rules out the second. I'd thought I could maintain that distance in the context of the arrangement in Roman's contract.

But that was before I met the children.

I'm potentially endangering them every day by not telling Roman the truth about my past. The journalist outside the café was just another reminder of how close I always am to possible exposure, to forces coming after me who won't stop at anything—including torturing children—to get what they want.

I touch my shoulder, feeling the old scars beneath the tattooed cage.

I know what the Orlovs are capable of.

The right thing to do is tell Roman the truth about my past and take the consequences. The problem is that, unlike Abby, I don't believe that telling him the truth will result in some kind of utopian happy family. Despite her assurances, I can't see any evidence to support her theory that he cares for me. Roman might fuck me like a dying man having his last drink, but he hasn't said one word that indicates he feels anything more than lust.

Besides, telling him the truth will almost certainly mean the end of my role with the children. If emotional intimacy isn't on the table—and he's made it blisteringly clear, in black-and-white print, that it isn't—then I face a choice: betray my family or continue to place the children in danger.

Opening up to Roman will expose Papa and me to grave danger, not to mention Alexei. And given that I now know Roman has ties to Miami, it's more than possible he will trade us to the Orlovs.

Continuing to lie, however, means putting the children in direct danger.

Which means that it's no choice at all.

Even a short time living within Roman's protective bubble has been a blissful respite from the exhaustion of constant vigilance. From a life where I've never been able to confess either my fears or my dreams to anyone. From looking over my shoulder every minute of every day. The comfort of a security guard outside my door, which is locked by a code only I know, is a relief nobody can understand unless they've slept with one eye open for years on end.

But that doesn't justify endangering three innocent children who have already seen more than enough. Watching Roman with the children yesterday brought home how selfish I've been, thinking I could have all this without anyone paying the price.

Roman's connection to Miami raises another possibility, of course. One I have to consider, even if it makes my gut churn.

Is it possible he's known who I am all along?

Logically, I know it is certainly possible.

But unlikely.

If Roman wanted to use or trade me, he'd have done it already. He certainly wouldn't have left me in charge of his godchildren.

No, I truly don't think he has any idea who I am.

But it's impossible that he could have grown up on the Miami streets and *not* heard of the Petrovskys. Or the Orlovs. Which means that if he does find out who I am, he'll know exactly what's at stake.

I heard what Abby said about his background, the way he and Dimitry met. Somehow it doesn't surprise me that even back then, Roman would insert himself between someone he considered innocent and any threat to them. It's what good men do. What honorable men do. And for all that Roman is ruthless, my gut instinct tells me he is honorable.

The Lucia part of me wants to trust him with the truth. If not for myself, at least so he can be prepared for any threat to his family.

But the Petrovsky part of me knows that the secrets I keep are not just mine. My father's life depends on me. My brother's, too.

Which means that I need to be careful, and I need to make sure that I have an escape route prepared.

I've still got an hour before I need to pick up the children. I change direction and head for Papa's villa.

When I arrive, Papa is in the middle of physical therapy. I

watch as he works with the therapist. It's only been a few days, but his speech is already easier, his body stronger. It hurts me to even think of taking him away from this, of putting us both back on the road.

It might not even come to that.

But I can't know that it won't either, especially after my run-in with that journalist and learning that Roman is from Miami.

I'll never forgive myself if things go wrong and I haven't taken precautions to protect my father.

After the therapist leaves, I sit beside him.

"Papa." I hold his hands. "Our contact in Argentina. Do you know how to get in touch with them?"

Papa tenses, his eyes on me sharp as lasers.

"*Da,*" he says curtly. He never allowed me to meet his contact when we were in Argentina. Sick and old though he might be, Papa will never stop trying to protect me, in whatever ways he is able.

"I got a burner phone." I slip the box under the rug covering his knees. "Can you place the call?"

He nods, but his face is creased with worry. "Dangerous."

"I know." I squeeze his hand. "But it's not safe to find someone here. Malaga is crawling with bratva. There's no chance we can get passports made without someone finding out."

Especially when I'm living in the home of the biggest pakhan in town.

I don't mention the journalist, Lance Ryder. I haven't forgotten that Papa thought he saw a man with a camera outside the motel. It's a coincidence I don't like at all, but I don't want to worry Papa any more than he already is.

"Get the passports sent to this address." I hand him a piece of paper with Abby's postal box on it. It's risky, I know, especially since she's clearly involved with Dimitry, however adamant she is that it's over. Either way, it's unlikely he's stooped to checking her mailbox.

"Leave—soon?" Papa is watching me closely.

"I don't know." There's no point in lying. "But I have the money to pay for passports now. I might not, in the future. I think this is best."

"Takes—time." I hate how worried he looks.

"There's no rush, Papa."

I mentally cross my fingers.

I *hope* there's no rush. If I'm wrong, and all of this has been some complex ploy by Roman to trade me to the Orlovs, then it's likely too late anyway. Either way, I can do this. Get new identities for us both. New names, new backgrounds. I've withdrawn enough cash from the account to run if we have no choice. Abby can always send the passports on to us.

I don't like thinking about any of this. But I've lived too long in the shadows to avoid harsh realities, no matter how improbable they might seem.

Papa and I have run too long, and risked too much, to get lazy now.

THE CHILDREN ARE YET to return when I get home. I'm still wondering if I can keep my secrets just a little longer, until I know we have passports and are safe. Then I think of Masha's little face and know that I can't justify secrecy one more moment.

I take the cover off my phone and take out the folded picture of Alexei I have tucked inside it. I cut it from a lurid tabloid piece about Russian bratva I found in a doctor's office. It's the lone picture I have of my brother. The photo was taken at some society event in Miami, barely a year ago.

I touch Alexei's face. He has an eye patch now, which tells

me everything I need to know about the ongoing torture he has endured. But he still looks so much like Papa it makes my heart hurt. He has the same hard body, grim expression, and fierce killer eyes. The face of a man who has seen too much death. More than anyone should have seen at only twenty-two years of age.

I unfold the brief biography attached to the photograph.

THE ORIGINAL ARTICLE had three other thumbnail images below the larger one of Alexei, one each of Papa, Mama, and me. I didn't cut those out when I took the article. Even though the photo of me was taken when I was fifteen, it resembled me enough to make me uncomfortable. The article itself gave me nightmares for weeks. Whoever wrote it knows much more than they should about our family history.

I trace my little brother's features. Despite the five-year age gap between us, Alexei and I were always each other's best friend. It was inevitable, really, given the cloistered life we led. I try not to allow myself to think of him, because when I do, the guilt is overwhelming. But sometimes I miss him so much it feels unbearable. Times like now, when the memories come in a flood that can't be held back.

"I'M NOT COMING with you, Darya." Alexei stands in the shadows, his face hidden from me.

"What?" I look at him in blank shock. "You have to. We escape together or not at all."

He shakes his head slowly. "This isn't your decision. And I won't change my mind, so there's no point trying."

"Look where we are!" I gesture angrily at the small tin boat tied

to a jetty just down from our own. "They'll find that tunnel the moment they know we're gone. They'll know you helped us escape—"

"No, they won't." In the pale reflection of the city lights off the water, Alexei's mouth is a grim line. "The guards outside our bedrooms were both paid enough to keep quiet until dawn. That gives me at least six hours to kill them both and get rid of their bodies. More than enough."

My mouth falls open. "Kill them? Are you mad? You're not a killer, Alexei. This isn't you."

"It has to be me." He steps forward, gripping my shoulders. "I need to become a killer, just like you need to become invisible. These are our lives now, Darya. If we want to survive, if we don't want to lose everything Papa worked for, this is the only way. I stay here and make peace with the Orlovs. You go and save Papa. You must."

I shake my head slowly. Reaching up, I touch the jaw that only recently sprouted the first signs of a beard. "They won't believe you. They'll torture you—"

"Worse than they already have?" Alexei gives a harsh laugh. "Pain I can take, Darya. Watching them torture you and Papa is far worse. You've been flirting with the guard on the gate for months. They'll believe it was him who bribed the other guards and let you go, just like we planned."

I look down at Papa, who is watching us in silence. "You don't agree with this, Papa. You can't." But I already know, looking at the faded eyes that are full of pain, what his answer is.

"You worked this out together." I look between them in shock. "You were just waiting until I was safely out to tell me. You always planned to go back."

Alexei nods grimly. "I'm sorry, Darya. But we knew you'd never agree otherwise. And this is the only way. Papa will die if we stay here. And it's only a matter of time until they decide to rape you, for fun if not for answers. The only surprise is that they haven't done it already. If we run together, the three of us will be caught before the *day is out. But this way, you have a real chance. The Orlovs won't hunt you as hard if they still have me to answer their questions."*

There's a hard determination in my brother's face that both breaks my heart and shows me the first indication of the man he is about to become. I can't bear the thought of him having to murder to protect me. Of him enduring Orlov's brutality so I don't have to.

I feel physically sick with guilt and shame.

"Go, Darya." Alexei kisses Papa on both cheeks, gripping his hands. "Please." It's then that his voice cracks, and I realize what it's costing him to do this, to force his father and me into the unknown night, armed with little more than some cash, a map, and an address in Argentina.

Every moment I delay is only making it harder.

"I love you, Alexei." I put my arms around his neck, trying not to cling to him.

"Keep running," he whispers, hugging me fiercely. "They won't ever stop looking, Darya, and they have money. It won't just be the Orlovs searching—it will be everyone who wants whatever reward they offer. Don't trust anyone. And never, ever tell anyone who you are. I'll find a way to defeat the Orlovs, eventually. And when I do, I'll come and find you. That's my promise to you."

"And I promise to become invisible." My whisper cracks, but I force myself to keep going. "I promise to keep Papa safe. To keep him alive. I'll disappear so completely nobody will ever find our trail, and I'll stay lost as long as you need me to be."

I WIPE MY EYES, staring at Alexei's face. Letting Roman in is one thing. Betraying the promises I made to my family is another.

I owe Roman the right to take care of his family. But I can't, and won't, endanger my own.

I will tell Roman some of the truth. Enough for him to make an informed decision.

I fold the article and slip it back inside my phone cover.

I just have to hope that doing so doesn't mean betraying everything I ran to protect.

2 3

LUCIA

By the time the children get back to the apartment, Maria has already set the table for lunch.

Five places.

My heart skips a beat. Does that mean Roman plans to join us?

The door opens behind me in answer.

"Just in time." Roman's deep voice sends a thrill down my spine. "How were rehearsals?"

"Masha is a cactus, apparently." I turn to face him, hoping none of my recent tension shows on my face. As soon as I see his split lip and the cut over his eye, however, all thoughts of the kids' respective parts in the upcoming Easter celebrations fly from my head.

"Oh my goodness!" I cross the room quickly. "You're hurt! What on earth happened?" I touch his face without thinking, then immediately realize my mistake.

Roman smells of the fight, raw sweat and violence that has nothing to do with the expensive suit he's hiding behind.

"I'm fine." He rears back from me as if he's been burned, glancing around the room. "Where are the children?"

"Washing up." My hands fall back to my sides, and I take a step back. "You're clearly not fine. At least let me dress that cut." It's completely unfair that the cuts only seem to enhance his physical attraction. Especially when he slips off his suit jacket and tie and rolls his sleeves up. I gulp, trying not to stare at the hard, tanned V where the shirt is unbuttoned, nor at the corded forearms. When I raise my eyes, he's smirking at me in a way that tells me he knows *exactly* what I'm thinking.

"It's nothing. Just a sparring match in the ring." Seeing my frown, he raises his eyebrows. "Doubting me, Miss Lopez?" There's a gruff intimacy to his voice that does very dangerous things to my body.

Thankfully, the children choose that moment to come back to the dining room. They stop dead in their tracks when they see Roman.

"What happened to *you*?" Ofelia asks bluntly.

"Well," Roman says, pulling out a chair for her and waiting until all three children and I are seated before taking his own, "Dimitry criticized your *alfajores*, so I thought I'd better teach him a lesson."

"You beat up *Dimitry*?" Mickey is looking at him with something like awe.

"What's wrong wiv my cookies?" Masha demands indignantly at the same time.

Roman's mouth twitches. He waits until the soup has been served and the chef has withdrawn before answering.

"Sarcasm, Mickey," he says, with something almost approaching a smile. "That means I was joking," he adds, winking at Masha. "Dimitry says your cookies are the best he's ever had."

She beams and tucks into her soup.

"So what did happen, then?" Ofelia hasn't touched her plate. She's still staring at Roman's face, and her own is quite pale. Suddenly I recognize the hard light in her blue eyes for what it is: fear.

"Your godfather is fine, sweetheart." I touch her arm briefly. "He and Dimitry had a sparring match in the boxing ring, apparently."

"Seriously?" Ofelia's eyes narrow, and she looks between Roman and me with a piercing glare so like his it makes me uncomfortable.

Both of us nod.

Seemingly satisfied, she picks up her spoon and clatters her soup around the bowl, shaking her head.

"Men are such idiots," she mutters. But I see the color slowly returning to her face, and my heart twists. Ofelia has buried her father and believes that loving her mother will place Inger in danger. Roman needs to understand how fragile she is, how deeply afraid of losing people.

Maybe I'll get a chance to explain that before he makes me leave.

"I'm a cactus," says Masha importantly.

"Shut up," Ofelia hisses to her sister. "He doesn't care—"

"I didn't know there were cacti in the Easter story." Pretending not to hear Ofelia, Roman turns to Masha inquiringly. "What does the cactus do, exactly, at Easter time?" He catches my eye, and I try not to laugh.

"I'm on the back of a twuck," Masha says. "We're singing."

"A float?" Roman's smile fades and he turns to me. "Did you know about this?"

My heart lurches uneasily. "I knew they were in an Easter production. I didn't know it was a procession."

His face darkens. The children exchange resigned looks that hurt me inside.

We sit in silence as the chef comes in and takes the soup

plates, replacing them with fish and salad. When he leaves, Ofelia says resentfully: "I suppose that means you won't let us go."

Mickey's head is down, hair flopping over his eyes. Masha is quiet for once, her eyes downcast. Ofelia stares flatly at Roman, her expression daring him to argue.

"It would have been nice," Roman says grimly, "if someone had advised me of what these celebrations entailed."

She folds her arms, having not touched her plate. "We told Stefania, the old au pair. She signed the consent forms."

"You mean you tricked her into signing them." Roman's face is flat and uncompromising. "Which, I imagine, is why she quit after less than a week."

Ofelia shrugs sullenly. "It's not *our* fault she couldn't read Spanish properly. Or understand Russian."

"You deliberately manipulated her." Roman puts both hands on the table and glares at her. "You know very well I would never have agreed to this."

She cuts her eyes to me. "Are you going to take his side?"

Suddenly all three children are staring at me.

Oh hell.

"Manipulating Stefania was unkind," I say quietly. "She clearly felt she had no choice but to quit after she discovered she'd been tricked into doing something she knew Roman wouldn't agree to. On the other hand"—I turn to Roman—"Stefania obviously chose to quit rather than face you and try to explain, just as the children chose to lie rather than come to you and ask permission."

"But—" Ofelia starts to protest.

"It's not your place—" Roman begins, his face thunderous.

I hold up both hands. "I'm not taking sides," I say to Ofelia. And"—I turn to Roman—"I understand that it's not my place to argue. But the parade is the day after tomorrow. The children already have parts and are clearly excited about being a part of it. Maybe we could at least find out what they're doing. Mickey?" Ignoring Roman's furious expression, I smile at Mickey. "Do you have a part in the procession too?"

His eyes dart nervously between Roman and me. "I-I'm doing all the audio programming."

Roman frowns. "What do you mean, you're *doing* the audio? Don't you mean you're helping someone?" When Ofelia tries to break in, he shakes his head, silencing her. "I asked your brother. Mickey?"

"No, I'm not helping." Mickey actually meets Roman's eyes, and there's the faintest touch of challenge in his voice. "I've set it all up myself, programmed the timing, everything." When Roman doesn't immediately answer, he goes on in a slightly stronger voice. "And it wasn't just Ofelia who tricked Stefania. We all wanted to be a part of the procession, and we knew you wouldn't say yes."

"Mickey," says Ofelia warningly, glaring at her brother.

"'Felia is real strict," Masha pipes up. "She watches Mickey an' me all the time."

I turn to Ofelia. "Do you actually have a part in the procession, Ofelia?" I ask gently.

She hesitates for a moment before answering, then shoots me a slightly defensive look. "No."

Roman's frown deepens. "Then why did you lie about it?" He gives her a hard look. "Are you trying to see some boy, Ofelia? Because if that's what this is about, then let me tell you—"

She pushes back her chair abruptly and stands, glittering eyes staring Roman down with absolute fury. "How dare you," she starts in a trembling voice.

"Oh, for goodness' sake." I touch her hand to stop her and give Roman a death stare of my own. "Haven't you been listening? Ofelia is there so she can watch out for her brother and sister." I turn back to Ofelia. "You tricked Stefania into signing that form because it's so important to Mickey and Masha, didn't you? But you couldn't tell the security guards about it, so you've been watching them yourself."

She gives me a little nod then lowers her head, staring down at the table, but not before I see the telltale sheen of tears in her eyes. At the other end of the table, Mickey's face darkens, and he turns to face Roman. "You always blame Ofelia for everything, but it's not her fault she gets in trouble. It's you who keeps sending her away to school, when all she wants is to be with us."

Roman stares at him, then at Ofelia's lowered head. Mickey returns his stare with a hard blue look of his own, which I can't help but admire. Expecting Roman to absolutely lose it, I'm rather surprised when he addresses Ofelia in a far gentler tone. "Is that true, Ofelia?"

"'Felia wants to stay wiv us." Masha glares at her godfather. Sliding from her chair, she slips her hand into her sister's. "Can we please be 'scused," she says, with remarkable dignity for a five-year-old.

"Ofelia?" I touch her wrist lightly. "Is that why you keep getting expelled? So you can be at home?"

She doesn't look up, just nods again, then gives a telltale sniff. I look around at the flushed faces and shoot Roman a warning look. "Can you give your godfather and me a little time to talk about this, guys? You can go downstairs and ask Chef if you can take your dessert into your rooms, if you like. Tell him not to bother serving us."

All three children stand, then pause, looking between Roman and me. "What is it?" Roman asks brusquely.

"Is she—will Lucia still be here after siesta?" Mickey asks, his pale face coloring.

Great question, kiddo.

Let's just add today's infractions to the list of difficult conversations I'm about to have. All I want to do is reassure him, but it's not my place to do so, and I won't give them false promises.

"Of course she will."

I stare at Roman in surprise. But he isn't looking at me or Mickey. He's staring at Ofelia's lowered head. If I didn't know better, I'd almost think he looked concerned.

The children file out, this time with Ofelia in the center, Mickey and Masha each holding one of their older sister's hands.

Roman frowns as he watches them go, then turns to me. "Make sure one of the guards is with them," he says curtly, "then come up to the penthouse. We need to talk."

LUCIA

Unsure exactly what to expect, I shower and dress again before taking the elevator upstairs. The last thing on my mind should be sex. Unfortunately, it seems to be almost the only thing on my mind, especially now that the end of my employment looks uncomfortably in sight.

The elevator doors open to a quiet penthouse. I can hear the shower running and almost turn and leave again. The thought of a naked Roman only a few walls away is extremely disturbing. In the end I hover uncertainly in the corridor, checking my appearance in the tall mirror. I'm wearing a white halter-neck sundress with a blue floral print. It's conservative enough, if you don't consider the lacy underwear beneath it, or the fact that it doesn't allow for a bra.

Stop thinking about him taking it off.

It's more likely that this will be the last of my new

wardrobe I'll ever wear. I sigh and bid a mental goodbye to the endless unexplored hangers in my closet downstairs.

"Take a seat." I spin around as an unsmiling Roman, clad in denim jeans and a white T-shirt, hair still wet from the shower, leads the way into the dining room. He pulls out a seat at the formal dining table and I sit down, swallowing uneasily.

This feels uncomfortably formal.

"Do you think what Ofelia said is true?" Roman asks without preamble. He's sitting off to my side, facing me, one ankle slung over the opposite knee. He's barefoot, drumming his fingers on the table. "Has she been getting kicked out of school just so she can be home with the other two?"

"From everything I've seen so far, I'd say the answer is yes. She's very protective of them both." When he doesn't immediately answer, I continue tentatively. "I'm sorry I didn't realize what the rehearsals were for. I was working off the notes left by the last au pair, who said the security detail had been taking them to and from rehearsal. The kids told me I wasn't required, and I believed them. I won't make the same mistake again."

"It isn't your fault." Seeing my surprise, Roman half smiles. "I might be a ruthless employer, Lucia, but I'm not an unfair one. We both got played on this one. I think the real question is, what do we do about it now? It's not safe for them to be in that procession. Holy Week crowds are huge."

"I'm sure a security guard could sit with Mickey," I argue. "And I could always ride the float with Masha, who, let's not forget, will be disguised as a cactus."

I attempt a smile.

"Security would be able to walk beside us, I'm sure." I remember belatedly that I'm supposed to be having a much different conversation right now, one that would certainly eliminate the option of me riding the float with Masha. But somehow that seems less important than mending the uncomfortable rift that opened over lunch. I'm rather taken aback that he's asking for my opinion at all. It's not like CEO Man to bother consulting anyone else. "Please let me fix that cut for you," I add. "The shower's made it bleed again."

Roman touches his eyebrow, looks at the blood on his finger, then wipes it impatiently with the back of his hand. "I told you, it's nothing."

"Nothing that should probably have stitches." I look around the penthouse. "I assume there's a first aid kit in here somewhere?"

He tilts his head in exasperation. "You're not going to let this go, are you? In the kitchen, over the stove."

I walk in and fetch it, then come back. He's still frowning at the table, fingers playing a rapid tattoo. I take out antiseptic and a cotton ball and approach him with caution, holding both up. His mouth twists wryly, but he doesn't argue as I set to work cleaning it.

"Ofelia is booked into school here for the final term," he says as I work, "but I have her registered at a London boarding school next year. Mickey, too."

I dab away, but don't answer. There's a packet of butterfly stitches in the kit. I open them while I wait for the antiseptic to dry.

"They need to get a good education," he says. His breath is warm on my skin, his jeans rough against my bare leg as I lean over to apply the stitches. "And they're better off not getting used to being here. They'll move back in with their mother as soon as she's finished in the US."

I swallow my profound objections to that plan and focus on the first part of his remarks. "Speaking as someone who spent quite a lot of time in boarding schools," I say cautiously, "they aren't always the best environment for a child with a disrupted home life. There are a lot of good international schools here. Surely Ofelia and Mickey could attend one of those? At least until their mother gets . . . settled."

"Maybe." He smells so good. Clean, fresh, and oaky, like a forest after rain. It's dangerous inhaling him. Even more dangerous to actually look at him. I stay focused on sticking his cut together, trying not to notice the way his eyes are roaming all over me. "I'll agree to the parade," he says abruptly. "After security have done a thorough assessment and given me a plan. The school issue I'll take under advisement."

"That will make the children very happy." I finish applying the stitches and go to step back, but Roman's hand snakes out, encircling my wrist. He uncrosses his legs and pulls me between them.

"And that matters to you?" His eyes are dark, his hands resting on my hips.

I gulp. A dull pulse begins to throb between my legs. "Of course it matters to me."

"Let's hope," he murmurs, his thumbs stroking leisurely over my hip bones, "that you take all aspects of your employment as seriously. Nice dress, by the way." He slides his hands down to the hem and then onto my bare legs. "Although I think I'd prefer to see it off."

I gulp. *Don't get distracted.* "There are—er—some other things we need to talk about."

"And we will. Later." His hands travel slowly up my legs, sending fire through me, until they come to rest tantalizingly close to where I need them. Abruptly he pulls me down, so I'm straddling him, his hands resting under my ass, my legs spread indecently wide. The hard bulge under his denim presses against the thin covering of my underwear. He rocks me slowly against him, my clit rolling up and down his huge shaft. I'm helpless in his grasp, my entire world centered on the fire between my legs, the need to have him inside me.

"You left this morning." His lips trace fire along my neck. "Why?"

He switches his mouth to the other side. I bite my lip in an effort not to moan.

"You said . . ." I gasp as his mouth moves lower. ". . . no pajama parties."

His cough of laughter jolts his cock against me in a way that makes me wetter than I already am. "I don't recall you wearing pajamas, *milaia*."

He rolls me over his length again. "Fuck, you're wet." His voice has a rough edge. "I can feel your heat all over me, little *vedma*. What if I put my mouth on these?" One hand comes up to my nipple through the dress. "Would that push you over the edge?" I gasp and arch toward him, grinding down harder on his sheathed cock. He thumbs the nipple so slowly I want to scream. "Well, well, Miss Lopez," he says huskily. "No bra? Somebody really does need to come."

I moan. *Is it possible to come just from dirty talk?* I feel like I'm already on the verge.

"Next time," he growls against the curve of my breast, "wait for my order before you leave my bed." His tongue traces the crevice between my breasts, still trapped in the sundress. "You do understand orders, Miss Lopez, don't you?"

Fuuck.

"Yes." My voice is breathy.

"Good. Then take your tits out of that dress before I tear it off."

I reach behind me and untie the halter neck. The dress falls away, revealing my naked breasts. His sharp intake of breath, and the sudden leap of his cock beneath me, send me spinning into a whirlpool of deepening desire.

I want him. I want Roman so fucking much I can't stand it. Some distant part of me is horribly aware that this might be the last time I get to do this, and that makes me shameless and desperate.

Taking his face between my hands, I kiss him.

Every other time we've kissed, we've been deep in it, already lost on our way to the final destination. This time is different. Slower. Entirely involved, just his mouth on mine.

I might have started it, but he takes control immediately, holding me hard on his cock, his lips taking mine with such devastating skill I'm writhing shamelessly, my bare breasts crushed against him. His tongue swipes my mouth, and I moan in the back of my throat, pushing harder into him. The kiss loops and surges, intense, deep, and all-consuming. His hand is in my hair, my mouth entirely at his mercy as he plunders it. The world shrinks down to the heat of our open mouths, the thudding pulse between my legs, my aching breasts. I'm a quivering ball of mindless desire.

He takes his mouth from mine and bends me backward, taking first one nipple then the other until I'm straining against him. My pussy is so fucking wet and swollen my underwear feels uncomfortably constrictive. I want everything off, want to feel his naked skin against my own.

"Take it off," I gasp, tugging at his T-shirt.

"So impatient." His throaty laughter vibrates maddeningly against my nipple. "But that isn't the way this game works, Miss Lopez." He pulls my dress over my head and rears back, staring at me. I'm naked but for lacy French panties, legs spread indecently wide, arched against his denim-covered cock with my nipples swollen and begging for his mouth.

"*Yebena mat*, little vedma." His voice is gravelly, his eyes burning hell fire. "Do you have any idea how fucking hot you are, Lucia? Look at yourself." He turns me around so I'm facing the mirror over the bar and settles me back down with my ass against him, my legs draped wide over his own. I barely recognize the girl in the mirror. Her lips are swollen, her eyes almost closed, nipples flushed and damp from Roman's mouth. His hand comes around and slips down the front of my panties. I cry out as his fingers find my clit. His other hand settles on my nipple. He puts his mouth against my ear.

"Don't close your eyes, little *vedma*," he murmurs. "See how fucking hot you look. How turned on you are." He slips a finger inside me, and I moan, trying to spread my legs wider, push it deeper. "This reminds me of the first day I touched you, in my office." He finger fucks me slowly, his thumb pressed against my clit, the iron length of his cock hard up against my ass. "You were so wet, *milaia*. But I think you're even wetter now. You're like a furnace inside."

"Please," I gasp. In the mirror I can see the powerful muscles in his forearms cording as he fucks me with his hand. It's mesmerizing. And it's driving me insane.

"Please what?" he rumbles in my ear.

"Please let me fuck you."

"No." Abruptly he lifts me up and slips my underwear off. He hitches me up, then lays me down on the marble dining table. He grins darkly. "First, I want to eat."

He covers me with his mouth, and all coherent thought is lost.

He eats me like I'm a creamy dessert on a spoon made of glass, licking every last crevice with delicate certainty. My hands thread in his hair, trying to press his face closer, but he teases me with wicked patience, sliding his tongue first up one side then the other, his tongue swirling slowly around my throbbing center like it's the chef's masterpiece. His fingers press the outside of my folds, pushing my clit up toward him, and he licks the length of me, barely millimeters from it with devastating precision, always just denying me that final satisfaction. When finally he encloses my clit in his hot, wet mouth, I throw my head back and scream.

His hands slip under my ass, his mouth devours me, and I

can feel my orgasm about to break like a tropical storm. Just as I feel the first ripples approaching, Roman rears back to standing, bringing me with him, my legs around his waist.

"Not yet," he says, eyes glittering. "I have to fuck you." There's no trace of teasing in his voice now. Nothing but the same urgent, dark need that is rippling through me. I pull his T-shirt off, he unbuttons his jeans, and I moan as his impossibly hard, swollen cock breaks free. I eye it greedily as he kicks his clothes aside and bends me over the table, spreading my legs wide. His harsh intake of breath as he holds my hips and stares down at me turns me on almost as much as the sight of his rearing cock in the mirror. I keep my face turned so I can watch as he slowly strokes the head of it down my wet opening, one of his hands splayed on my lower back. It's incredibly hot watching his masculine perfection, hard as the marble table itself, holding himself in check with iron control, his face darkly intent as he slowly teases us both.

I want to watch him forever. He's so damn beautiful, all corded muscle and taut control, his hands on me strong and sure. For the briefest moment I think of the horrible prospect that this might be the last time I am with him like this, and even the thought of it breaks my heart.

There's so much more to him than the autocratic CEO I met in the café. I can see the scars on his body in the mirror, the marks of the life he's led. I want to tell him that I understand scars. That I understand why it's so hard for him to open up to the children, even though I sense he wants to do that more than even he knows. I want to tell him how my heart flips every time he looks at me, just like my body surrenders at the mere thought of his touch. The blunt head of his dick slides over my clit and I groan, so close to the edge that I can barely see.

"I want this," I say hoarsely. "I want you so much, Roman."

He stills for a moment, poised at my entrance, his eyes in

the mirror narrow and dark. "Say it again," he says roughly. "Say my name. Tell me what you want, Lucia."

"I want your cock inside me, Roman." I'm losing it, even the sound of the words sending me closer to orgasm. "I want you to fuck me, Roman. I want you more than I've ever wanted anything . . ."

He thrusts into me with a hard roar, filling me so deeply and completely that there is nothing more than this. My eyes close and all I can do is hold on as he drives into me, over and over. I almost came the moment he entered me, and now I feel like I'm on a slow-rising wave, my orgasm building from the very base of my spine.

Then he slips his hand around to stimulate my clit. "Come for me, *milaia*."

And I do.

It explodes from the very depths of me, gripping me with an intensity that leaves me utterly breathless. I'm lost in ecstasy, seized by an endless wave of spasms that only seem to increase as he drives deeper and deeper into me. He thrusts to the hilt and holds himself there as I close around him, my whole body shuddering. Then he pulls out once, thrusts back in, even harder. White light explodes behind my eyes, and my body reaches for something more, a place I've never felt before, like a second layer of orgasm.

"*Fuuuuuck!*" I scream, and that's when I feel him lose it.

His thrusts grow almost brutal. One hand gathers my hair, tugging my head back. "You're mine, Lucia," he says roughly. "Say it."

"I'm yours." I'm beyond thought, beyond argument. "I'm yours, Roman. Only yours."

He roars and thrusts impossibly deep inside me, then holds still, his cock pumping with his release, each spasm drawing another echo from my own body.

It feels like ages when I finally become aware of the marble crushing my breasts and realize I've had my eyes closed. I stay like that for a moment. Roman is still inside me, his hands tracing my back. One finger halts on the scarred tattoo. I tense, waiting for the inevitable questions.

Instead, he slowly withdraws from me. I'm not entirely sure I can stand without his hands. My knees are weak as a kitten, and I feel completely disjointed. I turn and fall face down on the sofa, not least to hide my eyes from his. I'm afraid of what he will see in them.

I hear him rustling at the bar. A moment later he is standing in front of me, jeans on again, open at the top button. The bulge behind the material looks as huge as when he was inside me. Part of me wants to just reach for him and disappear back into the mindless sexual abyss. I feel both utterly relaxed and at the same time, already turned on for the encore. His eyes trace my body, lingering on my ass. For a moment I toy with the idea of rolling over and spreading my legs, just to see what he'll do. Something tells me Roman is far from done.

Before the idea becomes action, he hands me a frosty glass with a gin twist. I prop myself up on my elbows and sip it, my legs crossed behind me at the ankle. He sits on the coffee table next to me with a Scotch, his eyes still roving up and down my prone figure.

"I think you should take siesta here," he says. His voice is deep and rich with the aftermath of his orgasm. It makes me want to come again, right now.

But that would be dangerous.

The problem is that I want to say yes, so badly that I'm weak with wanting him. I want to crawl into his bed and curl into him. It's so tempting, the thought that he wants me to stay, that he might feel even a part of the same magnetic lust I do. But no matter what just happened between us, or what insane attraction is drawing me to him, I still have to tell him the truth.

I have no idea how to broach that conversation. But something tells me I should at least be dressed when I do.

"I don't think that's a good idea." I put my drink down, stand up, and walk over to my dress. "The children will be waiting to find out what you plan to do about the procession."

His eyes narrow, but he doesn't say anything, just sips his Scotch. I pull my dress on, horribly aware of his eyes on my back. I'm trying to work out how to say what I know I must, when he takes the decision out of my hands.

"Do you want to tell me why you have the mark of the Orlov bratva on your back," he says conversationally, "or would you like me to guess?"

ROMAN

Lucia freezes like prey in the forest, her back to me. I can almost hear her thinking frantically through what she's going to say.

Part of me wants to hear it.

The other part wants, very badly, for this to be a terrible mistake.

The Orlovs killed my father. They took everything from me. And I will remember their sparrow tattoo for the rest of my life. I saw it on the hands that wrung the last breath of life from my father and left his body limp on the kitchen floor.

My body is still pounding with the aftermath of fucking Lucia. If I'm honest, what I really want is to do it again, right away. But I'm not a man who tolerates being lied to. A little elusiveness, I can tolerate. But the Orlov bratva tattoo? In the same building as my godchildren?

Lucia Lopez is lucky she's still breathing.

"I saw it the first time I had you naked." I talk to her frozen back, keeping my tone deliberately casual. I have my Glock close by, though the thought of using it on the body that even now has me half hard makes me feel physically sick. "I told myself it was just a coincidence. You've done a good job of changing the colors. And the cage helps. But minutes ago I felt the scars you've disguised with ink. Whoever inked that sparrow on your back cut you where the wings should join the body. So I think it's about time you leveled with me, Miss Lopez. What's an Orlov bratva runaway doing in my home?"

When she finally turns, her face is bloodless, the topaz light in her eyes hidden behind an opaque layer I can't read. I don't like that. I don't like Lucia going some place I can't follow. It makes me frustrated, makes me fucking mad.

I've done everything to make her safe. And yet still she won't let me in?

I should be worried about what her presence here means, not why she's withdrawing. But if I'm honest, I'm far more furious that she clearly doesn't trust me than about whatever game she may or may not be playing.

Bratva games I can handle. I've been handling business since before she could walk. Give me an army bursting through my door with guns, and I'll show you a cold-blooded massacre that I walk out of without a backward fucking glance.

Based on those scars, and the mutilated sparrow, Lucia is either an instrument of the Orlovs by force or running from them. Either way, I can help her. The fact that she seems to doubt my ability to do so isn't just aggravating.

It's downright fucking insulting.

I glare at her. I'm about to explain exactly why crossing me is extremely unwise when, to my surprise, she speaks up voluntarily.

"I was planning to talk to you about this today. Now, in

fact." Her voice shakes, but her eyes on mine are steady, her face oddly set. I resist the urge to give a scathing response. Instead I move from the coffee table to the sofa, lean back, sip my Scotch, and watch her.

What I really want is vodka.

But there's no way I'm showing her how much this is getting to me. I've already let my guard down way too much with Miss Lopez.

Or whoever the fuck she is.

I scowl. I *really* don't like being the one in the dark here.

"I thought I could get through this contract and then leave without endangering anyone."

Leave? I'm gripping my glass hard enough to shatter the fucking thing. The endangering part is just laughable.

But the fact she planned to *"get through this contract"*?

Planned to leave, seemingly without a second thought?

It takes every ounce of self-control I possess not to throw her down on the sofa and show her how mistaken she is, if she thinks she's ever going to be able to walk away from me.

"But then I met the children." Her eyes go liquid soft, her lips quiver, and her hands twist anxiously. "I'd forgotten, you see. What it's like. To—to be in a family. To care more about what happens to someone else than about my own safety. We've been alone so long— " She cuts off abruptly, her eyes darting to the side, biting her lip as if she's said too much. She breathes in sharply, gathering herself, and faces me squarely again.

"What I mean to say," she continues in a low voice, "is that my presence in your house may pose a danger to your children. And to you."

I try not to laugh at the danger part. It's not that difficult, considering how incredibly pissed off I am.

So it was the *children* who changed her mind?

Not me. Not the fucking insane sex we've been having. Not the way I make her feel, or anything I've done.

No.

For *Miss Lopez*, apparently it's the children who managed to trip the emotional wire. And while I should, probably, think that's an admirable thing, what I actually feel is unbelievably fucked off.

Which makes me feel even worse, because who gets jealous of *children*, for goodness' sake?

She's *supposed* to adore them. They're supposed to adore her.

But the fact that they all seem to adore each other, while I'm stuck on the sidelines like a spare dick at an orgy, pisses me off more than I can explain.

And I do not feel proud of that at all.

"I know you want answers."

She's brave enough, I'll give her that. By now, faced with my death stare and grim silence, even the bravest of my minions would normally have collapsed in tears or bolted. I can see the trepidation in Lucia's face, but she doesn't actually seem afraid. I'm not sure whether that makes her a complete fool or the most courageous person I've ever met.

"This is what I can tell you." She meets my eyes steadily. "I'm not working for the Orlovs. But they are hunting for me. They've been hunting me for many years, and they won't ever stop. I give you my word that I do not mean any harm to you, your business, or your family. I would never, *ever* do anything to harm you or the children. But, Roman."

Her voice cracks slightly on my name. I clench my fingers hard to stop myself reaching for her. She looks so ridiculously soft, standing there with her lips still swollen from mine, her hair tousled, and her dress still creased from where I threw it. I want to pull her close and never let her go. I want her to say my name like it's home.

Instead I force myself to just raise an eyebrow.

She swallows hard and goes on, her voice not quite steady. "I can't tell you who I am."

I almost throw the glass across the fucking room.

"Please believe me when I say it isn't because I don't trust you. It isn't that." Her voice begins to tremble, and I can see the tears she's trying to hold back.

I want to be furious.

I want to not want to hold her.

"But I've made promises to people I love that mean I can't tell you the whole truth. I cannot betray those promises, Roman."

There's an almost pleading note to her voice that is getting close to breaking me.

"If it were only me at risk, then I would tell you the truth in a heartbeat. Please believe that. But others have risked their lives to ensure I am standing here today. To betray their confidence would dishonor that sacrifice."

She swipes impatiently at her eyes and takes a shaking breath, forcing herself to meet my eyes again.

"I know you're powerful," she says quietly. "And I don't doubt your strength. But the less you know about me, the safer it is. For you and everyone you love. For your business."

Her eyes drop to the floor. "I understand that my life is in your hands now," she says dully. "You clearly know who the Orlovs are. I've told you what I can, hoping you won't trade me to them, but I know how business is done. I know that I have no right to ask anything of you, after all you've done for me and my—friend. But given that this is probably the last conversation we're likely to have, I will ask anyway, because more lives than my own depend on what you do next." She takes a deep breath and faces me squarely. "I would be very grateful," she says quietly, "if you gave us a . . . head start, before you make that call to Miami."

For the first time in many, many years, I'm utterly dumbfounded.

Scrap that.

I've never been this dumbfounded in my entire life.

I always know exactly what to do. Whether it's a gun pointed at my head, or my own pointed at someone else's, I know. I don't hesitate. I don't overthink. I know when to run, and I know when to stand. I never, ever question my instincts.

But right now, my instincts are shot to hell.

Because this isn't about what I know.

It's about what I feel.

And I am not a man who deals in emotion.

Emotions are a murky undercurrent. They drag a man under. Emotions disguise the truth and cause confusion. This moment is evidence of that. My silence is all the proof I've ever needed that emotions are the most dangerous enemy a man can face. I've avoided them since the day my mother left. I shut them down completely the day my father died.

And right now, I feel like I'm drowning in them.

I want to kill Lucia.

I want to love her so hard she won't ever think about running again as long as she lives.

And most of all, I want to fucking murder the bastards who did this to her.

"I've said enough," she mumbles, and I can tell the last of her shield is finally about to break. "Please. Will you tell the children goodbye for me? I—I'll go now." She stumbles past me, toward the elevator doors.

It's only when they open that I finally find my voice.

"Wait."

26

LUCIA

"Wait."

One word. Said in a rasping, gravelly tone so unlike Roman's normal speech that for a moment, I don't recognize it.

Is it his killing voice? Will I turn to find his gun pointed at my head?

I saw the killer in him as I spoke. Saw the white knuckles on his glass and the glittering fury in his eyes. I've seen men kill before. I know the expression they wear before they pull out a gun and spray somebody's brains over the wall.

I'm not sure what particular strain of insanity made me believe this moment could ever end any other way.

But it's too late to run from it now. I played my cards and lost. I knew I'd lost the moment he asked about my tattoo. Maybe I knew before I ever walked into the penthouse today.

Maybe I've known from the day Roman walked into the café.

And maybe part of me is just tired of running.

Perhaps, without consciously knowing it, I was ready to surrender. To accept that there was never any chance of winning the game I've been playing from the day I escaped Miami.

An old man, sick and close to the end of his life, and a girl born to pretty dresses and finishing schools?

Papa and I never really had a chance.

And now, whatever mad dream I've held on to is at an end. I just wish I'd had a chance to tell Papa goodbye. To tell the children this isn't their fault, and that they shouldn't be afraid. I close my eyes briefly, seeing Ofelia's brittle mask in my mind, the fear she tries so hard to disguise, and say a mental prayer of apology.

I hate that you have this life too. I'd have done anything, given everything, to protect you from that.

But it's too late for prayers now.

I turn around.

Roman's eyes still glitter with the killing rage. He's barely moved since I began talking. Now he puts the glass down on the table with deliberate care. It's chilling to watch, like a leopard silently moving a branch aside in the moment before it takes down prey.

"You signed a contract, Miss Lopez." His voice is low, silken, and dangerous. "I assume you read it through before doing so?"

He still hasn't moved. The elevator doors are open right in front of me. I'm fairly sure I can make it into them before he pulls a gun.

"I wouldn't try it, if I were you." His lips curl, but the ice in his eyes is nothing like the sardonic humor I'm accustomed to seeing. "Even if you made it out of this room, which, believe me, is very unlikely, you wouldn't get as far as the lobby before you were caught. Unlike the Orlovs, when something is mine, I ensure it stays that way."

He crosses the floor with a lethal swiftness, punching the button with enough savagery it's a miracle it doesn't break. The doors close silently.

"I'm going to ask you again, Lucia." He doesn't try to touch me. He doesn't need to. I couldn't move if I tried. "Did you read the contract? Specifically, the part relating to termination?"

When I don't answer, his mouth hardens into a grim line. "Feel free to nod, if speech has somehow failed you."

I nod mutely.

"Good." His eyes bore into mine. "Then you know you're free to terminate our agreement at any point you choose. Am I to understand that you wish to do so now?"

I'm too bewildered to do anything other than stare at him. *Is this some kind of cat and mouse?* Does he want to play with me before he kills me? I've seen how ruthless Roman can be. I'm certain, though I've never seen direct evidence, that he's killed before.

Naively, however, I've never imagined him being cruel.

"Cat got your tongue, Miss Lopez?" His eyebrows raise questioningly, though the hard glitter in his eyes hasn't diminished a bit. "You seemed to have no trouble speaking minutes ago. You said quite a lot, in fact. Let me see if I can refresh your memory."

He doesn't move, his eyes pinning me to the spot.

"You said that it would be *safer*, for me, my family, and my business, if I don't know your identity. You implied that I would trade you to the Orlovs. Then you said this is the *last conversation* we would have. Have I left anything out?" He pretends to consider. "Oh—wait." He snaps his fingers. "That's right. You also refused to tell me the truth. Because despite believing that I'm *powerful*, and assuring me that you *don't doubt* my strength, you apparently believe that I'm incapable of protecting you." His icy veneer has burned away, exposing the searing rage beneath it. Roman, in fact, is angrier than I have ever seen him.

And I've seen him angry.

His fists are clenched, his eyes no longer the glittering arctic but burning hellfire. Every muscle in his body is tightly coiled, rigid with tension. Yet he hasn't taken a single step toward me since he crossed the room. Despite the almost vicious sarcasm in his voice, I don't actually feel afraid of him.

With a sudden shock, I realize why.

Roman isn't angry at what I said.

Correction: he's angry, all right. He's fucking furious. And I'm pretty sure that it's taking every bit of his self-control not to do something pretty savage to my body.

But not because he's threatened by what I told him.

He's insulted by it.

I'm so stunned that for a mad moment, I almost actually laugh.

I've offended him.

I've just told the most powerful man in Spain—hell, for all I know, probably in all of Europe—that I don't think he's capable of handling business.

And now he's pissed.

Not just a little bit pissed.

The kind of pissed that would usually result in his employees being verbally savaged to the point of quivering, sobbing meltdown. Actually, probably far worse than that. None of his employees would ever dare to push Roman Stevanovsky to this kind of pissed. They'd all have the brains to shut the fuck up long before.

I, however, have just run roughshod straight over the red caution line, directly into the danger zone.

"I—I didn't mean to imply that you were . . ." I stammer.

"What?" he demands. "You didn't mean to imply that I need to be *protected*? That I'm somehow incapable of keeping my own fucking business safe, let alone my goddamn *family*? Or are you saying that you *didn't mean to imply* I would invite you into my home, ask you to care for my children, only to then trade you to a pack of butchers who torture young women and old men?"

He raises his hands in epic frustration.

"What, exactly, did you imagine I could possibly need or want so much that I would consider trading a human life for it? Particularly the life of a woman who is caring for my children? A woman that I—" He bites off whatever he was about to say, spinning around and stalking across the room, wheeling to stand with his back to me, hands on his hips, staring out the plate glass window. His shoulders lift and fall with a rapidity that makes it clear how hard he's fighting for control.

I know better than to approach him. I'm also reeling from his unexpected reaction.

I've lived in fear for so long, kept my secrets so close, that both the fear and the secrets have become a mountain inside me. It never occurred to me that to a man of Roman's power, that mountain might seem like more of a molehill. A minor obstacle, a problem to be managed. Just another threat, in a lifetime that has probably been filled with far worse threats than I've ever faced. His palpable indignation is a revelation.

But he doesn't know the full truth, remember, Darya Petrovsky whispers in my ear. *He knows you're running from the Orlovs— but he doesn't know why they want you.*

But even the Petrovsky fortune seems insignificant now, in light of his reaction. Why would Roman Stevanovsky trade me for a fortune? Whatever treasures lie in that vault might be considered priceless by most, but Roman has enough money to indulge any desire he might have for priceless treasures. He has no need to traffic me for riches.

Isn't that one of the very things that drew me to him in the first place? Didn't I, barely a week ago, collapse on the floor and fervently wish for the hellfire and power Roman possesses?

And yet now I've just stood in the face of that hellfire and implied it isn't enough.

Again, I feel the nervous urge to giggle. I'm being confronted with the wounded pride of one of the proudest men I know.

You fucking idiot, Darya.

"Roman." I don't move into the room, but I'm encouraged when he immediately doesn't cut me dead. "I didn't think—"

"No," he says curtly. "You didn't."

"I—" I start, then stop.

What do I say?

That I don't want to leave? That the last thing I ever expected was that he would want me to stay?

Does he want me to stay?

I don't feel like I have any right to ask for anything. And by his rigid stance, the last thing Roman wants right now is reassurance from me.

"I—I'm going to leave. Go back to my apartment," I add hastily. I pause, but Roman doesn't say anything. "I'll wait to . . . hear from you, before I go to see the children." I pause nervously by the elevator doors, part of me hoping that he'll turn around and tell me to stay where I am. Maybe throw me down on his sofa and punish me in his own way.

That thought is dangerous. It's also stupid. The chances of Roman Stevanovsky ever throwing me down anywhere, ever again, are less than slim.

The doors slide open and I walk into the elevator, trying not to think of how much that thought hurts.

The last thing I see before the doors close is Roman's back, stiff and uncompromising.

The elevator drops, taking my spirits with it.

27

ROMAN

I hear Lucia leave.

I don't trust myself to stop her. I'm almost afraid of what I might do if I get my hands on her right now.

The fact that she doubts my ability to protect her?

That makes me want to snarl like some primitive caveman and tear down the fucking walls.

As for thinking that I would consider *trading* her, like some kind of livestock? To the fucking *Orlovs*?

"*Fuck!*" I grip the back of one of the dining chairs, forcing myself to breathe instead of hurling it through the plate glass window. I'm beyond furious. I'm fucking *outraged*.

I have a dark, primal urge to summon Lucia back to my penthouse. To mindlessly tear her clothes off for the second time, then take my savagery out on her body until she knows, without any shadow of a doubt, who she belongs to. What it actually means to be *mine*. To own her so completely that she realizes how insane it is to even *suggest* that I might fail to protect her.

I grind my teeth, still battling for control.

The only reason she's not horizontal underneath me is because whatever tiny fragment of rational thought I'm capable of right now knows that, for once, sex isn't the answer.

Lucia is terrified.

That much was plain the moment I met her. Now, however, I've seen how deeply embedded the fear is within her. And despite my current fury, I know what that kind of terror does to a person. It colors every encounter. It makes every person a suspected enemy and every situation a potential trap.

I've felt the same fear she does. I spent years running from the Orlovs, the same enemy she's running from now. That should make all of this easier, but it doesn't. It makes it so much more complicated.

I have a thousand unanswered questions, but those can wait. Now that I know who is chasing her, her identity should be easy enough to work out. But I need to move carefully.

Extremely carefully.

I'm grateful for whatever instinct made me keep my inquiries about Lucia to a tight circle of people I trust. Now, more than ever, that is vital. There's no chance I will ever allow the Orlovs to get anywhere fucking near Lucia.

But as for me getting close to the Orlovs?

A surge of something dangerously like excitement thrills through my veins.

I put vengeance on the back burner twenty years ago. Initially, I didn't have the means to execute it. Later, I owed Yuri and Mikhail my loyalty. I wouldn't do anything to endanger them or involve them in a war that wasn't theirs. More recently, I've been focused entirely on Mercura and safeguarding my godchildren's future. War with another clan is not part of that plan.

But that doesn't mean I've ever given up the idea of revenge.

I've only delayed it.

I know that one day I'll hold Vilnus Orlov's life in my hands. Stare into his eyes as I watch him die. I know it with a stone-cold, unmoving certainty. Killing Vilnus Orlov is a marker on the road of my life, a milestone I can see in the distance, that I'm moving inexorably closer to every day.

Vengeance is the reason I've always known I can't have a family or children. The kind of vengeance I intend to take upon the Orlov bratva isn't the kind of thing a man comes back from. It's wholesale slaughter and destruction. Vilnus Orlov's end won't be found in a simple, anonymous bullet to the back of the head.

It will be no less than the destruction of everything he has. Of anyone who dares stand in his defense. Of every single thing he values.

The exception, of course, being his woman, if he has one, and his children.

Unlike the Orlovs, I do not punish innocents for the crimes, real or imagined, of those meant to protect them.

But I do want Vilnus to know I'm coming. I want him to watch, with increasing fear, as I draw ever nearer. I want him to fucking *know* who's hunting him.

It took me years to discover the names of the men who murdered my father. I had to be careful. The Orlovs combed the streets of Miami, looking for a boy they'd assumed wouldn't last a week. I could have run, like my father had ordered me to. But despite the danger, I knew even then that one day I would have vengeance. And so I watched and I waited. I followed the men with sparrow tattoos as they searched for me in buses, trains, and airports. I learned who they were, where they lived. The name Vilnus Orlov, when I finally discovered it, meant nothing to me. I didn't know why he and his men had killed my father or why they wanted me so badly. But even as a teenager, and despite my father's orders, I knew that one day I would watch every fucking one of them die.

By the time Vilnus Orlov is face-to-face with me, I want him so goddamn terrified he's pissing his pants.

And now that I know it was him, or those he commands, who carved those lines into Lucia's back, I want that revenge so badly I can fucking taste it.

There's only one *pakhan*. Whoever carved lines on Lucia's back acted on Vilnus's orders, and it's he who will pay for it.

"Fuck." I spin away from the window, anger pumping through my veins to an almost unbearable degree. The mere thought of those bastards standing over Lucia with a knife turns my blood to ice. There isn't a boxing ring in existence that could contain the kind of rage I feel.

There's only one way to combat this level of emotion, and it doesn't involve punching Dimitry around a mat.

It involves cold, hard rational thought.

Every fact I can acquire.

And then meticulous, strategic planning.

But first, it involves making sure Lucia Lopez doesn't bolt before I have a chance to do any of it. Snatching my phone, I punch out a message to her.

Do not even think about running. Until and unless I specify, you are my employee and bound by your contract. Please ensure the children are informed that I have given my consent to their involvement in the procession. I will contact you in due course regarding the issues you raised. Meanwhile, rest assured that your privacy will be entirely respected and your safety guaranteed.

My thumbs punch out the final sentence with enough force to bend the screen.

How could she ever think I'd hand her over to those animals? Or that I couldn't keep her safe from them?

"I'm yours, Roman," she'd said. Even the memory of it has my body roaring for urgent release. But clearly, she doesn't have any fucking idea of what being *mine* means.

One day, very soon, just as soon as my desire to strangle her with my bare hands fades enough to feel comfortable, I intend to remind Miss Lopez exactly how I take care of what is mine. Obviously my lessons thus far have fallen short.

That highly dangerous train of thought is interrupted by Dimitry's name flashing on my phone screen. I snatch it up and punch the button. "What," I snarl.

"What the fuck climbed up your ass?" Luckily for him, he doesn't wait for a response before continuing. "Pavel found a trojan."

I rake a hand through my hair and fight the urge to pour another Scotch. *Can this day get any fucking worse?*

"How bad is it?"

"He's not sure. I'm with him now. He did try to call you first, but clearly you were . . . otherwise occupied."

"Can it, Dimitry." Normally I'd hit him with a comeback, but I'm not remotely in the fucking mood. I hold my phone out. Sure enough, there's been a dozen missed calls during the time I spent with Lucia. I didn't even notice the fucking thing ringing.

It's five p.m. now. I make a rapid calculation. "I'll be there within the hour. Tell Pavel I want to know exactly what we're dealing with by the time I arrive."

"Should I call Luis—"

"I can fucking drive myself."

"Copy *that.*" Dimitry's clearly got the measure of my current mood.

I feel a vicious sense of satisfaction. Lucia Lopez might have doubts about exactly how dangerous I am, but I can guarantee that right now there are at least thirty tech heads shitting their collective pants in anticipation of my arrival.

I head for the shower for the second time in an hour, tension coursing through my body like an electric current. I turn the water to ice-cold and revel in the discomfort. I need to wash every trace of Lucia off my body, get her bewitching scent out of my skin and her face out of my mind, or I'll never be able to focus on whatever goddamn trojan virus has been sent to hijack Mercura. I eschew my usual suit, reaching for my bike leathers.

It isn't the quiet whisper of the Mercedes-Maybach I need tonight.

Despite the fact that late-night rain is forecast, I take the elevator to the basement and head straight for the MTT 420-RR road bike. It starts with a deeply satisfying roar. I raise the security door and hit the road at an indecent pace, weaving impatiently through the city traffic. I'm itching for the steep curves of the mountain roads above Malaga.

There's something about all of this that I'm missing, something nagging just at the edge of my conscious thought, like an out-of-focus picture.

I remember very little about the years before my mother left and my father was killed. Thinking back to it is like standing on a ship and watching a distant shoreline fade into fog. My view of the past is obscured by the storm of hardship that followed. Now, however, I feel a sudden need to remember as much as I can.

As soon as I kick the city lights, I open the throttle and feel the monster leap beneath me. The bike surges at my slightest touch, engaging every sense as I rocket up the steep road leading to Mercura. It's this I need, the wind whipping against my body, the fierce tension of being at one with a machine as deadly as I feel right now. Every mile of concentration strips away another layer of distraction. The faster I lean into the tight bends, the more distance I get from the chaos in my mind and body. It takes about twenty minutes of hard, ruthless riding to gain the almost utopian mental plateau where my mind is entirely free of conscious thought.

The place where the magic happens.

Some people, I know, open their mind through meditation, or perhaps hypnosis of some kind. But for me, my unconscious is accessed through complete mental and physical focus. Climbing a rock face with no harness. Jumping from a plane.

Or speeding up a twisted mountain road on one of the fastest bikes known to man.

I lean into the road and let the visions come.

I'M EIGHT YEARS OLD, and it's late at night.

I wake abruptly, to a strange tension that seems to hang in the air above my bed. I can hear the faint rumble of voices coming from downstairs. It's rare for my parents to have visitors so late at night. I slip from my bed and crawl out to the landing.

The kitchen door is slightly ajar. Cigarette smoke weaves out of it, blue in the dim light. I can see a vodka bottle and three glasses on the round wooden table. A man is sitting with his back to me. He's very tall, even taller than Papasha, with wide, strong shoulders. Despite his obvious strength, his voice is gentle as he addresses my father in Russian, and vaguely familiar.

"This is a bad idea, Aleksander." Long fingers stub out a cigarette in an overflowing ashtray, then light another. "Let me help you."

"Helping me means war." Papasha's voice is harsh with pain. "We have not come so far to lose our children again, Sergei."

"The Cardeñases are a Colombian cartel." The man's voice is contemptuous. "This is not war, not for me. It is nothing more than pest control."

"No!" My mother interrupts them. I realize, with a shock of fear, that she is crying. "You do not understand."

"I know you ran away from the Cardeñases in Bogotá when you were a girl, Rosa." The man's voice is calm. "I understand you are afraid of your family. But here in Miami, they are still small players. Please believe me when I say they pose little threat to me."

"Sergei." Papasha breaks in. "The Cardeñases have a Russian connection. Rosa's contact told her that is how they found her."

In the short silence that follows, fear wraps around my child's heart, the previously unknown terror of realizing those whom I had thought invincible are suddenly, incomprehensibly, afraid.

When the visitor speaks again, his voice is deeper, harsher. "Just because they're Russian doesn't mean they know anything about us, Aleksander."

"Why else would they trade Rosa's whereabouts to the Colombians?" Papasha sounds impatient. "Russians don't betray each other—unless they think they stand to gain something. And whether you deny them or not, Sergei, the rumors about you, and the contents of the vault, continue to swirl. Now we must assume the past has finally found us."

"Perhaps." The visitor pours vodka into glasses and raises his own. "Za druzhbun, brother."

"How can you drink to friendship?" My mother's voice is shaking. "Your entire family is also at risk, Sergei."

"And I will protect them," the man growls. "Just as I will protect you, if you will only let me." He lights a cigarette from the butt of the last and draws deeply. "What did your contact tell you about this Russian connection?"

"Nothing." Papasha shakes his head. "All we know is that the Cardeñases are coming for Rosa—and that it was a Russian who leaked her whereabouts." He empties his glass. "That is all I need to know. We both know what happens to those who wait too long to act. I will not make that mistake again."

"There is a difference between being smart and being reckless,

Aleksander." The man's voice is measured, but there is steel beneath it. "You know what happens when families are split up."

"The moment your vor begin asking questions, we will both have a target on our backs." Papasha pours more vodka. "If we act now, we have the advantage of surprise. Rumors may surround you, Sergei, but none know of the connection between you and me. If we act quickly, they may never know.

"But if you go to war with the Cardeñases on my behalf, or the hunt for the Russian informant becomes public, how long do you think it will take before people put two and two together?" He shakes his head. "I cannot ensure that vault stays closed, and our children stay safe, unless my wife is free to do what I need her to."

"Or you can let me hunt the bastards down," the stranger growls, "and kill them before they even get close."

"We said that once before." Papasha's voice sends a shock of fear through me. It's cold and hard, the voice of a man I don't know. "I will not live another Paris, Sergei."

The deathly silence that follows frightens me. It's full of ghosts I can't see and don't understand.

When the visitor finally speaks, his voice is resigned, quieter than before.

"Tell me what you need me to do."

Papasha leans across the table toward the other man. "Get Rosa out of the country. Give her a new identity, one that can take her anywhere she needs to go. Hide her tracks well, and don't tell me how you've done it, until and unless we know it is safe. She will take the key to the vault with her. If we're right, her disappearance will expose both her enemies, and ours. We can deal with them once and for all. Rosa will stay one step ahead of them until we are certain the danger has passed. And so long as that vault can't be opened, our children are protected."

"You cannot use Rosa as bait!" The man is almost pleading.

"I know how to run, Sergei." My mother's voice is sad but strong.

"I've done it before, I can do it again. But I can't run with Roman, and I can't protect him if they find us. Not like you can."

"Then let me take him to the compound—"

"No." Papasha's voice is firm. "That will only confirm the rumors. There must be no connection between your family and mine, or all of our secrecy has been for nothing. It's why I've always insisted we use the tunnels to visit you. If there's any chance it is Ilyan behind this—"

"Then he is a dead man." The visitor's voice is flat and deadly. "And I will find him long before he finds us."

"You don't know that. You can't."

There is another silence, a longer one this time.

"Sergei." Papasha speaks again, quietly. "I owe you my life. Not once, but a hundred times over." The visitor makes a harsh noise of dismissal, but Papasha speaks over him. "No. Let me finish. Even after we made it to America, we both knew this wasn't over. We changed our names, and swore to maintain a discreet distance from one another until we were certain we had either hunted down the danger, or outlived it. Now we have to face the possibility that danger is shadowing us again. You must remember the lessons our parents taught us: a door cannot be breached so long as the keys to it remain hidden."

"I built that vault first to protect our fathers' legacy, and then to protect our children from that same legacy." The stranger's voice rises with anger. "I made those decisions to save lives, Aleksander, not to risk those most precious to us."

"And this is me trying to help you do that!" My father's voice is uncharacteristically vehement. He draws a deep breath. When he speaks again he is calmer, but still strong.

"After Paris you took the legacy our fathers left us both, and made it your own. I have let you carry that burden alone, for too long. I'm asking this of you now in their name, as well as for myself: if we cannot escape that lethal legacy, then let me at least ensure our children do not pay the price for it. Let me do what I must to ensure *that all our children can live the life we dream for them, free of the past."*

"How is this freeing them from that past?" The man sounds exasperated. "I built that vault to protect us, not to hold us hostage—"

"And it won't. All I ask is that you promise to get my wife to safety. If all goes well, there will be no need to do anything more. But if it does not . . . then our children will have options. We will never live another Paris. And I know that no matter what happens, you will protect my son."

The man turns to my mother. "Rosa. Are you certain this is what you wish? It is a terrible thing, for a woman to leave her child."

"It is the only way." My mother's voice is shaking but strong. "Let us do what we think best, Sergei. Just promise us that our son will be safe."

"I will protect him with my life, Rosa." From the landing, I see the visitor's gnarled, twisted hand reach out and grip my father's, who covers it just as tightly with his own.

"I want this over, Sergei," my father says hoarsely.

"Very well." The man's voice is resigned. "You have my promise, Aleksander."

AN INDIGNANT CAR HORN SQUEALS, and I swerve just in time to avoid the blinding headlights, my heart racing. I pull the MTT to the roadside and pull my helmet off, taking deep gulps of clear mountain air. My body feels as if it is still on that landing, the conversation as clear in my mind as if it took place yesterday. It seems extraordinary that I could ever have forgotten it.

But I guess there was a lot that I tried to forget back then.

That long-ago night took place when I was still safe. When home meant *alfajores* on a Friday afternoon and days spent sitting quietly on a small stool at the back of my father's shop as he worked. Any memory of those days has, for many years now, lived in a box in my mind marked *before*.

That box was closed long ago, buried beneath a new, far harder reality.

What I do remember, with painful clarity, is that soon after I sat on that landing, my mother kissed me goodbye for the last time.

I left for school one day as a happy eight-year-old boy with a vague memory of a strange midnight conversation.

I came home to find my mother gone and my father sitting at the kitchen table, a half-empty vodka bottle on the table in front of him and eyes as dead as a winter sky.

After that, the days became lonely. Bewildering. And then they became frightening.

Two years later, I stood outside the kitchen window and watched men with red sparrows on their hands torture the life from my father's body.

Then I ran.

I grip the handlebars on the bike, breathing slowly and steadily to calm the sudden rush of childish fear and anger.

I've punched bags hard as any boxer and ridden at speeds most racers would fear to go, but I realized long ago that some emotions can't be outrun. They live in unseen places, emerging when I least expect them.

My right foot tingles like a reminder.

I haven't thought about the old tattoo on that heel in a long time.

I guess that's what happens when you take a trip down memory fucking lane.

It was my father who tattooed the small, neat series of numbers on the sole of my foot, only days before he died. Maybe he knew even then that time was running out. He made me memorize the name of the Swiss bank that held the safety deposit box the numbers opened.

"It is a precaution, moy syn, *nothing more,"* he told me as he worked. *"If I should die before your mother comes back, this is how you can find her. But you must be careful. You cannot tell anyone the whereabouts of this box, and you must never be followed there. Do you understand?"*

It was the first adult secret he entrusted me with, and the only reason I agreed to run when he ordered me to.

Either way, by the time I ran, Switzerland might as well have been Mars for all I was able to get there. It was only years later, after Yuri had adopted me and when I was certain the men with sparrow tattoos were long gone, that I finally made the journey to the Swiss safety deposit box that the tattooed numbers opened.

I went there hoping to find my mother, or at least a clue to her whereabouts.

Instead, I opened the box and discovered a priceless Fabergé egg.

I would have traded the former for the latter without a second's thought.

First, I went to the nearest Swiss bar and got rolling drunk.

Then I got back to business.

I gave up any last hope I had of discovering what had become of Rosa Cardeñas Borovsky. Instead, I eventually used the Fabergé piece as collateral for the loan with which Mikhail and I started Hale and Mercura.

Never once did it occur to me to look inside the egg itself. Now, that seems remarkably short sighted, but at the time, all I had seen was what *wasn't* inside that box.

But now, remembering that long-ago conversation, I wonder if my father might not have hidden something else inside that egg. He was a jeweler, after all. One who specialized in designing intricate locks. It's what made the Borovsky safes so famously impenetrable.

I remember the vault he built, just as I remember the

Miami compound where he built it. I ran there after his death, just as he told me to.

But after I saw men arrive at those gates with sparrow tattoos on their hands, I gave up any hope of finding sanctuary there. And the vault had never mattered to me in the first place, beyond the fact that my father had built it. In time, both ceased to matter to me.

I was too busy trying to survive.

As for the man who promised that night to hide my mother and to protect me?

I kick the MTT into life with unnecessary force.

That bastard failed.

So profoundly that I lost both my parents, and any chance at a normal life. He broke his promises to my family. He let killers come to my door. And wherever he took my mother clearly wasn't safe enough.

I turn the bike back onto the road and roar onward in a satisfying spray of gravel.

I don't know exactly what I've learned through recovering that particular memory. It brings little with it other than bitterness, and anger.

Whatever may or may not be inside that egg can fucking stay there, for all I care. And the name Ilyan means nothing to me at all. I'm not even entirely certain I remember the name correctly.

I tuck the memory back into the box it came from and close the lid.

None of it gives me any idea how to manage either Lucia Lopez or the motherfucker currently attempting to hack into my billion-dollar project.

ROMAN

By the time I ride the MTT into the Mercura basement, my mind is laser focused. My past, along with the problem of Lucia Lopez's true identity, has been tucked away in a box I will open later.

After I've taken care of business.

Because that, after all, is what I fucking do.

I walk into the ops center, stripping off my helmet and gloves as I go. "What have we got?"

Dimitry's eyes narrow when he sees my leathers, but he wisely doesn't comment. "Pavel?"

Pavel wipes pizza sauce from his beard and blinks nervously behind his glasses. He's wearing a Thor T-shirt. I cannot imagine anyone who resembles a superhero less, although the way he puts down pizza certainly rivals a fucking Viking appetite.

"We've isolated the breach and plugged it. We're working

the trojan through analytics now." At least he doesn't try to bamboozle me with tech speak.

"Explain to me exactly what happened."

"The virus came through the software center upstairs. That is, whoever wrote the virus sent it into the software center first. As you know, Mercura is maintained entirely separately, which is why we caught the trojan before it caught us. That said, whoever wrote it is clearly looking for something. And they know what they're doing. The trojan didn't get picked up until it hit one of our firewalls."

He goes on to explain, in increasingly confusing language, what actually happened. I hear him out. Sometimes it's worth putting up with geek speak just to get the full picture, even if I don't understand half of it.

Randomly, I think of Mickey and smile inwardly. He'd probably be able to explain the fucking thing better than Pavel can. I can't believe that a fourteen-year-old has been left in charge of programming the audio for an entire Holy Week procession. Making a mental note to let him know how impressed I am, I tune back into Pavel's recitation.

"So the bottom line," I cut him off as he starts to peter out, "is that somebody suspects we're doing more than software development here and is trying to find out exactly what is going on. Is that correct?" I look between the nervous faces surrounding me, all of which nod vigorously.

"Right. Given that I sprayed the walls with the brains of the last traitor, do we have any idea who this *mudak* might be?"

"They're not one of us," Pavel says hastily. "That much I can guarantee."

"You made that clear enough in your report. That doesn't change my question."

"We're running it through analytics, trying to track it back." Pavel is becoming increasingly nervous. "But like I said, whoever wrote it—"

"Knows what they're doing." I finish the sentence for him. "Let's hope they don't know as much as you lot do, or I might have to start paying them instead." I almost smile at the indignant expressions on their faces. They'll work doubly hard to find the problem now. Nothing pisses a tech head off more than being outsmarted. I could offer a million-dollar reward for finding the origin of the trojan, and it wouldn't motivate them any more than the sheer satisfaction of gaining revenge. In their own way, the tech heads are just as ruthless as any gun-wielding *pakhan*. I can respect that.

"We did find one clue." It's one of the younger guys. He's so skinny he looks like a big wind could blow him over, but he's got the killer look in his eyes that tells me he wants this bastard almost as badly as I do.

"Talk."

"The programmer did a good job of bouncing the virus around before bumping it into our system. But we've managed to track three hard points that give us the approximate location the programmer was when they first tapped into our system. They're too smart to still be there," the guy adds. "And it isn't a hundred-percent accurate. But they'll have needed an extremely fast connection, so that should narrow down your search." He turns his screen toward me. It shows a map with a fifty-kilometer radius.

At the center of which is Pillars nightclub.

Dimitry and I both look at the screen, then at each other. He doesn't have to speak for me to read his mind, because I'm thinking the same goddamn thing.

Are you fucking kidding me?

"Are you sure about this?" I look around the room, zoning in on Pavel.

"It could be coming from a yacht," he says uncertainly. "Although it would need to be one of the superyachts. This

285

kind of work would need a lot more than a simple Wi-Fi connection to set up."

"It didn't come from a fucking yacht."

"Right." Pavel looks between Dimitry and me. "Well, basically, whoever originally created the trojan uploaded it to an external site, then waited for someone at the software center to download it, thinking it was a required update. Dimitry's already taken care of that particular individual," he adds hastily.

I nod. No less than I would have expected.

"That initial upload point we're still trying to track back. But after they'd uploaded it, the programmer had to wait on the external site until someone took the bait. Fortunately for us, that took long enough to leave a trace. The position you can see on the screen is as close as we can get to establishing where they were at the point the trojan got downloaded."

"Good work." I grip Pavel's shoulder, trying not to grin when he flinches. "Keep it up, and let me know the moment you find anything else."

"Boss." The geeks exchange relieved looks as Dimitry and I exit.

"There's fuck all down at that part of the docks," I say as soon as we're out of earshot. "And only one place I can think of that has high-speed internet hardwired in."

"Only one place with someone dumb enough to be looking into your business, at least." Dimitry's face is equally grim. "Does this mean we're heading to Pillars?"

I pause at my bike. "I think that would be a mistake. At least for now. We need to let the tech heads do their thing first. Tipping Nikolai off that we know what he's up to will only confirm his suspicions and send him further underground. I'd rather the little *mudak* think he got away with it. It will embolden him to make even dumber mistakes. But I do want to know who he's using to do his dirty work. It isn't like

Nikolai has a whole lot of friends with enough brains to pull this kind of shit off."

"Pavel is already hard on that trail."

"Yeah, I did get that impression." We exchange a grin. For all our impatience with the tech heads, Dimitry and I have learned a healthy respect for their competitive nature—and their abilities.

Without them, there'd be no Mercura, and we both know it.

"The real question," Dimitry says, frowning, "is what the fuck Nikolai is looking for. Has he really got enough brains, balls, or resources to even suspect what we're doing out here? Let alone actually attempt to sabotage it?"

"Nikolai's always been jealous of Hale. He ran that meeting with Cádiz FC behind my back. He met that fucking pap, Ryder, for reasons I still don't understand. And he's clearly in closer contact with Inger than I'm comfortable with. Let's just say that combination adds up to a fuckton of trouble in my book."

Dimitry nods. "Agreed."

"Reach out to that kid from Pillars, the one who helped us out the other night. Gregor. Do it discreetly; we don't want Nikolai freaking out. Find out what he knows, if anything."

"Boss."

"While we're on the topic of that journalist. Ryder." I look sideways at Dimitry. "Have you got anything on him yet?"

"I had Pavel on it, as you asked. This blew up before I had any answers."

"And the little ratfuck himself? Ryder?"

"Gone." His grim one-word answer contains a wealth of frustration. "I had him covered until this morning—when he managed to run into Lucia."

What the fuck?

"She was meeting Abby," Dimitry adds before I can erupt.

"The men following Ryder saw him approach Lucia outside the café. They called me to ask what I wanted them to do, but before I had a chance to give them the go-ahead to grab the guy, Lucia had brushed him off and the fucker was gone. It took us an hour to pick up his trail again. By that time, he was on a flight to London. And before you ask," he says, "I had men waiting to meet him in London. Problem is, he never turned up."

"What the *fuck* does that mean?"

"As far as I can tell, he checked in and boarded. My guess is that he did a runner right before the plane took off. We haven't been able to find him since."

I digest this for a moment, with an increasing sense of unease.

"What did he talk to Lucia about?"

"Said he was a friend of Abby's. Made some comment about Abby going to Pillars, and that she keeps interesting company. But my boys said the real reason Ryder was there was to get a happy snap. He had his camera right up in Lucia's face, apparently."

My unease snowballs.

"I know, I know," Dimitry cuts in before I can speak. "We'll find him. And I'll get Pavel back on his trail tonight, trojan or no trojan."

Thunder lights the sky, and the first rain starts to fall. I straddle the bike.

"Nice night for a ride," Dimitry says, casting me a curious glance. "Boxing ring not enough punishment for one day?"

"Nope." I pull my helmet on, then my gloves. "Keep me up to date. And I do mean up to date. I want to know anything there is to know."

Dimitry gives me a shit-eating grin. "Then you'd better start answering your phone. Not like you to tap out for siesta."

That comment throws me straight back to my penthouse this afternoon.

Lucia, wearing nothing more than a scrap of lacy underwear, legs spread over mine, writhing in ecstasy on my hand and cock. Lucia, face down on my dining table, me thrusting into her until she's screaming my name and begging to come.

Lucia—with an Orlov sparrow on her back.

I scowl. "I thought I told you not to mention her."

Dimitry raises his eyebrows. "I didn't," he says mildly. "But I'll take that to mean I have Miss Lopez to blame for your time-out this afternoon."

"Fuck off, Dimitry."

His shit-eating grin doesn't move. "Copy that, boss."

2 9

LUCIA

It's late at night, and the children long in bed, when the baby monitor crackles to life.

"*No!*"

I jolt upright in bed at the first strangled cry. I'm not asleep anyway; I'm not sure I'm likely to sleep again anytime soon. I don't stop to pull on a robe, just fling open my door and bolt across the corridor, past the startled security guard and into the children's apartment.

Certain it's Masha, I go straight to her bedroom, only to find her starfished on her back, mouth open wide in sleep. A brief glance into Mickey's room confirms he, too, is fast asleep. Then I hear the sound again, a half-strangled cry of such anguish that it hurts to hear. I slip across the hall and open the door to Ofelia's room.

She's curled up in a tiny ball, and the sounds coming from beneath the cover are the choked whimpers of a nightmare. I

290

know that sound well. I've woken up more than once in the same position, making the same sounds.

"Ofelia." I say her name softly, standing slightly away from the bed so as not to frighten her. I switch the lights on with the dimmer switch low. "Ofelia, sweetheart, it's only a dream. You can wake up now. Ofelia." I keep murmuring quietly, until eventually the sounds stop. Slowly the figure uncurls beneath the covers. A moment later blonde hair emerges, smeared across her tearstained face. She stares up at me, her eyes still stark and haunted by her dreams.

"Lucia," she whispers.

"It's okay, sweetheart." I sit down on the side of her bed and pass her the glass of water on her nightstand. "You were having a dream, that's all. Just a dream." I smooth the blonde strands away from her face.

"Masha?" she says anxiously, her eyes darting around the room.

"Asleep. Mickey, too. They're both fine. Don't worry, you didn't wake them." Gradually her breathing calms, the frantic beating of her heart steadying. I gently rub the base of her spine, keeping my eyes down while she gains control of herself.

"I'm sorry I woke you," she says in a small voice.

"You didn't." That's honest, at least. "I couldn't sleep. I was sitting out in the living room and heard you."

"You were?" She frowns. "Dressed like that?" I realize, with a jolt of embarrassment, that I'm clad in nothing but a tiny silk cami and French panty set. No wonder the guard's eyes nearly popped out. My boobs aren't made for a no-bra situation.

He's lucky I was dressed at all. I've never liked sleeping with clothes on.

"I left my robe on the sofa," I lie.

"Oh." Her eyes go slightly unfocused, and she chews her lower lip.

"Ofelia," I say gently. "Do you want to tell me about your dream?"

Her eyes dart to me and away again. "It was the night Papa died."

"Ah." I know their father died in a car bomb, but little more than that. "Were you there that night? Is that what you were dreaming about?"

"No." Her head shakes on the pillow. "We were at home. At our old home. The one we had before . . . everything."

"Here in Spain?"

"Uh-huh." She nods slightly. "We were with Babushka Vera."

Yuri's wife. I don't have an overly good impression of Babushka Vera so far. From the muttered side comments I've heard when her name is mentioned, she holds extremely conservative, traditional views and is very critical of all three children.

"Was it Babushka Vera who told you about your papa?"

"No." She frowns. "The phone rang, and she answered it. After a moment she screamed, and then she went into her bedroom and locked the door. We could hear her crying"—her voice cracks slightly—"but she wouldn't let us in."

I refrain, with no small difficulty, from the urge to say something extremely sharp about Babushka fucking Vera.

"What happened after that?" I ask gently. "You don't have to tell me if you don't want to."

Ofelia knuckles her eyes like a child.

"It's okay." She stares at the floor for a few moments. I keep rubbing her back in slow circles. "After a while, Mama came," she says finally. "She tried to take Masha."

My hand falters for a moment, then continues.

"Masha was crying."

From the corner of my eye, I can see slow tears trickling down Ofelia's face.

"Mickey was yelling at Mama to stop, and Masha was trying to hang on to me, but Mama took her anyway and put her in the car. She had a convertible," Ofelia adds, her eyes cutting to me. "Papa wouldn't let us ride in it. There wasn't a proper baby seat, and he says—*said*—that Mama drove too fast. I was trying to tell her, and Mickey was trying to get Masha out of the car, but . . ." Her voice trails off dismally.

I can see the scene all too clearly. It's hard enough for me to imagine, let alone for Ofelia to relive.

"Mama told me to stay and look after Babushka Vera, but I didn't want to. I wanted to go with Masha."

"Of course you did."

"Then Uncle Roman came and made Mama stop backing the car out. He took us all inside and that's when he . . ." Her voice chokes.

"That's when he told you what had happened to your Papa?"

She nods, unable to speak.

"That must have been terrible." I keep rubbing her back. "Is that what you dream about? Roman telling you about Papa?"

"No." She shakes her head wearily. "I always dream the same thing. Always. I dream that somebody is taking Mickey and Masha away, and I don't know where they're going. And in my dream I can't—yell. I can't tell them to stop." She's weeping openly now, her body shaking with sobs. "I c-can't do anything to fight back. And they're crying, and they don't want to go, but I c-can't h-help them . . ."

"Oh, darling." I lie down on the bed behind her and cuddle her close, stroking her hair and murmuring soothing nothings until she gradually quiets again and the sobs become soft hitches of breath. We lie like that for a long time, until finally her breathing slows and I feel her start to relax.

"Lucia?" she says sleepily.

"Hm?"

"I'm glad you're here."

I kiss the back of her head, squeezing my eyes shut to stop the sudden tears from sliding out. When I trust myself to speak, I say, "Me, too, darling. I'm glad I'm here, too."

"Thank you for . . . procession . . ." She's drifting.

"I can't wait to see it." I keep whispering to her as she slides back into sleep, stroking her hair long after I hear the long, rhythmic breathing.

I lie in the darkness beside her for a time, digesting what she said. I'm unwilling to leave in case the nightmare reclaims her.

I'd already deduced that Inger, the children's mother, is quite a piece of work. But I still don't understand how any mother could turn up after the death of their children's father and not only keep the fact from them, but then try to split them up.

Not to mention Babushka fucking Vera, terrifying all three of them by screaming and then losing herself completely.

I try to remind myself that the woman had just discovered her son was dead; I want to feel sympathy for that. But my efforts to empathize with her are far outweighed by my horror at her abandoning three young children at the most terrible moment of their lives, to selfishly indulge her own grief.

In the few days I've spent with the children, it's become horribly apparent that they're entirely dependent on one another for emotional support. Their father, who appears to have been the most attentive of the various adult figures in their life, has been gone for two years. Since then, from what I can deduce from the files and sparse notes, they've been largely raised by a series of nannies, with the occasional visit to Inger's parents in the US or to Vera in London. Roman has been their prime carer during that time, but from what I can see, he's been distant at best, and despite his recent efforts, just plain absent at worst.

I will contact you in due course regarding the issues you raised. Meanwhile, rest assured that your privacy will be entirely respected and your safety guaranteed.

I've read his text message so many times I have it memorized.

I wonder if it's wise to let Ofelia believe I'll be here for any length of time. Given his fury in the penthouse, and the curt tone of his message, Roman seems just as likely to send me packing as he ever was.

I did as his message asked, of course. I gave the children the good news that they are permitted to take part in the procession. I cooked fajitas with them, took them out for gelato on the seafront, then tucked them in and waited until they were all asleep before returning to my own apartment. By the time Ofelia cried out with her nightmare, I'd been lying awake in the darkness for hours, turning over everything that was said between Roman and me.

I didn't come to any conclusions, of course.

What conclusions are there to come to? Roman will make a decision, sooner or later. When he does, he'll tell me. And then whatever way the chips fall, I'll have to work with it. In the meantime, I'm grateful that at least it seems he won't betray me to the Orlovs.

I touch Ofelia's phone on the nightstand and it lights up: just after one o'clock in the morning.

The witching hour is close.

That thought brings me back to Roman calling me *little vedma*, little witch. I wish I could say I hated the name, but I don't, any more than when he slips and calls me *milaia*, "darling."

It's unlikely that I'll hear anything like that again anytime soon.

The uncertainty makes me restless and impatient. It's an unfortunate side effect of having been the sole person deciding my and Papa's future for the past six years. I'm always considering the next step, always making a plan. I find it deeply discomforting not to know what, exactly, Roman plans to do with me. Despite his assurances about my safety, our conversation has left me in limbo regarding how he feels, both about me and my past.

I check Ofelia's breathing. It's deep and even. I slowly withdraw my arm and ease myself off her bed. I leave the lights on low in case she wakes up again and pad restlessly out into the living room. I'm wide awake, sleep a distant dream. I walk over to the wide window that looks down onto the street below, staring out at the city lights. The streets are quiet, only a rare vehicle traversing them. I watch as a motorbike roars down the road at high speed. To my surprise, it pulls into the driveway leading into the basement parking garage. The rider halts and puts his feet to the ground, stabilizing the bike as he points the clicker to raise the security door.

It's Roman.

I can tell by the way he moves, the shape of his body. Even from this many floors up, I know it's him. My body leaps in immediate response, an insistent pulse thudding between my legs.

Where has he been? With whom?

I know I have no right to answers to those questions. Nor even to feel this sense of anticipation. Our earlier conversation in no way changes the contract I signed, nor the boundaries around our relationship that Roman has made so clear.

I know I can't ask him for what I want. This arrangement is about his needs, not mine.

That doesn't stop me wanting him with a fierce, almost desperate hunger.

All I can hear is his low, rough voice: *"On your knees, Miss Lopez."*

Desire licks through my body, hot and demanding.

Right now I don't want to try to make sense of what Roman and I are. I don't want to think of plans or next steps.

I don't want to think at all.

I have a sudden, vivid memory of kneeling before him, his massive cock driving into my mouth and his rough voice guiding my every move.

My pussy spasms.

I'm so ready I feel like I'll explode the minute he touches me.

If he touches me.

ROMAN

ake her wait.

It's past one in the morning when I finally pull the bike into the basement parking garage. I've deliberately returned late.

Despite the pelting rain, I chose a circuitous mountain route back to Malaga. I took the bends at breakneck speed, pushing the MTT and myself to the limit to exhaust myself in both body and mind. And yet no matter how far and hard I rode, the savage demon of fury and desire rode with me, whispering dangerous temptations through the rain.

I'm still restless when I step into the elevator. My fingers itch to press the button for her floor. The decision to house the au pair and children on a floor separate to mine makes sense. I've never wanted them impacted by my activities, nocturnal or otherwise. At this particular moment, however, that good sense is a barrier to what I actually need.

Which is to fuck Lucia into quivering submission.

Her unwillingness to trust me still infuriates me beyond reason. A hundred miles of hard riding has done nothing to suppress the niggling fear that despite my command, I will return to find her gone. It's been an effort of will not to text her again or post extra security to monitor her movements. But doing so would mean admitting those fears to myself.

And besides—I'm done talking.

I'm resolved to uncover her secrets. Then to solve her problems, so comprehensively that there's no need for talking at all.

A dark part of me wants her to be blind to my decisions. Needs her to learn how fucking wrong she was to ever doubt me. To ensure she learns the lesson that there's nothing, and nobody, I can't handle.

Consider it punishment for doubting my ability to manage business.

The desire to exert total control over her doesn't change the fact that I'm almost vibrating with tension as the elevator approaches her floor. I grit my teeth and keep my bike gloves on as a deterrent against pushing that goddamn button.

The elevator glides to a halt anyway. I mentally curse my security guards. Cell phones exist for a reason. There's nothing urgent enough to demand my attention by forcing me to stop.

On the other hand, I'm in the mood for a savaging.

Someone is about to lose their job.

I'm almost relishing the thought of ripping someone a new orifice.

The doors slide open, and my furious rant dies in my mouth.

Standing right in front of me is Lucia, her almond eyes slitted with desire, cherry nipples thrusting through a scrap of silk only slightly bigger than the French panties that barely cover the sweet curves of her ass. Off to my right, a security guard is nervously looking anywhere but at us.

I want to kill him.

I want to tear her apart.

And my resolve is shot entirely to hell.

I close one gloved hand around her arm and pull her into the elevator.

"What the fuck," I snarl as the doors close. "That guard saw you—"

"I don't care." Lucia faces me, trembling. I can feel her heat and hunger, smell the sweet intoxication of her arousal.

It's everything I've resolved not to do. Not to mention utterly outside the rules of our contract.

Exerting every ounce of will, I don't move.

Send her away.

But her eyes are liquid pools of desire. Her bee-stung lips are slightly parted. And my cock doesn't seem to give a fuck about my resolutions.

My hand tangles in her hair.

"Give me your mouth."

Her lips part with a soft cry that licks fire through what's left of my brain and makes my dick pound. The wildness inside her finds the storm that's been coursing through my own body all day. That kiss pushes me over the edge of reason.

Fuck detachment.

I'm going to *own* Lucia Lopez. Teach her how wrong she is to even *dare* to imagine I don't know what she needs.

My gloved hands go under the lush globes of her ass. I lift her against the elevator wall and take her mouth hard, demanding surrender. She opens beneath my assault with a small, needy sound that sends me into orbit. Her naked legs hitch around my waist, and I pull her silken-clad heat hard against me, rolling her clit against the length of my throbbing shaft until she's moaning into my mouth.

Oh, I'm going to fucking *torture* her for this.

The elevator dings.

Kicking my helmet ahead of us into the corridor, I carry her out of the elevator. Lucia's mouth under mine is both yielding and demanding, a fiery oblivion of contradiction. Her arms wrap around my neck as I walk her toward the bedroom, her breasts crushed against me. I pull my gloves off as I go, throwing them to the floor, holding her ass one-handed.

The gloves might be off, but my control is firmly in place. Let her grind against me like a silken temptress. Let her think she knows what she wants.

Let her think she's in control.

She's about to learn just how fucking wrong she is.

I slip the fingers of one hand beneath her French panties.

Her pussy is molten, slick fire.

"You were waiting for me."

She nods against my neck.

"You thought I wasn't going to come for you."

Her lips find my ear. "I need you, Roman." Her voice is a whispered breath, barely there, and yet my name on her lips is somehow lightning through my body. She licks the place beneath my ear that drives me fucking insane and says it again: "I need you so much."

I can feel exactly how ready she is. How impatient.

I kick the door of my room open and throw her down on the bed.

She eyes me beneath lowered lashes as I shuck off my jacket and T-shirt, biting her lip as her eyes travel over my chest, down toward the buttoned opening of my leathers.

I can read the naked need in her eyes, in the way those delicious lips part, her teeth scraping over the lower one. I revel in it.

The memory of those lips on my cock has been haunting me for fucking days.

I kick off my boots. "On your knees."

Her breath hitches, and her eyes glaze over. She obeys as if she's hypnotized, crawling down the bed toward me, her eyes locked on my shaft. I unbutton my leathers and her pupils dilate, her breath coming short.

I release myself and she moans, coming to her knees on the edge of the bed in a voluptuous, sensual movement, her tongue darting out to moisten her lips as her mouth moves toward my shaft.

"Not yet."

"Oh!"

Her eyes close, her whole body frozen and quivering. A sadistic part of me wants to keep her there, frustrated and needy.

Except I know that isn't what she wants. What she needs.

And despite a deep desire to punish the living shit out of her, tonight is about leaving Lucia in no doubt that I understand exactly what she wants and needs. That I'm the *only* person who understands.

And the only one who can give it to her.

This penthouse, and my bed, are the end of the road. The place where the running stops and her secrets are laid bare.

I tip her chin up. "Look at me."

Her eyes open. There's no trace of the shield that lay over them yesterday afternoon, no shadow of fear or murky secrecy. There's nothing in the topaz depths but simple, naked desire and soft, delicious submission.

"I will always come for you, Lucia." I part her lips with my thumb, tracing the lower lip that haunts my every dream. "Never doubt that." My eyes lock on hers. "Never doubt *me*."

Her eyes glisten, then close. Her chin makes a tiny movement in my hand as she nods.

"Good."

I step away, and her eyes fly open.

Her breasts are thrust toward me, nipples pressing against the silk. The panties are dark beneath her slit, soaked with her arousal.

Her teeth scrape across her lower lip, her eyes limpid as she waits on my command.

I've never seen anything so fucking hot in my life.

"Take your clothes off." My voice is a low growl.

Her body shivers like a current of electricity just ran through it. She obeys immediately, pulling the lace over her head, revealing her gorgeous tits and rosy, swollen nipples. Her panties slide over the peach of her ass, and she kicks them aside.

"Knees apart."

She gasps, her eyes locked on my dick. When she spreads open for me, her lips are puffy and slick with need.

"Open your mouth."

Her eyes flutter closed, and her tongue licks the wet fullness of her lower lip as she does as she's told. I slide my shaft between her lips.

Her mouth is velvet heat. I hold myself in control with iron discipline as I ease into the open, wet cavern. Her soft groan vibrates maddeningly against the throbbing head of my cock, her hand straying down over her belly.

"No." I catch her wrist and push her hand away. "You don't get to come that easily, little *vedma*. Not tonight. Not until I order you to."

Her pelvis jolts in response, and she makes an inarticulate cry in the back of her throat that makes my cock jerk in her mouth.

I push further into her. "Tell me whose orders you take."

She moans, her crimson lips opening impossibly wide to take me.

"Tell me!" My voice is hard and controlled, barely containing the danger beneath it.

"Orrrs," she garbles around my shaft.

"Yes. Mine." I withdraw slightly and she whimpers, nodding as she sinks her mouth down greedily onto me. Her hips are rotating in a slow, sensual circle as she tries to gain the stimulation I'm denying her. Moisture trickles down the inside of her thighs, and her swollen mound begins to part, opening to reveal the throbbing button at the center. Her hands reach for my leathers, tugging at them impatiently. I push her hands away, withdraw from her mouth entirely, and peel them off, kicking them aside.

Her mouth is wet and swollen, her eyes narrow slits of lust. She's staring at my cock, her hips still moving in the slow circles that drive me fucking crazy, as if she's already imagining I'm inside her. She licks her lips hungrily, groaning aloud when my cock leaps in response. When I steer the head back toward her mouth, she covers me eagerly, moaning in satisfaction as I sink between her lips.

It's even better than I remember. Lucia's mouth is almost as hot as her pussy.

Almost.

I'm barely holding on. But there's going to be time for proper restraint, later. This first round is just a lesson in surrender. The punishment will come afterward.

"Use your tongue."

"Ah," she manages, a small, high sound of desperation that has my balls clenching in response. She lashes her tongue around the head and lathes my length, wet heat swirling over every inch. Her ass is moving rhythmically, seeking a touch I won't give her.

I grit my teeth.

"I told you not to come," I rasp.

"AH!" The blush I love explodes over her skin, turning every inch of her to rose-colored heat. I can read it perfectly. Both her impatience and her helpless, squirming need.

"Is this what you were thinking about tonight, little *vedma*?" She moans around my length, trying to push me further in. "Being on your knees, with my cock in your mouth?"

"*Aah!*" Her incoherent scream shivers along my shaft. Her hips start rocking again, more urgently this time. Eyes closed, lost in sensation, she slides her mouth up and down my length, her tongue swirling maddeningly around and underneath the head, tracing the veins. Every pass sends a rush of blood to my groin, bringing me close to the edge.

"I told you not to come yet."

Her hips jerk, then quiver to a halt. She's on the edge of coming, whether I touch her or not.

I pull out of her mouth abruptly.

"Look at me," I growl.

She obeys immediately, staring up at me through glazed eyes, her swollen, wet lips open. She's so close to coming her body is already rippling with it.

"*Khuy*." My control is starting to splinter.

"On your back."

She falls back on the bed, arching her hips toward me.

"Lie still. Hands over your head." I reach into the bedside table for a silken cord and bind her hands, just tightly enough to keep her there.

She trembles. Her legs are straight, her entire body still, waiting.

"Eyes closed." I lift her head and tie on the blindfold.

I stand back, drinking in the exquisite sight of her naked body on the very edge of orgasm.

"I'm going to teach you what I mean when I say you're mine, Lucia."

She quivers, every nerve straining toward me.

"It means I'm the one who sets the rules. It means you don't need to see what I'm doing to know that I'm taking care of you. And most of all." I put my mouth close to her ear. "It means that I demand your absolute, and utter, surrender. Nod if you understand me."

She moves her head, sucking in her lower lip in a way that makes me grind my teeth.

"Spread your legs."

She gives a small cry and obeys. Her pussy glistens before me in open invitation, her belly tight with readiness. I force myself to stand back from her. It's a sweet form of fucking torture.

"I'm going to give you what you need, Lucia."

"Uhhh," she moans, raising her hips toward me.

"I know you don't want my fingers."

She sucks in her breath, biting her lip.

I move around the bed and put my lips so close to her ear that she can feel them. "I know you don't want my mouth."

"Ah!" Her pelvis jerks upward, her knees rising, her legs widening. I move back to the end of the bed, fisting myself slowly, drinking her in. "I know," I say in a low voice, readying myself, "exactly what you need."

Her dripping slit visibly spasms, and I'm done waiting.

I fill her, suddenly and completely, pinning my lips together to restrain my own bellow of pure fucking bliss. I speak in a low, calm tone that has absolutely nothing to do with the mind-bending level of lust I'm managing.

"I know exactly what you want, little *vedma*." I thrust deep into her, and she screams again. I hoist her legs, rocking her higher. "You want to come with my cock deep inside you."

I close my eyes, feeling her slight movements with each stroke, angling myself to hit the parts within her and without that she needs. She cries out higher with every thrust, her legs wrapped around me, urging me deeper within.

Next time, I'll tie her legs.

"You can't hold it, can you, *milaia*?"

Her mouth opens in a garbled cry.

"I can feel how close you are." I pick up the pace. "And I know *exactly* how to get you there."

I slip my thumb onto her insanely swollen clit and drive my cock all the way home, locking into place deep inside her.

She doesn't just come.

She comes apart.

Her walls spasm fiercely. I plunge even deeper, and she screams and shakes, her body rising to tangle with mine, her legs gripping me urgently. Over and over the spasms wrack her body, and I ride the miracle as long as I can, until I finally erupt, pumping in a seemingly endless wave of ecstasy.

"Fuck," she gasps, as we come down from the height. Her body gradually stills beneath mine, her limbs going limp.

Despite fucking her into oblivion, my body is still wired to hell. And seeing her lying there on my bed, arms over her head and eyes covered, her mouth swollen from my cock and her body still wet and open, sets the demon within me into hellfire mode.

I move slightly inside her, and her eyes flutter open in surprise. "You're still hard? After *that?*"

"That," I say, shifting inside her again so she gasps, "was just the fucking warm-up, *milaia.*"

I SPEND the next hours taking Lucia apart, one delicious morsel at a time.

Marking every inch of her body as mine.

I trace her scars and find the places that cause her to squeal, and those that bring forth mewling cries of submission. I deny her the ability to see or move and take dark pleasure in exploring every part of her as she writhes on my bed. I take her to the edge then deny her my touch until she's a moaning, screaming mess. I fuck her with slow, deliberate precision, every thrust exorcising the savage demon that has twisted my mind since our conversation yesterday.

Only when dawn is close do I free her ties. By that time the world between us is a storm, a place in which we are both lost. The wracking intensity of our mutual ending shakes me to the core and leaves me wondering who, exactly, learned a lesson.

As light creeps into the room, I'm standing by the bed, looking down at Lucia. She's sprawled face down and fast asleep, tangled in the sheets, hair strewn over my pillows.

There's something deeply satisfying about having her here, in my bed. Where I can see her. Touch her. Inhale her scent.

Watching her sleep and knowing that, so long as I do, she can't run.

Despite the all-nighter, my body feels oddly exhilarated, as if I've inhaled oxygen at a mountaintop. I feel like I could wrestle a lion and win.

I know it's time to send her back downstairs; the children will be awake soon.

I tell myself I'll do it after I've had a shower.

Then I stand under the water, staring through the glass at her sleeping body until sunlight has chased the night away.

LUCIA

"Owww!" Masha glares at me.

"Sorry," I mutter around the pins in my mouth. "But you have to stay still."

"You keep pricking me!"

"Well, that's what you get for being a cactus." I wink at her, and Masha gives me a gap-toothed grin. "Also," I add, "I did tell you sewing is *not* my forte."

"What's a fortay?" she asks, turning obediently as I pin her costume.

"It's a strength," Ofelia supplies from her seat on the sofa. "But you're wrong, Lucia. The costume looks good." She gives me the wary smile that still breaks my heart.

Ofelia is opening up, slowly. But she still lives behind a wall, one I'm not sure anyone will ever truly breach. Her eyes never stop watching her siblings, and caution is an ever-present shadow behind her eyes. The real miracle to me is that despite her multiple expulsions, and the harsh discipline I can read between the lines of the outraged comments in her reports, Ofelia's unconditional devotion to her siblings has never wavered. Every day I know her increases my respect for her. She may be only fifteen, but grief and responsibility have given her a quiet dignity. It infuriates me that a myriad of school teachers and boarding house mistresses have misconstrued Ofelia's pain for arrogance, her disobedience for attention seeking.

Most of all, it shocks me that after several days I've yet to hear any of the children have a conversation with their mother, or any other member of their family. In fact, their phones are remarkably quiet. No texts from friends or hidden phone chats. Roman's godchildren rely on each other. They are each other's support network and friendship group. Even at rehearsals, they keep themselves slightly apart from the crowd, instinctively drawing closer to each other.

Tomorrow is the actual procession. Roman has assured the children he will attend.

He hasn't communicated much to me. Actually, we've barely spoken since the earth-shattering night in his penthouse. Not that speaking has been required. I've been summoned each night, and sometimes during siesta. Sex has become my every meal.

I'm not complaining. I don't want to talk any more than Roman does. Our time together is an oasis, a fantasy land where all that matters is my body, his body, the way we fit together. I've never known anything remotely like what happens between us when the door to his penthouse closes. In fact, it feels like something in me has been unleashed. I try not to overthink it, just as I try not to think of where this all will end. I've just been floating along on a permanent cloud of oxytocin that effectively numbs logical thought. For once in my life, I've been more than content to bid logic goodbye.

"So this afternoon is our final rehearsal, right?" I stick the last of the pins into Masha's costume.

"Yes." It's Mickey who answers. He has his head in his laptop, frowning in concentration. "And some of these times are still off."

I plop on the sofa arm and ruffle his hair. "You'll have time to test them out this afternoon. If you're still stuck after that, we'll ask Roman for help."

Mickey and Ofelia both snort derisively. "Yeah, right," he mutters. "As if he'd know one end of a computer from the other."

I deliberately don't react. Despite Roman joining us for meals, and a tentative thawing of the vibe between him and the children, I'm increasingly aware of the wariness with which they regard him. It's expressed in a myriad of ways. One of the most common, particularly from the older two, is in snarky asides like this one. The fact that they say them aloud in my presence, however, I take as an encouraging sign that they actually want to be contradicted. It's a delicate line, where I need to allow them to express their true feelings while also forging a bridge of understanding. Aware that three sets of eyes are watching me closely for a reaction, I remain beside Mickey on the sofa and tap his shoulder lightly. "Did you know that Hale has an entire software development facility full of computer specialists?"

That gets their attention. Mickey swings around to look at me, frowning. "Hale is mainly a property development company. That software place is just a sideline."

"Sure." I reach over and key in a website I found in one of my many online searches about Roman. "But Hale Tech employs a lot of people. I'm pretty sure that if you needed any technical help, Roman would be able to get it for you."

"Hey." Ofelia points to a bearded man onscreen. "We know him."

"That's Pavel!" Mickey's eyes light up. "He was a good friend of Papa's. He gave me my first laptop. He's like, the absolute best at coding. Hey, Ofelia, do you remember when he made all the lights in our house go on and off?" The two go off into fits of laughter. It's the most wonderful sound I've heard in a long time, and I make minor adjustments to Masha's costume as the older two tell their younger sister the story, talking over each other in their eagerness. "Pavel's *so* cool." Mickey's eyes shine. "He used to teach me loads. It's been ages since he's come over," he adds wistfully.

"Well, maybe we could ask Roman if Pavel can come here for lunch one day," I suggest.

"That would actually be awesome." He gives me a smile that is by far the most enthusiastic I've seen from him.

"If Roman agrees," mutters Ofelia, her eyes sliding to mine then away. It's going to take more than promises to melt the protective barrier of ice around her heart when it comes to Roman.

"Well, let's see if you can get through the procession first. If you're stuck this afternoon, we can call him. Otherwise, we'll talk to Roman about it after the procession. How's that?" Mickey nods emphatically, Ofelia with rather less conviction. Masha is still busy admiring her cactus outfit in the mirror.

"Okay." I sit back and admire my handiwork. "Let's go and try this masterpiece out."

<hr>

I'M SITTING in the vast auditorium adjacent to the Russian Orthodox Church, surrounded by a chaos of parents, costumes, and children, when my phone buzzes.

It's from Papa's nurse, Carlos, who I've come to like a lot.

Juan is anxious today. Is a visit possible? I think it would calm him.

I tense, staring at the screen. My first thought is that he's been upset by the horrible pap photographer who accosted me outside the restaurant, but I dismiss that almost instantly. Papa's villa is set back from the road, concealed behind high walls and abundant foliage. Anybody trying to get a picture would only manage a blurred shot at best. Besides, after our fateful discussion about the Orlovs, Roman has posted a formidable security detail at the villa. I won't pretend I'm not grateful for his caution, even if he didn't discuss it with me first.

I mentally run a checklist of what might be upsetting my father. *Is his anxiety over the contact in Argentina?*

Part of me wants to text Papa immediately. I know he will never message me himself, no matter what has happened. He doesn't trust phones, even the burner phones I get him. There's no point asking him what's wrong.

I tap the phone against my leg, trying to think. I'm not sure whether I should tell Roman or keep it to myself. Papa is surrounded by security. And regardless of what Roman now knows, bringing him face-to-face with Papa is an absolute no-go zone. There's no way the two of them won't instantly know what the other is. Part of me knows that the meeting is probably inevitable, especially now that Roman knows who is hunting us. But I'd rather avoid it as long as possible, not least because I shudder to even imagine Papa's reaction once he realizes exactly who has hired me.

There's also a good chance I'm simply panicking over nothing.

The dress rehearsal is in full swing. There's no way I can leave, especially given that the villa is almost an hour by car from here. I won't have any free time this afternoon or evening, since the procession is tomorrow.

There's also no way I'm going to rest easy until I know what's bothering Papa.

Damn it.

I make a snap decision and text Carlos.

Will call in on the way home in an hour. Children with me. Would rather they don't meet Juan. Is there anyone who can watch them for a short time?

Carlos answers immediately. *No problem.*

I try to put my worries out of mind for the rest of the rehearsal. Ofelia and I stand beside Masha's float and mimic her teacher to help her remember the movements for her cactus dance. Mickey has his head down for the entire thing, his face fixed in fierce concentration as he manipulates three screens at once.

"Mickey is incredibly talented," his teacher says when I compliment her on the production. "He knows more about the technical staging than our so-called experts." She gives me an approving smile. "You're clearly doing good things. I've never seen the children so happy."

"Oh, no," I say hastily. "This is all Ofelia's doing. She's the one who got her siblings involved and made sure they came to rehearsals."

The teacher raises her eyebrows. "Actually, it's Ofelia I was talking about. Look." She nods at Ofelia, who is currently adjusting Masha's costume. "She's actually laughing. I don't think I've seen that girl smile once since she came here. Until you showed up." She gives me a kind smile. "You're clearly doing a great job. Keep it up."

Her comments leave me with an odd lump in my throat. Being told that the children look happy makes warmth steal through my body like a drug, lulling me further into the dangerous state of comfort and safety I continually remind myself isn't permanent. But even my stern self-talk melts away when all three come rushing over at the rehearsal's conclusion, eyes shining.

"I done all my dance," Masha says importantly, taking one of my hands and skipping a step.

"She got all the movements right." Ofelia is smiling, hanging on to Masha's other hand.

I squeeze Masha's hand but aim my comments at Ofelia. "You did brilliantly to teach her all that. She was watching you all the way through."

She colors with pleasure. "The costume you made is perfect," she says, giving me a rather shy glance.

"Gah!" I roll my eyes. "Let's just hope it actually holds together until it's done." Ofelia laughs.

I turn to Mickey. "How did you do?"

"All the transitions worked perfectly," he says with quiet satisfaction.

"Your teacher told me that you know more than even the stage manager."

Mickey colors and turns away. "Oh, I don't know about that," he mumbles. But he walks a little taller as we leave the auditorium, nodding shyly to some of his classmates.

"So." I say, as Luis closes the car doors. "I know you're probably starving. Would it be okay if we made a quick stop on our way home? A friend of mine has been unwell, and I want to check in on him briefly." Seeing the children's faces grow wary, I add, "Roman has security at the villa, and the nurses caring for my friend are hired by Hale, so it's not a secret, okay?"

"Oh." Ofelia and Mickey exchange a silent glance, then nod, their faces clearing. Their visible relief makes my heart twist. I wonder how many times they've been asked by the adults in their lives to keep secrets. Not for the first time, I feel a fierce desire to protect them from the manipulations of unworthy adult figures.

"So is this man, like, your boyfriend?" Ofelia asks the question seemingly casually, but all three sets of eyes slide toward me.

"Hardly." I grin. "Juan is almost ninety and is in a wheelchair."

"Oh!" She sits back in her seat, looking even more relieved. "Oh, well, that's good, then." Braced for questions about who exactly Juan is, I'm completely taken aback by her next comment. "I don't think Roman would like it very much if you had a boyfriend."

"Nope." Masha shakes her head vigorously.

"Ha," Mickey says, but he's grinning, too. "Yeah. Can't see Roman liking that *at all*." The three children look at each other and giggle. Rather flustered, and entirely unsure what to say, I decide that silence is the better part of discretion and say nothing at all.

To my relief, Luis changes the subject, and we talk about Holy Week for the rest of the car ride.

LUCIA

arlos meets us at the door. The children's faces light up when he greets them by name.

"I remember you." Ofelia's relief is apparent. "You cared for Babushka Vera when she was sick last year."

"Then you probably remember Anna, in the kitchen." Carlos smiles as he takes Masha's hand. "She's baking a cake. Would you like to see?"

Thank you, I mouth to him over their heads as the kids head eagerly for the kitchen. He smiles and waves me away. *He's on the terrace,* he mouths back.

I go upstairs and find Papa staring fiercely out at the distant sea. He starts when he sees me. "*Docha.*" He frowns, checking his watch. "You have time?"

His speech has improved even more. Once again I feel the tug of mingled pleasure and concern.

I love that he is here and getting the help he so badly needs.

I hate that at any moment it might all disappear.

"I have time." I sit down beside him, taking his gnarled hand in my own. "How are you?"

"Hmph." He grunts, not looking at me.

"Is something bothering you?"

"*Nyet.*" But the answer is too curt to be reassuring.

"Did you see something? Is there someone watching you?" I scan the area, but I can't see down to the street. I can't imagine where he would have seen anyone.

"*Nyet.*" He shakes his head. He's frowning, and I can sense his tension. His fingers move restlessly on the blanket, his eyes avoiding mine. I feel increasingly uneasy. "Papa." I lower my voice. "Is it your contact in Argentina?"

He makes a noncommittal noise, turning his head to hide his expression.

That's it.

"If you can't get ahold of them, don't worry," I reassure him. "If we can't get new passports, it doesn't matter. It's not as urgent as I thought it might be." I feel a sneaking sense of relief at saying that, which in turn makes me feel guilty. I can't afford to get complacent, to place my faith blindly in Roman. At the same time, every day I spend cocooned in this newfound life makes the thought of running again loom darker in my mind. Which incites a different kind of guilt.

But Papa is shaking his head. "Not that," he says, again without his customary hesitation. There's a dark edge to his face that sends a real glimmer of fear down my spine. There's something he doesn't want to say, and that worries me more than anything.

"Please." I kneel in front of him, forcing him to meet my eyes. "Tell me what is wrong."

He takes a deep, ragged breath and passes a hand over his face. His eyes, when they finally meet mine, are shadowed with such pain it hurts me inside.

"Alexei," he says roughly.

I'm momentarily so shocked that all I can do is stare at him. We've had no contact with Alexei from the day we left Miami. To my knowledge, we had no way of contacting him even if we wanted to risk it. So when I answer, all I can do is repeat the name, my voice little more than a whisper.

"Alexei?"

Papa nods. Fear grips my heart.

"Is he—oh, God. Is Alexei . . . ?" My voice trails off, unable to speak the dreaded words.

"*Nyet, docha.*" Seeing my fear, Papa grips my hand. "He is alive."

Oh, thank God.

"My—friend. Argentina." Papa speaks slowly, with a lot of hesitation, but still more coherently than he has in months. "Alexei—contact them."

I frown. This is an entirely new development. Papa has never allowed me anywhere near his contact in Argentina. In fact, he's been positively militant in keeping their identity a secret. When we first got to Argentina, Papa was still well enough to speak coherently. It's only since his recent strokes here in Spain that his speech has been so badly affected. Back then, he was insistent that I remain entirely removed from his contact. At the time, I was new enough to our changed circumstances to accept his command without question. In the years since, however, I've pushed more than once for information. Papa has always staunchly refused to say a word.

To discover, after all this time, that the Argentinian contact is a potential channel of communication to the brother I love and miss so deeply feels like something akin to betrayal.

"You've been in contact with Alexei?" Releasing Papa's hands, I sit back, battling to keep my anger under control.

His mouth tightens. "Never—until this." The truth in his

expression calms me somewhat. "Emergency," Papa manages. "Only contact—if emergency."

"Ah." It's beginning to make sense. "You gave Alexei the details of your Argentinian friend and told him to contact them only in the case of an emergency?"

Papa nods vigorously.

"Then what is the emergency? Did your contact tell you?"

His hesitation increases my mounting anxiety. His mouth is a grim line, and I can sense the battle he's fighting inside himself. "Papa." I grasp his hands again. "You told me once that nobody can fight an enemy they don't know about. I need to know what dangers we might face. Please, trust me with this?"

I can feel his reluctance, his internal fury that he must share information like this with me, his daughter, whom he still believes it is his job to protect. Part of me is impatient; after all these years, surely I've earned the right to have a seat at the decision table? But a deeper part of me, perhaps the part that recently witnessed Roman's fury at my mistrust, understands instinctively how hard this is for my father. I force myself to wait patiently.

When he finally does speak, however, a childish part of me wishes I could have remained in ignorance forever.

"Alexei," he rasps, the words dragging from him like blood from a stone, "says—Orlovs—coming." His blue eyes fix on mine, the reluctant truth in them striking my heart in two. "He say they—know—we here."

Fear grips me hard enough that I'm temporarily unable to speak.

"Too—late—to run." This last is said heavily. It's this, I realize, that has stopped Papa from saying anything to me. He's done the math. He knows that if Alexei has given this warning, then people are here, in Malaga, looking for us. And if they're this close, then Papa is right: it's too late for us to run.

"They found us?" My voice is barely a whisper.

He drops his head. "*Da*," he says heavily. "I—think I
—knew."

I know what he means. There have been too many coincidences lately.

The robbery.

The man Papa saw with a camera.

The journalist asking questions.

I think I knew, too.

I think I've known for a while that the Orlovs were closing
in. Maybe that's why I took Roman's offer, and why I confided
in him after so many years of diligent silence. I think that
some part of me accepted the truth before my conscious mind
was able to face it.

The problem now is what I'm going to do about it.

Before I have a chance to even start thinking of solu-
tions, the door behind me bursts open and Masha comes
running onto the terrace, a frowning Carlos following close
behind.

"Luce! Luce!" Beaming, she holds up her prize, a startled-
looking gecko dangling by his tail from her tiny fist. "I
caughted him," she tells me proudly.

"I'm so sorry," Carlos says behind her. I shake my head,
waving off his apology.

"My goodness," I say, putting my arm around her from my
position on the ground in front of Papa. "Where shall we put
him, darling?"

Masha's face falls. "Wanna keep him."

To my surprise, I hear Papa snort in amusement behind
me. I turn to find him regarding Masha with an indulgent
smile I can't remember seeing since I was a tiny child. He
holds out his hand. "Show," he says.

Entirely unbothered by such a brief order, Masha proudly
holds out the lizard, which Papa solemnly inspects. "I found
him in toilet," she says importantly.

He nods as if this is the most normal occurrence in the world. "Name," he says, in his rasping voice.

Masha cocks her head to one side consideringly. "Potato," she says finally.

Papa's cough of laughter is much louder this time. "Tato," he repeats, his laughter increasing to a shaking guffaw. "Tato!"

Shaking his head, he laughs so hard that eventually Masha bursts into a pack of giggles, which in turn sets me off. And that is how Ofelia and Mickey find us, a few moments later, all three of us in peals of laughter, repeating the word *potato* over and over.

"Gecko," I gasp, pointing at the bemused lizard, who is still hanging from Masha's hand.

"He's named Potato," Masha announces happily.

Ofelia and Mickey, however, laugh only briefly. They're staring at Papa. And by their wary expressions, they're already reconsidering their earlier relief.

"Who is that, Lucia?" Ofelia asks me in Russian. Too late, I realize that Papa is clad in a short-sleeved cotton shirt that clearly reveals the faded tattoos on his forearms. Tattoos the children would know all too well, especially the rose entwined with barbed wire that is almost identical to the one Dimitry wears, a symbol of a youth spent in jail.

Papa's eyes narrow at the Russian words, but when his eyes cut to me, he looks resigned rather than surprised.

Mickey is staring at Papa with a hard expression. "You're Russian," he says flatly. "He understood you," he adds, speaking to Ofelia, who has gone very white and is uncharacteristically silent. Mickey moves subtly to stand in front of his sisters, pushing Masha firmly behind him as he faces Papa.

Papa meets Mickey's eyes evenly. "*Da*," he says, his voice courteous despite the ever-present rasp. "*Ya Russky.*" *I am Russian.*

"We don't know you." Mickey's eyes move warily between

Papa and me as he pulls out his phone. I know he's contacting Roman. Ofelia is staring at me, eyes narrowed.

I turn back to Papa, my tension ratcheting up with every second. I don't know what to do. I wasn't expecting this moment, or at least, not yet. I particularly wasn't expecting how it would feel to see the children looking at me with the wary suspicion I've worked so hard to break through. It hurts, far more than I imagined it could.

Seeing the question in my eyes, Papa shakes his head. It's a small movement, but the resignation in his eyes tells me all I need to know. *It's too late. For lies, for subterfuge. It's too late to run.*

"Ofelia." I turn to her, forcing a smile to my face. "I'd like to introduce you to someone very important to me." Mickey turns, frowning, the phone still in his hand. I can see Roman's name on the screen, but he still hasn't pushed the call button. "This is my father," I say gently. "His name is Juan."

"Juan?" Ofelia glares at me. "That's not a Russian name."

"No." I don't attempt to lie. "My father has many enemies. He is old and very sick, as you can see. So now he lives under a different name, so that people can't find him." I have the full attention of both Mickey and Ofelia now.

"What about you?" Mickey's normal reticence is completely gone. His eyes bore into me just as fiercely as his sister's. "Do you have a different name, too?"

"I do." There's no point lying now. "But I would rather not tell you what it is. Not because I don't trust you." I look between them as steadily as I can, though my hands are shaking and my heart is thudding. "Because our names are a secret that is dangerous for anyone to know."

"Does Roman know about this?" Ofelia's voice is brittle as ice.

"Yes." I nod at the phone in Mickey's hand. "You can call him, if you like. I'm very sorry that I've made you feel unsafe or worried. But I would never, ever want you to keep secrets from your godfather. Call him," I say again, this time more emphatically. There's no point in any more subterfuge. Roman is going to be furious; but then again, this moment was always going to come.

In a way, it's simply a relief.

"*Syn*." We all turn to face Papa. He is sitting stiffly upright in his chair, looking directly at Mickey, whom he has just addressed as *son*.

He holds out his hand. "*Govorit' pravdu*." *Speak the truth.* Despite his gravelly voice and slight hesitation, there's no doubting the command in his words. "*Eto pravil'no*." *It is the right thing.*

My heart lurches. How many times have I heard my father say that? To men, when a difficult job must be done. To my brother and me, on the night we left Miami. Simple words, but ones that carry so many memories they bring tears to my eyes even now. I blink hard, willing myself not to lose composure in front of the children.

Mickey hesitates, staring at my father's hand. He glances at me, then at his sister. Whatever Mickey sees in her face is enough to make his mind up. Stepping forward, he grips Papa's hand. "I must call my godfather." His eyes are dark and grave, his Russian far more formal than any I've heard, and he meets my father's eyes steadily.

Papa nods as seriously as if Mickey was one of his *vor*. "*Konechno*," he says simply. *Of course.*

Mickey nods, then releases Papa's hand. His eyes meet mine briefly, then cut guiltily away. "Mickey." I start forward, but Papa frowns at me, and I stop. "It's fine, Mickey," I say quietly. "It's the right thing to do, as Papa said."

"Papa?" Masha pipes up, her lovely blue eyes staring at my father curiously. "Your papa?"

"Yes, darling." I kneel beside her, gently removing the

unfortunate Potato from her fist and placing the gecko in a nearby ceramic garden pot. "This is my papa."

Masha goes closer to Papa and touches his old, wrinkled hand tentatively, as if doing something very brave, then looks up at him. He smiles at her and turns his hand over so she can inspect his palm. She does so, tracing the old lines on it with fascination, then, without a moment's hesitation, climbs up his long legs to sit on his lap. "My papa is dead," she says, staring at him solemnly.

Papa nods gravely. "*Mne zhal'*," he says. *I'm sorry.*

Masha regards him for a moment, then suddenly beams again. "Can we play with Potato?"

My father laughs softly, nodding toward the ceramic pot. Clambering down, Masha runs over and pulls the unfortunate gecko out, then brings it over and climbs back onto Papa's lap.

I turn to Ofelia. "I'm sorry," I say softly, under cover of their laughter. "Truly. I didn't want to keep secrets from you."

"Whatever." She shrugs, her face shuttered and cold. "I don't care."

Her words cut like a knife, but I have little time to think of anything to say, because Mickey turns back to us, his eyes dark. "Roman is on his way," he says quietly.

ROMAN

"Uncle Roman." It's extremely rare for Mickey to call me. Let alone address me as "Uncle." I frown out the plate glass window of my Hale office, my entire attention on the phone in my hand.

"What is it?" Unease makes me sound harsher than I might have liked. "Mickey?"

"Lucia brought us to the villa where Babushka Vera stayed. You need to come, Uncle Roman. The man here is Russian."

A thousand questions run through my head, but every one of them is superseded by the fear I can hear behind Mickey's unusually forceful tone.

"You're safe, Mickey. I know the man there." I mentally cross my fingers at the lie, all the while running through the security measures I've taken in case I might be mistaken.

No. Even if I don't know the identity of the man Lucia is

caring for, he is cocooned in security I have provided. The children are safe at the villa, that much I can be certain of.

"The security guards at the villa are mine, Mickey. Do nothing. Just wait, and I'll be there in fifteen minutes."

"Uncle Roman."

"Yes?" I'm already stepping into the elevator.

"Lucia said that isn't really her name?" The uncertainty in his voice makes it more of a question than a statement.

I close my eyes briefly.

"Yes, Mickey. I know that." I make my tone deliberately calm.

"Oh." The confusion and hurt in that one simple sound makes me wince.

"I'm on my way, Mickey. Just relax, okay? There's nothing you need to worry about. Do you understand?" I keep the line open until he cuts it at his end, by which time I'm already in the Maybach and pulling out of the basement. I race through the siesta-quiet streets, the speed matching my thoughts.

The truth is that since I discovered who Lucia is running from, my only concern has been ensuring her safety. The most peaceful moments I know are when she is in my bed, naked, her body mine to own and hold. In only a matter of days, I've begun to listen for the sound of her laughter floating up from downstairs. To count the minutes until I can summon her to my penthouse.

And in my need to satisfy myself that Lucia is safe in my care, I've managed to neglect the three people for whom I am legally, morally, and emotionally responsible.

Not neglect their safety, of course. I could be drugged and bound and still ensure my people are fucking safe.

But I've conveniently overlooked the fact that this revelation was always going to be inevitable. I've allowed them to become attached to Lucia, all the while knowing that eventually this day of reckoning would come.

Dimitry's warning rings uncomfortably clearly through my mind: *"It's about damn time you did something more than just keep them safe. They need more than just a nanny, Roman. Especially one who might leave at any minute. They need a father. And a mother. One who actually gives a shit about them."*

I grip the steering wheel hard enough to turn my knuckles white, grinding my teeth. I really, *really* fucking hate to admit when I've messed up.

I take care of my people. I make certain they're safe. But Dimitry is right: in the case of my godchildren, "safe" means a lot more than placing guards on the door.

The kids lived through the trauma of their father's brutal death, the raids that imprisoned their grandfather, and Inger's blatant neglect. Vera has the emotional intelligence of an amoeba, while Inger's parents prefer cruise ships to relationships.

And then there's me.

I run an orange light, ignoring the indignant shriek of car horns.

Without any discernible effort on my part, I've been enjoying something of a proxy relationship with the kids, enabled and facilitated by Lucia. I've even felt self-congratulatory about having made such a good choice. As if they were simply another task taken care of.

Best geek minds in the world? *Check.*

Best security guards in the business? *Check.*

Best au pair? *Check.*

And let's not forget why exactly you hired her.

Although on that particular point, my logical mind wavers. I didn't ask Lucia to sign that contract simply because I had to have her in my bed. In some ways, it would be easier if I had.

No.

I asked her to sign it because some part of me *knew* the

name. If she's such a good *friend* of yours," she says, putting enough emphasis on the word *friend* to make it clear she hasn't let that part of the explanation go, "then why do you have to keep her real name a secret?"

Mickey nods emphatically at this. His eyes aren't quite so X-ray probing as his sister's, but they hold the same sensitive awareness as his father's once did. If I could always read a room at a glance, Mikhail was always able to read the emotions at play within it. Mickey seems to have inherited the same ability.

"I'm not going to try to sugarcoat this for you." I lean forward, holding each of their eyes in turn. "You already know that our family faces . . . risks that others don't."

Perhaps once, I wouldn't have alluded so directly to the nature of our business. But these kids have had a front-row seat to the brutality. There's no point in trying to pretend our world is something other than what it is. The fact that not even Masha turns a hair at this comment is proof enough of my point.

"Lucia comes from the same world we do," I continue quietly. "Her family has suffered similar tragedies to ours. I wanted her to feel safe again, just like I want you three to feel safe."

There's an odd relief in actually saying that aloud. And when I do, it feels simple. It feels right.

"She said her father has enemies."

Her *father?* I conceal my surprise at Mickey's remark. My brief impression of the man in the wheelchair was of someone old enough to be Lucia's grandfather. But at least this revelation makes Mickey's comment easy to answer.

"Masha," I say gently, seeing her squirm restlessly on the sofa, "would you like to play with Mr. Potato again? You can go outside and ask Lucia to help you, if you like." The fact that she instinctively looks to her siblings for consent, rather than taking my word, is yet another twist of the knife.

I have a lot of fucking ground to make up.

I wait until she's left before addressing the two very shuttered faces in front of me. "Lucia and her father do have enemies. Very dangerous ones. They are living under different names so those people can't find them."

"Then why did you take them in?" Mickey's question is uncharacteristically harsh. "If they have dangerous people chasing them, doesn't that mean we're in danger, too?"

And now we're at the pointy end.

I meet his eyes steadily. "Do you believe I would ever place you, or your sisters, in danger, Mickey?"

His mouth twists. "No, but—"

"But Papa would have said the same thing." Ofelia cuts her brother off. Glaring at me, she folds her arms. "You can't keep us safe, no matter what you say. Nobody can keep anyone safe. And bringing *her* into our house just makes our lives even more dangerous than they already are."

As usual, her barbs are precision designed for maximum damage. Usually I shut them down with equally harsh rebuttal. But that hasn't worked in the past, and it sure as hell won't work now.

"I can understand why you believe that, Ofelia. And in some ways, you're right." She reels back, her eyes narrowing in surprise. "I can't guarantee that you will be safe every day of your life. That would be a foolish promise to make, and you are clever enough to know that. But that's the key here, *umnyashka*. You're clever." I nod at Mickey. "You both are. Look at what you did today. You identified a risk, and you took action by calling me. You didn't wait passively for someone to notice the danger for you. Instead you looked for it, and despite your affection for Lucia, you acted on your instincts. That's what intelligent people do, Ofelia. I've known men twice your age who wouldn't have acted that quickly. You've both seen danger close up and suffered the results of violence. You've both learned from that. But here's the important part."

Two sets of eyes, one deep cobalt and grave, the other piercing, dark arctic blue, stare back at me. To my astonishment, Mickey and Ofelia actually seem to be hanging on my every word.

"Knowing that danger exists doesn't mean we run from it. Identifying risk doesn't mean we choose a life of seclusion and defense. To do so means we would hide behind high walls for the rest of our lives, never daring to go outside, or"—I crack a smile—"take part in a Holy Week parade."

Their faces thaw slightly.

"Most importantly, when a friend is in danger, we don't turn our backs on them. We don't let them face that danger alone. We take them in. Make them feel like family. And we do everything in our power to ensure they are protected—even if that means keeping their identity a secret."

Ofelia's eyes widen, and she turns instinctively to look out onto the terrace, to where Lucia is on her hands and knees with Masha, scrabbling through the plants for the elusive Mr. Potato. Mickey has colored slightly, his eyes fixed on my face.

"I thought I was doing the right thing for Lucia and her father by keeping their secret." I hold Ofelia's eyes. "But when I'm wrong, I say I'm wrong. I realize now that I could have trusted you with that secret, and been certain that you would keep it. Nobody understands family better than both of you. You both protect Masha every day. You have each other's backs without question. I should have known you would have Lucia's, too."

Mickey is nodding vigorously, and Ofelia has hectic spots of color on her cheeks.

"I was *really* mean to her," she mutters, glancing shame-facedly at the door.

"I wouldn't worry about that. Lucia absolutely adores you." I give Ofelia a smile, and for once, she tentatively returns it. "She will understand, probably better than anyone, why you were so afraid."

"But if she's in so much danger," says Mickey worriedly, "how are we supposed to protect her?"

Oh, no.

"That's my job." I pin them both with a serious look. "I want you to always be thinking for yourselves, to be smart and accountable for your own safety, as I said. But keeping this family safe is my job. That includes Lucia.

"I need you to trust me to do that. I realize that after what happened to your father, you might find that hard to believe. I understand that. Believe me when I say that I, too, learned lessons from that experience. I can promise you this: your safety is my primary mission in life. I do nothing without considering it, first and foremost. And that goes for Lucia and her father, too. Do you trust that I will do everything in my power to keep you safe?"

Ofelia and Mickey look at each other, then back at me.

"Yes," Mickey says.

"Yes." Ofelia actually nods at me. "I do."

"Thank you." Reaching across the table, I take one each of their hands. "And for my part, I promise that I will be honest with you both from now on. The first example of that is what I'm about to say now.

"It's safer for Lucia, and for our family, if we all continue to call her and her father by the names they use. I know it's asking a lot, and I hope you know I wouldn't ask it if I didn't believe it was strictly necessary. But Lucia is our responsibil-ity. Our family. And what do we do when someone is family?"

"We protect them," say Ofelia and Mickey in unison.

I nod. "Exactly. Are you willing to help me protect Lucia and her father?"

"Yes." They answer without hesitation.

"Good." I squeeze their hands, and they return the pressure. "Then let's go outside and show them how a real family takes care of one another."

ROMAN

"**L**ucia." She's kneeling on the tiles, poking about in the bushes with Masha, presumably in search of the elusive Mr. Potato. She jerks around at her name, her eyes darting worriedly between Ofelia and Mickey.

She isn't concerned for herself, I realize. Lucia is worried about the children.

"I'd like to have lunch served here, so we can all eat together."

Her face is a picture of confusion. She looks at the children, then glances behind her, at the old man in the wheelchair.

"Ofelia." I turn to my goddaughter. "Would you guys like to take Lucia in and show her how we set the table? And Masha, perhaps you might like to pick some flowers to go in the center?"

Ofelia smiles shyly at Lucia. "I'd like that."

"I can pick flowers," says Masha proudly, immediately heading for the doors.

Ofelia slips a tentative hand into Lucia's, leaning her head on her shoulder briefly. "Sorry," she mumbles.

"Oh, no." Lucia kisses the top of her head. "Don't be, darling."

Mickey takes her other hand. "Me, too," he says quietly.

Lucia's eyes mist over. She glances at me over their heads. *Thank you*, she mouths.

I smile. *You're welcome.*

They move toward the doors. Lucia looks back briefly at the long, lean figure in the wheelchair, but she doesn't linger. She knows as well as I do that this meeting is best done without an audience.

I wait until the glass doors click closed before speaking.

The old man is watching me. Despite his age and obvious infirmity, there's no doubting he was once a formidable figure. His shoulders are still rangy and tough, his spine ramrod straight. He's well over six feet, with hawkish features, fierce blue eyes, and the alert attention of one well used to danger.

I walk across to him and offer my hand. *"Dobro pozhalovat' v moy dom." Welcome to my home.*

He takes my hand, nodding sharply. His grip is strong. I smile internally. Nothing in the man's manner indicates that he is anything other than my senior. I might as well be one of his *vor*, come to pay tribute, rather than the man who effectively holds his life in my hands. In Russian tradition, it's never proper to shake hands over a threshold. Increasingly, the old traditions matter less, but today I find myself rather relieved that this first meeting with Lucia's father is taking place outside. I feel oddly aware of the formalities, as if I were sitting at my father's table once again, being instructed on the correct manner of address.

The man gestures to a chair on the other side of the garden

table, on which a chess set is laid out. I take the seat. A moment later, the terrace doors open and Ofelia emerges with a silver tray, atop which is a Russian samovar, two filigree glasses, and a small plate of halva. "Lucia asked me to bring tea," she says, looking between us curiously.

The old man smiles at her. "*Eta ochen' mila s Vashey starany.*" *That's very kind of you.*

She returns the smile, coloring slightly, and leaves us.

The older man pours tea, once again as if the house were his. Only after we have sipped from our glasses does he meet my eyes again. "So," he says, in labored, heavily accented English. "My daughter—living in—your home."

It's a hell of an opening. His words are slightly staggered, and I remember that Pavel said he had suffered a stroke. Despite his slow, hesitant manner of speech, every word rings with the authority of a man accustomed to command.

"Your daughter is safe in my home."

The man's lips harden. "My daughter—not—safe —anywhere."

I nod slowly. "I understand that the Orlov family is searching for you."

The blue eyes narrow, studying me closely. I meet them steadily. Finally, the man raises his tea glass and takes a sip, his eyes not leaving mine. When he lowers the glass, his lips twist in something approaching a wry smile. "Name—on passport— is Juan Ortega," he says, this time in Russian. His eyebrows raise slightly. "But you—know—that."

Oddly enough, his speech, though slow, seems to be improving with every rasping word.

I tilt my head slightly. "I am Roman Stevanovsky."

Juan's eyes narrow, and he studies my face curiously. "Stevanovsky." He repeats the name slowly. "Hale Property."

"*Da.*"

"Heir to Yuri Stevanovsky." It isn't a question. Anybody who reads an expat paper knows my name, and about Hale Property. But this man also knows *what* I am, and to which clan I belong.

He might be old, but he's still tapped in.

"Yes." I'm accustomed to men assuming that I am Yuri's son. I'm not certain why it should make me uneasy that Lucia's father assumes the same thing, but it does. I dislike lying to him, which is ironic, given that he is living in my home, under a fake name, no less.

He fixes me with a stern glare. "Why—are we—here?"

Now we get to business.

I push the plate of halva across the table and pour more tea. "The children's nanny quit at short notice before the holidays. Lucia was working in the café across the road from Hale. I knew she spoke Russian, and she's clearly well educated. She was working a lot of hours for very little money. It seemed a logical solution."

My tone is even enough. I meet his eyes as I speak. And the man is in a wheelchair.

Given his narrowed eyes and steely glare, however, I suspect that none of that would be a deterrent from him doing his best to kill me, if he doesn't like my answer. He'd never make it out of his chair, obviously. But that doesn't mean I don't fucking respect the intention.

"All—this?" He gestures around at the villa, plainly questioning why housing him is part of Lucia's employment. I hope that's the only aspect of the arrangement he questions. I have no desire to defend the less honorable part of the contract. I suspect that might result in a test of the killing theory.

And if I'm being entirely honest, lately I haven't been too proud of that goddamn contract myself.

"I work unpredictable hours," I say, pushing that uncomfortable thought aside, "and require Lucia to fit in with my schedule. The villa was empty. Again, it seemed logical."

"*Logical.*" The old man sits back in his chair, eyeing me skeptically. "What—about—Orlovs?"

I can tell it hurts him to ask. This is a man who clearly would once have murdered any man who came for his family. Something tells me he'd still do his damndest to try, bare-handed if necessary.

"I have no interest in trading you to the Orlov family." I hold his eyes steadily. "My home is yours. Unless and until you decide to leave, you and your daughter are under my protection."

His mouth tenses. Something hard flashes in his eyes, a piece of the warrior he clearly once was. I don't need to imagine the insult such a man might feel at my offer. But if I've read him right, and I am sure I have, Lucia's father is also a realist. His eyes shift sideways, considering what he might say. I remain quiet, waiting. When he turns back to me, his face is set and hard.

"They—know." He meets my eyes directly. "Orlovs. That we are—here. Orlovs—coming."

The fuckers are coming?

Savagery surges through me in a primal rush.

Come, you bastards.

"Let them come." Despite my customary restraint, even I can hear the edge of war in my voice.

Juan nods, but his face is grim. "Your children." He addresses me with a quiet dignity, despite his rasping voice. "Not safe with—us."

I turn my tea glass in slow circles on the table. "Lucia said as much. I will tell you what I told her." I stop the tea glass and meet his eyes directly. "I protect what is mine. No matter who, or what, comes at me."

Nothing more. Either this man understands that I can take

care of my own or he doesn't. I'm long past the time when I justify anything I do. To anyone.

There is a pause, during which the old eyes study my face keenly. I don't flinch from the scrutiny, and after a time, Juan inclines his head. It's an oddly poignant gesture. That of a proud man accustomed to offering, rather than accepting, protection. His nod is one of resigned acceptance, but definitely not of surrender. I can see the mind still active behind his eyes. It almost makes me smile.

Juan Ortega, or whoever he truly is, will reluctantly accept my help.

But he hasn't given up on whatever still drives him. I suspect he won't until he is in his grave. Somewhat to my surprise, I find myself rather admiring Lucia's father. And I'm not a man who takes a liking to many people, let alone admires them.

"I understand you can't share your identity. I will accept that—for now." I lean forward. "But not indefinitely."

The man searches my face carefully. After a time, he raises his eyebrows slightly and tilts his head in acknowledgment. "So," he says, with a hint of his earlier wry smile. He nods at the chess board. "Shall we play, then?"

LUCIA

We take lunch on the terrace, beneath a trellis dripping with purple wisteria. The air is scented with citrus and jasmine from the trees, and the terracotta tiles are cool underfoot. The table is wrought iron topped with Moroccan tiles, and is currently covered with a variety of dishes, silver cutlery Ofelia took from an old wooden box, and linen napkins in monogrammed rings. The samovar has been replaced by pottery jugs of watered-down wine and a soft drink for the children.

"I'm a cactus," Masha is telling Papa proudly. "Luce made my costume."

"A cactus." Papa nods solemnly over his soup, his blue eyes twinkling.

"We do the cactus dance. 'Felia," Masha says authoritatively, "show Deda the dance."

Ofelia and Mickey both tense, looking nervously around

the table. My knife clatters onto my plate. I glance furtively at Roman, unsure what he's going to make of Masha referring to Papa as "Grandfather."

"Perhaps another time, Masha." Roman grins, seemingly entirely unconcerned by the familiarity. "Deda and I have a game of chess to finish after lunch." He's seated at one end of the long table, Papa at the other. I'm sitting opposite Masha, who insisted on sitting next to Papa. Ofelia is next to me, Mickey on the other side.

"Okay." Masha wriggles in her seat. "May I be 'scused? I want to find Mr. Potato."

"Mr. Potato will be fine for a little while." I smile at Anna as she clears our plates. "Let's wait until after we've eaten, shall we?" I put some salad and chicken on Masha's plate, cutting the meat into smaller pieces.

"Mickey," Roman says, turning to his godson. "Tell me about the sound you've set up for the parade tomorrow. What program did you use?"

I've been too worried to really look at Papa since the moment Mickey called Roman. I've been caught in a nervous storm, unsure both of how Roman would handle the situation and, perhaps more pertinently, how Papa would react to meeting Roman. As relieved as I was to emerge onto the terrace and find them amicably playing chess together, the lack of guns blazing is still a far cry from domestic bliss. I'm not sure what my proud father is going to make of being called grandfather by children he's only just met.

But when finally I dare to glance at him, I find no trace of the grim, hawkish man calculating the odds, nor of the hard expression that precedes an argument. Even the polite mask he reserves for carers seems to have been dropped. Instead of being upset by Masha's use of the word *Deda*, Papa's face is strangely soft.

"Will you help me look for Potato?" Masha asks him, spearing a piece of chicken.

Papa's mouth twitches at the corners. "After—chess—Deda needs—siesta." Masha knocks over her cup, and he catches it just in time, setting it gently back upright. "Masha—siesta—too," he says, smiling at her.

Masha pouts. "Chess is boring."

"*Nyet.*" Papa shakes his head. "Lucia learned—when she was—your age." His eyes flicker to me. Suddenly I am back in our Miami home, sitting in a courtyard not unlike this terrace, my brother and father laughing as they try to teach me the names of the pieces.

Alexei. My heart clenches as I remember my conversation just before Roman arrived. Alexei has been in touch. Has tried to warn us. Anxiety races through my system again, the permanent reminder that no matter how calm this setting might be, danger lurks just beyond the terrace.

"Prawn," my father says softly. I look up to find him watching me, his eyes shadowed with memory.

"Prawn?" Ofelia looks at me curiously.

I swallow hard to clear the lump in my throat. "I couldn't remember what the little chess pieces were called," I explain. "So my brother called them prawns, because there's so many of them in the sea."

Mickey's head lifts in interest. "You have a brother?"

Oh, crap. "Yes," I mutter, glancing surreptitiously at Papa. His lips press together, emotion flickering behind his own eyes. He glances at Roman. Something passes between them, the kind of silent understanding I recall seeing between Papa and his men, years ago.

"Ofelia," Roman says, breaking what was about to become an awkward pause. "After lunch, perhaps you could play piano for us? Masha can show us her dance before I take you home for siesta."

Ofelia flushes with pleasure. Papa asks her how long she's been playing, and the awkward moment passes as conversation resumes.

Lunch passes pleasantly. Afterward, Papa and Roman resume their game, and Ofelia sits down at the piano inside, beginning to play as Mickey and I clear the table, waving Anna away. "I can take care of the dishes," I say, smiling at her. "We've kept you late enough as it is. Why don't you go home, join your own family for lunch?"

Mickey and I wash up to the sounds of hilarity upstairs, as Masha demonstrates her cactus dance moves, encouraged by Ofelia. I hear the low rumble of my father's laughter. I can't remember the last time I heard him laugh. It's a bittersweet joy, one full of memories, of the life we once led and of a happiness I thought forever lost.

It seems incredible that I should hear that sound again. I feel almost overwhelmed by the surreal nature of the gathering, like I'm living a day in someone else's life. It's hard to trust the feeling of happiness, especially when I remember who we are running from and the fact that we are still living under assumed names. My two lives are merging, and yet still there remains so much that is unsaid, so many secrets that must be kept.

And I still haven't spoken to Papa.

Roman comes into the kitchen as Mickey and I are finishing up. "Can you go and catch Masha for me?" He smiles at Mickey, who returns it. I don't know what, exactly, Roman said to the children earlier, but whatever it was seems to have completely reset the dynamic, for which I can only feel grateful. He waits until Mickey has left before turning back to me.

"We'll leave, give you and your father some time to talk," he says quietly. "Come back when you're ready. There's no rush. Take all the time you need."

"Roman." I fold the tea towel slowly. "I didn't mean for this to happen. The carer called me—"

"It's fine." There's an odd gleam in his eye, a slight tension in his body that I don't quite know how to read. "I'm glad I've met your father. I think it's better, like this. And I was long past due to have an honest conversation with the children."

"Did you?" I frown, trying to imagine what an *honest conversation* might have looked like.

His mouth quirks. "Honest enough. I skipped over Ofelia's question about whether or not you were my girlfriend."

"Oh," I manage. It's more of a gasp than a word. Color floods my face.

"I left that part out of my discussion with your father, too."

"Uh." That one doesn't sound much better.

He's leaning against the sink, his arms folded, watching me with a faint smile, as if he knows exactly how unsettling I'm finding this entire conversation.

Not to mention how unsettling I find his nearness. There's something intensely intimate about being together in such a domestic space, the children's laughter echoing off the tiles and the scent of cooking all around. Seeing Roman in a kitchen, shirt sleeves rolled up and tie loose, feels dangerously good, like the promise of forbidden fruit.

"I'm going to attend the parade with you tomorrow."

I gulp. "You are?"

"Yep." He nods, his smile widening at my surprise. "Masha is quite insistent that I should see the cactus dance. And I'd like to bring Pavel, one of my computer geeks, to watch Mickey work. He was the one who bought Mickey his first computer."

I don't miss the faint gleam behind his eyes, nor the long finger tapping against his arm. Roman has reasons for attending tomorrow beyond watching the children perform,

I'm sure of it. But after today's emotional roller coaster, I don't feel overly inclined to ask too many questions.

And I've still got Papa to face.

"So." He pushes off the sink. Glancing around to ensure we're alone, he kisses me once, hard, on the mouth, leaving me breathless. "Until the morning, then."

"I'm sorry I didn't tell you the truth."

Papa and I are sitting either side of the chess board, a bottle of wine between us. I know he's not supposed to drink it undiluted. On the other hand, there's no chance I can get through this discussion without a drink, and I figure he can use one, too.

Papa gives me a rather old-fashioned look. "You told me —nothing."

I color, staring at my wine.

"You—knew. Roman—bratva." It isn't a question.

"*Da.*" I answer in Russian. "I knew."

"Hmph." Papa snorts and takes a long swallow of his wine. "Vodka," he mutters under his breath, casting me a sideways look that I pointedly ignore. He knows better than to ask me directly. Watered-down wine I might tolerate, but there's not a chance I'm letting him near a vodka bottle. Hard spirits are completely off the doctor's checklist of approved substances. "Why lies?" He eyes me over his glass.

I take my time answering.

Because I knew you'd never agree.

Because I couldn't face running.

Because I thought there was a good chance you might kill Roman before he ever said a word.

"I didn't want to worry you," I say eventually.

"Ha!" His derisive snort is not unlike Roman's indignation

a few days earlier. He shakes his head impatiently. "Dangerous," he mutters.

"I know." There isn't much I can say to that. "But you said it
yourself, Papa. The Orlovs know we're here now. We couldn't
run even if we wanted to. This way we are safe. At least for a
while."

"Roman—knows." Papa is frowning at the table, and I can
tell his mind is racing in a thousand directions. "Orlovs."

*Which explains why Roman was twitchy as a bug on crack in the
kitchen.* Probably also explains why he's bringing a tech geek
to the parade tomorrow, along with, undoubtedly, a small
army of security.

I take a deep breath.

I'm exhausted.

This day feels endless. This week, even. The tension is like
a wire getting cranked tighter and tighter, threatening to snap
at any moment. What chaos might then ensue is a terrifying
prospect.

"Did you tell him about Alexei?" I ask.

"*Nyet.*" He passes a hand over his face. He's getting tired,
his voice rasping, his words slurring slightly.

I cover his hand with my own. "You should rest, Papa. It's
good that Roman knows the truth. At least that way he can
protect the children."

"*Da.*" Papa's face softens, his eyes meeting mine. "Good to
see you with—children, Dayushka."

"Ha." I try for laughter, but the emotion in Papa's eyes stifle
it in my throat. He grips my hand wordlessly. I feel in his
touch all he can't say, the regret that it should be somebody
else's children calling him *Deda* instead of his own grandchildren. That this life has deprived me, as he sees it, of a family of
my own.

"I'm happy here, Papa," I say quietly. "Happy with the
children."

"Happy," he rasps, his eyes on me rather more knowing than I might like. "Happy with—Roman."

"He's my boss, Papa." I avoid his eyes.

"Hmm." He releases my hand. He doesn't push it, but his silence speaks volumes. We sit for a short time in silence. When he speaks again, Papa's voice is cracked with exhaustion. "Glad you have—man. Protection." He nods slowly, his eyes sad. "Keep you—safe."

I know what he means. I might be safe, at least for now, but Alexei isn't. And both of us know that so long as the Orlovs have my brother, neither Papa nor I will ever truly know peace.

"We'll get Alexei back, Papa," I whisper, gripping his hand again. "I promise you we will."

He nods, but he doesn't answer, and the resignation in his eyes hurts me deep inside.

We sit on the terrace and watch the day fade, slowly drinking the rest of the bottle in a silence full of all that we have lost. I stay long after Papa has fallen asleep, tucking the blanket around him and watching the night grow. The city lights reflect off the water beyond. I wonder if my brother is somewhere here in Spain, watching these same lights.

"Alexei," I whisper to the sultry coastal breeze. "I'll find you, brother. Somehow I'll find you and give us back our home."

The wisteria vine quivers above me, my promise lost to the night.

36

ROMAN

"It's dangerous." Dimitry taps his fingers impatiently on the steering wheel of the Maybach. We're in the parking lot of the Russian Cultural Center, amid a milling crowd of costumed children and anxious parents. "If what you say is true, the Orlovs could be anywhere. Today could turn into a goddamn bloodbath, Roman."

"Which is why every man we've got is doing security detail." My eyes follow Lucia and the children as they step out of the car ahead of us. Luis holds the door open, scanning the crowd cautiously.

There are two other cars, one ahead and one behind us, from which men have already exited and are now discreetly herding my family into the center. Pavel glances at the Maybach, his bearded face anxious. He is made for scanning data, not crowds. And he knows damn well that today's little excursion is way out of his comfort zone.

But I want him here, just as I want the hidden guns and watching eyes of my *vor*. I doubt the Orlovs will make a move in broad daylight. But it isn't just them who worry me.

"Nikolai is coming today," I tell Dimitry as we exit the car. Lucia is twenty paces away. She's wearing an understated white linen dress teamed with tan mules. It's an elegant, simple outfit that nonetheless does nothing to hide the sensual curves of her body.

Christ, I want her.

It took all my self-control not to summon her to the penthouse last night. I managed it partly because I needed to organize security for today and partly because I suspect she faced a very challenging conversation with her father after we left the villa. I'd give quite a lot to know what was said between them, but for now, at least, other problems have superseded my curiosity.

"Why the fuck is Nikolai coming?" Dimitry's tone is thick with disgust. "Pavel successfully tracked that trojan back to Pillars. Even if he doesn't know who uploaded it yet, it was certainly done with Nikolai's permission. That little *mudak* needs to be kept as far away from your family as possible."

"And if he gets even a hint that I'm keeping him away, our best chance of discovering what he's actually doing will be gone."

Dimitry glances curiously at me. "You're oddly calm for a man facing a possible shoot-out and family betrayal."

I know I am, and he's right: it is odd. But since my conversation with Lucia's father, I've been existing in the edgy, expectant vacuum that precedes an eruption. I can feel the storm coming. There are clouds hovering over every aspect of my life: my burgeoning relationships with Lucia, her father, and my godchildren; the trojan virus attacking Mercura; the journalist who has disappeared, seemingly into thin air; and above all, in the news that the Orlovs might be somewhere close.

I'm existing in the stillness before the chaos.

All I can do is watch, wait, and prepare.

I might look calm. Inside, however, I'm like bottled lightning—just waiting for the right time to strike.

"I'm going to join the kids. Keep your phone close."

Dimitry's indignant expression makes me grin as I turn toward the center.

Inside the crowded auditorium the noise is deafening. Pavel is off in the corner with Mickey, already deep in conversation. Seeing me come in, Mickey shoots me one of his rare smiles and gives me a thumbs-up. I can't help but feel rather pleased by that. It's only been a day, but suddenly the kids don't seem to see me as enemy number one anymore.

A bawling child runs past me, chased by a harried-looking parent. "How the fuck do teachers do it," I mutter to Lucia as I catch up with her.

"I'm pretty sure they drink a lot." She smiles, adjusting Masha's costume. Somehow I feel calmer just being close to her.

Dangerous, Borovsky, dangerous.

This whole domestic arrangement is dangerous, and not just because of the chaotic crowd. I'm getting involved, way more than I ever intended, both with Lucia and the kids. And at the same time, it's a seductive danger, the kind that reaches out with the comforting smell of *alfajores* and afternoon dinners and lulls me into believing it's a life I could actually live.

Get your head back in the game.

"You're wearing a mask, right?" I say, scanning the crowd.

"I've got it." Ofelia pushes through the crowd, waving two lion masks. "One for Luce, one for me."

"Lions," I say dryly, eyeing the masks, "and cacti? The

mystery of Golgotha gets more mysterious with every passing moment."

"Hush." Lucia elbows me warningly. "The teacher slash director is in earshot. It's her baby, so be nice."

I roll my eyes. Ofelia, looking between us, giggles.

By the time the floats are arrayed and the children in place on them, I'm in as much need of a drink as I am of blissful silence. "Don't you dare," Lucia hisses, seeing me look longingly toward the bar, where several of the fathers have already decamped. "You will walk beside the float with Ofelia and watch every inch of the cactus dance."

"Who's employing who?" I grumble, but I let Ofelia take my hand anyway. She leads me behind Lucia through the crowds to Masha's float. Lucia kneels down behind a clump of fake grass right behind Masha, who keeps turning around to talk to her, which leads to Lucia repeatedly turning Masha back in the right direction.

It's exactly the kind of scene I've spent years staying the fuck away from. And yet for some reason, I *like* being here. Most of all, I like being here with Lucia.

Better make the most of it. There's only four and half months left of that contract.

I shift uncomfortably. I don't like thinking about that fucking contract. Increasingly, even remembering it makes me feel slightly sick. I particularly don't like thinking that goddamn piece of paper is the only reason Lucia's here.

"Masha!" Ofelia waves at her sister, and Masha beams from the small round hole in her cactus costume. On the front float, Mickey, with his headphones on and face fixed in concentration, hits a button, and the music begins. Pavel, beside him, claps him on the shoulder and gives me an extremely nerdy thumbs-up. Mickey follows the direction of Pavel's gesture and sees me. I wave, returning Pavel's dorky thumbs-up, and Mickeys face lights up in a brief flash of surprised pleasure before he turns back to his laptop. The screen on the back of his float explodes in color and then begins a complicated series of psychedelic patterns. I can't help but admire his concentration. The kid's barely fourteen, and he's coordinating a complex light and sound show with timings for over fifty acts. There's a quiet certainty about the way he conducts himself, a solemn maturity, that impresses me, but he also has his father's kindness. Watching him bestow a rare smile on an anxious girl who has the wires mixed up, gently untangling them for her, I think that Mikhail would be extremely proud of the young man his son is becoming.

Ofelia is running beside the float, vigorously repeating the movements for the cactus dance so that Masha can copy her. Between Ofelia and Lucia, Masha manages to remain in position and at least look like she vaguely knows some of the choreography.

"Why are there lions and a fucking cactus in an Easter parade?" Dimitry mutters, coming alongside me.

"No idea. Still haven't made sense of it. Just cheer like you understand," I say out of the corner of my mouth, waving and smiling at Masha.

"There's a lot of cameras." He nods at a journalist running alongside the floats on the other side of the road. There's also the usual barrage of cell phones being held up, filming the entire thing. I was right the first time. The entire event is fucking security nightmare. Despite my men scattered through the crowd and walking close to the float and to Ofelia, I don't like it. I don't like it at all.

"Any sign of our friend Lance yet?" I scan the crowd, looking for the English bastard's face.

"Nope." Dimitry shakes his head. "But there's an incoming to your left that's almost as much fun. Christ." He inclines his head to where Nikolai, hair slicked back, flanked by more muscle than a Kardashian, dripping ostentatious gold and wearing a shiny tracksuit and sneakers, is making his way through the crowd toward us. "What did he do, go shopping at Gangsters"R"Us?"

"Roman!" Nikolai shouts above the music, giving me an oily smile.

He throws his cigarette to the ground as he approaches, almost stubbing it out on the foot of a small child.

"Nikolai." I swallow my distaste. "Subtle," I say, nodding at the muscle clustered around him.

"Crowds aren't safe, Roman, you know that." Something about the way he says it, a slightly cocky edge, makes my unease grow.

"Expecting trouble, Nicky?" I keep my eyes on Masha's float as I speak, watching Lucia's crouched figure and the little dancing cactus. I move slightly closer, so I'm barely a pace from where Ofelia is running alongside.

"I'm like a Boy Scout, Roman. Always prepared."

Oh, this fucker is definitely up to something.

"I was surprised you decided to come today." I speak without looking at him.

"I could say the same about you." Nikolai has fallen in step beside me. I move aside, putting a little distance between us and getting even closer to the float. "I wasn't aware you were so dedicated to my nephew and nieces." He shoots me a sideways glance, but I don't take the bait.

He should take the hint and leave it there.

But nobody ever accused Nicky of being smart.

"Or is it," he says slyly, "that you just can't stay away from that hot au pair you hired? Never pegged you for the type to fuck the help, Roman."

I shoot Dimitry a brief look, but it's unnecessary. He's already moved to take my place next to Ofelia.

Twisting the ass end of Nikolai's silky tracksuit bottoms high enough to make his voice squeak, I push him silently ahead of me through the crowd. His men are a moment too late to stop me, and by the time they wise up, my own have them well in hand.

Dumb fucks.

"That gun in your pants is in my hand now," I murmur in Nikolai's ear as I thrust him off the main road and into a side alley. "And if you think I won't use it on you, fucking think again, Nicky. I've got plenty of reasons already. All I'm looking for right now is a good excuse."

I spin him around and thrust him up against a brick wall. Two of my men have taken up guard at the end of the alley. "Get back to the float," I order them sharply. "I've got this."

"Boss." One of them starts to argue, frowning.

"Fucking go," I snarl. "If this is a distraction and my family suffers, you'll pay for it. Understand? *Go.*"

They do.

"Now." I get right up close to Nikolai's face. "What the fuck do you think you're playing at, Nicky?"

"What?" he whines. "I was just making a joke, Roman. I didn't know you were so worked up over your nanny."

"You seem to have an unhealthy fascination with my au pair, Nikolai. Why is that?"

He spits to one side. I slam him harder against the bricks, and he scowls. "There are a dozen agencies you could have hired a nanny from. Instead you hired some illegal *blyat* from a café. Who also just happens, apparently, to speak Russian. It's a weird coincidence, you have to admit. Inger certainly thinks so," he adds with a sly expression.

"Ah." *I fucking knew it.* "So Inger has you doing her dirty work, now, Nicky?" I drop him to the ground and let go of him. "Taking orders from a woman? Tsk, tsk." I wag a finger in his face. "I wonder what Yuri will think of that?"

His face tightens. "Inger and I just care about Mikhail's

children. About making sure they're safe and that they get what they're entitled to."

I almost laugh aloud. "If Inger gave a single fuck about the kids, she'd have been here for the past two years, and for the fourteen before that. She's never given a fuck about who I hire to look after her children, so I don't know why she's suddenly taking such an interest now. As for making sure they're safe?" I crowd Nikolai until he's hard up against the wall again. "Are you honestly questioning my ability to do that?"

I can see the fear in his eyes, but for once, he doesn't back down. "You didn't keep my brother safe," he says. "Mikhail died—and you did nothing to stop it."

For a moment I'm actually too stunned to react.

Then I punch Nikolai twice with full force, direct to the face.

He slumps to the ground, his nose bleeding profusely.

"How fucking dare you." I'm so furious my voice shakes. "I yelled at Mikhail to get out of the driver seat the minute the ignition didn't turn over. A dozen men heard me, and not all of them together could hold me back from pulling him out of the burning car. Mikhail was my goddamn *brother*. I'd have given my own life for his a hundred times over rather than lose him."

"Ah, yes," Nicky sneers, holding his nose. "The famous story of how you took a bullet for him. But that bullet worked out pretty well for you, Roman, didn't it? Just like the raids seven years ago that put my father in prison. From Miami backstreets to a Spanish penthouse in less than twenty years. That must be some kind of fucking record."

"Do you have a fucking death wish, Nikolai?" I stare at him, trying to work out what the hell is going on. "Where the fuck is all this coming from?"

He stares back at me, his mouth working, eyes darting this

way and that. "I know you've got something going on in that software facility," he says finally. "And there's no way you started Hale without some kind of backing. After Otets went to prison, our business was shattered—so where did the money for Hale come from? And now you have Mikhail's children, his *heirs*, locked up in your penthouse under your so-called *protection*."

His tone has become more injured as he's gone on, and when he speaks again, it's with the petulant, spoiled tone that has always set my teeth on edge.

"You and Mikhail always shut me out. When I was younger, I didn't understand enough to ask questions. And then at first, when you palmed me off with Pillars, I was too happy to actually have a part of the business that it didn't occur to me to complain. But I'm Yuri's *son*. I'm Mikhail's brother. You're not even family, Roman. And now you're running an entire business in secret, and you don't even trust me enough to tell me what it is. You control Mikhail's legacy, not to mention his children. Put yourself in my shoes, Roman. Wouldn't you be suspicious, too?"

His voice is a petulant whine by the time he finishes, and he stares sullenly at the ground. The raucous sounds of the parade are beginning to fade into the distance. The midday streets are quiet, all the shops closed, residents out watching the spectacle.

I could kill him now, and nobody need ever know it was me.

It's fucking tempting, but I dismiss the thought as soon as I have it. Pain in my ass or not, Nicky is family, to both Yuri and the children. And family is family. Even if I'm technically not part of his, as he's just made abundantly clear.

"I suppose you're going to kill me now," he says dully.

"It would be my right." I glare at him. "I doubt even Yuri would question it if I did. He's killed men for far less than the disgusting accusations you just made."

But my mind is whirling as I speak. There's something else

going on here, something I can't quite see. Nikolai isn't smart enough to connect all these dots. Somebody is pulling his strings. If I want to find out who, I need to keep him alive, and at least pacified.

Tread carefully.

"You're right, Nicky." I deliberately speak in a calm, even tone. His head jerks up in surprise. "I haven't involved you in the family business as much as I should have, but only because I thought you were happier running Pillars than wearing a suit in a corporate office. But of course you want to visit the software facility and understand what we're building there. I can take you up to see it this week, if you like. I hadn't realized you were interested in tech."

Nikolai's eyes narrow. "You're trying to tell me it's just a software company you're running up there?"

"I'm not trying to tell you shit, Nicky." I allow my impatience to show. "I'm offering to show you, which is far more than you deserve, after accusing me of killing Mikhail."

"Well, did you?" he asks suspiciously.

"Of course I fucking didn't. And get up off the ground." I grasp his arm and pull him to his feet, resisting an extremely strong urge to punch him again. "I offered to bring you with me the night we caught the men who planted that bomb. I even offered you the right of pulling the trigger. It was your choice not to be there, Nikolai. If you had questions, that was the night to ask them. But if you still have doubts, then ask the men of yours who were there that night. They'll tell you those men admitted what they did readily enough. As for the start-up money for Hale—you might remember that Mikhail and I went to war after Yuri was jailed."

I almost manage to keep the sarcasm out of my tone, but going by Nikolai's sulky expression, he got the message clear enough. When Yuri went to prison, Nicky was the same age I'd been when I took a bullet for Mikhail. He knows as well as

I do that he could have insisted on going to war with us. Instead, he was too busy trading off Yuri's fame, hanging out in nightclubs, making friends with the celebrities who frequent his club now.

"We won a lot of bank in those wars. What we didn't have, we borrowed. Then we worked, Nicky. We worked fucking hard."

No chance I'm ever mentioning the Swiss lockbox. Not even Yuri knew about that. Nikolai sure as fuck never will.

"As for the children—I never asked to be made their legal guardian. And you of all people should know how hard I've worked to get Inger to take responsibility for them. Having her take permanent custody of her children has been my sole goal for two years, and still is. I have an email trail to prove it, should you require it."

Although as I say those words, an uneasy feeling steals through my chest. I've always told myself I want Inger to take the children. I've been convinced that is the only workable option. But in a rapid shuffle of mental pictures, I see the three children covered in flour and caramel, dancing with Lucia in the kitchen. I hear Mickey's grave voice down the phone, asking me to come to the villa because something is wrong. I think of Masha's little hand in mine, and Ofelia's reluctant smile.

For the first time, I find myself wondering if it's truly the right thing to send them back to their mother.

In fact, I realize with some surprise, I don't fucking like the idea of handing them over to Inger at all.

I tuck those thoughts away and bring my mind back to the task at hand.

"The children are your blood, Nikolai. You can see them anytime you want. They aren't 'locked away,' as you put it. They're simply safe, as Mikhail would want them to be. And as for their inheritance?" I step closer. "If you ever," I say, giving him the death stare and lowering my voice to the menacing growl that has made far better men than him piss their pants, "*ever* fucking imply again that I would cheat Mikhail's children out of the legacy he built for them, I will kill you. I won't talk to you. I won't justify myself. You'll just be dead, Nikolai. That's it. That's all." I stare the little *mudak* down. "Do you understand me?"

He shivers. "*Da,*" he whispers hoarsely. "Yes, *pakhan.* I understand. I'm sorry."

I hold his eyes long enough to let him see the murder in mine. It isn't hard. It's all I can do to stop myself putting a bullet between his eyes right now.

Eventually I stand back. "Right." I nod curtly toward the street. "In a minute, I'm going to rejoin the parade, and you're going to fuck off. But before you go, I'd like you to answer one question, Nikolai." He meets my eyes sullenly. "What made you ask these questions now?" I watch him carefully. "Why, after all our family has been through, would you come at me with accusations that could get you killed? What is it, exactly, that you think I'm hiding from you?"

Nicky's eyes dart this way and that, looking for an escape. Finally, clearly realizing there isn't one, his eyes meet mine then slide away. "It was something a friend of mine said," he says sulkily. "Miguel."

I frown, taken aback. "Perez? The Cádiz keeper?"

"Yes." He purses his lips. "Miguel has this journalist friend, a guy called Lance Ryder. He's done a few good pieces on Pillars, given us good exposure. Then last week, Miguel set up a meeting with the Cádiz manager, like I discussed with you." He gives me a rather defensive look, but since this is old news, I just nod. "Miguel brought Lance to the meeting. He said it was because Lance was doing a profile piece on him. He assured me it was all off the record."

I bite my tongue to stop myself asking how anyone, even

fucking Nicky, could be so dumb as to believe a journalist would listen to a meeting about a potential money laundering operation *off the record.*

"But after the meeting, Lance started asking all kinds of questions. About Hale, and especially about the software facility. He said the tech center is a front for something else. I told him I had no idea what he was talking about, and he said you gave me Pillars to keep me busy, so I wouldn't ask questions. He implied that you were hiding whatever it is even from Mikhail. He asked about how Mikhail died, and how Otets got caught. But most of all, he was asking about that girl from the café across the road, the one who's your nanny now. It was weird, Roman." He meets my eyes, genuine confusion in his. "He asked if my father ever told me about something called the Naryshkin Treasure."

"The what?" I make Nicky say it again.

"Then you've never heard of it either?"

I shake my head. "No fucking idea."

"Oh." Nikolai looks relieved, and a bit shamefaced. "Well, Lance seemed to think your nanny knows something about it. He implied that the two of you are conspiring in some way. He hung around for a few days, working in one of the private rooms, asking all kinds of questions. At first I didn't really care, since he was taking good pap shots and Pillars was getting good publicity out of it. But in the end I didn't like some of the things he was saying, so I stopped answering his questions." He looks at me hopefully, as if I'm going to give him some kind of fucking approval for doing the bare minimum to show me loyalty.

"You told me all this came about because Miguel said something," I prompt.

"Oh. Yeah." Nikolai wipes some of the blood from his nose. "The thing is, a few days after I kicked him out of Pillars, Lance just disappeared. I mean, I called him to ask if he wanted an exclusive on an event at the club, and his phone was disconnected. Nada. I asked Miguel where he went, and he said that Lance is running from you." He glances at me. "Apparently, Lance told Miguel that your men were following him. Miguel said that Lance knows things about your business at the software facility, and things about your past, that you'd kill to keep secret. He doesn't know what," he adds hastily. "Miguel doesn't know what Lance was chasing down, just that he said Miguel should warn me you aren't to be trusted. That's it, Roman. That's all I know." He eyes me warily. "I know I should have told you before now, but—"

I wave that off impatiently.

Nikolai is finished as far as I'm concerned.

I might stop short of putting a bullet through his brain, but he'll be on such a short fucking leash for the rest of his life that he might begin to wish I had. That isn't what interests me now.

"Did you end up finding out anything about this Naryshkin Treasure that Lance was so obsessed with?"

"The treasure?" Nikolai frowns in confusion. "Oh, no." He shrugs, giving me a rather bemused look. "I mean, it's obviously just one of those stories you hear, right? Journalists make them up all the time about Russians, especially rich ones." Then his face takes on a shrewd expression. "Wait. Is that why you had men following him? Do you think he's onto something?"

"Of course not." Nikolai's blatant greed is about as subtle as a fucking sledgehammer. Nonetheless, better I nip it in the bud. The last thing I need now is Nicky getting curious. "I'm just wondering why he thought I was involved. No," I say, as if dismissing it. "I had Ryder followed because I knew he attended a meeting at Pillars, and I knew he was a journalist. I was worried he would damage us in some way."

It isn't entirely untrue.

"Oh." Nikolai has the grace to look ashamed, and I don't feel remotely fucking guilty about it. "Thank you for looking out for me, Roman."

"Yep." I nod curtly toward the main road. "Let's get back to the parade. You're going to say hello to your brother's kids, then you're going to get the fuck out of my sight. Are we clear?"

"Yes, *pakhan*." He lowers his head sullenly. "Crystal."

37

LUCIA

Roman has disappeared.

His presence is like some kind of magnetic field; I always know when he's nearby. One moment he was there, barely a pace from Ofelia, and my world felt ordered and safe. The next, the air felt somehow loose, slightly chaotic, and when I looked at the place where he'd been, I found Dimitry instead.

"Da-da-da." Masha dances dreamily in time to the music. Her performance is over for now, and she's just singing randomly along to the music blaring from Mickey's speakers. The crowd roars as a gymnast flips on the back of a truck, and I swing around, startled.

I really don't like crowds.

I might have fought for the kids to do this, but that doesn't mean I don't find the entire thing nerve-wracking. A hundred phones are recording us. I can hear Russian accents from every part of the crowd. It makes sense, of course. Every Russian in the whole south of Spain has come to celebrate at the biggest Russian church in the region.

I'm really starting to question my sanity in thinking this was, in any way, a good idea.

And where the hell is Roman?

I raise my mask slightly and catch Dimitry's eye. *Where is Roman?* I mouth.

Dimitry frowns and indicates that I should lower my mask. I do, but not before he sees how worried I am.

Nikolai, he mouths back.

Hm. So that was the thin-faced guy in the tracksuit with all the steroid-junkie bodyguards. It's hard to believe that Nikolai belongs to the same family as Roman. He looks like some street thug who got lucky, a distant cry from Roman's lethal elegance.

"Masha!" Ofelia is waving to her sister. "It's time to do your dance again."

I hear the familiar strains of the cactus song, a particularly grating tune created by Masha's teacher that I hope never to hear again. The music rotates through each float, enabling each group to perform their particular piece for the crowds. This is the fourth time we've done the cactus dance during the procession. It's possibly the thousandth time I've done it this week.

At least the lion mask hides my face.

But as I turn Masha to face the front yet again, I can't help but smile as I watch a beaming Ofelia make exaggerated gestures beside the float and hear Masha giggle delightedly as she follows her sister's lead. "Look, Luce," she burbles happily. "'Felia dancing."

"Yes, she is, *myshka*." I catch Masha as she teeters at the edge of the float after a slightly too enthusiastic spin. The exhausted teacher shoots me a grateful look. "You're doing such a wonderful job," I say to Masha. "Just be careful when you turn, darling." I keep a handful of the cactus costume bunched in my hand, just in case.

Masha has a habit of darting off in any direction at any given moment. It's one of the reasons I know Ofelia needs to be here, close by, keeping an eye on her. I want Ofelia to gradually start trusting me to take on that role, to begin to have a life for herself. The other girls her age are on floats themselves, or in the crowd in a group of friends. Ofelia seems to know none of them and care even less, even though I've noticed more than one of the young guys looking her way admiringly. Even clad in cornflower-blue shorts and a white sleeveless linen blouse, wearing simple sandals, Ofelia is breathtakingly beautiful.

It's as if she knows their life isn't for her, I think sadly. I know how that feels. As ever, I hate that she is experiencing the same detached solitude I did as a teenager. Then I think of Roman promising he will reconsider her schooling options, and my heart lifts a little. *Maybe I can make it different for her.*

But all of that depends on if this strange life I'm living will become something permanent.

I can't tell.

It's all happening so quickly, and there's been so little time to discuss anything, even if Roman actually wants to, which I'm entirely unsure about. In another week the children will be back at school. Perhaps things might settle down a little then.

Or perhaps the Orlovs will come before that.

I push that firmly out of my mind.

"Luce!" Abby emerges from the crowd to stand by Dimitry, waving frantically at me.

I wince at her use of my name, but give her a small wave back. A frowning Dimitry says something in her ear, and she quickly lowers her hand and looks around nervously. I hate this, that even my friends have to worry about simply greeting me in public. At the same time, I can't help but notice how close she stands to Dimitry, and how he angles his body to include her in his circle of protection.

I'm glad.

I like Dimitry, and I *love* Abby. Whatever is going on between them, I hope they're getting to a good place.

Abby leans forward and says something to Ofelia, who returns her smile shyly after getting a nod of approval from Dimitry. The two girls walk together by the float, Abby making Ofelia and Masha laugh by trying to imitate the cactus dance. The parade is entering the wide-open plaza that is the finish point, the floats taking up their positions in a square at the edges. Balloon sellers and food vans vie with street performers in a mad clash of color and hilarity. Our float finds its way to its marked spot at the far corner, and the teacher, the other parents, and I lift the excited kids down one by one. I still can't see Roman anywhere. I'm starting to feel uneasy, despite the legion of men in dark glasses standing in loose formation at a careful distance.

"I need to pee," Masha announces, loud enough to make one of the other cacti nearby giggle.

"Okay." I take hold of her hand and turn to Dimitry.

"There are portables set up over there." He nods toward the edge of the square. "We'll come with you. I've got men on Mickey." We set off through the thronging crowds, Abby and me on either side of Ofelia and Masha, with the men in glasses spread out around us. There's still no sign of Roman. We reach the restroom trailer, and Ofelia screws up her nose.

"I'm good, thanks," she says. "I'll wait out here with Abby."

"I've gotcha, girlfriend." Abby grins at her. "Wait until you start going to music festivals. Believe me, these are luxury by comparison."

"Don't even start on those stories," I warn her, seeing

Ofelia's eyes light up with interest. "Music festivals are a hard no. For at least a few years."

"Ha. Just because you have no life." Abby winks at Ofelia. "I'll wait until she's inside to tell you about the time I . . ."

She's incorrigible. Shaking my head and laughing, I head Masha toward the trailer stairs. One of the security guys has a look inside, but backs off hastily when he's met with an indignant chorus of female protest.

"We'll be fine," I assure him, walking Masha up the stairs.

We survive the queue, during which Masha's hopping from one leg to another grows more urgent. I unbutton her costume in preparation, sighing with relief when we finally get an empty cubicle. Afterward, we emerge and stand by the row of sinks as Masha washes her hands and I button her back up again.

"Darya."

I momentarily freeze at the low male voice, then force myself to slowly begin buttoning again, my fingers not quite steady. I'm only just aware of the tall figure immediately to my left, completely concealed within a purple dinosaur costume.

"Don't run. I can help you get a message to Alexei. He's here, you know. In Spain."

I keep my head down, not reacting at all. I know the voice; it's the same paparazzi journalist who was chasing me outside the café. The fact that he knows my name, and my brother's, is terrifying. But there's no chance in hell I'm making this worse by playing into his game.

"Luce." Masha stares at the dinosaur with a confused expression. "Dino talkin'."

"Not to us, darling." I stand up, her hand firmly gripped in mine. For a moment I consider exposing the dinosaur as a man, but that will only create a panic, which might be exactly what he wants. Better that I ignore him entirely.

"You should talk to me, Darya. You're trusting the wrong people—"

"Excuse me." I push my way through the queue of chattering people, hoping none of them heard the whispered conversation. I stumble down the stairs, pushing my mask up as I do, heading straight for Dimitry.

"Purple dinosaur," I say. He takes one look at my face and heads for the stairs without bothering to even ask what's happened, directing his men to the other end and ignoring the shrieking women.

I know that it's a risk, given that the journalist clearly knows more than he should.

But this is about Masha's safety. Ofelia's.

That bastard came at me in a public toilet, for goodness' sake. He could have snatched me or helped someone else do it. Masha would have been all alone and terrified. They might even have taken her, too. I grip her hand tightly, my heart pounding.

Ofelia clings to Abby's hand, Masha to mine, and we stand in a protective circle of Roman's muscle. We're still standing there when Roman pushes through the crowd toward us, the thin-faced Nikolai stumbling in his wake. Nikolai's nose looks like it's recently had a fist in it.

Roman takes one look at my face, and his own hardens. He turns to the security men, who begin to explain without being asked. They're still explaining when Dimitry pushes his way back to us, his expression thunderous. He mutters something in Roman's ear, then catches my eye and shakes his head curtly.

"The door at the other end was unlocked," he says. "The guy was gone before I got there. And before you ask," he says to Roman, "we checked it before they went in. He must have already been inside."

Roman moves close to me and lowers his head, so I can

speak directly into his ear. "It's a journalist. He was after me," I say quietly. "I think his name is Lance."

He nods. To my relief, he doesn't ask me about the encounter. Instead he gives several short, low-voiced orders, and some of his men disappear into the crowd. "I don't want to scare the children," I murmur to him. "Or ruin their day."

Roman leans down and rights Masha's crooked costume. "You remembered all the movements for your dance," he says, smiling at her. "I saw you."

"'Felia helped," Masha says, beaming.

"I saw that, too." Roman gives Ofelia a reassuring smile. "Don't be scared," he murmurs to her, when her stiff face doesn't relax at all. "It was a journalist, and we've taken care of it. Okay?"

The color slowly comes back into her face. "Okay." But I notice that she doesn't object when Roman takes her hand.

"Hi, Nicky." Abby greets the tracksuit guy with noticeable reluctance.

"Abby." His eyes rest on her curiously. "Does Miguel know you're here?"

"It's really none of Miguel's business where I am," she says coldly.

Well, that's a good thing.

"Lucia." Roman gestures to the man unsmilingly. "This is Nikolai, the children's uncle."

Not *my brother*, I notice, as I shake Nikolai's hand. Not even *Mikhail's brother* or *Yuri's son*. His eyes are too close together, and he looks at me with far more interest than I'm comfortable with. His handshake is limp and slightly moist. Even the children seem less than enthusiastic in their greetings.

"Hey, Uncle Nicky," says Ofelia, keeping her eyes down and her body turned toward Roman's as Nikolai greets her.

"Hullo," says Masha uncertainly. Neither girl offers him

their hand, and I notice he doesn't try to kiss them, as is customary.

We walk together over to the sound trailer.

"Wait here," Roman orders Nikolai curtly. He brings me and the girls over to the trailer, then leaps up onto the back of it in an athletic jump that makes several of the nearby women cast him admiring glances, and a couple of the men look sour faced.

"Amazing job." Roman claps Mickey on the shoulder. "It went without a single hitch. Well done."

"There were a couple of last-minute problems," Mickey says, smiling shyly. "I was lucky Pavel was here."

"Not at all," says Pavel cheerfully. He's a very round guy, wearing a Tin Tin T-shirt and cotton candy in his beard. "You had it all under control, man. I just checked your work. He did good," he adds to Roman. "Real good."

"I saw." Roman puts an arm around Mickey in a loose hug. "Brilliant effort. Wasn't it, girls?" Leaning down, he hauls Ofelia up onto the trailer. I hand Masha up to him, and he places her gently down and then extends his hand to me. Dimitry helps me up, and for a moment we all stand in a small group, hugging Mickey one by one.

"You were amazing," I whisper to him.

"Thanks." His eyes are shining. I notice that Roman has taken Pavel aside and is having a low-voiced conversation that I'm almost certain involves the missing purple dinosaur.

Roman waits until we're all done congratulating Mickey, then nods briefly at Nikolai. "Your uncle wanted to say congratulations."

"Oh." Mickey's face goes rather guarded. "Thank you," he mutters, barely looking at Nikolai.

Wow. These kids really don't like their uncle.

"Thanks for coming," Roman says to Nikolai. "We'll catch up soon."

It couldn't be more of a dismissal if he'd thrown him out of the plaza. Nikolai clearly gets the message, because he doesn't argue, just mumbles a goodbye and leaves. I notice his steroid boys are missing. My guess is that Roman took care of them.

"So, guys." Roman draws the kids and me into a huddle. "I have a surprise for you."

The children eye him warily.

It's as if they're just waiting to get kicked again, I think sadly. I wonder how many times lately a "surprise" has been a euphemism for being shipped off somewhere they don't want to go.

"Do you remember my finca in the mountains, where we went for Mickey's birthday?"

The kids' eyes widen. They nod.

"Well, we're heading up there today. We're going to spend the rest of the Holy Week holidays there. What do you think about that?"

Masha immediately starts jumping up and down, but Ofelia's eyes narrow. "Where will you be?"

Smart girl.

But Roman just smiles. "With you, of course." He ruffles her hair. "And guess what? We're bringing Deda up with us, too." He meets my eyes over the children's head. I should be cross that he's made that decision without me. But I'm not. I'm just relieved that we'll be out of the city, away from crowds like these and whoever is hunting for us.

I smile at him. "That sounds wonderful."

38

LUCIA

"Catch, Lucia!"

I hit the blow-up ball flying toward my face, laughing as I duck beneath the pool surface.

The water is balmy, April sun beaming down from a cloudless, deep blue sky. The infinity pool is perched on the edge of a rocky cliff, the distant Mediterranean Sea glittering far below. Mountains rise behind the white walls of the renovated farmhouse, rippling into the distance on either side of the estate. It's called Finca de Carrascas, named after the holm oak forest that surrounds it. Bright pink bougainvillea crawls along the walls, and the air is redolent with the scent of the clematis, jasmine, and citrus plants on the patio behind us.

"Hey, Masha!" Mickey calls. His sister turns around just as he runs and hurls himself into the pool, sending water cascading over Masha and Ofelia, who squeal in delight.

"Deda!" cries Masha. "Watch me!"

Papa smiles from his dry seat on the patio, applauding as Masha pulls herself up on the side of the pool, then jumps back into Ofelia's waiting arms.

I lie on my back in the deep end of the pool, gazing up at the sky, peace stealing through my body.

"Hey." A shadow crosses me, and I turn my head to find Roman grinning down at me. His hair is slicked back, water running in rivulets down the rippled, tan breadth of his chest. He's wearing nothing but dark red swimming shorts that sit just under the V of his navel. Every scarred, tattooed inch of him is rigid muscle.

A bolt of pure, unadulterated lust rips through me.

Christ.

I roll over, ducking my burning face under the water.

I'm used to wanting Roman. Accustomed to the sudden, vicious rushes of lust that take me by surprise. But Roman in a suit and tie is one thing. An almost familiar temptation by now.

Roman wearing nothing but swim trunks and a shit-eating grin, water running down his gleaming body, is a whole other world of lust altogether.

I emerge to find him with an even wider smile and an evil gleam in his eyes. "Water nice, Miss Lopez?"

Two can play at that game.

I swim over to the steps and walk out, adjusting my white bikini. I stretch languorously as I reach for my towel, enjoying his sudden intake of breath and the way his eyes darken.

It's only been a few days since the parade, our hurried packing, and the late-night drive up to the villa, but it already feels as if we've been here for months. The privacy, endless days of sunbathing and swimming, and meals taken together as a family on the patio, have only served to increase the intensity of my attraction to Roman.

Particularly since we've been steadfastly keeping to our own bedrooms.

Despite Papa being in a separate villa fifty meters from the main farmhouse, the nights here are deathly quiet, and the children's bedrooms are located just across the courtyard from ours.

Not great for screaming, and Roman and I both know how loud I get.

By the look on his face currently, he's not enjoying the forced celibacy any more than I am. I'm not going to lie; I get more than a little thrill from that thought.

"So." A grinning Abby bobs up to the surface at my feet. It was Roman's idea that she join us. Going by how often she and Dimitry have been sneaking off in the midafternoon, I'm guessing they've moved on from whatever was blocking their relationship before.

"Dimitry and I are going to child sit tonight," she says. "You and Roman are going out. No arguments." She heads off my protests at the pass. "We offered, and Roman agreed."

I glance at Roman, coloring. Close as our domestic arrangement is, I've always been firmly in the au pair role around the children and Papa. Roman and I spending time alone sends a pretty clear message that there's more to the situation than what we've presented.

"You need a break," Roman says, his eyes dark and caressing on my skin in a way that makes my breath catch. "We both do."

"A break." Dimitry breaks the surface, grinning. "Is that what we're calling it now?"

Roman opens his mouth in what I'm quite sure was about to be an obscene rebuke. He catches himself at the last minute.

"Dinner," he says, in as dignified a tone as he can in the face of Abby and Dimitry's visible amusement. "Somewhere nice."

To my surprise, the kids don't so much as blink when I mumble that Abby and Dimitry will be watching them that evening. Even Papa just waves me away with a slight smile. I'm rather taken aback that nobody questions why I might be spending a social evening out with my boss.

I take my time dressing. Finally, encouraged by Abby, I settle on a full-length midnight-blue dress in velvet silk with a soft cowl. It exposes most of my back and a great deal of cleavage.

"Are you sure this is okay for dinner in a mountain village?" I turn doubtfully in front of the mirror. "I feel a bit overdressed, particularly with high heels."

"Nope." Abby grins. "Trust me, this is perfect."

"Hang on." I meet her eyes in the mirror. "What do you know that I don't?"

"I know nothing." She holds her hands up with a wide-eyed, innocent look that does nothing to reassure me. When I eventually emerge into the living room, the kids are draped over the furniture, still wearing their swimsuits, playing some board game with Dimitry and Papa that seems to involve a lot of shrieking and accusations of cheating. They all stop when I walk in.

"You look gorgeous," says Ofelia, in somewhat unflattering amazement.

"Pretty!" Masha claps her hands together, bouncing up and down in excitement.

"Wow," says Mickey shyly.

"Yes, well, better get a good look at her now." Roman appears in the doorway.

I suck in my breath.

If I thought him earth-shattering in a suit, his bespoke tux ratchets up the hotness to a whole new level.

"We won't be home by the time you go to bed, so say goodnight. Don't crumple her," he warns them sternly, as the kids converge for hugs. I look over their heads to Papa. The expression on his face almost ruins my makeup. I stop by his chair and kiss his creased cheek. "Goodnight, Papa," I whisper.

He touches the small, plain studs at my ears. "Your mama— would be—proud," he whispers, and I know he's thinking of the Fabergé teardrops I left in my bag. They don't match this dress. I pull back in time to see him lock eyes with Roman.

"I'll take care of her," Roman says courteously in Russian. He puts his hand out.

My father takes it and nods, for all the world as if he were giving permission. I'm grateful to Roman for that, for giving Papa that courtesy.

"You look stunning," Roman says, smiling at me. "But that dress is missing something."

"What?" I turn this way and that, wondering if I've left the tag on the dress.

"These." He holds out a velvet-covered box, grinning, and opens it.

I gasp. Inside, nestled on a bed of midnight satin, are a pair of inch-long diamond and sapphire earrings. They match my dress perfectly. I look up to see Abby grinning like a maniac.

"You knew," I say accusingly. She just shrugs, still grinning. The kids all cluster around, making admiring noises.

I take out my studs, and Roman replaces them with the earrings. His large fingers handle the delicate clasps with surprising sureness. I glance at Papa. He's watching Roman, a strange expression on his face that I can't quite read. When he sees my face, he gives me a brief nod, but his smile is slightly fixed. His eyes slide to Roman, then back to me.

I know this isn't the way he imagined me being taken to dinner by a man. But it's the life we have, and I hope he can come to peace with it.

Roman gestures to the door. "Shall we?"

DINNER IS in a restaurant inside a cleverly renovated ancient mountain castle.

"It dates back to the Moorish occupation," Roman explains as he hands the car keys to a smiling valet. "Although, like most castles in Andalucia, it was Visigothic before that, and probably Roman even before that." He holds out his arm, and I slip mine through it. "There's a wonderful flamenco performance during dinner, with local dancers. I thought you'd enjoy it."

"It sounds wonderful." Slightly overwhelmed by the entire thing, I allow him to lead me through the stone archway.

The restaurant is in a courtyard surrounded by arched colonnades. A fountain trickles in the center, and flowering plants climb over the stone pillars. A stage is set up at one end with instruments, clearly awaiting performers. Our table is set on a private terrace at the rear of the courtyard, though with a clear view of the stage. The terrace juts out over a dramatic cliff. In the distance the Malaga lights twinkle. I like that they're far away. The night is still but for a light breeze, and the low lighting allows the stars to gleam down.

"To us," Roman says, after the champagne has been poured. He holds my eyes as we drink.

"Thank you for the earrings." I stammer slightly, flushing again. I'm still not sure what to make of the extravagant gift.

"You're welcome." His mouth curls in a smile that, for once, is neither sardonic nor slightly cruel. "They suit you." He gestures around the terrace with his glass. "All of this suits you."

Not entirely sure how to respond to that, I take another sip of champagne, searching around for something to say. I feel oddly shy, which is incongruous, given how intimate we've been with each other. "The kids love it at the finca," I say finally.

"I don't want to talk about the children tonight." He sits back as the waiter brings out a selection of tapas that look divine. "Or about the journalist," he goes on, "or the Orlovs, or about my work. Tonight, I just want to enjoy being here, with you."

He traces my hand with one long finger, and I shiver. His voice is low, his eyes intense, and I want to tear his clothes off.

"I think," he says, "that it's about time we got to know one another a little better."

I tense, and he continues stroking my hand, not taking his eyes from my face.

"I don't mean to frighten you. Or ask you anything you don't want to tell me. I just want to learn a little more about you, Miss Lopez." He grins, and I start to feel more relaxed. "Like for example, how did you learn to make such good coffee?"

I laugh. I can't help it.

"Well," I say, looking at him shyly, "it was actually my mother who taught me. She was Colombian. She insisted on having a professional standard machine in our kitchen at home. Then, later, Papa and I were living in Argentina for a while. I needed work by then, so I found a job in a coffee shop. I was so bad at it," I admit, and he laughs softly. "No, really. I was. The first day I broke three glasses. I thought I'd be fired, but luckily they kept me on. I didn't know the first thing about how to operate a cash register, or carry three plates, or anything, for that matter. It was a steep learning curve."

I find myself telling him about those early days, when Papa and I were still living in a tiny apartment in a rundown part of Buenos Aires. "I had three jobs," I say. "I was cleaning, as well as working in a bar and at the coffee shop. We were trying to save money; I didn't have a lot of choice. But I kind of liked it,"

I say when his smile fades. "I'd always envied kids who had paper rounds, you know? Or a part-time job. They seemed so . . . free, compared to us." I halt, aware that I've probably said too much. To my relief, however, Roman doesn't push me for an explanation.

"I was the opposite." He gives me a wry smile. "My father had me working for him from as early as I can remember."

"Really?" I try not to push him too hard, but I'm fascinated. "What kind of work were you doing?"

"He had a shop. He . . . mended things, and made others. He made jewelry, too." He nods at my earrings. "In fact, he made those."

"These?" I'm so taken aback that I can only stare at him. I touch the sapphires tentatively.

"Yes." Roman lifts a piece of tapas to my mouth and watches as I eat it. "I used to sit in the back of his workshop and fetch his tools. He would make me watch what he was doing, then imitate it. My father always said that the only way to learn was to teach the hands first, and the mind would follow. Sometimes he got me to work blindfolded."

"Wow." I don't ask what, exactly, his father was making. It's the fragile rules of our conversation—to tell each other our stories, without actually divulging anything specific.

"My mother was Colombian, too." Roman smiles at my surprise. It's nice to think we have that in common. "She worked as a dressmaker. Her workshop was at the back of my father's. So a lot of my childhood was spent running around with parcels under my arm, doing deliveries for both of my parents. She was a great cook, too," he adds. He gives me a small smile. "She used to make *alfajores* every Friday afternoon, when I came home from school."

"Oh!" I remember the way he looked the day he came in to find me baking with the children. "So you really did know what I was making that day."

He grins. "I could smell those cookies all the way up the elevator. You'll be making them again, trust me."

"How old were you when—" I stop when I see his face cloud over. "Abby told me you and Dimitry met when you were very young," I say instead.

"We did." His smile has faded, but to my relief, he doesn't shut down completely. He waits until the waiter has served the next course, a delicious array of spiced chicken and pomegranate. "My mother had to . . . leave, when I was young. A couple of years later, my father was . . . he died."

What he doesn't say could clearly fill an encyclopedia, but I play by the rules and don't ask.

"After that I was on my own. I met Dimitry a while later, and we kind of stuck together. Then, when I was sixteen, I met Mikhail. His father, Yuri, took a liking to me. When they left the States and came back to Spain, they brought me with them." He shrugs. "The rest is history, I guess."

We talk as the various courses come out, not about anything in particular, just getting to know one another in a way we haven't been able to before. I tell him how much I loved playing piano when I was younger, and about the art that Papa collected, the galleries we used to go to. He tells me that he loves going to auctions, finding little-known treasures others miss. "That's where I found those earrings," he says, nodding at them. "My father's pieces turn up every now and then. Not many people recognize them. Some of them are expensive, others not so much, but to me, they're all pieces of my past, and incredibly valuable. I buy them anonymously," he adds, grinning. "I don't want to push the price up."

I laugh aloud at that. I realize, to my surprise, that I'm having the nicest night I can remember in a really long time. If ever. This is a side of Roman I've never seen before, a glimpse into the man behind the ruthless mask and corporate exterior.

I'm not entirely certain why he's trusting me with this part of himself, but nor do I feel inclined to question it.

After dessert, the lights go down, and the musicians walk onto the stage to a round of applause.

"They sing first," Roman murmurs to me across the table. "Then the *flamenca* will come out."

I've seen a lot of flamenco performed since I've been in Spain. There are performances at every fiesta and on almost every street corner. But when the male singer cries the first, low strains of his song, chills run down my spine.

"It's called *cante jondo*," Roman says in my ear. *Deep song.* He's moved our chairs to the front of the table, so we're side by side, and his lips touch my ear as he speaks.

I shiver.

The singer's words soar into the night like a paean to Spain. He sings of dusty olive orchards, red under the dying sun. Of love lost and found, and generations bound to the earth. His words are both tragic and beautiful, and so clearly a love song to the country around us that they are incredibly moving. By the time the rapid clapping of the other musicians begins, and the steady drumbeat rises, signaling the *flamenca's* entrance, I'm utterly spellbound.

Dark eyes lined with kohl, her hair pulled back in a large chignon, the woman begins to dance. She isn't a young woman, probably somewhere in her forties, and her body is rounded with age. But somehow her years and curves only add more intensity to her dance. Her feet fly in rapid, intricate steps, the metal soles of her shoes rapping out a complex rhythm. Her body ripples in elegant, sensual movements, telling the story that is being sung. More than anything, it's her face that entrances me. Frowning in concentration, her eyes intense and gleaming with fierce triumph, she whips herself and the audience into a gradual frenzy. By the time her flying feet and the rapid clapping reach their climax, I'm breathless, every nerve in my body alight.

We burst into a sea of applause, and I turn to Roman to find him watching me, his eyes dark with desire. It's like a spark to the smoldering need inside me.

"Let's get out of here," I whisper.

39

LUCIA

Roman doesn't take me back to the finca. Instead, taking my hand, he leads me through the castle and into an elevator operated by a valet. We stand with our backs against the wall, staring at the valet's white-jacketed back, not daring to look at each other as the elevator rises a couple of floors, then opens silently. I step out as Roman tips the man and walk over the flagstone floor. Rustic as the apartment is, with a vast wrought iron candelabra overhead, the wood and glass decor is sophisticated and subtle. The doors are open onto the terrace, which is almost as wide as the one we dined on. Candles burn behind filigree sconces on the wall, casting decorative shadows over the stone. Off to our right, light and chatter spill from the dining room, the sound of background flamenco guitar poignant on the night.

"It's beautiful," I breathe, leaning over the stone balustrade.

"So are you." I turn to find Roman standing in the doorway, staring at me. He crosses the terrace in a few strides, pulling himself up short a pace from me.

"There's something I need to say." His voice is slightly hoarse, his eyes on mine particularly serious, and I feel a faint flutter of anxiety. "It's about that contract."

I tense. I can't read his intention, and I try not to worry about what is coming next.

"I've tried to honor that," I say nervously. "I know it's been difficult. With Papa and everything else." I'm stammering.

"No, Lucia." He shakes his head impatiently. "What I mean is that I don't want—dammit." He rubs a hand over his face.

Is he actually uncertain of himself?

The concept is so alien I can't quite imagine it.

"Wait," he says curtly. He turns, going into the apartment, and I stand awkwardly on the terrace, wondering what is coming.

Trying not to imagine the worst.

He returns a moment later, holding the contract up in front of him.

"When I gave you this," he says quietly, twisting the paper into a funnel, "I meant it as security. Money and protection for you. Convenience, I guess, for me." His mouth twists in something like distaste. "A few weeks ago, I thought that would be enough. But now . . . well, now it's different."

His voice is oddly halting. He takes a deep breath.

"I guess what I'm trying to say—rather badly—is that I don't want you to be here because of a contract. I want—well, I want it to be your choice."

He halts abruptly, staring at me. "Say the word, Lucia," he says roughly, "and I'll drive you back to the finca tonight and send you to your own bedroom. Nothing will change in relation to the money I'm paying you or your place in my home. Nobody ever needs to know that there was anything between us other than a work contract. You have my word I'll never breathe a word to your father about it. In fact," he says, eyeing the offending funnel of paper with rather disgusted eyes, "if it was up to me, I'd burn the damned thing here and now and never speak of it again. But it needs to be your decision." He holds the papers out to me. "This contract is your security. If you want to keep it, then that is up to you. I just want you to know that whatever you decide, I'll honor your decision."

I'm so taken aback that for a moment I don't say anything at all. The funneled contract hovers in front of my eyes.

Finally I take it.

The papers feel cold and unpleasant in my hand. I flick through them, not really seeing the words on the pages. The signature on them doesn't seem like mine, or rather, I no longer feel like the person who signed my name. So much has changed since the day I first read the words in that contract that I barely recall how I felt then, even though it was only weeks ago.

Back then, Roman was a stranger. One I wanted, yes, and desired more than I ever have any man. But one who terrified me, too.

And now?

Now I've lived in his home. Slept in his bed. Fallen in love with his children, and watched them slowly come out of their shells. Watched Roman himself change. He's still the hard bastard I met. More so, perhaps, than I'd even guessed. As ruthless as any of the men I was raised with. Fiercely protective of those he loves and, undoubtedly, just as savage when anything of his is threatened.

But I've also seen another side to him. The man who knew when it was time to give more of himself to the children in his care. Who made sure Mickey knew he was proud of him, and who found a way to build a bridge to Ofelia's heart. The man who managed to meet my father in a way that preserved Papa's dignity and earned his respect.

More than the nights I've spent tangled in his sheets, or the way he makes my body melt with little more than just a look, it's those aspects of Roman that have lowered my defenses. It isn't the money he's put in a bank account for me that's made me feel safe.

It's him.

Being close to him.

Knowing that I can trust him.

"Say something," he says roughly, his eyes dark hollows in his face.

I don't though. Instead, I walk over to one of the sconces on the wall. Holding the papers up to it, I let them catch light. I carry the flaming papers across to the terrace and let the night breeze tear the embers from my hands, watching them float away into the night. When the last paper starts to crumble, I drop it onto the stone terrace, where it curls into ash.

I turn to Roman. "I didn't sign that contract because of the money," I say quietly. "I didn't sign it to keep myself safe, or because I was running from the Orlovs. Maybe, at the time, I told myself that was why I was signing it. I told myself that I'd do anything to keep Papa and me safe. And I told myself I could walk away, at any moment. But that was a lie, Roman. I was lying to myself."

I step closer to him, wrapping my arms around his neck. "I don't want to run away from you," I whisper. "I don't even know that I could anymore."

His arms snake around my waist, though he still holds me slightly apart.

"I can't promise you anything," he says hoarsely, "Other than what I already have. I don't know how much I can . . . I won't make promises I can't keep, Lucia."

"I know that." I hold his eyes with my own. "Neither of us

can make too many promises, Roman. Our lives don't allow for them. But for now, we're here. Together. And there's nowhere in this world I'd rather be."

I press my body gently against his, and he groans softly, his arms tightening around me. I can feel his resolve crumbling, and the knowledge that it's me doing that to him gives me a fierce, almost heady rush of power.

He wants me. Roman truly wants me.

Somehow, it's different from before, from all the fiery encounters of power and lust that have carried us here. "I won't run from you, Roman." I hold his face in my hands. "Not unless you tell me to go. That's the one promise I will make."

Something flashes deep in his eyes, a savage gleam that sends fire through my body. "Good," he says roughly.

Then he kisses me.

It isn't like before. Nothing like the fierce need that has had me squirming desperately every time it's begun. This is slow, deep, and sweet with the promise I've made and the world that we've begun to create. His lips say all the words his voice can't. He holds me like I'm as fragile as his father's earrings, his hands splayed across my bare back, and kisses me on and on, until the sensation blends with the wild flamenco guitar on the night, and I'm lost.

He slips the dress from my shoulders, his lips tracing every place his fingers touch. He walks around my body, trailing his hands over my bare skin, peeling my underwear off me and slipping off my high heels, kissing his way up my leg, from instep to inner thigh, until I'm clutching his shoulders and moaning, my legs parting, craving his touch. The light mountain breeze plays over my bare skin, like tiny fronds stimulating my flesh.

"Take your clothes off," I whisper, pulling impatiently at his jacket. For once, he doesn't smirk or give me orders. He lets me pull at the bow tie and throw his jacket aside, to unbutton his shirt and push it impatiently from the broad shoulders I've dreamed about touching all week.

"I've been watching you." I kiss his neck, his chest, as I pull at the buckle of his belt. I slip his trousers and shorts down, sliding down his body to remove his shoes and socks with them. He stands like some ancient marble statue, scarred and magnificent, powerful legs slightly parted and his fists clenched, allowing me to savor him. He's hard and swollen, his cock raging toward me, but I want to be slow. I want to make this last.

"It's been fucking torture watching you half naked in the pool." I walk around his body, my fingers roaming all over him, owning the territory I've only dared to sample before now. I cup his hard buttocks, pressing my aching breasts against his back, and he turns his head to watch me through half-slitted eyes. Only his clenched fists and taut, corded muscles betray the restraint he's exerting. "I've spent every night aching for you. It's like you woke my body up, and now . . ." I press my mouth to the soft place beneath his ear. "Now," I murmur, lightly touching my tongue to his skin, "I can't put the fire out, Roman. It's like you're inside me. Even when we're apart, I can feel you. And I want you. I *need* you, Roman. All the time."

His arms encircle me, and he captures my mouth with his own. I can feel the barely restrained need in his touch, in the rock-hard length of him throbbing against me. I'm wet and aching, but I also want this, the leisurely exploration of hands and mouth, the languorous pleasure of being entirely unhurried. There's a sweet torture in forcing my own desire to wait, to submit to his slow, sure kisses, the subtle stroking of his hands along my hips, my waist. He unpins my hair and lets it tumble through his fingers, growling in the back of his throat as he twines handfuls of it and draws my head back to mouth my neck. Moonlight spills across the terrace, turning his body to carved marble and the night to utter magic.

When finally he hitches my legs around him and carries me to the bedroom, my mind is gone, lost in a sensual river of desire. He lays me gently across the vast bed and lowers himself beside me, one muscled leg thrown over mine, locking me down as he catches my breasts with his mouth. I strain against him, moaning softly, and he holds one nipple and then the other in the heat of his mouth, plying them with his tongue until I'm half lost with it. My hands clutch at his hair, the breadth of his shoulders, pressing him to me and myself into him. His cock burns against my hip, and he doesn't push me away when I reach for him, groaning onto my nipple when I grasp his shaft and start slowly pumping him. He tortures my breasts until I'm writhing beneath his leg and his cock is a throbbing weapon in my hand.

"I don't want to wait," I gasp, arching up.

He raises his head and smiles darkly. "I know what you want, Lucia. Haven't you learned that by now?"

Hooking my leg over his arm, he enters me smoothly, deeply, and so surely it takes my breath away. "You're so swollen," he mutters, surging into me. "There's nothing like this, Lucia. Being inside you. Your heat, your scent . . ." He plunges deep into me, and I wrap my legs around him, pulling him even deeper. We stay like that for an endless moment, rocking slowly together, inexorably pushing us both toward the pinnacle.

"I can always tell when you're close," he murmurs in my hair, pushing up just a fraction so he hits that place inside me that makes me scream aloud. "And that first scream," he growls. "You don't know how much I love hearing you fucking scream, Lucia."

"It's you," I gasp, my feet locking at the ankles, trying to pull him even further into me. "It's like you're touching every place inside me. You're so big, Roman. So fucking hard . . ." He withdraws and thrusts into me, hard, and I scream again.

"That's it," he growls in my ear. "You can feel it coming now, can't you, *milaia*? I can feel you, starting to come on my cock . . ."

I scream again, his words throwing me over the edge. The spasms start deep in the base of my spine, spiraling up exquisitely slowly, and he holds himself deep inside me, rocking slightly, drawing out the ecstasy until it's almost unbearable. "Fuck, Lucia," he mutters in my ear. "I've never felt anything so tight and hot in my goddamn life."

"*Argh!*" I'm lost, barely even aware of my own screams as the waves crash over me. Roman is roaring above me as he thrusts deep and holds, his searing heat exploding inside me, pumping with every contraction of my body around him.

The climax is shattering, a mind-blowing, full-body explosion that takes a long time to settle. When finally Roman withdraws from me, I open my eyes to find him staring at me, his face shadowy and oddly grave.

"Sleep, *milaia*," he whispers, kissing my forehead. "I'll be here when you wake."

Too tired to argue, too happy to want to, and too satiated to do anything but obey, I close my eyes and drift off, safe in the hard circle of Roman's embrace.

ROMAN

I'm in the shower when my phone rings. I ignore it, not least because I currently have Lucia's legs hitched around my waist, fucking her slowly against the tiles as water cascades around us. Abby and Dimitry have taken the children for a walk, and Lucia's father is off doing his physical therapy. Since the night in the castle, we've stolen every moment we can, and some we really shouldn't have. The kids have stopped looking for Lucia in her room in the morning and instead taken to knocking on my door and commanding us to get up. Even Ofelia seems to have accepted the new normal without so much as a flicker of an eye. Only around Lucia's father have we been discreet, although that old bastard doesn't miss a trick, so I'm pretty sure he knows exactly what's going on.

I'm not sure how I'd feel about that in his place. But I'm too old to apologize to anyone for taking what I want. And I'm too far gone to pretend I don't want Lucia. Every moment of every day, in every possible fucking way I can.

"Oh," she gasps now, bucking against me. "Oh, Roman . . ."

I thrust harder into her. Christ, she feels exquisite. It's as if I've spent a lifetime eating dinner, without ever understanding what food really tastes like. Lucia is a banquet that never ceases to enthrall me. Making love to her is endlessly fascinating, an all-consuming desire that is fast becoming an obsession.

I hold her ass and rock slowly deep inside her. This is where I lose myself. This moment when I'm so far into her body that I don't know where I end and she begins. And somehow, every time I get here, it feels new.

"Roman . . ." Her eyes flutter closed, and her mouth opens. I cover it with my hand to muffle her screams, grinning darkly as she bites down on the flesh of my palm. I'm getting better at knowing exactly when she's going to shriek the house down.

Her body begins to quiver and shake, her muffled screams vibrating against my hand. The phone rings again just as I erupt inside her.

"*Khuy.*" I pull reluctantly out of her, kissing her swollen mouth. "I'm sorry, *milaia*. I have to take this."

"Uh-huh," she says dreamily, swaying underneath the water. I wash off and step out of the shower, the sight of her body, flushed from lovemaking, making me half hard again as I towel off.

"This better be an emergency," I snarl into the phone, still staring at Lucia. She's watching me through slitted eyes, soaping her body in a way that's doing nothing to make my cock go down.

"Well!" Inger's shrill indignation manages to deflate my hard-on faster than an ice bath. I walk into the bedroom, closing the bathroom door behind me, and pull on some clothes.

"What is it, Inger?" I do my best to keep my voice level.

"It would have been nice to be informed that *my children* were taking part in a public performance. I don't recall giving my consent for—"

"You were informed." I cut her off mid-rant. "Every decision I make about the children is emailed to you directly."

"I *work*, Roman. I can't be expected to open every email your assistant sends." Her whining tone sets my teeth on edge. "It was only because darling Nicky texted me photos that I—"

"*Darling Nicky?*" I laugh scornfully. "Darling Nicky was at the parade for a total of about five minutes, and believe me, the kids were a lot happier when he left."

"Don't be silly. They love him. They spent all that time with him last summer on the *Guapa*, Yuri's yacht." Her tone is faintly accusatory, which really makes me gnash my teeth.

Yuri's fucking yacht was one of the red flags that brought the authorities down on us in the first place. The fact that it took me almost six years to convince him the *Guapa* was an extremely dangerous, not to mention fucking expensive, indulgence that we do not need still pisses me off. Maybe it's the street kid in me, but toys for the sake of appearances have never appealed to me. I can't see the point in maintaining a floating goddamn palace just so that everyone knows I'm as rich as *Forbes* already reports me as being.

The fact that Nicky flew over to the States, without bothering to inform me, and took Inger and the kids for a month-long jaunt around the Caribbean, on a yacht I was still paying for, pissed me off beyond recognition. It still does.

In the end I brought the damned thing back to Spain and lived on it until the penthouse renovations were finished. Partly to piss Nicky off, but mainly because I figured I might as well make use of it. I finally managed to convince Yuri to sell the *Guapa* six months ago, which pissed Nicky off even more, since I'm pretty sure he'd been planning to use it as party central the minute I vacated it.

I hear the shower stop running. I need to wrap this up. "What do you want, Inger?"

"Well." Her voice takes on a sulky edge. "I told you I'd be coming back to Spain for a visit soon. For the Russian Cultural Society Benefit."

"Sure," I say blankly. I vaguely remember her saying something about it.

"Well, it's on in two months. I know how hopeless you are with these things, so I'm going to contact your assistant to put it on your calendar. I want you to escort me, and I want Ofelia to come, too. It's about time she started to attend charitable functions. And I've been a patron of the RCS since before she was born. It's part of her heritage, Romie."

I roll my eyes. Inger cares as much about charitable causes as she does about cockroaches. She just likes having her photograph taken and playing the part of Mikhail's grieving widow, despite the fact that they'd been divorced for some time before his death. Taking Ofelia just adds to the photo opportunity.

"Sure," I say again. I can manage one benefit, if it means keeping the peace. "Let my secretary know the dates."

"Ofelia will need a gown. Get that nanny to take her shopping. Although, going by her lion mask in Nicky's photos, she's got about as much fashion sense as I'd expect from a South American illegal."

The bathroom door opens, and Lucia's magnificent naked body emerges, flushed from the shower. I grin darkly. "That's true enough. Lucia's not really one for clothes."

Lucia throws her towel at me and I duck, grinning.

"Well, then find someone who is. Anyway, Romie, I have to rush. Send kisses to the children."

"Sure." I hang up and throw the phone onto the bed, then put my arms around Lucia and start kissing her neck.

"Roman!" She pushes me away half-heartedly. "The children will be back any minute. We can't."

"We can." I pull her against my hardening cock.

"Who was that you were telling about me wearing no clothes? Oh," she gasps, as I slip a finger inside her.

"That," I say, marveling at how wet she is, "was the children's god-awful mother, Inger. She thinks that your lion mask means you don't know one end of a clothing store from another. I told her that clothes aren't really your specialty. Not that I'm complaining, mind you."

"Roman!" Her indignation only makes me laugh more. "You can't joke about things like . . . *ah*," she squeals, as I find her still-swollen clit. "No." She struggles feebly, although she's half laughing. "What did Inger want?"

"Some stupid charity thing she wants to take Ofelia to." I tear my shorts off with one hand, keeping my other inside Lucia. "Don't worry, it's months away. She probably won't turn up anyway."

Then I turn my attention to her mouth, swallowing any further protests in favor of far more important things.

———

When the phone next rings, the children are laughing in the kitchen with Lucia and I'm attempting to get some work done in between dips in the pool.

"Pavel." I stare at the laptop screen, studying some numbers, listening with half an ear.

"I've found something." The gravity of his tone gets my full attention.

"Speak."

"I think you need to see this."

I frown. "Can it wait a day? It's our last night. We're heading back to the city in the morning. The kids start school the day after tomorrow."

"Sorry." Pavel doesn't sound it. "But I think you'd rather see this as soon as possible."

Damn it. Pavel knows better than to fuck with my time. If he says I need to see it, then I do.

"Fine." I glance at my phone. "I'll be there in half an hour."

I end the call and go to the bedroom, pulling on jeans and a shirt as I go. The research facility is barely ten miles from the finca, which is one of the reasons I bought it in the first place. I'm all about convenience.

"Hey." I touch the base of Lucia's spine as I come into the kitchen. She jumps, casting a nervous glance at the kids. I grin. I actually love how she jumps every time I touch her when they're around. And the kids are starting to enjoy it, too. Ofelia rolls her eyes.

"Oh my goodness," she says with exaggerated sarcasm. "Like we don't all *know* what you guys are up to. You're not exactly subtle."

Lucia's face flames red. "Um," she mumbles.

Masha looks up with interest from some food mixture she's half covered in. "Why your face red, Luce?"

"Because she's been a bad, bad girl," says Abby cheerfully, winking at me. Dimitry guffaws in the corner, then hastily tries to conceal it with a cough.

"Abby!" Lucia shoots daggers at her friend.

"Oh, I don't know." I kiss Lucia's cheek, which makes Masha giggle. "I'd say she's been pretty good, actually."

"Roman!" Lucia gasps in horror.

"OMG." Ofelia clamps her hands over her ears. "Children are present, people."

"Gross." Mickey shakes his head, but he's grinning at his laptop screen.

"Hey, Mickey." He raises his head. "Want to come hang out with Pavel for a bit? I've got to go to Hale Tech to check something out." The way his face lights up makes me feel a hundred feet tall.

"Yeah," he says enthusiastically. "That'd be super cool."

"Right." I kiss Lucia again, thoroughly enjoying the volcano of color on her face. "We'll be back for dinner, okay? Sorry about this." I shake my head at Dimitry when he stands up. "All good, brother. I'd rather you stay here."

"Copy that." He sits down again, pulling Abby between his knees.

"Double gross," mutters Ofelia, shaking her head as she waves me off.

I take the Maybach, since Luis has the day off.

"Wow," says Mickey as we pull out of the garage. "This car is *so* cool."

I realize, with a now familiar twinge of shame, that I've never actually had the kids in my car before. *So many things I've never shared with them.*

"I'll teach you to drive it another time, if you want."

"That would be *awesome*," he breathes.

"Then it's a deal." I wink at him as I take the Maybach around a bend rather too quickly. "But maybe we won't mention that part to Luce or your sisters, okay?" He nods so emphatically I almost laugh.

"So you've been to the software facility before," I say. "You know the deal—you can hang out in the tech center while I talk to Pavel. I'll send him in to you when we're done."

"Uh-huh." He gives me a sideways look. "But I'm not allowed down in the server center, right?"

I glance at him, rather taken aback.

"I'm not an idiot, Roman." He meets my eyes steadily. "I could hack into the Spanish government's mainframe when I was twelve. I know you've got a whole thing going on underneath the facility."

"Huh." I'm not entirely sure what to say to that.

"Papa used to take us there all the time when we were little," Mickey goes on. He's watching me carefully, as if weighing how much he can say. I keep my eyes on the road and let him talk. "When Mama first left, before all the nannies."

All the nannies. I try not to wince. *I should have fucking been there.* But I'd been too busy back then, too focused, to consider offering my help in looking after the kids. Anyway, I'd always stayed away from Mikhail's domestic life, except for birthdays and Christmas. I didn't want to get involved. To be relied on.

"I guess Papa thought we were too young to understand what we were seeing," Mickey is saying. "Ofelia didn't get it. She wasn't really interested, anyway. And Masha was just a baby."

"But you did understand?" I glance at him.

"Not at first. It wasn't until last year, on the yacht, that I started to get curious."

"The yacht?" That gets my attention. "Why was that?" I try to keep my voice casual.

"It was something Uncle Nicky said to Mama. He thought we were all asleep, but I was still awake, gaming on my computer. I wasn't trying to listen," he says, slightly defensively. "But they were talking right outside my room."

"It's okay." I smile reassuringly at him. "You're not in trouble. What was it you heard?"

"Uncle Nicky was complaining that you don't include him in everything, and Mama asked what he meant, because you'd given him that nightclub. Pillars. Anyway," he goes on, "Nicky said that he should 'have a piece' of the software facility. Mama asked what was so special about the facility, and Uncle Nicky said that you don't dig up acres of mountain behind a high-security fence if you're just making software." He shrugs. "Then just recently, Luce mentioned something about it. I know what a server center is, and I started to think back to when we visited with Papa. I figured it out, I guess. Also, the facility produces *really* boring software. Like, kid's stuff." His contempt is so like that of my tech heads that it almost makes me laugh.

Except for the fact that what he's saying is dangerous enough to put me on high alert.

"Did you mention any of that to Nikolai?" Despite my best efforts, I can hear the tension in my voice.

"Of course not!" Mickey's indignation is too raw to be fake. "I'd never tell anyone about what you and Papa do. Did," he corrects himself quietly, and I feel a pang of sadness. It should be Mikhail sitting here, talking to his son, teaching him about the family business.

But Mikhail isn't here. You are. And Mercura is Mickey's family business.

I didn't intend to start involving Mickey, or any of the kids, in Mercura, or any of our businesses. They're just kids. But suddenly I realize how naive that is. They're already involved. They've lost their father, and their grandfather is in jail. They spend their lives surrounded by security, and in the knowledge that they're in danger.

"I've looked it all up online," Mickey says, as if to confirm my thoughts. "I know why Deda Yuri went to jail. I know what they say about Hale Property, that it's just a front for our other businesses." His casual use of the word *our* is strangely touching. "And I know that you . . . well, I know that the men who killed Papa aren't alive anymore."

I shift uncomfortably in my seat. "Mickey, I—"

"I'm glad those men are dead." Startled, I look at him properly. His face is set and hard, oddly mature for the boy he still is. "I know it isn't right to feel that way," he says quietly. "But they killed Papa. At least now they can't hurt Ofelia or Masha."

There's no bravado in his tone. He's not trying to impress me or act tough. He means every word.

I've always known Mickey is fiercely intelligent. His report cards are off the chart, and Pavel has mentioned more than once that his abilities are above average. A year ago one of his teachers actually suggested that Mickey was wasting his time in her classes, and that his abilities in math and science already outstripped her own.

But until now, I never realized that he's strong, too.

Mickey isn't a child playing on computers. He's a young man who has lost his father and never really had a mother. And he's a brother who is determined to keep his sisters safe.

He might be only just fourteen, but I can already see the man he's going to become. A man his father would have been truly proud of.

No thanks to me.

I'm just sorry I didn't see it earlier.

"Mickey." I pull the car into the Mercura parking garage and switch it off, turning to face him. "I'm sorry you've had to work all this out on your own. And there's nothing wrong with feeling glad those men are dead. You're right," I say steadily, speaking to him as I would to any man. "They can't hurt you anymore. Sometimes we have to deal with enemies that way. I don't like it, and I know you don't. But that is the life we lead. Sometimes, it's necessary."

He nods slowly, his eyes on mine big and solemn.

"I don't want to lie to you about what is underneath Hale Tech. I always intended to tell you about it, one day. I guess I just wanted to protect you for as long as I could. To keep you safe. Because what we're doing here is dangerous, Mickey. I need to know that you understand that."

"Dangerous." He cracks a smile that takes me by surprise.

"You're explaining to *me* how dangerous technology can be? Seriously? You can't even convert a PDF document."

I laugh aloud at that, shaking my head.

"I underestimated you, Mickey. I'm sorry, okay? But what you're about to see would mean the end of us all, if anyone ever finds out. I can bring you inside it. But once I do, there's no going back. I'm not sure your father would have approved of me doing that, while you're so young. And I'm pretty sure Lucia would kill me if she knew we were even having this conversation."

"I'm not a kid, Roman." Mickey's eyes narrow, and I see a steel in them that I never really noticed before. "I have an IQ of 180. That makes me technically a genius, in case you don't know that stuff." He half smiles. "I act a lot slower than I am. It's easier that way. People leave me alone."

I look at him curiously. "How did I not know all this?"

He shrugs. "Because people see what they want to see. Even you. And what most people see is a geeky kid in glasses who can't talk to people." That makes me actually laugh out loud.

"Well, Mickey," I say, opening the car door and stepping out, "come with me. You're about to meet a whole lot of people just like you."

41

ROMAN

Mickey slips into the tech head group like he was born into it. It's almost amusing, how fast they recognize one of their own. Within minutes he's glued to a screen, laughing at some joke I don't understand and completely absorbed by whatever the fuck the little symbols on the screen mean. I haven't explained Mercura to him yet. There'll be time for that, although I suspect that by the time we leave, he'll probably know more about how it works than I do.

I leave him to it and follow Pavel into the private office. "It's good to see Mickey here." He touches a key, and the screen bursts into life. "He's too smart for light and sound shows at a parade, boss."

"I'm starting to get that." I lean over his chair. "What am I looking at?"

"An academic paper by one Lawrence Carter Rydell." Pavel

grins at me. "Aka paparazzi journalist Lance Ryder." The journalist's shiny smile appears onscreen, and my fingers tighten on the back of Pavel's chair.

I'd love to shove those gleaming white teeth straight down the fucker's throat.

"What you told me at the parade, about the Naryshkin Treasure, was the missing link. It turns out that Lance is just the name he uses as a byline on pap pieces, which is why I couldn't find anything on him before. Lawrence Carter Rydell, however, is the very posh son of an aristocratic British mother and wealthy American father. He grew up between London and Miami. Daddy was a hedge fund man, Mummy had the posh connections. Lawrence was educated at Eton, then later, Oxford. This was his final paper." He clicks back to the academic paper.

"'The Redistribution of Imperial Russian Wealth in the Soviet Union,'" I read aloud. I frown. "So this fucker studied Russian history?"

"Not just history. He studied linguistics, learned to speak Russian fluently. Even spent time in Russia. According to this paper, his particular area of interest was the so-called Naryshkin Treasure. I've sent you a copy in case you're interested."

"So our boy likes Russian treasure stories. What's this got to do with him chasing Lucia?"

"Everything." Pavel clicks again, this time to a news story. "Ten years ago, Lawrence's nice life came crashing down when Rydell senior was found dead in his Miami mansion. Turns out he had a small gambling problem. And Rydell senior wasn't just using his own money. He also dipped into the hedge fund he was managing, to the tune of several million. Gambling is mostly illegal in Florida, so his favorite places to lose money were high-stakes private card games. Clearly he got in too deep with the wrong people. His death was supposedly a suicide."

I scan the article briefly. "Bratva hit," I say curtly when I finish.

"Since the Russians run nearly all the card games in Florida, it definitely looks that way. Lawrence certainly thought so. He went on a one-man mission to track down his father's killer. His family was completely bankrupt, and after his father's disgrace, none of his old connections wanted anything to do with him. He started writing freelance articles about Russian crime families. He pitched them to the likes of the *New York Times* and *Washington Post*, but nobody really gave a shit about some Russians running a game in Miami. He wasn't subtle, asked questions in the wrong places, and caught the attention of the wrong people. The only reason he didn't wind up in a ditch like his father was because nobody actually printed his articles.

"Then he started pitching the tabloids instead and found his audience." He clicks again. "This was the last article he wrote under his own name."

My heart stops.

Lucia's face is front and center on the screen.

She's a lot younger, sure, but it's unmistakably her.

"Darya Petrovsky." Pavel's voice has a satisfied edge. He spins in his chair, clearly pretty happy with himself. "She's the daughter of Russian bratva legend Sergei Petrovsky, who, I'm guessing, is the old man currently hanging out in your finca."

All I can hear is my father's voice: *"Go to Sergei Petrovsky's compound. He'll take care of you . . ."*

The room spins around me, past and present colliding in a weird slipstream. Pavel's voice seems to come from a long distance. I have to force myself to concentrate on what he's saying.

"According to this article, Darya and Sergei disappeared

from Miami about six years ago." Pavel clicks to the next page. "The Petrovsky bratva virtually ran Miami until Sergei's first stroke, a decade ago. He lay in a coma for months. Nobody thought he'd survive, which is probably why there was a coup, led by this guy. Vilnus Orlov."

He enlarges one of the pictures. My gut churns as Vilnus fucking Orlov's brutish, narrow-eyed face stares back at me.

"Problem was," Pavel goes on, "Old Man Petrovsky didn't die from his stroke. Orlov had killed all of the Petrovsky brigadiers and was in control of the Coconut Grove compound. There was no reason to spare the old man, yet instead of killing him, Orlov brought him home to the compound. The reason why Orlov didn't just knock off his rival is a mystery that fascinated Lawrence." He clicks back to the photo of Lawrence Carter Rydell. "He had a whole stack of wild theories about the Petrovskys, who, incidentally, he blames for killing his father. This article claims that for four years after Sergei's stroke, the Petrovskys and Orlovs all lived together in the Petrovsky compound in Coconut Grove. Just one big unhappy family. Except for Lucia's—I mean Darya's— mother, that is. Her body turned up on a Miami beach about two years into the party. She'd clearly been enduring torture for a long time. She was covered in scars and had been repeat- edly sexually assaulted."

I want to punch something. I want to hit something so badly I have to clench my hands into fists to stop myself putting them through the nearest wall.

All I can see are the scars beneath the Orlov tattoo on Lucia's back. The thought of Vilnus Orlov putting his hands on her, of taking a knife to her beautiful body, makes me so fucking dangerous that I almost don't trust myself to speak.

"Go on," I say through gritted teeth, glad Pavel can't see my face.

"Lawrence clearly attracted a bit too much attention with

this article. He was shut out of Russian circles, probably had his life threatened. He disappeared from the Miami scene and reemerged a year or so later in London, under the name Lance Ryder. Had a whole new ID made, changed the way he looked. He didn't lose interest in the story, but he did get smarter. He made his latter pieces more puff and gossip, clickbait shit nobody takes that seriously. Like this one a couple of years ago, when he photographed Alexei Petrovsky attending a Russian Society ball in Miami. Alexei is Lucia's—Darya's —brother."

I study the picture. Alexei resembles his father. Blond, tall and rangy, with Sergei's hawkish features and deep-set blue eyes, although one is covered by an eye patch.

Courtesy of the fucking Orlovs, no doubt.

"Ryder makes a big deal out of the fact that despite being a prisoner of the Orlovs, Alexei Petrovsky still apparently runs his father's empire, albeit on a tight Orlov rein. And this is where Ryder's old academic papers meet the modern tabloid world." He clicks again, and then, with a dramatic flourish, indicates a tabloid headline on the screen. "Behold," he says theatrically. "Ryder's theory about the Petrovsky family."

Is the Naryshkin Treasure Buried Right Here in Miami?
The secret reason the Petrovsky crime family have survived the bloodiest coup in bratva history.

I SCAN the tawdry article beneath a grainy photograph of Alexei, trying to keep a neutral expression with no small effort.

"So," I say curtly when I'm sure my voice is steady. "Ryder

believes Sergei Petrovsky is, in fact, Sergei Naryshkin. The son of a prince, raised in a Russian gulag. He theorizes that Prince Naryshkin had a fortune in pre-revolutionary treasure, hidden in a vault beneath the Naryshkin family estate in Russia that the communists couldn't manage to break into. Ryder theorizes the old prince taught Sergei how to open the family vault. When Sergei left the gulag, he broke into the Naryshkin estate and escaped with the fortune locked away there, including some missing imperial Fabergé eggs."

I don't allow myself to think about the Swiss lockbox.

I know, without any doubt, where one of those missing imperial eggs is.

And the name Sergei, while not unusual, is too much of a coincidence to sit easily with me.

"Ryder thinks the eggs are the reason the Petrovsky clan rose so rapidly in the Miami crime world," I go on, working hard to keep my voice steady. "According to this article, he thinks the Orlovs launched a coup on the Petrovskys to gain control of the rumored treasure, but for some reason couldn't find it. So they kept first Sergei, and now Alexei, alive because they have either information or the means to access what the Orlovs want. That's also why they tortured Sergei's wife, trying to make him talk."

"More importantly," says Pavel, glancing at me, "Ryder thinks that's why Sergei and his daughter ran from Miami. His theory is that Sergei left Alexei in charge and saved his daughter from suffering the same fate as her mother. But when they disappeared, they took either the fortune itself or the means to access it. Ryder's theory is that Alexei is the Orlovs' ace in the hole to trade for it when they eventually catch up with Sergei and his daughter."

I stand back from the screen and eyeball Pavel. "And you believe this shit?"

He shrugs. "Ryder does. He's a rich kid who found himself

bankrupt. Went from having membership at every club that matters to being refused entry to any of them. He's been reduced to grubbing a living from snapping pics of Z-list celebrities he despises. He wants to believe in buried treasure, and my bet is that he's trying to get a piece of it. From where Ryder sits, I think he believes he's actually entitled to it. He's definitely obsessed with the story." He meets my eyes somberly. "And he knows Lucia is Darya, boss. That much I think we need to be sure of."

I drum my fingers on the back of his chair, my head spinning.

"Oh. I almost forgot. There's one other thing," Pavel says. "It's about the trojan virus." He throws me a manila file. "You can get Mickey to explain the details if you want, but basically, the upload didn't come from Pillars. That is, the user hijacked their high-speed connection, but the actual upload came from a mobile location close by. Most likely a yacht at the marina."

"Ryder?"

"Our best guess is yes," he says, "but we don't know for certain. Going by his obsession with Russian bratva, though, I think it's a pretty good guess."

"That's a problem."

Pavel looks uncomfortable. This is the part of my business he stays out of. It's a conversation for me and Dimitry, rather than the tech heads. "This is good work, Pavel." I stand up, clapping him on the shoulder, and he looks relieved. "And you know what the best part is?"

He looks at me uneasily. My lips twitch. I'm never really going to tire of fucking with the tech heads. "Now," I say genially, "you can get the fuck on with the Mercura launch, instead of playing detective."

The relief on his face is almost comical. "Thank God," he says fervently. Then, clearly realizing how he sounded, he looks at me nervously. "I mean—that is, I didn't mean—"

"I should fucking hope not," I say sternly, suppressing my laughter with no small effort. I wish Dimitry was here. These moments are just wasted when I'm alone. "Go on, then," I add, nodding at the door. "Fuck off."

Pavel scurries out, leaving me with a picture of Lance Ryder—or whatever the fuck his name is—and an absolute fuckton of questions.

IN THE END, though, I decide my questions are going to have to wait.

If I've learned one thing over the years, it's to trust my gut. And my gut says I need every fucking piece of this puzzle in my hands before I start piecing it all together. So I shove Lance Ryder and the Naryshkin Treasure into my mental vault and instead apply myself to the one thing currently demanding my attention: Mickey.

"And Pavel gave me an actual job to do, but I don't think he thought I'd be able to do it, but I did, in, like, five minutes."

I've never heard him speak so much, nor so breathlessly. I shift gear around the bend and keep listening.

"And so Pavel said I should come back, and they'd show me more about what they're doing, but he said it was up to you. But, like, can I?" Mickey turns to me, his eyes shining. "I mean, I know I don't know exactly what you're working on there, and I get that you can't tell me, but even if I could do small bits . . ." His voice trails off hopefully.

I've been thinking about this in the back of my mind since our conversation on the way to the lab. Instead of answering immediately, I pull the car to the side of the road, so we can have a proper conversation. "Tell me something, Mickey. Have you ever had a girlfriend? Or boyfriend," I add hastily. "Whatever. You know what I mean."

He stares at me, his face slowly coloring. "Why would you ask me that?" he mumbles uncomfortably.

"I'll tell you why. Those guys you were hanging out with in the lab? Most of them started working for me when they weren't that much older than you are now. My people found them in basements and school classrooms, hacking into the same kind of shit you're undoubtedly hacking into now. That's the thing about the fun little games you've been playing, Mickey. Sooner or later, someone notices. It's just a question of who and when. And when someone offers a teenager a huge fucking salary and unlimited access to all the tech they need, do you think anyone ever says no?"

He frowns. "I guess not."

"Nope. But these are guys who've spent most of their lives in front of a screen. Most of them were geeks at school, too focused on what they were hacking into to care much about friendships, let alone relationships. Want to know what those guys spend every minute doing when they're not working for me, Mickey?"

He nods, but by the color on his face, he knows what I'm about to say.

"They're either watching porn, gaming with long-distance and usually unobtainable people they'll never meet, or creating avatars of the objects of their desire. Let me tell you what they aren't doing. They aren't actually dating. They're not out in the world, learning how to interact with other people. They're living off pizza and soda instead of taking care of their physical bodies. Typing instead of talking. And the closest most of them have ever come to actually making love to anyone is on the other end of a virtual reality headset."

Mickey's eyes are glued to my face. He gulps nervously but doesn't say anything.

"I know you're far too smart for school. So sooner or later, you're going to have to make a choice—do you want a career in academia, in government, or in private business? If your goal is to win the Nobel, then you need to stop hacking and get into academia. If your goal is to work for the government, well." I grin. "You and I probably need to part ways pretty soon." He laughs at that. "And if you want to run the business your father left behind, then you need to listen to what I'm going to say."

"I don't care about academia," Mickey says. "I mean, I get the importance of the piece of paper. But I don't want to go into research. And I definitely don't want to work for any government agencies." His lip curls in a way that reminds me so much of Mikhail it's uncanny. "History doesn't have much nice to say about government agencies."

I chuckle. "Probably not. Okay, then. Here's what I think we should do. You keep going to school. Play the game. Keep your head down, like you have been doing. Stay under the radar, but start enjoying being there. Take up a sport, go to school dances. I can help you," I say, when he looks uncomfortable. "I'll make a deal with your school so you only attend part-time. I'll tell them you have a private tutor or something. Two days a week, you come to the lab and work with the tech kids. Start learning the family business. I'll make sure you get to do all the illegal stuff you can handle, but you'll do it in my center, under Pavel's supervision. No more hacking with your friends at school, or from home. And you agree to let me help you get fit and strong." I fix him with a stern look. "You've seen enough by now to know that our business gets violent. If you want a place in it, you need to learn how to handle your-self. Are you prepared to commit to that?"

Mickey bites his lip uncomfortably. "What if I'm no good at it?"

"Ha!" I laugh. "You know how big Dimitry is, right?"

He nods.

"Well. When I first met him, Dimitry was a scrawny kid

who couldn't land a punch. He was getting beat on all the time."

Mickey's eyes widen. "Seriously?"

"Yup." I wink. "But don't ever tell him that I told you that. So what do you think?"

He's already nodding enthusiastically. "Yes. I can do that. Yeah, that would actually be super cool."

"Good." I turn back to the wheel and pull the car onto the road.

"Uncle Roman?"

"Hmm?"

"Do you think that if I . . . get fit, and do . . . what you said, like with school dances and stuff, that I might have a girlfriend one day?"

I grin. It amuses me that after the confident young man I spoke to in the car earlier, I'm now talking to the uncertain teenage boy who is desperately in need of reassurance. "I think I can guarantee that you will, mate."

He digests that for a moment.

"Uncle Roman . . . about Lucia."

Darya, you mean.

My hands clench the steering wheel, but I keep my voice even. "What about her, Mickey?"

"She's your girlfriend, right?"

I keep my eyes staring straight ahead, trying rapidly to think of how best to answer that one.

"We don't mind," Mickey says quietly. "None of us do. We like her. I just thought you should know that."

"That's good." I grip the steering wheel and start taking the bends a bit faster. "I'm glad you like her."

Except that after everything I've just learned, I'm not so sure that I should be glad about that at all. I'm not sure that allowing the kids to get attached to Lucia is even safe. And as for her being my girlfriend, as Mickey put it?

The truth is, I don't know what the fuck Lucia is to me now.

Darya.

Ever since she came into my home, I've been gradually breaking every rule I've ever set for myself. Some of them I don't regret, like making the kids my priority. Part of me has always known I should have taken more responsibility for them, and now that I have, I know it's the right thing to do. For better or worse, Mikhail left his children in my care. At the least I owe it to him to make sure they're safe and loved.

But when it comes to how I feel about Lucia?

Darya.

I wrench the car around a corner with enough speed to make Mickey give me a side look.

Fuck.

If she knows even half of what Pavel has turned up, then Darya Petrovsky has been lying about a lot more than just her identity. And as much as I don't want to face it, there's more than just a chance that her presence in my house is no accident.

I need time to read through Lawrence Carter Rydell's paper. To find out about the Naryshkin family. Whether or not the journalist's theory is right about the name change to Petrovsky. And if so, what connection there might be between the Petrovskys and the Borovskys.

Because if my hunch is right—and they're rarely fucking wrong—then the Sergei I once overheard talking to my father in the kitchen is actually Sergei Petrovsky, aka Sergei Naryshkin, heir to a legendary fortune.

The same man who my father trusted to get my mother to safety, and whose secrets he fucking died to protect, is now living in my villa. And his daughter is sleeping in my bed.

Can that really be a coincidence?

My entire focus all this time has been on making Lucia feel

safe. Gaining her trust. But she's never trusted me enough to so much as tell me her real name.

Now I'm left wondering if I've been played.

If she's an enemy, I'll find out. I've never let emotions get in the way of business, and I'm not about to start now.

Except that the thought of putting a bullet between those beautiful almond-shaped eyes makes me sick to the gut. And even the suspicion that she might have been playing me all this time is like feeling the earth crack under my feet.

Worst of all, I've got nobody to blame but myself. For breaking my own rules. For letting her into my home without knowing everything I needed to. For making this about anything more than just sex.

I should have stuck to that contract. Better yet, I should have fucked her and then walked away.

But it's too late for that now. Lucia—*fucking Darya*—is in my house now. In my children's lives. Which means I'm going to have to just let this one play out, at least for a while. No matter how furious I am.

I grip the steering wheel hard and take the bends home at a high enough speed to turn Mickey's face white.

I have no fucking idea who to trust, nor how to make sense of any of this.

42

LUCIA

"**I** thought you might like to have dinner with us."

"I can't." Roman cuts me off before I've barely finished speaking. "We're flat out here. Some other time." He hangs up before I have a chance to argue.

What the fuck?

I stare at the blank phone screen in frustration. It's been like this since we got back to Malaga. Correction: it's been like this since the day Roman and Mickey went to Hale Tech together.

I have no idea what happened between them, but something clearly did. For starters, Mickey's now doing three days a week at school instead of five and spending the other two cloistered somewhere with Roman, not that either of them have bothered to explain to me why or what they're doing.

Far more upsetting is that in the two weeks since we got back, I've gone from spending every night in Roman's bed to sleeping alone. The nights he joins the kids for dinner, he mostly gives me the evening off. On the odd occasion when our paths actually cross, he's polite but incredibly distant.

Every bit of the intimacy we shared at the finca is gone. I don't know why, and I don't know how to breach the gap.

I open the oven and put a tray of cookies inside. Baking always calms me. I've baked enough lately that Chef has begun complaining that I've made him redundant. I've just finished a tray of *alfajores*, not least because they remind me of Roman. Part of me is hoping he'll smell them from the elevator again and come in, like he did the first day I made them.

Maybe he just got tired of me.

I haven't wanted to face this particular option, but it's kind of an inescapable logic. One moment Roman was taking me for dinner, saying that he wanted it to be my choice to stay with him and making love to me like I was a precious ornament.

The moment I made it clear that I actually *wanted* to be with him, he disappeared.

Classic emotional avoidance.

I was a challenge, nothing more. Roman got what he wanted and then lost interest.

I pull out the bowl of bread dough I've left rising on the windowsill and tip it onto the flour-covered countertop. I need to pummel something.

Is he seeing someone else?

I punch the dough with a lot more force than is required. Even imagining some other woman putting her hands on Roman makes me want to tear them both apart.

Which is dangerous. Roman isn't mine, no matter what we were before we came back to Malaga. In the end, what have we really had? A fuckton of amazing sex and a few cozy family moments. It's hardly the love affair of the century.

Even if it felt that way. Even if that week, it finally felt like I had a family.

Because whatever he was playing at when he handed me back that contract, I'm still technically just an employee.

Turning the dough over, I slap it into shape, biting down on the tears that keep threatening to spill. Abby's been calling daily, but I really can't confide in her. Papa keeps asking where Roman is. And he's recently started to watch me with a concerned look that doesn't bode well, so I've been avoiding him, too. Which is hard, since Masha has become so attached to him that she's constantly bugging me to visit. Worst of all, Ofelia is far too perceptive for her own good. She, however, doesn't ask me questions. She just watches me when she thinks I'm not looking, with wary, worried eyes that break my heart. I know she's afraid I'm going to leave. The worst thing is, I can't reassure her that I won't. I don't want to lie to her. And the way Roman's been behaving, I'm not entirely sure I won't be evicted at any moment.

Damn it. I toss the bread dough this way and that, kneading it into oblivion. *This is what happens when you open up, Darya.* I brush impatiently at my eyes. *You never should have let your emotions become involved. You shouldn't have agreed to this craziness in the first place.*

I'm almost glad when Abby calls. "You and I are hanging out tomorrow night," she announces. "No arguments. I know it's your night off, and I never get to see you anymore."

"That's probably because you're spending most nights underneath the tasty bodyguard." My voice is cheery, but I can't help feeling a twinge of envy. The irony is that the more distant Roman and I become, the closer Abby and Dimitry seem to be getting. From what I can tell, they're basically head over heels in love.

I should be happy for Abby.

I *am* happy for her.

But it hurts that barely two weeks ago, I was in exactly the same place, or I thought I was. Now I just feel lonely and confused.

"Well, there is that." Abby chuckles dirtily. "But I miss you, Luce. I want to catch up. Hear all the goss on CEO Man."

"You may as well call him Roman. You did spend an entire week dunking him in his pool."

"Nah." Her Australian accent toughens up. "He might be putty in your hands, but I gotta say, he's always gonna be CEO Man to me. That bastard is one tough nut to crack."

Curiosity gets the better of me. "What makes you say that?"

"Just that he's been riding Dimitry at work night and day ever since that week in the mountains. And by the multiple black eyes I've dressed, he's been taking Dimitry apart in the boxing ring on a regular basis, too. If I hadn't seen how hot he is for you when we were up at the farm, I'd have been worried for your safety, girl. But I do wonder how on earth you put up with him. He's so . . . grim."

I might have declined her invitation to go out. I'm not much one for partying, at all. But if I'm honest, the opportunity to pump Abby for information about Roman is too tempting to pass by.

"So," I say, keeping my tone deliberately light, "what have you got in mind for tomorrow night?"

"You mean Rapunzel's actually going to leave her tower?" Abby squeals. "That's fucking incredible. Okay. I know you hate going out, so what about a girl's night in? I'm thinking cocktails, get a meal delivered."

"Fine," I say, laughing. "But we're not going out. And definitely not to Pillars nightclub, okay?"

"Not a chance," she says scornfully. "I don't ever want to see that prick Miguel again. Did you know he was actually seeing two other girls at the same time he was seeing me? Unbelievable."

"Actually, I can. You know I never liked him. Dimitry is a hundred times better."

"I know, right?" Abby sighs. "I'm in real trouble with that one, Luce. Anyhow. I can't wait to tell you all about it tomorrow night. Come over in the afternoon, as soon as you can get away."

"Sure." I think of the Orlovs hunting me, the journalist who tracked me down at the parade, and what Roman might make of me heading out without security.

Then I remind myself that I'm not doing anything wrong. A night at Abby's is hardly hitting the town. I've done okay at looking out for myself for six years. And besides, Roman hasn't even remotely concerned himself with my whereabouts for over two weeks, and I've been just fine.

To hell with him.

He probably won't even notice I'm gone.

———

"You look amaaazing!" Abby kisses me on the cheek and drags me upstairs into her apartment. I've always loved her little walk-up. It's a cozy, bohemian space with a black-and-white-tiled floor, doors that open onto a tiny wrought iron balcony, and Abby's art equipment strewn around everywhere. It smells of paint and turpentine, with secondhand furniture and a sagging old couch that's perfect for curling up on.

"So." She opens a bottle of wine and pours us both enormous glasses. "Tell me everything."

"I'd rather hear about you and Dimitry." I clink glasses with her. "How's it all going?"

She tucks her legs underneath her. "Well, the sex is fucking amazing." I laugh and settle back to listen. Abby barely draws breath for the next hour, telling me all about how she and

Dimitry gradually got to know one another. "And I mean, it's good now," she says, "but he keeps so many secrets, you know? Like, I honestly don't know anything about what he does, really, other than that he works for Roman and is his regular punching bag."

She eyes me over her glass. "I don't suppose there's any point in asking you about it," she says half hopefully.

"No, I'm afraid." I shake my head, avoiding her eyes. "I know about as much as you do. I'm the au pair, and that's about as far into Roman's business as I go."

"Bullshit." Abby sits back, staring at me with rather less humor than a moment ago. "I get that you won't tell me the truth about your life, Luce. But at least be honest about what Roman is. Because I might be a lot of things, but I'm not an idiot. You two are a lot more than work associates, or at least you were two weeks ago. And Roman isn't just the CEO of Hale, any more than you're just a waitress from Argentina."

I swallow my wine, unsure what to say. Abby and I have always avoided the topic of my past. Hers too, for that matter. The last thing I was expecting was a full frontal assault.

"Look." She puts her glass on the rickety coffee table. "I have Google, Lucia. I know all about the Stevanovskys. I know Roman is the head of their organization, and so I'm guessing Dimitry is one of his . . ." She waves her hand in the air. "I don't know. What do they call it in the Russian bratva?"

"*Vor*." After so long, the word tastes strange on my lips. "They call them *vor*. Warrior."

"There you go." Abby picks up her glass again with a smug look. "And now we're actually talking."

"I can't talk about any of this, Abby." I turn my glass in my hand, feeling deeply unsettled. "If you've been googling Russian bratva, you know how dangerous their world is. So if you invited me here tonight to try to find out about Dimitry, I'm sorry, but I'm going to have to leave again."

"Their world, Luce? Or yours?" She leans forward, taking my hand. "I didn't invite you here to cross-examine you. But I'm frustrated. I feel like I'm living in the middle of something I don't understand. I'm falling in love with a man I barely know. And I've been screwed over so many times . . ." She shakes her head. "I'm just scared, I guess."

I'm just scared.

Heat rushes through my body. For a moment I think I might actually throw up. Then suddenly I'm freezing, so cold I'm actually shivering.

I burst into tears.

It takes me completely by surprise.

One moment I'm sitting on the couch, the tight knot of tension I've lived with for years a hard ball in my belly, trying to work out how best to answer Abby. The next moment, I'm crying. Red-faced, can't catch my breath, ugly crying. The kind of tear storm I haven't had since I was a small child.

I cover my face, unable to look at Abby. I will myself to stop, but I can't. The tears come thick and fast, shaking my whole body.

"Oh, baby." She scoots up the sofa and wraps her arms around me, rocking me soothingly. "I'm sorry."

"Not your fault," I sob. "Mine."

"No," Abby says, holding me. "It isn't your fault at all. Whatever this is, it isn't your fault."

I can't answer her. All I can do is cry.

"Let them come," she murmurs. "Just let it all out."

I don't know how long I stay like that, Abby saying soothing things, my tears completely soaking her shoulder. Finally the storm begins to subside. "It's going to be okay, Luce," she says, still holding me.

It's her use of my name that finally turns the tears off.

"Lucia isn't my name." I pull away from her, meeting her

eyes briefly. Abby just hands me a tissue. I blow my nose, not looking at her.

"Well, that's not exactly news." She gives me a wry smile.

"I know you suspected. It's not because I don't trust you that I haven't told you. It's just not safe." I shake my head. "Not for anyone. I guess for a while, I thought . . . I was. Safe. With Roman." I take a deep, shuddering breath that hurts my throat. "I think I got used to that feeling. But now . . ." My voice trails off.

"Now what, Luce?" Abby frowns at me. "By the way Roman was all over you at the farm, I'd say you were better than just *safe.*"

"He hasn't touched me since we left the finca," I whisper. "He barely looks at me, Abby. I think he regrets ever getting involved with me at all. And I have no idea why, or what I did." My voice breaks on the words.

"Oh, darling." She pulls me fiercely close as the tears come again, this time slowly, just steady weeping that won't quit.

"It was what you said about being scared." I breathe deeply, trying to still the sobs catching in my throat. "I've been scared for so fucking long, Abby. And I thought I wasn't anymore. That I didn't have to be." I shake my head, the tears slipping silently down my face. "Now I just can't face it," I say brokenly. "I can't face running again. Being scared all the time."

"Then don't," she says, rubbing my back. "I can help you, Luce. You don't have to run."

"You don't understand." I pull back, wiping my eyes tiredly and shaking my head. "This isn't something you can help with. I appreciate you offering, more than I can say. But I mean it. There's no way I can involve you in this." I grip her hand, suddenly afraid. "And you can't tell Dimitry. About any of it. Promise me, Abby."

"Of course I won't tell him." She is frowning worriedly at

me. "But I don't like this, Luce. Does Roman actually know the truth? About . . . whatever it is that you can't tell me?"

"No." I shake my head, sniffing back the tears. "Well, some of it he does. But not my real name. Not who I am. Not because I don't trust him. I do, Abby. I trust him more than anyone else I've ever met. But there are other people at risk. People I love. And their secrets aren't mine to tell, no matter how much I might want to."

She hands me the wineglass, and I take a deep gulp, then another. Right now, the thought of being lost in an alcoholic mist is incredibly appealing.

"For the record," Abby says thoughtfully, "I think you're wrong about Roman. I know assholes, Luce. And much and all as I think CEO Man is as grim as fucking winter, I don't think even he could fake the way I saw him looking at you. Which means that what you really need to do is talk to him."

"Ha." I swallow more wine. "He'd have to actually be around for me to do that."

"Well, then." She gets a calculating look on her face. "Maybe we just have to make him be around."

"No games, Abby." Even the thought of it makes me feel tired. "Whatever Roman's problem with me is, he isn't a man who takes kindly to being played."

I shake my head tiredly. I feel exhausted. Wrung out, completely emotionally drained.

"Let's just hang out here and drink wine." I reach for the bottle and top up my glass. "To be honest, all I really want to do tonight is get toasted enough to forget about the whole damn thing. Just for one night, I don't even want to think about Roman Stevanovsky. I just want to be Luce and Abs."

"Okay." Abby nods, giving me an understanding smile. "Then let's find that junky Spanish radio station you love, open another bottle, and do really bad dance moves in my kitchen."

We clink glasses, and I give her a watery smile. "That sounds amazing."

"Oh my goodness," I gasp, straightening up and rubbing my burning thighs. "Forget the gym. I should just drink and dance like this more often."

"Like nobody's watching, babyyyy," Abby says, waving her hands dreamily in the air. "Who needs a nightclub? This radio station is ridiculous. It's the bomb."

"I know." I dump more wine into my glass. "How is it that Spain can have an entire radio station dedicated to obscure '80s music the rest of the world has forgotten about? It actually makes Spotify redundant."

"One of the many reasons I straight-up love this country." She waves an empty bottle in the air. "That, and the fact that the vino is cheap. Which is lucky, since we've run out."

"Nooooo!" I flop onto the sofa. "This was poor planning on our part, Abs."

"We could go out dancing?" she says doubtfully.

"Nope." I shake my head. "Even if I was sober that would be a bad idea."

"Fine. There's a shop on the corner. I'll be back in twenty minutes." Abby reaches for her bag.

"No." I grab her hand. "I don't mean to be overprotective, Abs. But it isn't just me who's in danger right now."

She rolls her eyes. "Oh, man. You're as bad as Dimitry. He insists on picking me up from work every night. He even got all the locks on the apartment changed."

"I'm glad, Abs." I squeeze her hand. "Dimitry's a good man. I'm glad he's looking out for you."

"Yeah." She shoots me a shy smile. "Me, too. Ha!" Her eyes gleam suddenly. "Talking of that, maybe now is a good time to test his instructions that I should call, no matter the time, if I am, quote, *even thinking* about going outside on my own at night."

"You're shameless." I shake my head, laughing, as Abby takes out her phone. "Do you mind not mentioning that I'm here?"

"My lips are sealed." She punches out a text message. "Or rather my thumbs are. Oh, look, my experiment worked!" She beams at me. "Liquor delivery on the way."

ROMAN

"**I**f you think I'm getting back into that boxing ring, you can fucking think again." Dimitry glares at me. "I don't mind being your punching bag, Roman. But twelve days out of fourteen is starting to push the friendship. And Abby's starting to wonder why I turn up with a new black eye every couple of days."

"Suit yourself," I snarl, heading for the ring. "I'll find someone else to spar with."

"Good luck." He crosses his arms and raises his eyebrows. "Look around, brother. There's not another soul in the place. They've all started running the minute they see you walk in."

I glare around the studio.

Motherfucker's right. The place is empty.

"I'm going to give you some advice," Dimitry says. "And don't bother giving me the death stare. You know it doesn't work on me anyway."

"I'm not fucking interested."

"I don't give a shit." He moves in front of me. "Whatever's happened between you and Lucia, you need to fix it."

"Don't say that goddamn name." I thud my fist into a nearby bag, only barely restraining myself from landing it on Dimitry's face. "Ever. Don't ever say that name again."

His eyes narrow. "Wow. That might be a bit of a challenge. Seeing as, I don't know, she's *living* with you?"

"With the children. Whole different thing. And not for much fucking longer, so I wouldn't get attached." I thud another fist into the bag.

"Bullshit, Roman. If you wanted her out, she'd be gone already."

"Don't"—*thud*—"want"—*thud*—"to upset kids." I unleash a lightning left-right cross that sends the bag flying.

"Oh, right. So you're keeping Lu—keeping her around just to keep the kids happy." Dimitry leans against the wall, studying me, his arms still crossed.

"That's right." I avoid his eyes and keep thumping the bag. "They've had enough disruption already."

"And this has absolutely nothing to do with whatever it was Pavel uncovered about her."

I stop punching abruptly and swing around to face him. "What do you know about that?"

"Nothing, until just now." Dimitry's grin is at total odds with the sharp look in his eyes. "But I figured you must have found out something, and clearly I was right. Have you asked her straight-up about it?"

I kick the bag in frustration and walk across the deserted studio, not least so I don't have to face him. "There's no point," I mutter.

"Really." His tone is so derisive I turn around, scowling at him.

"Yes, fucking really." I've spent two weeks reading every

goddamn thing I can find on the Petrovskys. I've devoured every word of Lawrence Carter Rydell's paper and read every other skeezy article he's written. And I'm about ninety percent certain that the little fuck's theory is dead-on.

But I'm also a hundred percent certain that he doesn't know who the fuck *I* am. I plan on keeping it that way. And that means getting Darya and Sergei Petrovsky out of my life as soon as possible. Just as soon as I work out exactly what they know and what their game is.

I just haven't quite managed to find out yet. But asking Darya directly will only give the game away. And as far as I'm concerned, Miss fucking Petrovsky has already played me for long enough. I don't plan on giving her any more string to tie me up in. Which means not touching her at all.

Which has been fucking torture.

I thump the bag with particular vehemence.

"Do you remember," Dimitry says thoughtfully, "what you said to me that first night after we ran from the halfway house? When we slept under the overpass?"

I roll my eyes and belt shit out of the bag. "Spare me the psychotherapy, *mudak*."

"I knew that family services would be out looking for me," he goes on, completely ignoring my warning. "And I was shit scared of being taken back into care."

I can't help but remember him the night we met, a scrawny kid in clothes from the juvie bin, running silently through the streets at my right shoulder. Part of me thought he'd run out of breath long before we got clear of the kids chasing us. Part of me almost hoped he would.

And I was secretly relieved when he didn't.

I focus on the bag, punching a steady rhythm.

"You told me I had a choice," Dimitry goes on. "One was to go back to the halfway house and take whatever came. We both knew that with a juvie record, I wouldn't get a foster family, or not a good one. But you never said that. You just said that if I wanted to go back, you'd take me. I asked you what the other choice was. Do you remember what you told me?"

I punch methodically, ignoring him, but in the back of my mind, I can still see us as we were that night, huddled in the dirt, sharing a tin of beans and jumping at every sound. It was a lifetime ago. It feels like yesterday. I remember how that overpass smelled, like piss and fear and loneliness.

"Do you remember?" he asks again.

"Of course I fucking remember." I punch the bag so hard it flips up into the air and turn to face him. "I said I could help you disappear so they would never find you. Since you're here pissing me off right now, clearly we know what choice you made. So the fuck what?"

"Yeah, I guess that's the part you would remember." Dimitry pushes off the wall and grabs the bag, bringing it to a halt and eyeballing me around the side of it. "But you said a lot more than that. You told me that disappearing meant living in the shadows, maybe forever. Never trusting anyone with my name or story. You told me the only way to stay safe in the shadows was to bury my past and forget who I'd been up until that moment."

"I was a kid." I grab the bag and push it hard enough to knock him out of the way. "I was probably fucking high, if I was gabbling on with that crap. You should have clipped me in the mouth, like I'm fucking tempted to do to you right now."

"You've never been high in your life." Dimitry stands aside and lets me punch. "Every word you said was the truth, and you knew it. Yes, I chose to stay. But not for the reasons you think. Not because I was scared of going back to the halfway house, even though I knew it meant more beatings, and probably more rape."

I wince. I still hate thinking about the shit Dimitry went

though before I found him. He's never directly said the word *rape*, although the nightmares he had when he was a kid gave me a pretty good idea of what he'd endured. I keep punching, not looking at him.

"I stayed because up until that point, I thought I was the loneliest, saddest motherfucker in this world. But that day, I realized I'd met someone even lonelier than I was."

I stop punching and stare at him incredulously. "Are you trying to tell me you stayed out of fucking *pity*?"

"Of course not." Dimitry holds my eyes steadily. "I stayed because it amazed me that anyone could have lived for years feeling as lonely and lost as I did then, and still find it in themselves to defend a dumb little kid they didn't even know. I fucking trusted you, Roman. I'd have followed you anywhere. Off a goddamn cliff, if you'd told me to. Not just because you were a scary motherfucker who I knew could keep me safe, but because I knew that even if you had buried your past, you hadn't buried your soul with it. That was more than I could say for anyone else I met back then."

The bag swings between us like a metronome. The studio is dead silent but for the creaking of the chain as the bag goes back and forth. Dimitry and I stare at each other, and weirdly, given his impressive bulk and hard face, in his eyes I can still see the scared kid who huddled close to me that night, so skinny his bones stuck into my side. I remember how fucking brave I thought he was, how despite the cigarette burns and the bruises, the dark shadows in his eyes and the way he jumped at every sound, he never once complained.

Most of all, I remember how it felt to finally have someone by my side. Someone who was my responsibility to care for and keep safe. Dimitry won't ever fucking know it, but the truth is, it was him who saved me back then. He gave me a reason to wake up every day and fight for a better future, for us both.

"What's your point, Dimitry?" It's not quite a snarl this time. *Fucking past. Fucking emotions.* Lately, it feels like I'm living in a toxic swamp filled with both.

"My point is that you never stopped being lonely. Not when Yuri adopted you. Not when you built Hale. Not even when you made enough money to buy all the women you could want. No matter what you've achieved, part of you has always lived in the shadows. Right up until the day you moved Lucia into your home. And fuck you," he says, holding up his hand to ward off my protests. "I'll say her name if I want to. She's a beautiful girl, Roman, and she fucking adores you. Whatever your problem is with her, you need to sort it out— or you'll be living in those shadows forever. And that's not tough, Roman. It's just fucking sad."

We stare at each other over the punching bag for a full minute. Then I pull my gloves off and throw them at my bag.

"Fuck this," I growl. "Let's go and get drunk."

44

ROMAN

It's been a long time since I've been in a bar.

Dimitry and I picked one far away from the beach bars and tourist haunts, the international hotels and the trendy nightclubs. This is a backstreet taverna, where old men eat peanuts and throw the discarded shells on the floor in the bar while their wives gossip in the dining room, juggling babies and small children. Music blares from a television in one corner while a bullfight shows on the other. In the dining room, some game show plays on a third. The various televisions compete with the raucous conversations. Amid it all, the barman serves endless drinks while his wife serves up superb plates of tapas to accompany them. Dimitry and I lean against the bar with our beers, though he doesn't quite match my intake.

"I thought we were getting drunk," I say when I down my fifth, along with a vodka shot, and he's still on his first.

"Abby's out tonight." He turns his bottle on the bar. "I just want to make sure I'm sober in case I get a late-night pick-me-up call."

I give him a sideways look. "That's all getting a bit serious, isn't it?"

Dimitry shrugs. "Maybe."

I don't ask any more questions. Frankly, I've had more than enough emotional discussion for one day. I focus on the drinks and the bullfight. It's been outlawed in the north of Spain, and plenty of people protest it wildly. But in Andalucia, bullfighting is a religion. And unpopular as my opinion might be in some circles, I fucking love it. Nobody who hasn't sat in that sawdust-filled arena and watched the terrifying dance between bull and toreador can ever really understand the drama and passion. But in this traditional southern bar, every man, woman, and child gasps and shrieks at each pass, applauding both man and beast with equal fervor.

"*Khuy.*" Dimitry frowns at his phone.

"Pick-me-up time?" I ask sarcastically, trying to suppress a faint twinge of something horribly like jealousy.

Why the fuck am I jealous?

It isn't like I want Lucia—*fucking Darya*—texting me late at night. I just shut her down this afternoon, for Chrissakes.

So why does it piss me off so much that it doesn't seem to bother her at all?

Apart from necessary communication relating to the children, Lucia hasn't crossed the line with me at all. No sudden lingerie-clad appearances in my elevator. No demands as to why I haven't been calling her to my apartment. Nothing at all, in fact, other than some concerned sideways looks, but even those she's kept largely to herself, no doubt to save worrying the kids.

Which only makes it fucking worse.

And I'm sick and tired of trying to work out what to call

her in my head. Darya, Lucia—I don't actually care what her name is, but I really fucking hate that when I was deep inside her I was calling her by a name that she knew wasn't truly hers. It's as if I was sleeping with a lie this whole time. Making love to a body, but not a soul.

And the fact that you're referring to it as making love should be enough to make you end this thing right now.

Not to mention souls. It's fucking Dimitry's fault, talking about all that bullshit before we came out.

"Hey." He shoots me an uncomfortable look. "I've got somewhere I've got to be."

"Well, I'm not hanging around to drink on my own. You can drop me off on the way."

"Actually, I'm going in the opposite direction. I've got to, errr . . . drop something off at Abby's place."

"You're doing her shopping now?" He's pissed me off enough tonight that I'm taking a rather evil satisfaction in making him squirm.

"She has a girlfriend around, and they've run out of booze." Dimitry meets my eyes rather challengingly. "With everything that's happening with that journalist, et cetera, I told her I didn't want her heading out at night on her own, so she called me to ask if I'd mind coming over with a couple of bottles."

I'd give him shit about it, except that it's exactly what I'd do in his shoes, and he knows it. "Yeah," I mutter, spinning the glass in annoyance. "Fair enough." I glance at him. "You stopping there?"

"No. They're still drinking, apparently. Want to come?" Dimitry finishes his beer and pulls out his keys. "We'll drop the car off afterward, keep going."

"Sure." I down the last of the bottle. The drinks have barely taken the edge off. "Why not."

Anything but the inside of that goddamn penthouse, with Lucia sleeping one floor beneath me.

"I'LL JUST BE A MINUTE." Dimitry pulls up beside a crumbling apartment block in a run-down part of town and grabs the bottles he just picked up at a corner store. Crossing the road, he presses a buzzer, and a few moments later, Abby opens the door. The way she wraps herself around Dimitry annoys the hell out of me.

I'm just contemplating leaning on the car horn to make my point when a movement in a lit window above the doorway catches my attention.

Behind a flimsy curtain, a woman is dancing. Her arms are raised, every sensual curve silhouetted perfectly by the light behind her.

And I know exactly who it is, since those exact curves have been torturing my every dream for the past fucking two weeks.

What the fuck is she doing in this part of town, dancing like that where anyone could see her?

I'm out of the car and across the road before I've even thought it through.

"What the fuck," I bark at Abby. "What is Lucia doing here?"

"Hey." Dimitry glares at me. "You don't talk to her like that."

For the second time that night, I'm tempted to take a swing at him. But by the rather dangerous gleam in his eye, I'm guessing that would cause the kind of scene none of us need. "Then move," I say curtly, glaring at Abby. "I need to talk to Lucia."

She folds her arms and glares right back at me. "Not a chance."

I almost laugh. Even Dimitry looks uncomfortable. "Abby," he begins.

"Uh-uh." She shakes her head, still staring me down. "It's taken two bottles of wine and some solid hours of crappy Spanish rock to make that girl stop crying. There's no way I'm letting you undo all my good work."

That pulls me up short. "What do you mean, stop crying?" I frown at Abby. "What's she crying about?"

She looks at me like I'm a particularly imbecilic toddler. "What the fuck do you *think* she's been crying about, you idiot?"

Dimitry shoots me a worried look. "Hey, Abs—"

"No." She holds up a hand to stop him. "Don't get in my way, Dimitry. This idiot needs to realize what he's done." Her death stare could almost rival my own. "I've known Lucia for more than two years," she says fiercely. "In that time I've seen her frustrated, annoyed, exhausted, and occasionally angry. But even at her most desperate, do you know what I've never seen? I've never seen her cry. Not until tonight."

She prods me in the chest with an accusing finger. "Not until *you* made her feel scared. I told her to trust you, did you know that? I thought you could be trusted. But now she's in there with red eyes and a broken fucking heart, terrified she's going to have to run again. All because you got what you wanted and then kicked her to the curb. And let me tell you, Mr. CEO Man." She hiccups. "If I lose my best friend because you're a selfish prick, I'm going to come for you. I don't care how—*hic*—scary you are."

I'm stunned into temporary silence.

"Hey, sweetheart," Dimitry says, slipping his arms around an unsteady Abby. "I think maybe you've had enough to drink." The worry has gone out of his face, though. The motherfucker is actually struggling not to laugh.

"He's not—*hic*—going upstairs," Abby says belligerently, staring at me.

"Yes, he fucking is," I mutter, casting Dimitry a look. "Please remove her."

"I know that look." He grins as he lifts Abby and places her carefully below the steps. "He's going in, Abs, even if it means going through you. Sorry."

I wait until she's out of the way and leave her arguing with Dimitry as I climb the stairs. I take them slowly, trying to make sense of what the fuck Abby just said to me.

Lucia—scared?

Crying?

Planning to fucking *run?*

Because I *broke her fucking heart?*

Does she honestly believe that I "got what I wanted, then kicked her to the curb"?

Or is this just another game?

Only an uncomfortable feeling in my chest says that it isn't.

I pause outside the half-open door.

"Abs," Lucia says uncertainly from inside the room, "is that you?" The faint tremor in her voice breaks the last piece of my self-control.

She's scared. She's scared because of me.

"No, it isn't Abby." I push the door open. Lucia is backed up against the tiny kitchen sink, her eyes wide with fear. When she sees me, the kitchen knife in her hand clatters to the floor.

"Roman," she whispers, slumping against the counter. "I thought—I was scared that you were someone else."

"Well, I'm not." I eye her across the room, anger and tension making my voice hard. "But I could have been. What the hell were you thinking, coming to this part of town? There isn't even a decent security system on the door, for Chrissakes. I could have been anyone."

"I didn't think you'd . . ." She swallows, breaking off. Abby wasn't wrong about the tears, I realize. Her eyes are puffy and swollen. And why haven't I noticed how tired she looks?

There are dark shadows under her eyes. She swipes impatiently at them, but not before I see the twin tracks leaking slowly down her face. She goes to move toward me, but she's clearly drunk her own weight in wine, because she stumbles.

"You've drunk too much." I grab her before she falls, steering her to one of the wooden kitchen seats. "I'm going to take you home. You need to sleep it off. We can talk in the morning."

"No . . . point." She shakes her head wearily, not bothering to brush the fresh tears from her face. "This was a mistake."

An odd fear seizes my chest, overriding the anger. "It's always a mistake to drink that much wine," I say curtly. "Come on. Let's go home."

"No." Her shoulders shake. "It's not my home, Roman," she whispers, looking at the floor. "And I don't want the children to see me like this. They're already scared." She gulps, then takes a deep breath and meets my eyes. The shattered expression in hers breaks something deep inside me. "You've been very generous," she says hoarsely. "But you don't need me anymore. The kids trust you. And I know you'll look after them. I think it's better if you just . . . let me go."

All the things I want to say, all the questions that have been racing around my brain, clash in my throat. I stare around at the tiny apartment, Lucia's small cloth backpack in the corner. Somehow I know there's money in there, a change of clothes. Maybe even another fake passport.

Lucia is getting ready to run. *Because of me.*

I pick her up in one movement, ignoring her gasp of protest. "I'm taking you home," I say roughly. "We can talk there."

45

LUCIA

I stare out the back seat window during the car ride back to the apartment. To my embarrassment, and probably because of the vast amount of wine I've consumed, the silent tears just won't stop. Dimitry drives. Roman stares stone-faced ahead. He doesn't say a word when the car pulls up in front of the building, just slams the door, opens mine, and propels me ahead of him into the building. Putting his arm around me to shield my face from the doorman, he herds me into the elevator. He hits the button for the penthouse floor without releasing me. I stand in the safe haven of his embrace, closing my eyes and inhaling his familiar scent, impressing it on my mind for the coming days, when I'll have only the memory of it to comfort me.

I know we've hit the end of the road. I've seen it coming every day since we got back from the finca. I suppose I should be grateful he's at least doing it in person.

"I'll make coffee," he says curtly when we get to the penthouse. "If you want a moment to freshen up."

I half laugh, half cry. Roman isn't a tears man, I already know that. And clearly he doesn't want to deal with whatever emotional breakdown I'm having right now. I weave my way to the bathroom and turn the water on cold, trying to shock myself out of the weak, weeping mess I've become. I can't seem to stop crying. I feel both ashamed and too tired to try to fight it.

At least he hasn't got rid of my robe. *Or not yet, at least.*

I wonder why I even thought of it as *my* robe? A hundred women have probably used it before me.

That makes the slow tears start again. I mop them up, silently willing myself to get it together.

I wrap myself in the robe anyway. It was mine for a few weeks. *That's probably a record for Roman Stevanovsky.*

I come into the main salon and pick up the steaming coffee on the dining table.

"You promised me you wouldn't run." Roman has his back to me, staring out the window.

I curl up in a small ball on the leather sofa, trying not to think of the times he's thrown me down on it, tearing my clothes off in his haste to take me.

Those days are gone, sister.

I blow on the coffee, holding the hot cup between my hands, trying to stop the slow, rolling tears that just won't fucking quit.

Roman turns around, his eyes narrowing when he sees my face. "Why are you crying?" he says accusingly.

I almost choke on my coffee, but I don't yet trust myself to speak. And I don't want to make the situation any worse.

"You need to start explaining yourself to me, Lu— " He cuts off abruptly halfway through saying my name and turns swiftly away.

Oh, fuck.

I'm frozen in place on his sofa, the burning-hot cup in my hands forgotten.

He knows.

I'm as sure of it as I've ever been of anything.

He knows who I am.

It's not like I didn't figure this would happen eventually. Roman isn't the kind of man to let a secret like that lie. And he's got all the resources he needs to run down every lead until he gets answers.

Suddenly it all makes sense. His abrupt withdrawal, the way he hasn't been able to so much as meet my eyes for almost two weeks. The way he's managed my time so I barely spend any of it alone with the children.

He doesn't trust me.

The tears start again, silent and thick, running unheeded down my cheeks. Whatever happened earlier tonight with Abby was just a small breach in the dam behind which my emotions are kept. But now I can feel the entire wall crumbling, the long years of terror and silence threatening to pour out of me in a torrent I'm only barely holding back.

"How long have you known?" My voice cracks. It's painful to speak.

Roman swings around, frowning.

"You found out who I am." I gulp a scalding mouthful of coffee in an attempt to gain control of myself. "I couldn't work out what I'd done. I thought you'd . . . grown tired of me." I shake my head tiredly. "But it was that all along, wasn't it? You know who I am, and now you realize that I was right. You know it isn't safe to have me around your children. I told you, Roman." I put the coffee cup down with a slightly shaking hand. "I tried to warn you. It could have been Masha they took that day at the parade. It could have been any of the kids. You're just starting to realize it now, aren't you?"

As I speak, the tears dry up. There's no point shedding them anymore. Tears are a luxury I can't afford. I know Roman won't throw me to the Orlovs, or at least, I think I know that. But I know he won't let me stay, either.

At least I know why now, I think dully. Oddly, that helps.

Roman's face is closed and hard. I stand up shakily. "I'm going to go downstairs and pack," I say quietly. "I'll be gone before morning. Papa too."

I make it halfway across the room when his voice stops me. "Say it."

I turn, confused. "Say what?"

"Your name. Fucking say it. Out loud."

I shake my head, the tears that just dried up threatening again. "You know I can't do that, Roman. I promised—"

"What about the fucking promises you made to me?" He hurls the words at me furiously. "To the kids? What about those promises—or don't they matter to you?"

I stare at him in astonishment. "Of course they matter!"

"Then why?" He crosses the room and stares at me with hard eyes. "Why didn't you just tell me? Why, even now, won't you trust me enough just to say the words aloud?"

"What's the point?" I say dully. "You know what my name is. You know who I am. Why do you need to humiliate me by making me break my word as well? At least leave me with that." The tears start to spill again. "You can tell me to leave. I understand that, Roman. But please don't make me betray the people I love. My word . . . that's all I have now. The only thing I have left that's actually mine."

A faint crease appears between his eyes. "That's it?" He's staring at me with an expression I can't read. "That's the only reason you have for not telling me?"

"What other reason would I possibly have?" I'm tired and confused, and I don't understand why he's pushing this.

"Fine," he says stiffly. "Then I'll say it. Your name is Darya Petrovsky."

It's unsettling, hearing my name spoken aloud after so long. First by Ryder, now by Roman. The only other person who's used it for six years is my father, and even then, rarely. It's like having part of myself called up from the grave. I've buried Darya Petrovsky so completely that being called by her name feels dangerous, makes the world around me feel shaky and uncertain.

"Yes," I whisper. The tears are coming now. I know I can't hold them back. "That was . . . that used to be my name."

"Your father is Sergei Petrovsky, *pakhan* of the Petrovsky bratva in Miami. Your brother is Alexei Petrovsky. Still living in your family home. *Pakhan* of your family, in name, if not in fact."

"You've done your research." It's a feeble attempt at pride, but my shaking voice undermines it.

"Why did you come to Malaga?" His face is still hard, still closed. I wish he'd just let me go. I don't have the energy for this fight. *Not when I have to get ready to run.* The dread rises up again, thick and choking.

"What does it matter now?" I turn away from him again. "Please, just let me go, Roman. I've got a lot to do—"

"Tell me why you came to Malaga."

Bewildered, tired, and with wine still churning uneasily inside me, I throw my hands up in exasperation. "Because we didn't have enough money to run any further, Roman, alright? Because by the time we made it from Morocco to Spain, my father was close to death and I was almost broken." The dam breaks, tears spilling down my face. "That's it, Roman. I don't know what you expect me to say."

"And the contract with me." He steps closer, his eyes relentless on mine. "Why did you sign it, really? You told me once before that you knew what I was. What did you mean by that?"

"You're bratva!" I stare at him, tears running down my face. "I knew what you were the moment I saw you, okay? Is that what you want me to say? Do you want me to admit that I *wanted* your protection? Then yes, Roman. I did. But I never would have asked you for it. I never would have asked you for a damn thing. Even after we . . . after what happened, that day in your office, I wouldn't have asked for it. But then you sent me that contract. I know I shouldn't have signed it, okay? I always knew it would end up like this. I know you can't have me in your house, around your children. I tried to tell you. I did. I tried to warn you." Now I'm sobbing, but I'm past caring. I'm so far past it that I can barely stand up.

I have nothing left to lose.

"But you were so sure," I say brokenly. "Papa . . . he told me it was dangerous. He wanted to run. It was my fault, Roman. My fault that we stayed."

"Wait." His hands cup my face, his eyes searching mine. "Your father wanted to run, after he found out who I was?"

"Of course he did," I say dully. "He knew it was dangerous for us to stay. For you, as well as for us. I think he'll be . . . relieved that we're going."

Roman stares at me, his eyes almost black. There's none of the fire and fury I'm used to seeing in them. He looks almost as tired as I feel. All I really want to do is reach for him. And every moment that I can't is like another dagger to the heart. "Please," I whisper. "Just let me go, Roman."

But he doesn't.

"Abby," he says roughly. "She said you thought I was . . . tired of you." His mouth curls in distaste. "*Kicking you to the curb* is the expression I believe she used."

"That's what I thought. Before I realized that you knew who I was. Abby doesn't know about any of this," I say, slightly defensively. "She doesn't know my name, or where I come from, or even understand what you do. Don't blame her."

"I don't give a fuck about Abby." His thumbs stroke my cheeks, remarkably softly given his fierce expression. "What I do care about is why you could ever think that I would just . . . discard you."

"But you are going to do that." I lift my shoulders helplessly. "All we're talking about is the reasons *why* you're going to do it."

"No, Lucia, I'm not." He shakes his head, holding my eyes. "And I'm going to keep calling you that, by the way, because I don't know who the hell Darya Petrovsky is. But I do know Lucia Lopez." He cradles my face. "I know the Lucia who came into my home and changed it overnight. Changed *me* overnight. The girl who captured the hearts of my children the day they met her, and mine almost as quickly." He draws me close to him and kisses me softly on the lips. "I didn't pull away from you because I want you gone, Lucia. I pulled away . . . Well, some day I'll tell you about the life I lived before I met you. It made me . . . hard. And made it hard for me to trust anyone. I thought that you'd found me deliberately. Targeted me, for some reason."

I pull back from him, frowning through my tears. "Why would you think that?"

"It doesn't matter now." He laughs rather unsteadily. "I just . . . I was scared, Lucia. Fuck." His thumbs wipe the tears from under my eyes. "Please don't cry. You don't know how much it breaks my heart to see you cry."

"Why were you scared?" I can barely speak. I take his hands from my face and wrap them around my body, pressing myself close to him, trying to reassure myself that he's actually here. That this horrible night isn't going to end in me fleeing into the night, alone and afraid. "What could possibly scare Roman Stevanovsky?"

"Ha." His laugh is choked. His head goes back, and he takes a deep breath before looking at me again. "The past leaves scars, Lucia. Loving you . . . I guess it felt like asking for another one. Especially when you wouldn't trust me with your name. I guess I thought you were playing some kind of game with me."

I stop his words with my mouth. The kiss is long and sweet, and by the time I pull away, my tears are gone and the familiar fire is starting to burn. "You said *loving* me," I say softly. "Do you mean that, Roman?"

"Yes." His answer comes immediately, without hesitation. "Yes, Lucia. Darya. Whatever name you use doesn't matter. Whoever you are, I love you. I think I fell in love with you the day I saw you standing by that goddamn coffee machine. The ten minutes in the morning when I walked in and tried to make you blush were the best of my entire day. I spent hours thinking about how to get that blush from you, did you know that?"

I laugh shakily. "Not as long as I spent thinking about how to outsmart you. Did you know it took me an entire day on the phone to get bottles of Novoterskaya water in, after I heard you savage your assistant for not having it?"

He grins. "Do you know the only reason I savaged her was to see what you'd do?" His smile slowly fades. He touches his lips lightly to mine. "I don't want to hide this anymore, Lucia. We can work out the details another time. But I don't want these fears between us anymore. I want you here, in my house. In my bed. With my family. No contracts, no end date. I just want you here. Can you do that?"

"Yes, Roman." He catches my mouth and it opens beneath his, my body melting into his embrace. "Yes, I can do that," I murmur against his lips. "Because I've loved you just as long as you've loved me." I pull back so he can see my eyes, and the naked need in his takes my breath away. "I love you so much it almost broke me tonight, when I thought you wanted me gone. I love you so much that I signed away my freedom and my body, because if that was the only way I could have you, then I'd take it. I've risked my father's life and my own to be with you. And I'd do it all over again, if it meant I got to be here, with you and the children."

"In that case," Roman says roughly, "I think it's time we're done talking, don't you?"

Picking me up, he walks me down the corridor and into the bedroom.

ROMAN

"**U**ncle Roman!" Masha's indignant tones pierce straight through the bedroom door. "Hurry *up!*"

Lucia leaps under my hand as if it's a cattle prod. "Get up," she hisses.

"No." I catch her around the waist and throw her back beneath me. She gasps as I run my tongue along her collarbone. "Stay quiet," I murmur, pinning her beneath me with my leg, "and maybe they'll go away."

"We can *hear* you," says Ofelia in a bored tone. "Lucia, I can't find my blue halter top."

"And I'm supposed to be at the lab in half an hour," adds Mickey.

I look down at Lucia's swollen lips and the cherry nipples already hardening under my touch. "Later," I murmur, sucking one of them before she slips out from beneath me. "We never should have given them the code for that elevator," I grumble as I head for the shower.

"It was your idea." Lucia steps in ahead of me. "No," she admonishes, dancing out of reach of my hands. "Seriously, Roman. Ofelia is meeting her friends at the fiesta, and Masha's been promised churros. We need to move it." I wait until she's out then turn the water to icy cold, trying to kill my raging hard-on. You'd think that two months of having Lucia in my bed, the shower, and on any available surface at every spare moment would have lessened my desire for her.

You'd be wrong.

When I emerge from the shower, she's already dressed in a white sundress which, by my reckoning, I could remove in about three seconds. "Are you going to see your father this afternoon?" I ask, calculating the timing of a siesta special.

"Yes." She glances sideways at me, and I suddenly regret having brought that particular topic up. "You know, Roman, it would be nice if you would actually talk to him."

"I need to get Mickey to the lab." I turn away, buttoning my shirt so I don't have to see the sadness cloud her eyes. I know Lucia doesn't understand why I avoid her father. But over the past two months, we've won a tentative peace. Lance Ryder has stayed lost since the parade. There's been no sign of the Orlovs. Mercura is almost at launch date, with no further problems.

Best of all, Lucia and I have been happy. Not just sexually mind-blowing, which we always were. But actually fucking *happy*. As in, race home from work already looking forward to what I'm going to find happy. Cooking as a family happy. Helping kids do their goddamn homework happy, although in Mickey's case, it's more like him tutoring me.

And most of all, devouring Lucia's body every night happy. Which, if I'm going to be honest, is more like ecstasy than happiness. Sex with her is a drug I cannot get enough of. And lately I've been thinking nonstop of how I nail that down permanently. As in, a diamond ring on her finger and my baby in her belly kind of permanent.

Except there's the small matter of our respective fathers. More to the point, the fact that my father died to save hers. And that my mother disappeared forever due to Sergei's failure to protect her, as he promised my father he would.

I can understand Sergei wanting to protect his children and guard their inheritance. Respect it, even.

But that doesn't mean I can forgive him for failing to help my father protect his.

And right now, my only goal is to protect the fragile happiness in my home. That means continuing to call Lucia by her assumed name, so the children aren't confused. It means giving all of us time and space to gradually relax and find a routine and dynamic that works.

And on top of all that, I'm still running a multibillion-dollar business, with the Mercura launch date edging ever closer.

Bottom line?

I don't want to rock the boat. I'll face Lucia's father soon enough and explain who I am. Probably around the same time I take Lucia to pick out that diamond ring.

But not yet. Not while the Mercura launch date is just around the corner, and I've only just begun to trust that when I get home every night, Lucia will be there.

"About *time*," Ofelia says impatiently when Lucia and I finally emerge. She's perched on the countertop in my kitchen, eating a tostada and sipping fresh-squeezed juice. Masha is kneeling on a stool beside her, covered in pulp, and Mickey is opposite them, laptop open on the other side of the counter.

"You guys know you have a perfectly good kitchen down-stairs." I gently shift Masha out of the way as I go to the fridge.

"Not to mention a chef whose actual job it is to make your breakfast."

"He did make it. We just brought it up here. Except for the juice," Ofelia adds. "But we couldn't be bothered going back down to get it, and you had oranges in your fridge."

"*Had* being the operative word." I eye my bare refrigerator shelves and close the door again. "Come on, Mickey. Looks like I'll be hitting the café at work. Have you got your gym bag?"

"Yep." He closes his laptop and jumps off his stool. After only two months training with Dimitry and me, he's already begun filling out. He moves with an athletic confidence, no longer the gangly, awkward kid who couldn't look me in the eye. He's swapped his glasses for contacts and cropped back the floppy curls so his eyes are actually visible. Mickey won't ever be a jock, but going by the way the girls who came over for Ofelia's sixteenth birthday sleepover last week ogled him, I don't think he'll be reduced to creating an avatar when it comes to getting laid in a few years.

"Hey," Ofelia says as we reach the door. "Don't forget that stuff you said you'd do for my project."

Mickey nods. "On it."

Lucia frowns. "Ofelia, you can't get Mickey to do your project work for you."

"She's not, don't worry," he says. "It's just a computer bit that will make it look better, that's all. Bye."

His sisters wave as we leave, and Lucia throws me a shy smile. Even after two months, and with the kids more than aware of where Lucia spends her nights, she's still wary about open displays of affection in front of them. Normally I thoroughly enjoy exploiting that discomfort, but I'm still fighting to keep my cock under control, and that sundress is way too tempting to be safe.

"So," I say as the elevator drops to the basement level, "what's this project you're working on for your sister?"

"It's just a boring family tree thing. Don't worry." The look he casts me is almost amused. "You and Lucia aren't in it, since you're my adopted uncle and Lucia is . . . well, not officially family."

I should feel relieved by both of those things. Oddly, however, they thoroughly piss me off. Which makes no real sense.

"I'm just going to spend some time up in the lab before I go down to work with Pavel, though," Mickey goes on. "The software program I need is up in the research facility."

"Yep." I shift my mental focus to Mercura issues. Given the current murky waters surrounding both my and Lucia's backgrounds, I'd rather not dwell on family any more than necessary.

"So we're set for launch next month." Pavel pushes his chair back, rubbing his face and yawning. He's been working ridiculous hours the past few weeks. All the tech kids have.

"Does that mean it's time for invitations to go out?" I tap my fingers on the table, looking around at the exhausted faces.

There's a collection of nods, but Pavel, I note, looks slightly uneasy. Which means there's a problem. I narrow my eyes at him, and he shakes his head, a movement so infinitesimal that it's obvious he doesn't want the others noticing. "You need to do it in person," he stresses, "as discussed. You let one of these links go digital, and we're exposed. This is the high danger end. Every minute between the moment you have those conversations, until we go live, is a chance for us to be undermined. We've done our end to keep Mercura locked down. This part is up to you."

"I'm well aware of that, Pavel." I glare at him. Having respect for the techies is one thing. Being told how to manage fucking business is quite another. "Trust me. The people using this system aren't going to be any more interested in exposing it than I am."

"Fair enough." His expression doesn't change, but there are a few knowing smirks around the table. I don't mind that. Sometimes I think the tech kids are more excited than I am at fucking over the corporate banking systems. And given that they've all got a financial stake in ensuring it goes off without a hitch, their confidence is pretty much assured. It's unlikely any of them are ever going to find a pot of gold like Mercura, and they know it. These kids are going to be set up for life after the launch.

I might use bullets when necessary, but I've always believed that, in most cases, honey works a lot better than a bee sting. I nod at the table, and they file out.

"What the fuck, Pavel," I growl as soon as they're gone. "You think I need to be told how to run security?"

"You do if someone is a step ahead of us." The way he glances around to make sure we're alone sets my teeth on edge, but there's only the buzzing of the long banks of machines. "We might have a problem. More than one, actually." He turns the laptop screen around so I can see it. Unease crawls down my spine. Alexei Petrovsky's one-eyed face stares back at me. He's standing on the deck of a yacht, beside another face that's vaguely familiar, but which I can't immediately place.

"After I turned up the stuff about the Petrovskys," Pavel says, "I put a hidden search in place that locates anything that appears online about them. This cropped up about an hour ago. For once, this isn't our friend Ryder's handiwork." He nods at the photo. "This is a Miami-based online gossip site that enjoys tracking the rich and semifamous. Apparently our friend Alexei has been spending time on a superyacht that recently docked in Miami." His eyes swivel to mine. "I'll give you one guess which yacht."

A glance at the screen only confirms my worst suspicions. "What the fuck is Alexei Petrovsky doing on the *Guapa*?"

It can't be fucking coincidence, I know that much.

"Here's the thing that's really interesting." Pavel opens another window, this one the records from a Spanish port authority. "Remember that trojan we managed to lock out a couple of months ago?"

"Given that it almost cost me several billion dollars," I say sarcastically, "I think it's safe to say that I remember, Pavel."

"Yeah. Well." He reddens and clears his throat uncomfortably. "My point is that according to these records, the *Guapa* was in the Malaga marina at the time."

My head snaps around. "What the fuck? How did we miss that?"

"Well, first because you'd already sold it six months ago, to that Swedish software developer." He nods at the man standing next to Alexei on the screen. "Lars Andersson."

"Who wanted it because of the tech capabilities I'd set up on board," I say slowly, my brain starting to put it together.

"Exactly. He had it sailed to Italy, where it changed hands again—this time to a shell company based in the Caymans."

"Bratva money."

"We should assume so, given Alexei Petrovsky's presence on it. Petrovsky, or Orlov, money, which is untraceable, of course." He clicks back to the Port Authorities record. "According to this record, at exactly the time that trojan got into our system, the *Guapa* was being refueled in Malaga. And given the equipment on board, not only could a clever operator have uploaded that virus, they could also have moved that yacht around enough to make it almost impossible to trace."

"Fuck." This is far, far worse than anything I'd previously

imagined. "So you think this Lars Andersson knows something about Mercura? And that he's working with Alexei Petrovsky?"

"Andersson's sold the yacht, so he might not have been here at all. This just came up, as I said. I haven't had time to look into it properly." He takes one look at my face. "I know, I know. Keep digging. Be discreet." He shakes his head tiredly. "It's a hell of a coincidence. But it doesn't make a whole lot of sense, boss. Lars Andersson could match any of the techies in this building, and then some. He's basically a fucking genius. If he wanted to get into Mercura, I hate to say it, but he'd *be* in."

"For fuck's sake." I rub my face again. "Either way, I don't like the thought of him being anywhere near Mercura. Stay on it, Pavel. Actually, throw everything you've got at it. This could seriously fuck us."

In more ways than one.

"Boss."

"What?" I try not to snarl. I truly do. This isn't Pavel's fault.

"I know you want all this Petrovsky stuff kept on the down-low. But I'm going to need help on this. I'm swamped already."

I frown. "You can get some of the tech kids on it, Pavel. This isn't a background check—"

"No." His answer is swift and certain. "I trust them, boss. But Lars Andersson is like a fucking god to most of those kids. He's the classic tech start-up boy wonder, started in his parents' basement when he was a teenager, had his first multi-million-dollar deal by the time he was sixteen. There's no way I'm giving any of them the chance to have so much as a shot at outsmarting him. It's like dangling heroin in front of an addict. None of them will be able to resist doing dangerous shit."

"You could have mentioned all this when I sold the fucking yacht to him," I say tightly.

Pavel gives me a rather old-fashioned look. "As I recall, your only comment when I mentioned Andersson's line of work was that you, quote, didn't give a fuck what tech bullshit he did, so long as his money was good."

Unfortunately, that does sound like me.

"Dammit." I glare at him. "Tell me there's no way he could have found traces of Mercura on the equipment on board."

"Not a chance." Pavel's already shaking his head. "My people replaced the entire system with new equipment. The *Guapa* was sold with all the same capabilities, but absolutely no trace of prior activity. If Andersson is working on this, then it's his own doing."

Which doesn't make me feel any better at all. And doesn't solve the problem of who I can trust to help Pavel.

"Can I make a suggestion?" he asks hesitantly.

I nod curtly.

"Mickey."

"What?" I stare at him in disbelief. "Mickey's a fucking kid."

"So was every tech in here when they started. Mickey is also a genius. And he's been working alongside me for months. He knows how I work. He's fast, and he learns even faster. He's exactly what I need. And you trust him."

I drum my fingers on the table, thinking. Mickey will be on school holidays in just over a week. He's already been accepted into multiple schools for next year. And God knows, there's nowhere he'd be happier than holed up in the Mercura basement with Pavel.

And Pavel's right. I *do* trust him.

"I'll set it up," I say.

LUCIA

"And you and Masha will be here?" Ofelia chews her lip nervously.

"We're not going anywhere, darling." I indicate the enormous pile of churros on the plate in front of us and the pot of chocolate that is currently decorating Masha's dress. "We'll be watching you from here. And Dimitry's got security under control. Don't worry," I say in a lower voice. "They'll stay out of sight. Your friends will hardly know they're there."

"Yeah, right," Ofelia mutters. "Like they're ever more than five meters away. It's okay," she adds, seeing my face. "I know the security guys are necessary. I just hate that they're always around."

"I know." I squeeze her hand. I do know. I also wouldn't even consider being in this plaza if it weren't for Dimitry and his men.

It's the annual festival celebrating the pilgrimage to El Rocío. All of Andalucia takes part. Those making the pilgrimage parade through the streets in a flamboyant display of flamenco dresses, oxen-drawn wagons, and proud Spanish caballeros on prancing horses. Many of the women in their dresses are perched up behind the men on horseback. The wagons wind through the streets accompanied by flamenco music and the rapid, rhythmic clapping that propels it. The pilgrimage can take several weeks, depending on where the pilgrims begin from, and the starting day is always a huge fiesta. We're sitting in the plaza from which this particular procession will begin, and it's already a riot of color. Normally Roman would be hovering anxiously at anything like this. But it's been two months since there's been any sight of Lance Ryder, or the slightest indication that the Orlovs have any idea that we're here. Security is still tight, but lately, I've begun to relax slightly.

Maybe the information Papa got was wrong. It's even possible that we've managed to either throw the Orlovs off the scent or that they're simply not game to take Roman on. If I had to lay money on it, I'd guess the second one. Either way, I've breathed a lot easier since Roman found out who I really am. And I've been so damned happy lately that part of me simply doesn't want to think about what could go wrong.

"Hey, Luce." It's a small gaggle of girls who have, to my vast relief, recently become Ofelia's friends. They're sweet girls she met at the Russian Cultural Center when Masha and Mickey were rehearsing for the Easter parade. Their Russian heritage eases many of the issues that divide Ofelia's life from that of normal Spanish kids, including the ever-present security detail. Despite the fact that many of them come from significant wealth, they're all very much normal teenagers. It's been a relief to see Ofelia drop her previously sophisticated dress, which made her look far older than her years, for simple outfits like the halter top and shorts she's wearing today. Nothing can disguise the tanned length of her legs or extraordinarily beautiful face, but at least with her hair tied up in a simple ponytail and no makeup, she looks like a beautiful young girl instead of a runway model. She's just turned sixteen. I don't even want to think about how stunning she's going to be in another couple of years.

"Hi, girls." I give them a little wave. I've gotten to know most of their mothers or, in most cases, their nannies or security details. I recently hosted nearly all of them for Ofelia's sixteenth birthday sleepover, a *Vampire Diaries* marathon that kept them squealing and crying into the small hours. It was also Ofelia's first sleepover.

Mine too, for that matter.

A sixteenth might normally be a grander occasion, but Ofelia didn't want it to be. I think she was more excited about having an actual sleepover than a grand affair in a ballroom. Like most of her friends, she's lived a very sheltered life, one that hasn't often involved outsiders.

The apartment has become more of a welcoming space to visitors, but Roman's penthouse remains strictly off-limits to anyone but family.

Family.

That's how it's begun to feel lately. And I love it, but it terrifies me, too.

"Wow." A couple of girls spot Dimitry walking toward us and giggle nervously. "He's *so* hot."

"Hands off, girls," says Abby cheerfully, pushing through the crowd and kissing my cheek. "He's mine."

"Come on." Ofelia tugs her friends' hands. "Dimitry's boring. Let's go."

"Did you hear that, darling? You're boring." Abby pulls a face at Dimitry, but he doesn't smile. He is in work mode, his eyes roaming the plaza nonstop.

"I've got five guys around you," he says to me. "I'll stay on Ofelia and her friends with my guys."

"Okay." I shoot him a smile. "Thank you."

"Churros," says Masha, around a mouthful of batter and chocolate. She holds out a sticky fist to Dimitry, who laughs. "Not now, sweetheart. But thank you." He nods at me and moves off into the crowd.

"You two look cozy." I give Abby the ghost of a wink.

"So far, so good." She helps herself to churros. "At least now that I'm working full-time at Pillars, I'm out of that horrible café."

"I still can't believe Dimitry agreed to you working there."

"I think he figured it was the lesser of two evils. After he saw Revolting Pete grope me, he was ready to agree to anything. And Gregor's a good boss. He pays well, and none of his men grope the staff."

"Gregor?" I frown. "I thought Nikolai ran Pillars."

"He's away. Gregor's in charge, and he's a decent bloke. I think that's why Dimitry got me the job."

"I'd give anything to have been there when Dimitry knocked Pete out," I say longingly. "You still haven't told me exactly what happened."

"It was magical." Abby sighs blissfully. "Dimitry came to pick me up. Normally he comes in and waits by the bar for me to finish, but he got a phone call before he left the car. I was cleaning the bar down, and Pete came in to hand out the tips. You know how he does."

"Oh, I do." It used to be our daily nightmare.

"So I'm leaning over, picking the bottles up off the shelf—I might have been giving Dimitry a bit of a show," she adds mischievously, "since I knew he was outside, probably watching me through the window. Pete, however, didn't get that particular memo. So he pulled his usual trick of pressing right up against me, pretending to reach for a bottle. Gave my ass a good grope while he was at it."

"Gross." I shiver. That particular detail is an all-too-familiar experience.

"So the next minute, Dimitry's literally thrown Pete over the counter, and he's hit the floor. Right before Dimitry's fist hit his face. Multiple times. Ah." She sighs. "It was a beautiful thing, Luce. Wish you'd been there."

"Me, too." I savor the image for a moment, moving the chocolate pot away from its precarious perch on the edge of the table. "That's your last one," I tell Masha sternly. "Leave some for Abby and me."

"Full anyhow," Masha says, giving me a chocolate-smeared grin. "Can we go see *los caballos*?" She's fluent in Spanglish. Sometimes Russian slips in there, which Ofelia likes to call Spanrush.

"We can see the horses in a bit. We're going to wait for Ofelia to come back. I brought your coloring book." I clean her up, get some crayons, and leave her to it. Masha will happily color all day.

"So how is it at Pillars?" I ask Abby curiously. "Don't you see Miguel all the time?"

"No. He's over in the States with Nikolai. Cádiz is doing some showcase matches in Florida for advertising dollars during the offseason. Which, from what Gregor says, means plenty of yacht parties with models and paparazzi. Good riddance," she says darkly. "To both of them. I don't think Gregor likes Nikolai too much."

"Uncle Nicky," says Masha, not looking up from her coloring book.

"Yes, darling." I stroke the hair back from her face. "Nikolai is your Uncle Nicky."

"Uncle Nicky an' Inger on a boat," she says.

My hand pauses. Masha never refers to her mother as

Mama, no matter how often her siblings correct her. "That's right," I say, stroking her hair back. "You were on a boat with them last summer."

"No." She's still coloring. "Las' night, when 'Felia Face-Timed. They on Deda Yuri's boat."

"Oh," I say, frowning. Masha doesn't offer any more information, and I don't push her. Abby looks at me curiously, but I shake my head and put a finger to my lips. The noise in the plaza ratchets up a level as the flamenco dancers start up right in front of us, precluding any further conversation.

I don't interfere with the kids' FaceTime sessions with Inger. For starters, they're rare enough to seriously piss me off. From my observations, the kids are fortunate if they get more than a brief call every couple of weeks, usually when Inger is out with friends and wants to show off her "darling children." I've also noticed that the kids never mention me by name when they're talking to her. I take it from their reticence that bringing anybody to Inger's notice might not be the wisest idea, so I keep my distance.

That said, the fact that Inger's hanging out with Nikolai strikes me as a little odd. And I thought Roman said that the yacht had been sold.

None of your business, Lucia.

Lately, I've stopped calling myself Darya, even privately. Somehow, I've become much more *Lucia* than I ever was Darya. I don't miss being Darya. I don't miss the cheap rooms and choking fear, the ever-present packed bag and never-ending struggle for survival.

Lucia gets to bake, as often as I could wish for. She spends every night being taken apart in ever more fascinating ways by a man she loves more than I ever knew it was possible to love someone. She gets smeary good night kisses and shy smiles from three beautiful children whom she falls more in love with every day. And most of all, Lucia gets to watch her father slowly coming back to life. Even if he does incessantly ask where Roman is, which is a bit awkward.

If it wasn't for the fact that my brother is still in the hands of the Orlovs, life would be perfect.

Well, that, and Roman's sudden and rather strange aversion to spending time with my father. Which is beginning to really bother me.

I haven't forgotten that Roman comes from Miami, or that his mother was Colombian. In the years before Vilnus's coup, my father was at war with some Colombians. He never talked about work, and I only know that much from snippets I overheard from my security detail, which was increased during those years. I'm not naive about my father's reputation back then. His world was just as violent and bloody as Roman's. More, maybe. There's more than a slight chance that Roman's family suffered at my father's hands, even indirectly. But I wouldn't know, because for all that my past is now in the open, Roman has remained as closed about his as ever. I can't blame him. From the scars he bears, it clearly wasn't an easy time.

"Have you made that doctor's appointment yet?" Abby says in an undertone, casting me a sly glance. Her question jolts me out of my ever-present confusion over why it is that Roman seems to have developed an active dislike for my father and throws me straight into the other problem I've been doing my best not to think about at all.

"I never should have told you about that," I mutter, feeling the color start rising up my chest. "I'm a few days late, Abs. That's it."

"And you've been shagging CEO Man nonstop for months. Do the math, Luce."

"I'm not going to start panicking just yet. And don't you dare say a word to Dimitry."

"My lips are sealed." Abby mimics zipping them. "But I

don't know why you're worried. CEO Man is head over heels for you, anyone can see that." My blush turns into a full-blown red canvas.

"We'll see." I'm not remotely certain that Roman's current obsession with my body will extend to caring for another life growing inside it. Besides, I've never been regular.

And you also haven't exactly been religious about taking the pill lately, my mind reminds me. It isn't intentional. It's just that between juggling three kids and being up all night with Roman, my routine has gotten a little out of whack. Even so, I need to get a test.

Whenever I get a chance to be alone for a minute, which is just about never these days.

Thankfully, Ofelia chooses that moment to return, and we settle in to watch the parade.

"MICKEY and I are going to be late getting home." Roman's tone is businesslike. He's clearly busy.

"It's all good. The girls are both exhausted anyway, so we might just have an early bite and I'll get them to bed."

His voice lowers. "That sounds like the best plan I've heard all day. I'll message when I'm on the way and drop Mickey off in the apartment." He hangs up before I can say anything, not that there's any need to. I'm already planning what to wear. I've begun to seriously appreciate the shopping expedition I went on right at the beginning of our "arrangement." The extensive lingerie selection has definitely come in handy.

I wait until Ofelia and Masha are down, then choose a scarlet combination with boyshort panties and a push-up corset. I throw a slip dress over it for the sake of the security guys in the corridor and head for the elevator.

In the penthouse, I head into the kitchen and make a small

platter of tapas, ready for when Roman gets home. He likes telling me about what Mickey's been up to, and increasingly, where his own projects are at. He doesn't go into detail, but I know he's got a big launch coming up that's been taking up a lot of time.

I carry the platter out and put it on the bar, then go to the bedroom to swap my dress for my robe. The cleaners must have moved it. Lately there's been such a mess of clothes in the penthouse that they sometimes get my stuff mixed up with the kids'.

I walk down the corridor, checking each room, but I can't find it. I try the handle on one door, but it's locked. I frown, trying it again.

That's weird. Oddly enough, now that I think of it, I've never seen that door open. *It must be some kind of storage thing.*

Eventually I find my robe under the bed, crumpled up from the last time Roman tore it off. *Oh well.* I smile to myself. *There goes that idea.*

My phone buzzes. *Five minutes away.*

I grab one of Roman's shirts from the closet and throw it over my lingerie, undoing most of the buttons. I finish the look off with a scarlet tie, then prop myself on one of the dining chairs, put my stilettoed heels up on the marble table, and wait.

The elevator dings a moment later. Roman strides into the dining room, then comes to an abrupt halt when he sees me. A dark smile replaces his rather grim expression.

"Nice tie."

"Thanks. The man who chose it has really good taste." I hold up the Scotch bottle. "Drink?"

"Hmm." He looks me up and down. "I'm not sure what I need more right now, Scotch or you."

I swing my feet off the table and walk slowly toward him,

dangling the bottle between my fingers. "You could always have both at the same time."

"Tempting." His arms whip out and pull me against him. He's already hard. He kisses me so thoroughly that I almost drop the bottle, and when his hand roams beneath my ass, I feel the first moisture slick my thighs. "But," he says, pulling back and giving me a wicked grin that says he knows *exactly* how wet I am right now, "I'd rather savor both, I think. Make me a drink while I shower?" Slapping me lightly on the ass, he saunters down the corridor, throwing pieces of clothing to the floor as he goes, throwing a sly glance over his shoulder.

Bastard.

I pour him a Scotch and figure two can play at that game. By the time he comes out, I've lost the shirt and tie and am seated on one of the barstools, legs crossed demurely.

"Mean." He takes the Scotch, eyeing me slowly up and down. My breath catches. I love this, the game before we begin. Every day it's different. Every day it blows my fucking mind.

He's wearing nothing but a towel, and I can already see the rigid outline of his shaft pushing against it.

"I made tapas." I indicate the plate on the bar.

"I don't give a fuck."

I giggle. He's staring at my breasts, pushed indecently high by the corset. Tossing off his Scotch, he moves toward me and tugs the scarlet ribbon holding the corset together, sucking in his breath as it falls away. "I'd far rather eat you."

I moan as he lowers his head to them, pushing my thighs apart with his hands so he can stand between them. He holds me steady on the stool, which is good, since the moment his mouth hits my nipples I'm in serious danger of falling off. "Mmm," he mutters around first one, then the other. "You taste delicious." He pushes my breasts together, his tongue roaming across them, driving me mad. "I swear these get better every time I touch them."

I reach for his towel, and he steps just out of reach. "Not yet."

He lifts me up onto the bar in a swift movement and spreads my legs wide, placing his thumbs just beside the lacy edge of my underwear. I push my mound toward him, aching for his thumbs to move closer. "Always so impatient," he says, shaking his head, but the dark fire in his eyes betrays that his own control is starting to crack.

I love this too. Love watching him begin to lose it. But he's proven, over and over, that he can hold on way past when I lose it. And I've paid for trying to best him by spending hours being held on the brink of orgasm. I'm in no mood for that tonight.

"I've been thinking about fucking you all day," I murmur in his ear. I feel his muscles go taut against me and smile to myself. "I've been thinking about your cock—"

He covers my mouth with one hand. With the other, he pulls my underwear off. "No more talking," he warns me in a low voice. "That's cheating."

So much for my careful lingerie planning.

I give a burble of laughter behind his hand, which turns into a moan as his mouth hits my wet, aching center. My legs go over his shoulders and my head goes back, his fingers dipping into my mouth as he licks me slowly, with the devastating precision that always completely undoes me. His tongue skirts the swelling button at my center, lathing each side but never giving me exactly what I want, until I'm squirming and moaning under his attack. My hands are in his hair, urging him closer, but the corded muscles in his neck says he won't be pushed anywhere he doesn't choose to go. I'm already so close to orgasm it will only take a swipe of his tongue to get me there.

"Mmm." He pulls back just as I'm about to tip over the edge. The towel is bulging to breaking point. I reach for it eagerly, but Roman steps out of the way. He pours himself another Scotch and takes a mouthful, staring at me spread across his bar. I swell under his eyes, my whole body aching for him.

"Bedroom," he orders.

I slide down the bar and head down the corridor, still wearing my heels. I cast him a backward look, just to pay him back for the one he gave me when he headed for the shower. He follows me down the corridor, eyes dark and intent on my ass, Scotch still in his hand.

I turn when I enter the bedroom, reaching again for the towel. He lets me grab it this time, and I tear it away, moaning as his cock surges up to his abdomen. I take it in my hand, slowly pumping him, so swollen between my legs that it's almost impossible to move without groaning.

He slips his fingers beneath me, swearing softly as he feels me open for him. Lifting an ice cube out of the glass, he runs it down my throat, then over my nipples, lingering on each one. The Scotch and ice sting my flesh, making me gasp. He licks the moisture off, slowly. My hand movements are becoming more erratic. He pushes my hand away and picks me up, carrying me high over his head to the bed then lowering himself down, still holding me above him like he's a weight lifter, slowly bringing me down until he's lying on his back with my legs planted either side of his face; then he gets to work with his mouth again.

I grab the back of the headboard, writhing on his face and the hands cupping my ass, crying out as he teases me. Still he won't touch the core of me with his tongue, teasing every part of me with strong, sure strokes, but holding back from right where I need it. His fingers slip inside me, delicately opening me for his tongue, but they're not enough. His hands lock me in place, not letting me near what I really want, holding me just far enough off his tongue that I can't grind down on him like I need to.

"*Ohhh . . .*" The buildup is starting again. I'm squirming, my body spinning out of control. "I don't want to come like this," I gasp, rocking my hips back and forth over his tongue.

"No." He lifts me up, pushing me off his face. "You want to come like *this*." He slams me down onto his cock, and I scream as it fills me. "That's it, *milaia*," he murmurs, letting me rock out of control on him. "Scream for me." He pushes upward and I shriek again, pushing myself hard on him so my swollen clit rubs against his pubic bone. "Fuck, you look beautiful like that," he growls, surging up into me. I move, faster and faster, and he lets me ride him, murmuring to me as it starts to hit.

Just as the spasms seize he rears up, wrapping his arms around me as his cock pumps deep inside, my breasts crushed to his chest. His mouth takes the next scream from mine, and as my body shakes, his cock pulses his release.

"I love you," he murmurs into my hair. "Fuck, I love you, Lucia."

LUCIA

"What about this one?" I hold up a cream silk evening gown that perfectly complements Ofelia's skin. For a girl with classic Russian coloring, she tans like a Mediterranean beauty, her skin turning a lush buttery caramel in barely ten minutes' exposure. I spend half my time running after her with sunscreen and a hat.

"I don't know." She eyes it doubtfully. "Mama might not like it."

"Would you rather wait until she's here to choose? She might like to take you dress shopping herself."

"No." She goes quite pale. "No, I don't like shopping with her." Something about her swift answer, and the way she turns back to the rack of dresses to hide her face, sets off alarm bells. I hesitate, eyeing her stiff shoulders. Anything to do with

Inger is dangerous ground, particularly where Ofelia is concerned.

"Well, the Russian ball is still a week away, and your exams are over. We've got time. We can look again tomorrow, okay?"

"'Kay." Ofelia gives me a small smile, but her eyes slide away from mine. My unease ratchets up a notch.

"How about we go for coffee and *piononos*?" I tuck my arm through hers. Masha's pre-school doesn't finish up for another week, so Ofelia and I have a rare gap of time to be alone together. We both love *piononos*, syrupy sponge cakes rolled around rich fillings, but since our favorites are those soaked in almond liqueur, we don't tend to have them when Masha is around.

Her eyes light up. "Yum."

We wander through the cobblestoned alleys of Malaga's old historic center, our security detail keeping a respectful distance, and take outdoor seats at one of the specialty *pastelerias*.

"Are you looking forward to the ball?" I ask after our cakes and coffee arrive.

Ofelia shrugs. "I guess." Her eyes are opaque, expression carefully neutral. When I first met the children, it was the default mask she presented to the world. These days, however, the only time I see it is when Inger comes up in conversation.

Hence the alarm bells.

"A lot of your friends will be there, too," I say encouragingly.

"Ha." Her laugh is completely humorless, with a slightly bitter edge. "Because *that* will help." She looks away, stirring her coffee mindlessly, not touching her *pionono*.

Figuring that's the best opening I'm likely to get, I go in. "Have you had a falling out with your friends, Ofelia? Is that what this is about?"

"No." She shakes her head. "No, my friends are cool. But I doubt they will be after the ball."

I frown. "Why is that?"

Her eyes flicker to me then away again. "You don't get it," she mutters. "You don't know what those things are like."

It's my turn to laugh without humor. "Actually," I say quietly, "yes, I do."

Her skeptical gaze rests on me, her coffee stirring becoming more determined. "Oh, you do, huh?"

Oh, baby. You have no idea.

Some of my worst nightmares stem from public events exactly like the one she's dreading.

"Do I know what it's like," I say, trying hard to keep my voice even, "to be paraded before a media scrum, forced to smile and describe what designer I'm wearing, with camera bulbs clicking in my face? Yes."

Ofelia's eyes narrow.

"Do I know what it's like to have a hand pressing into the base of my spine, prodding me sharply in a painful reminder to say exactly what I'm expected to and nothing more?" I close my eyes briefly, the memory of Vilnus's spiteful eyes, insidious whispers, and sharp fingers sending a chill through my body. When I open them, Ofelia has stopped stirring her coffee and is staring at me. "Do I know what it's like," I say softly, "to dread getting into the limo when it's all over, only to be . . . punished, for what I got wrong?" I cover her hand with my own. "Then yes, Ofelia. I know *exactly* what those events are like."

Her eyes glisten with sudden tears. She blinks furiously and swallows, dropping her gaze. "I hate them, Luce," she whispers. "And if Mama stayed away, most of the press wouldn't even care. But she *wants* them there. She has journalists on speed dial, and she expects me to . . . to . . ."

"Perform for them," I say gently.

Ofelia nods. "She gets so angry if I get it wrong. I know she won't like my friends. They'll all be in, like, normal dresses. But Mama will want me to look like her."

"You mean like a . . . model?"

She snorts. "You don't have to be polite, Luce. I know what she looks like."

I keep a diplomatic silence. I'm not going to lie—I might have cyberstalked the kids' mother once or twice. Inger's fashion sense is bratva chic, tacky luxury at its most ostentatious. The girls Ofelia has befriended in Spain belong to the far more settled Russian elite, who either stopped flaunting their wealth long ago, or, like my father, never did in the first place.

Until Vilnus Orlov came into my family's life, I'd never been paraded in front of paparazzi. Quite the opposite.

Like Roman, my father had taken every precaution to keep his children out of the limelight. The events we attended were quiet afternoon teas at the Russian club, private gallery showings, or invitation-only lunches and dinners with the grandchildren of exiled Russian aristocrats. Most at those events came from impoverished families who'd lost everything when they escaped the revolution. But lack of fortune had never affected their cultural inheritance.

Everyone at those tables spoke multiple languages. They read Tolstoy in the original and knew their Rachmaninoff from their Tchaikovsky. In fact, some of the attendees of those lunches were the descendants of the intellectuals we discussed.

Every person in those rooms, no matter how dire their financial circumstances, knew exactly how to dress.

Some had scoured every thrift store in the city to rescue a classic Chanel piece or a vintage Yves Saint Laurent. If they wore expensive jewelry, it would be one piece, worn with quiet pride, that had survived the family's flight from Russia.

Even three, sometimes four, generations after the fall of the Russian aristocracy, there remained among the exiles a fierce intellectual pride. I ate lunch with the daughters of poets and political activists, princesses and counts. I learned how to serve tea correctly, and the fine subtleties of language that distinguished the old, lost Russia from the ostentatious new one rapidly emerging from the fall of the Soviet Union.

Entry to those rooms could not be bought, no matter the wealth of the new oligarchs who tried. It was gained by quiet conversations between those who recognized each other. My father was born after the revolution and raised in a gulag, and yet he belonged utterly among those exiles in a way a hundred newly made oligarchs never could, as did Alexei and I.

Vilnus Orlov never will.

Neither, I know, will Inger. And unfortunately, Ofelia knows it too.

I come back from the past to the present, and to Ofelia's brimming eyes. I squeeze her hand. "We can choose a dress together, darling. And I can talk to Roman, if you like."

"Do you think he'd listen?" She rubs her eyes and looks at me hopefully.

He damned well better.

"I can try, Ofelia."

She sniffs, giving me a watery smile. "I wish you could come with us."

I feel a sudden, unpleasant shock, even as I return her smile. The fact that she doesn't even consider my attendance at the ball a possibility is like a bucket of cold water in the face of the fantasy I've been living these past months.

It's a stark reminder of my place in Roman's household.

We finish our cakes and wander through the streets in companionable silence, but my inner self is in turmoil.

Roman avoids my father.

He hardly ever takes me to public events, other than those that are part of my role.

Only days ago, at the fiesta, I was thinking of how it felt to be part of a family.

But regardless of how many nights I spend in his bed, how close I am to his children, or how many times he tells me he loves me, that single line from Ofelia has made one difficult truth brutally clear.

I'm not part of Roman's family. I'm not his partner. I'm a secret, something to be hidden away behind closed doors.

And I have no idea where that leaves me.

I think of the unboxed pregnancy test stuffed in the bottom of my drawer. With a cold shock, I imagine running again, but this time with a baby in my arms as well as a crippled old man.

And despite all that Roman has said to me, the many reassurances he's given, I can't help but wonder if what that journalist said was right.

Am I trusting the wrong people?

49

ROMAN

"Why the fuck are you at Pillars?" I frown at my phone. It's nine a.m., and Dimitry was supposed to be at my Hale office an hour ago.

"There's an issue with an order that hasn't shown up. I'm just lending Abby a hand to sort it out."

For fuck's sake. I forgot Dimitry's girlfriend is working at the nightclub now.

"That's Nikolai's fucking job. Wake the lazy prick up."

"Nikolai's away. I told you that, remember?"

"Of course I fucking remember." I'm getting annoyed. "But that was weeks ago."

"Yeah, and he's still away. Gregor's been running the show, but he's working twenty-four seven. He was still up from last night, trying to work it out, when Abby got here this morning. I just sent him to bed, told him I'd sort it out. Abby's here on her own, and she doesn't have all the contact numbers."

I press my fingers to my head, staving off an imminent headache. "How is Nikolai still away? Is the little prick on permanent fucking vacation?"

"No idea. Gregor said he's in the States, something to do with Cádiz FC doing showcase matches."

"Hmm." I'll be making a call sooner rather than later. "Do what you need to, and let me know when you're done."

"Copy."

I hang up, drumming my fingers on the desk. Nine a.m. is too early to call Miami, and I've got bigger priorities today. I make a mental note to call Nikolai when I'm done.

I'm restless, on edge. I glance at my phone.

No message from Lucia.

Usually she texts me a few times during the day, just an image of the kids or some small message of love or support. Although I often don't have time to do much more than simply like the message, unconsciously I've begun to look forward to receiving them, especially on days as important as this one. She knows that today is the first meeting with the clients I've handpicked to utilize Mercura. The absence of a message makes me uneasy. I pick up the phone and call Luis.

"Boss."

"Are you with Lucia?"

"Yep. And Ofelia. Dress shopping again." He almost succeeds in not sounding bored.

"All okay?"

"Yep." He lowers his voice. "Anything I need to look out for?"

"No, no. All good." I hang up, feeling a bit foolish and admonishing myself for being a possessive prick.

I feel as if I've barely seen Lucia in the past few days. I can't exactly blame her for that. In the lead-up to today's meeting, I've been coming home after midnight most nights. Part of me always hopes to find Lucia waiting for me, wearing one of those delicious fucking lingerie sets that I get to tear off. But school has finished for the summer, and I know she's been flat out with the kids. I make another mental note, this time to take her out somewhere special. I need to make the most of my time with her before Inger shows up.

Fuck knows I don't want Inger to get even the faintest idea of Lucia's importance in my life. That way lies serious trouble. Inger sees the parts of my life I allow her to and gets access to nothing more. She's selfish, temperamental, and incredibly disruptive for the children—but she's also their mother. It's a fine line to walk. Walk it I do, for the kids' sake, but there's no fucking way I'm letting her anywhere near Lucia.

I thrust my personal issues to the side and focus on the presentation I'm about to give. It feels strange to be in the Hale offices. I've been so absorbed with the Mercura launch I've spent hardly any time here for weeks now. But that's the thing about running a legitimate business front: in order for it to look legitimate, sometimes you actually have to show up. And the Hale offices are perfect for today's meeting. Nobody watches who goes in or out of Hale's revolving doors.

A dozen limousines winding up a Malaga mountain to an obscure software facility, however, is a different matter entirely.

And I don't need anyone looking into Hale Tech. Not even the people who are about to make a fortune out of it.

"Mr. Stevanovsky." The receptionist's voice crackles through the intercom. She's lasted longer than any of her predecessors, not least because I've spent so little time here. "The first of your guests has arrived. I've sent her to the boardroom."

"Let me know when they're all here."

I stand at the window, staring out at the city below but barely seeing it. Pavel isn't keen on me having this meeting before he and Mickey have tracked down what they need to.

But I've trusted my gut for a long time, and right now, it's telling me to act.

The longer we sit on Mercura, the higher the chance it gets uncovered or a competitor beats us to it. And although Pavel and Mickey have been working night and day, they both shake their heads whenever I ask about the trojan and the possibility of Andersson being involved. I get the feeling they both know more than what they're saying, but I also know Pavel won't waste my time by talking before he's got a complete picture.

I wait until I get confirmation that all twelve have arrived, then stand up, shoot my cuffs, and head for the door.

It's time to fucking do this.

"That's the proposal, in a nutshell." I look around the gleaming boardroom table. The Russian faces looking back at me would make government agencies across half a dozen countries shit their collective pants.

A stone-faced young man who took the bratva into Thailand and now runs one of the largest criminal associations in Southeast Asia.

A Russian Jewess who is ex-Mossad and now runs a team of the world's deadliest assassins for hire.

Sitting next to her is a man named Makari Tereschenko, with whom I've done a lot of business over the years. He's an ex-Russian FSB agent and now heads up the world's biggest private mercenary army. According to my research, he and the ex-Mossad agent have been unofficially doing business for over a decade.

A few extremely brutal *pakhans* who run most of Greece, Turkey, Lebanon and Syria despite decades of relentless scrutiny trying to expose them.

Zinaida Melikov, Russian heiress who reportedly

murdered her own father before taking over his London-based bratva organization and building it into the most deadly in that city.

The heads of two competing Paris bratva clans, neither of whom acknowledge the other.

And, just to round it off, a couple of Russian arms dealers whose real names were buried long ago.

Between them, the people sitting at this table control around eighty percent of the world's illegal financial transactions.

That's excluding the government-sanctioned deals, of course. That's a whole other business, one anyone with half a brain stays the fuck out of. The people at this table manipulate government agencies. We don't deal with them. That's the thing about governments: they can be brought down overnight, along with the fragile protection that bribery buys from them.

That's a mistake Yuri made, and not one I will ever repeat.

"I've explained as much of the tech side as I'm willing to. Any one of you can decline my invitation. There's no bullet waiting for you if you do, on that you have my word."

I smile coldly.

"Of course, if you attempt to sabotage me, that guarantee is null and void."

"You say there is almost a month until launch." One of the Paris *pakhans* leans forward. "Why bring this to us so early?"

"Because it will take that long for you to liquidate what you hold elsewhere and divert it creatively so it enters our system without detection. Between us we control the GDP of several small countries. The disappearance of that money will shake the international markets. That's why my proposal is to stagger our respective investments. The key to making this work is to do it without drawing any attention."

"Then what, exactly, are you expecting from us today?" It's

Zinaida, the London heiress, with whom I've done business more than once, and who, in my humble opinion, is possibly the most dangerous person sitting at the table.

Psychopaths are a whole different level of ruthless.

"Before I give you the answer to that, I need to know if you're buying in or not."

There's a general murmur of uneasiness and shifting of seats around the table.

I wait until they've all settled and are looking at me again.

"You all know the dangers of a money trail in the digital age." I open my palms. "Every one of us has faced threats to our business because some journalist *followed the money*. We all know that diligent accountants pose more of a threat to our operations than any rival or government agency.

"This proposal is for a currency that is ours alone. We control it. It's not publicly listed. Nobody can find it without an invitation, and that invitation can be revoked after a single transaction if you choose. Resources funneled through it are completely untraceable, gone before there's any record they ever existed in the first place. Like I said in the proposal: I'm offering you a world where nobody can ever follow your money again." I nod curtly. "I've given you all the information I can. If you want to leave, now is the time. Those still seated in five minutes will receive their invitations."

I don't move. I don't offer to break for coffee.

All phones were checked before entry and everyone scanned for technical gizmos. Everyone at this table understands the stakes.

The minutes tick by.

Nobody makes eye contact.

I particularly avoid looking at Zinaida. She and I spent a night together, a long time ago, before Yuri was imprisoned. It wasn't an experience I have any desire to repeat, but I've never forgotten what she told me back then.

"You should kill Yuri and his son, before they get you killed. Weak men die, Roman, and they take others down with them. You're the strength in Yuri's operation, and he knows it. That's dangerous. Most of all, you should ask yourself: why did Yuri take you in? What does he have to gain? Because if you think it was the bullet you took for his son, you're a fool. Work out why he wants you—but do it soon. Then put bullets through anyone who stands in your way."

Given Zinaida's notorious reputation for savagery, at the time, I dismissed her warning as the dysfunction of a psychopathic mind.

Still, I've never forgotten it. Over the years, I've developed a healthy respect for Zinaida, even occasionally enjoyed a vodka with her. And for some reason, perhaps simply because I'm currently fed up with both Nikolai and Yuri, her warning feels oddly pertinent.

The five minutes are up. I put the Russian and her warning out of my mind.

"So." I look around the table. "We're all still here."

They nod.

"There are twelve envelopes sitting on the side table." I gesture to the neat stack. "There are no names on them, no particular order. Inside each one is a device that holds a digital code. Once you activate it, you will be inside the system and able to access further directions. Each device is for a one-time use only. We will activate them inside this room, after which you will all watch them be destroyed.

"Ladies and gentleman." I smile around the table. "Welcome to Mercura."

AFTER THE TOASTS have been drunk and formalities completed, the room empties out—all except the ex-FSB agent who runs the mercenary army. Of all those invited to today's meeting, Makari Tereschenko is the only one I would describe as a true friend.

"Glad you said yes, Mak." I proffer my hand and he grips it. There's nothing bone crushing in the shake. Mak Tereschenko is a man who has nothing to prove, to me or anyone else. He's also one of the few men who can match me in the boxing ring, but it's more than that. I know the stories about how he came up in the FSB, and if even half of them are true, the man's legend is well deserved. I also know for a fact that at least three members of the G7 alliance have him on speed dial.

"It's a good offer." His voice is clipped and cool, upper-class Brit with not a trace of Russian accent. The man was a chameleon for a long time. These days, I hear he owns a stately pile of stone in the English countryside, which no doubt pisses off every old Etonian in the district. "And besides —I haven't forgotten that I owe you."

I frown. "That isn't a debt, Mak. I told you that at the time."

He tilts his head politely, flat black eyes as inscrutable as ever. "Your tech guys found the money trace on the Malian deal. If you hadn't tipped me off, we'd have faced an ambush, not to mention an embarrassing international situation. I owe you, Roman, and I pay my debts." He takes the glass of Scotch I offer. "It's the first time I've seen you since then. Like I said, Mercura is a good deal, one that will benefit me. My buy-in has nothing to do with repaying my debt." He hands me a thick cream card. It has nothing on it apart from a gold-embossed phone number. "This card is a one-time offer. All the resources at my disposal are yours, without question, for a one-off situation when you may need them."

I tense, and he half smiles. "Don't be insulted. I know you have resources of your own, efficient ones at that. But we both know there's a world of difference between security and an army. And a man with a business the size of yours never knows when he might need an army." He nods at the card. "If you ever need it, my army is yours."

I swallow my instinctive protests. A favor from a man like Tereschenko is a matter of honor, and no less than I would have done in his shoes. I take the card. "I appreciate it, Mak."

He almost smiles. "Knowing you as I do, I imagine you'll be making that call sooner rather than later, Stevanovsky. Either way, look me up next time you're in the UK. I've got a new set of wheels that makes your MTT look like a fucking tortoise."

50

ROMAN

"**A**ll of them said yes?" Dimitry is poised on the edge of my desk, swinging his leg and grinning. "So we're up and running."

"Not exactly. We're entering the most dangerous period now. During the investment phase, Mercura will be at its most visible. This next month is when we're at the greatest risk of discovery." I glance around uneasily. "I don't even like talking about this here. Let's keep those discussions for the lab." I glance at my phone. "Which is where I need to be as soon as possible, to give Pavel the good news. You coming?"

"Absolutely." He jumps off the desk.

I give him a sideways look as the elevator drops to the basement. "No more errands to run for Abby?"

"Nope." He gives me a shit-eating grin. "All done, but thanks for checking in on me."

I hold up my hand, and Dimitry throws me the keys to the

Maybach. I'm in the mood to drive. I'm fired up after the meeting, adrenaline from the danger and the win flooding my body. What I really want is to drive straight back to the penthouse and fuck Lucia until neither of us can breathe, but I'm guessing she's still dress shopping with Ofelia. I glance at my phone. Still no message.

Is she seriously that busy that she forgot the launch was today?

I swallow my unease and direct my frustration where it's more useful. "Tell me." My voice echoes around the concrete parking garage. "What the fuck is so important in the United States to keep Nikolai out of the country for so long?"

Dimitry grimaces as he folds his bulk into the passenger seat. "Why don't you call the little prick and ask him yourself?"

"I'd prefer a little more information gathering before I do that. Has Gregor said anything?"

"Gregor's too busy trying to juggle Pillars, the girls, and Nicky's gambling rooms to worry about what Nikolai's actually doing. All he said is that Cádiz is playing a round of showcase matches with the Southern States Soccer league. The team has based itself in Florida, which is probably why the little fuck is hanging around. Plenty of girls, booze, and parties."

Plenty of fucking Orlovs, too. I tap the steering wheel uneasily. *Not to mention the* Guapa *is currently docked in Miami.*

"You think he's up to something?" Dimitry's always been able to read me too easily.

I shrug. "Maybe."

"You know both Nikolai and Mikhail went to college in Florida. That's the reason we met Mikhail in the first place. Nicky is probably just hanging out with his idiot rich-boy friends, showing off the football club he thinks he owns, and flashing his gangster credentials around."

"Probably."

Except it's Miami.

Dimitry gives me a curious look. "Care to share your thoughts?"

"After we've spoken to Pavel."

He shrugs. "Suit yourself."

———

"So it's good news." I grin around at the tech kids, all of whom whoop and high-five. "But I don't need to tell you how intense the next month is going to be. If you thought the last couple were hard, then stock up on the soda and pizza, because the next one will be one all-night session after another."

I'm not sure what it says about the geek squad that they all look positively happy about that.

Dimitry catches my eye, and I suppress my answering grin with an effort. "Go on, then," I say genially. "Fuck off. Get to it." I catch Mickey looking at me hopefully. "Fine," I say, casting my eyes skyward. "You too."

"Hey, Mickey." Pavel halts the kid mid-flight and hands him a memory stick. "I want you to run that trojan again, see if you can make sense of that pattern you found. Use the operations center so it's secure." He nods at the room where the tech kids are currently clustered, all congratulating each other on the fact that they now get to play with Mercura in real time.

Mickey's eyes light up. He takes the stick like he's been given the keys to the Maybach. He barely looks at me in his haste to hit his laptop. Pavel has kept Mickey focused on unraveling the trojan and tracking Lars Andersson. The Petrovsky part of the story I'm doing my best to keep him away from, aside from the bare bones of Darya's identity.

Mickey loves Lucia. I'm not keen to fuck up that dynamic.

"Thanks," I say when he's gone.

"Yeah, well." Pavel looks disgruntled. "Mickey should actually be the one telling you this, since he tracked it down. It's starting to get awkward, boss. That kid is smart—very smart. It's hard hiding things from him."

"It was your idea to involve him."

"That was before he started to find shit I didn't see coming." He casts side eyes at Dimitry, then back to me.

"Dimitry's up to date on Lars Andersson."

He nods, but raises his eyebrows significantly.

Oh, fuck. That means there's some kind of crossover. Still, Dimitry's going to need to be briefed anyway.

"Keep going," I say curtly.

"Well okay, then." Pavel brings up a school class photograph. "Guess who attended boarding school in London at the same time as Lars Andersson?" He points to a face, then enlarges the photo.

"Is that Alexei *fucking* Petrovsky?" I stare at the screen, something hard and unpleasant growing in my chest.

"I'm afraid so." He clicks again and brings up a digital record with the school logo. "And, predictably, if I might say so, it gets worse." He points to the screen. "Alexei and Lars roomed together for two years. Quite the buddies, it would seem." He pulls up an array of photos, each of which shows the young Alexei and Lars in a variety of scenarios. "Rowed in the same crew. Ran cross-country together. They even visited one another's houses—here's a photo of Alexei celebrating Lars's thirteenth birthday with Lars's parents, in Stockholm. The last photo of them is this one in the *Old Collegian*'s magazine. They were both fourteen at the time." It's a photograph of the two grinning boys in school uniform, showcasing the school's new computer lab. "It was this photograph that Mickey found, and how he tracked the association in the first place."

Pavel gives me a worried look. "I know you wanted him to

focus on Andersson's movements, but there wasn't much I could do once he found the connection. He's like a dog with a bone once he gets hold of something." I can hear the admiration in his tone.

I don't like Mickey knowing any of this, but I can deal with that later. I tilt my chin at the screen. "Go on."

"Barely a month after that photo, Sergei Petrovsky had his first stroke, and Alexei was pulled out of school and brought back to Miami. He never went back, for obvious reasons. Two years after that, Lars got his first software deal and left the school also. There's no further record of contact between the two—until the sale of the *Guapa*. Like I said, the yacht was officially bought by a shell company in the Caymans. But Mickey tracked the money, and the company is an Orlov front, like we thought."

I just grunt. That much is obvious.

"Lars Andersson boarded a flight from Sweden to Italy a couple of days before the yacht changed hands. The next time he used his passport was in Spain, at the Madrid airport, when he flew back to Sweden."

I can feel Dimitry's eyes on me. I try to breathe deeply. "So despite having sold the *Guapa*, Andersson remained aboard it all the way from Italy to Spain. Including when it refueled here."

"And he wasn't alone." Pavel casts me a wary glance. "According to the flight manifests, Alexei Petrovsky flew into Italy on the same day as his old buddy Lars."

"*Pizdozh.*" I glare at the screen.

This is bad. Really fucking bad.

Dimitry frowns. "But why would Orlov send Alexei in person for the *Guapa*? Don't rich assholes usually just pay a skipper to move their yachts?"

"That's the fucking billion-dollar project question." I drum my fingers on the back of Pavel's chair. "However Alexei managed to get there, clearly the scheming little fuck was planning to meet up with his buddy Lars."

"It looks like it." Pavel glances at me. "I think you can safely assume that buying the yacht was Alexei's idea, one he somehow got the Orlovs to buy into. The real question we need to be asking is why?"

"That's not the question," I say tightly. "We have one of the world's best tech experts aboard the most high-tech yacht in the world, in the company of a man with very questionable loyalties. Despite the reputation English boarding schools have for rampant homosexuality, somehow I doubt that Alexei Petrovsky and Lars Andersson were fucking each other in the sunshine."

"Why would Alexei Petrovsky be working with Andersson to bring you down?" Dimitry shifts restlessly as the car winds down the mountain road in the darkness. "He hates the fucking Orlovs. If he wants his sister back, wouldn't he befriend you?"

"Not if he thought he could use me to get his family back."

His eyes widen. "You think he's coming after Mercura? Planning to trade it to the Orlovs for his father and sister?"

Among other possibilities.

"I think there's a chance."

I depress the accelerator as we hit the steep curves, leaning the car into the corners.

"Holy shit." Dimitry gives a low whistle. "What a clus- terfuck."

"Yup."

I'm glad I sent Mickey home earlier with Luis. I need time to think this shit through.

"There's a loose cannon the size of Lars Andersson potentially trying to fuck us," I say grimly, "right when Mercura is at its most vulnerable phase. And Alexei clearly knows Lucia is in Spain. When Ryder found Lucia in that public bathroom during the parade, he claimed he could get a message to Alexei. He also told her, and I quote, that Lucia is 'trusting the wrong people.'"

"Yeah, you told me. But since when do you trust journalists?" Dimitry's tone is dismissive. "This Ryder fuck is a little *mudak* who wants to stir up trouble. For all we know, he's not even in contact with Alexei. Why would you believe a single word he says?"

Because he knows more than he should, about too many things.

But I'm not getting into that, not even with Dimitry.

There'll be time to deal with Ryder and his theories once Mercura is safe. For now, what matters is securing the future, not digging up the past.

And if protecting Mercura means having to kill Alexei Petrovsky, then I'll do it.

Whether he's Lucia's brother or not.

I speed the car up. I feel restless and reckless.

There's a storm coming.

I can fucking feel it.

Tomorrow morning, I'll get to the bottom of whatever the fuck is going on. But tonight, I need to let off some steam. I definitely need to stay away from Lucia until I've got this thing under control.

"Hey." I give Dimitry a sly grin. "Remember that vodka we used to drink, back in Miami?"

"Graf vodka?" He laughs. "God, I haven't drunk that for years. And it was the best, too. Why don't they stock it in Spain?"

"I've got a bottle stashed in the penthouse." I shift gears and go even faster. "Whatever else is going on with this Andersson shit, I got Mercura off the ground today. Fancy a celebratory drink?"

"Seriously?" He raises his eyebrows. "I thought you'd be celebrating a bit . . . err . . . differently."

So did I.

But ruthless prick though I might be, I'm not entirely sure even my poker face can handle making love to Lucia while I'm contemplating putting a bullet through her brother.

"You in or not?"

Dimitry shrugs. "Abby will be working until the early hours. Hell, yes, I'm in."

51

LUCIA

"It's perfect." Ofelia eyes herself shyly in the mirror. "Thank you, Luce." Her dress is the cream silk we tried on several days ago. It's sleeveless with a cowled halter neck and drapes elegantly to the floor, making the most of her height without overemphasizing her slender curves or exposing too much skin.

"I think it's missing something." I pull out the velvet bag with my mother's Fabergé earrings and tip them into her hand. "These should match perfectly."

Ofelia's eyes widen, her mouth a perfect O of surprise. "They're so pretty," she breathes, fastening them in her ears and turning her head this way and that.

"They belonged to my mother." I kiss her cheek. "She'd have loved to see you wearing them."

"Oh, I couldn't." Ofelia fingers the earrings longingly. "Are they horribly expensive?"

"Not at all," I lie. Those at the ball who recognize the earrings for what they are will respect her for wearing them. Those who don't will simply think them a tasteful choice for a young girl.

"Ofelia, come—Wow." Mickey slides to an abrupt stop, staring at his sister in somewhat unflattering amazement. "You look really good."

"Really good," she repeats sarcastically. "Gee, thanks."

"But I'd take it off if I were you." He looks over his shoulder and kicks the door shut. "The doorman just called. Mama's downstairs."

Ofelia stiffens. "Oh, shit." She gives me an apologetic look. "Sorry, Luce."

"That's fine." I try not to appear nervous.

Why the fuck didn't Roman tell me she was coming?

"Why don't you change out of the dress, and I'll put it away for you? You can get Masha," I add to Mickey, already unhooking the cream dress. "She's coloring in her room."

"Okay." He shifts uncomfortably from one foot to the other. "Um—I'm not sure if Roman knows Mama is here or not. Somebody should probably call him."

"Sure." I force a smile. "I'll take care of it, Mickey. There's no need to worry."

I'm not sure who I'm trying to reassure.

He leaves. Ofelia's gone quite pale. "I thought she wasn't supposed to get here until tomorrow."

"She probably just wanted to spend time with you." I force myself to smile, despite the uncomfortable prickling sensation under my skin. "Or maybe take you shopping."

"I need to do my hair," she says worriedly. Instead of her normal shorts and T-shirt, she reaches for a tight-fitting black Versace dress that shows a vast expanse of leg and a pair of very high heels. She exchanges my earrings for gold chains with the Gucci logo hanging from each end that drip down from each ear.

The outfit ages her by approximately a decade, particularly when she piles her hair up in a distressed bun and adds mascara and lipstick. It's also completely inappropriate for a lunchtime outing.

Roman will have a fit.

But I'm not getting between Ofelia and her mother, particularly given our recent shopping expedition.

"I'll head upstairs when she gets here," I say quietly. "If you need me, just call."

She nods distractedly. It kills me to see her tension.

The elevator dings, and a moment later I hear a piercing shriek. "Mickey! Masha, darling! Look how big you've gotten!"

I wait until I hear them all move to the kitchen, then slip down the corridor to the elevator, taking it up to Roman's apartment. I hit call on his number as I go, my heart thudding uneasily.

He doesn't answer.

I write a brief message instead: *Inger is here, in the apartment with the children.*

I stare at the screen, but the message stays unread. I try not to let it upset me.

Is it really possible that he didn't know she was arriving?

In the penthouse there's an empty vodka bottle on the dining table, with two glasses and the remnants of several cigars. The scene makes me feel vaguely uneasy. Then again, everything lately seems to do that.

Roman came home after midnight last night. Instead of summoning me, he just sent a message saying he'd see me tonight. I know he had a big presentation yesterday, so I'm guessing that ran late. Clearly, going by the empty vodka bottle, it went well.

Equally clearly, he celebrated his success with someone

that isn't me.

That hurts. More than it probably should, since going by the cigars, it's unlikely he was drinking with anyone other than Dimitry.

It still hurts.

Normally I would have messaged him good luck yesterday. But since Ofelia's comment about "wishing" I could attend the ball, I've been feeling more and more insecure.

Roman has rarely answered my messages from the beginning, usually just putting a thumbs-up on them. It never bothered me before. I know how busy he is; sending a photo of the kids or a short message was just my way of keeping him connected to the family as he was working.

But now I can't help but think that the only times he ever messages me is either for logistical arrangements or to summon me for sex. We haven't actually gone out for a meal together, minus the kids, since the night at the castle. It's always lunch or dinner in the apartment, followed by a bedroom liaison in his penthouse, whether during siesta or late at night. Again, it never bothered me before. But he's known about this ball for weeks and never mentioned it to me at all. If he's planning to attend, and I can't imagine a man in his standing in the Russian community wouldn't, it isn't with me.

If I needed further proof of his indifference, he doesn't seem to have missed my daily updates. Last night's late message is the only one he's sent, other than the normal arrangements for the kids.

What makes it far worse is that my period is now almost a week overdue. And that terrifies me beyond rational thought. I still haven't brought myself to actually take the test.

The sound of footsteps makes me start. I relax when I see Maria, the maid who always cleans the penthouse. "Hola, Maria." I force a smile.

"Lucia." She looks unusually worried. "Is everything alright with Mr. Stevanovsky?"

"Why wouldn't it be?" I feel a twinge of alarm.

"It's just that room," she says in rapid Spanish that betrays her nerves. "You know, the one that is always locked."

"What about it?"

"Well, the door was open this morning. Just a bit, but it's normally shut, so I thought maybe it had been left open for me to clean. I didn't mean to look inside," she adds hastily. "I just glanced inside briefly. But—and I know this is none of my business—I noticed that the safe inside it is open. And it's empty." Her anxious eyes meet mine. "I promise you I didn't take anything out of it," she says nervously. "I would never steal anything—"

My alarm ratchets up a notch.

"Of course you wouldn't," I say immediately. "Mr. Stevanovsky knows that, Maria. It's why you're the only person who cleans for him. He trusts you completely. Please don't worry."

"But that room, it's never open. What if someone broke in?"

"I'll call Mr. Stevanovsky and clear it up." I smile reassuringly, despite the uneven thudding of my heart. "Please don't trouble yourself. This will just be some kind of misunderstanding, I'm sure of it."

"Okay." She looks relieved. "I'll just finish clearing up that bottle, and then I'm done."

"Oh, don't worry." I wave her off. "You go. I'll finish up here." She argues for a few moments, but in the end, she goes.

I take the bottle and glasses into the kitchen and wash the glassware slowly.

Don't go prying, Lucia.

Whatever he has in that locked room is absolutely none of my business. Doors are locked for a reason.

But what if he was broken into?

I know damned well I'm just going for excuses here. There's no way anyone broke into Roman's penthouse without him knowing. And he was clearly here himself last night.

Nonetheless, my feet are already carrying me down the hallway.

Turn back, Lucia. Spying on your lover is about as low as it goes.

The door is only just open. Maria clearly felt as guilty as I do right now and tried to leave it as she found it. It's to her credit that she mentioned it at all.

Will you mention it, Lucia? Will you tell him you came and spied?

I push the door slightly open.

The room is windowless and entirely empty, but for a large, heavy, rather old-fashioned safe. It's actually quite beautiful, with ornate decorative wrought iron that reminds me of something. But I'm more concerned with what Maria noticed: the door to the safe is wide open, the shelves completely bare.

Maybe he emptied it for the business deal yesterday.

I suppose that would make sense. Although, to be honest, I can't imagine the sums of money Roman deals in fit easily into a safe, even a large one.

And again: none of your business, Lucia.

I need to get out of here. Whatever is going on with the safe is Roman's affair, not mine.

Then I see the brass nameplate on top of the safe. And suddenly, I know exactly where I've seen that particular style of wrought iron before.

Shock runs icy cold through my body, followed by a hectic rush of heat that leaves my heart pounding. I cross the floor nervously and run my fingers over the name engraved on the plate.

Borovsky.

How many times have I seen that same nameplate, on the door to my family vault back in Miami?

Vilnus Orlov's voice rings through my ears as if it were yesterday. *Tell me how to open it, Darya . . .*

I leap back as if I've been burned. Even touching the nameplate makes me feel sick and frightened.

I back out of the room, staring at the safe, and carefully close the door exactly as I found it, my heart pounding.

Why the hell does Roman have a Borovsky safe locked up in his apartment?

I know all too well how rare they are. Collector's items, in fact, that sell for millions of dollars. Notoriously the hardest safes in the world to crack. A fact of which I am painfully aware, having watched my mother be tortured to death in Vilnus Orlov's efforts to crack our Borovsky vault.

What possible reason could Roman have to own one?

I think back to the conversation we had during that wonderful, long-ago dinner at the castle. "I like going to auctions," he said, "buying up treasures other people miss."

Maybe the safe is just another one of those treasures?

I swallow, my throat dry. It seems like too much of a coincidence to simply be a chance purchase. And why hide it away in a secure room? If he bought the safe as a collector's item, why not display it?

No matter how I try to suppress my unease, it just won't go away.

My phone rings, startling the hell out of me. I'm almost desperately relieved to see Abby's name on the screen.

"Hey, chica," she greets me. I can hear a lot of noise in the background, and she sounds a bit rushed. "I can't talk for long, I need to get back to Pillars. Just wanted to let you know that I'm at the post office. That package you warned me about is in my box. What do you want me to do with it?"

The passports.

For Chrissake. Can today get any more stressful?

I almost feel sick even thinking about the package from Argentina. Somehow I managed to conveniently forget about asking Papa to order the new identities. *Well, not forget*, I think. *Just ignore.*

But I can hardly leave them with Abby.

I glance back at the slightly ajar door. Suddenly that secure room feels like the basement in a horror film, as if something evil has been released. All I want to do is get the hell out of here.

"You're heading back to Pillars now?" I ask.

"Yep. The boss is home today, apparently, so loads to do."

Of course he is. My mind is swirling crazily. Nikolai probably sat next to Inger on the fucking plane. Masha's casual reference to Nikolai and Inger recently being on Yuri's old yacht together is yet another thing I haven't had a chance to talk to Roman about. There just hasn't seemed to be the right moment. And besides, I'm not sure whether it's important or if it will just cause trouble.

How would I even know what's important? Like Roman and I ever talk about anything, other than what lingerie set I'm wearing.

I feel overwhelmed by the threads of my different lives, caught in a confusing tangle of past and present. I'm angry, and I'm scared.

Which is probably a symptom of pregnancy.

Oh, FUCK.

"Earth to Luce," Abby says impatiently. "Sorry, girlfriend, but I'm kinda on the clock here."

"Can you slip out about four?" It's two now. Going by what the kids have told me about previous visits, I'm almost certain Inger will want to take the kids out and show them off. I need to see Papa, but more importantly, I need to be out of this building. Away from everything to do with Roman and that damned safe.

"Yep." Abby's panting, clearly striding out to get to work.

"I'll meet you by the marina and pick the package up, okay?"

"Yep. Done." She hangs up.

I pass the kitchen and find myself staring blankly at the empty vodka bottle on the table. For the first time, I notice the label on it, and my tension level goes through the roof.

Graf vodka.

My father used to drink that brand—*back in Miami.*

He's complained more than once that it isn't sold here in Spain.

Roman always drinks Scotch.

So was it really Dimitry he was with last night, or was it someone else? Someone Russian, who just happens to drink vodka from Miami?

Ice-cold fear trickles down my spine.

My phone buzzes again, this time with a message from Ofelia: *Going out shopping with Mama. Got whole security detail with us.*

Not that any of that security detail bothered to let me know.

Then again, why would they?

Inger is the children's mother, after all.

I get back into the elevator and return to the apartments, now empty and silent. One lone guard remains in the corridor. "Hey, Bryce." I give him a small smile. "Kids went out okay?"

"Yeah. Luis's team is with them, and Inger had security of her own, too. Don't worry." He gives me a rather more understanding smile than I'm comfortable with. "Inger's visits are a nightmare tornado, but they never last long."

His sympathy only makes it worse.

"Sure," I mutter.

I go into my rooms, shower and dress, then go back to

Bryce. "Can you take me to the villa? I think I'll have lunch there today."

"Sure." He smiles easily and gives me a wink. "Don't blame you, to be honest. We all run like hell when Inger's in town."

"I didn't actually know she was arriving today." I'm desperate to ask where Roman is, but I don't want to be obvious about it.

"Mr. Stevanovsky probably didn't know, either. He's under the gun today." Bryce gives me another of those sympathetic smiles that makes me feel like a complete idiot.

I check my phone again, but there's no message from Roman.

Bryce pulls up outside the villa. "I'll be right here when you're ready."

"To be honest, I'm just going to hang here today. I can give you a call when I'm ready to go, if you like. No point both of us waiting around."

"Sure." He gives me his easy grin. "Just call me, then. I won't be far away."

Knowing he's probably watching, I head into the villa and close the door behind me.

Anna comes out. "Oh," she says, frowning. "Papa is sleeping. I can wake him up, if you like."

"No, don't worry." I smile at her. "I might just have a nap myself, if you don't mind. It's been a long morning."

"Of course!" She beams, ushering me to the guest bedroom and closing the door behind her.

I wait for about half an hour, until the villa is completely quiet. Anna, I know, will be curled up on the sofa, taking her own siesta. I creep downstairs and wait until the security guard passes the front door. I glance around, but to my relief, Bryce's car is nowhere to be seen.

I slip out and make my way toward the marina.

LUCIA

"Chica!" Abby comes rushing toward me, her smile faltering as she gets closer. "Oh, no. I know that look. What's happened?"

"Inger turned up." It's the easiest of my problems to explain.

"The dreaded mother? Oh, fuck." She gives me a sympathetic hug. "Was she awful to you?"

"I don't know. I hid in Ofelia's bedroom to avoid her, then escaped up to the penthouse before we accidentally ran into one another. I know it's cowardly." I shrug ruefully. "But the kids were already tense. I didn't want to make it worse."

"Smart, I'd say." Abby squeezes my hand reassuringly. "Listen, I can't stay long. Gregor's stressed out of his brain about Nikolai coming in tonight. There's loads of stuff to do. Dimitry usually helps, but he's been MIA the last couple of days." She grins at me. "I blame CEO Man. Apparently some deal came off and they got stuck into the vodka last night. It must have been some celebration. Dimitry didn't even make it home."

I force a smile as if I know what she's talking about. "Yeah, I gather it all went well." Even if I'm relieved to know it was Dimitry with Roman last night, it seriously irks me that Abby knows more about what happened than I do.

"Here's your package." She pulls a thick padded envelope out of her bag. It's post stamped from Seattle and has the logo of a popular online store on it. The description on the international sticker describes the contents as books.

"Thanks for this, Abs. They're for Papa." I hate how easy it is to lie to her. "He's starting to read again, but it's really hard to find books in his language here in Spain."

"You mean in Russian." She gives me a complicit smile. "I'm not totally clueless, Luce. It's pretty obvious where you're from." She mimics zipping her lips again. "But I know, I know. Secret squirrel and all that."

I swallow hard and give her a weak smile. "Thanks. I'm . . . sorry, Abby."

She waves me off. "We've all got our secrets, chica." She gives me a slightly pained smile. "Even me, believe it or not. I get it." She hugs me briefly. "I've got to go before Nikolai the Knob turns up."

I can't help but snort at that. Abby's always had a way with nicknames.

"Take care, okay?" She looks around at the slow-growing dusk. "I'm amazed CEO Man let you come down here alone. You should get back, yeah? Even I'm not a fan of the marina at night."

"Go, go. I'll be fine." We kiss goodbye, and I take off down one of the small alleys behind the dockside warehouses that lead back to the main road. It will only take me ten minutes to get back to the villa.

I'm halfway down the alley when I hear footsteps behind me. I speed up slightly, keeping my eyes on the streetlights up ahead. I wonder, rather tiredly, if I'll ever stop fearing the sound of footsteps following me.

They're getting closer.

Resisting the urge to turn around, I speed up into a partial jog. An old joke of Abby's runs through my mind: *Just because you're paranoid doesn't mean somebody isn't following you.*

Channeling Abs makes me smile. I'm almost at the main road.

"Darya."

Lance Ryder. I'd know that British private schoolboy voice anywhere.

My blood runs cold. I break into a run, but a hand closes around my arm, jerking me to a halt.

"Let me go." I swing around, trying to wrench my arm from his grip.

"I'm not trying to hurt you, Darya." His polished features are as smooth as ever, his gleaming smile as unsettling as I recall. "I'm trying to help you. Roman Stevanovsky isn't who you think he is."

"I don't care what you have to say." I'm trying to keep hold of my bag with the package in it while also twisting out of his hold.

"He's been buying up Borovsky safes at auction anonymously for years, Darya." His clasp on my arm is like a vise. "He knows who you are, and he knows why the Orlovs want you. Do you think it's a coincidence that he's got you in his home, under such close watch?"

Every word feeds the fears that have been churning inside me since I opened that door this morning. But fears or not, I'm not taking advice from a snake like Ryder.

"I told you to let me *go*." I finally manage to pull free of his grasp. "I don't know what you're talking about." I glare at him.

"I have nothing to say to you. Stay away from me, unless you want Roman to come after you himself." I back away down the street, still watching him.

"I'm not the only one who knows where you are, Darya." His eyes flash nastily. "If you trust me, I can help you. I helped your brother, Alexei. He's here, did you know that?"

"I don't know what you're talking about," I say again. I'm almost at the road. "Just leave me and my friends alone."

I back onto the pavement and collide with a passerby. My bag falls off my shoulder. "*Disculpe me*," I stammer, swiping my bag hastily off the pavement, my heart thudding.

"*Nada*." The woman steps around me, giving me a kindly smile.

I don't bother looking around for Ryder.

I just run.

I RUN the entire way back to the villa, looking over my shoulder every few steps. I can't see Ryder, but that doesn't mean he isn't still watching.

And much as I loathe him, I can't get his warning out of my mind.

Especially since I've seen the proof of Ryder's words with my own eyes.

Why would Roman buy up Borovsky safes?

One might be a coincidence. But several? Bought anonymously?

If Ryder's telling the truth.

Unfortunately, however, his claim matches Roman's own admissions to me too closely for comfort. Roman said he'd been buying up his father's jewelry for years.

Swap "jewelry" for "safe," and he's already told me the same story.

Anna, Papa's maid, opens the door to me with a smile that quickly turns to concern. "What happened? I thought you were still asleep! Are you okay, Lucia?" She glances behind me, frowning. "Where's your security?"

"It's nothing." I try to smile. "I had to slip out to pick up something from the post office. I didn't want to bother Bryce during siesta. Somebody tried to snatch my bag on the way home, and I got a fright, that's all. I'm fine."

"Oh!" She covers her mouth, ushering me inside. "You poor thing. You shouldn't have been walking alone, not at dusk. It's not safe, even in Malaga . . ." Chattering on, she seats me at the kitchen table and starts pouring me a glass of wine.

"Anna." I interrupt her. "Can we just keep this between ourselves? Papa would worry, and Roman will be furious if he knows I went out without security. I don't want Bryce to lose his job for something that was my own fault."

"Of course." She pats my hand. "But are you sure you're okay? Here." She pushes the glass of wine toward me.

I eye it warily. I've never wanted a drink more.

But as much as I want it, I can't help but think of the unopened test sitting in my drawer.

Damn it.

I'm suddenly fed up.

Between my pregnancy fears, Inger's arrival, Roman's silence, the Borovsky safe, and my encounter with Ryder, my internal stress barometer has hit peak pressure.

There's only one of those things I can actually control.

I resolve to take the test tonight. At least I can cross one damn thing off the stress list, either way.

Making a decision, however small in the grand scheme of things, helps calm me down. Gives me the illusion, at least, of control.

And being accosted by Ryder in a dim alley has put something else into perspective.

Not once has Roman made me feel endangered.

In fact, he's done everything in his power to do the opposite.

The last time I didn't trust him, I nearly lost him. Even the memory of that makes me shudder.

Ryder's hand on my arm was a reminder of the terror I've lived for six years. Roman gave me a way out of that, and he's never given me reason not to trust him.

Ryder, on the other hand, is a notoriously skeezy pap journalist who has repeatedly harassed not only me, but Abby, too. He told me once before that Alexei was here—and yet I've seen no sign of my brother. I know Alexei. If he was close, and knew I was in danger, nothing would stop him from getting a warning to me.

I need to talk to Roman.

That decision gives me an even greater sense of relief. Roman clearly has secrets. But I don't believe he's lying about how he feels about me.

I simply can't imagine anyone, particularly not a man as ruthless and passionate as Roman, being able to fake the intensity of feeling that exists between us.

Yes, he's been avoiding my father. But that could be for a myriad of reasons that have nothing to do with Miami or Roman's interest in Borovsky safes.

My father is a traditional Russian man.

Roman is *pakhan* of the Stevanovsky bratva, which is about as traditional as it comes.

Secret or not, given that our relationship began via a sex contract, in his shoes I wouldn't be too keen to face my father, either.

There's no question that he has some explaining to do about the Borovsky safe. And maybe, if he's from Miami, he might even have heard the rumors about the Petrovsky vault.

But I can't believe, in my heart, that the same man who has

let Masha spread caramel all over him, taught Mickey to box, and actually managed to connect with Ofelia can genuinely wish me harm.

My mind at least partially eased, I make my way up to Papa.

He's sitting just in front of the terrace doors, a plume of smoke rising from the cigarette in his hand, which he hastily stubs out and tosses in the garden when he hears footsteps, waving the smoke away. Clearly, he's managed to bribe one of the therapists. I've refused to buy him cigarettes for years.

"*Docha!*" He greets me with a slightly guilty smile, propelling his chair easily toward me, eyes bright and alert. It's astonishing just how much his condition has improved with the daily therapy sessions.

Despite the damned cigarettes.

But I'm not going to berate him about them today. There's too much else on my mind.

He glances behind me. "*Gde deti?*" *Where are the children?*

Papa has become very attached to all the children, particularly Masha, who can sit by him for hours, babbling away in Spanrush. The two seem to have a quiet understanding that exists amid the small flowers Masha likes to pick in the garden and the special rocks Papa collects to show her when she comes.

"Their mother, Inger, has come for a visit," I explain in Russian.

It's not a lie.

"Ah." He touches my hand, nodding. "Now I understand the troubles on your face."

It's always hard hiding my emotions from Papa. And it's been a long time since I've visited him alone. We often come here for lunch instead of going back to the apartment. The villa terrace is a pleasant place to eat, and the kids love the informality of Anna's cooking. Papa likes playing chess with

Mickey, chortling when Mickey inevitably beats him. And he loves listening to Ofelia play the piano. The villa feels oddly empty without them all here.

"*Docha.*" He's frowning. "I would like to speak to Roman."

You're not the only one.

But there's no time for all that now. "I'll bring him," I say, dodging the question. "Soon."

I brace myself for what I need to say. Part of me wants to keep the existence of the passports a secret. But some secrets aren't only mine to keep. It's Papa's contact who sent them, and he deserves to know they're here.

Holding my finger to my lips, I nod at the terrace.

Papa reacts immediately, his eyes growing sharp and focused. I wheel him outside, over to the low wall, and he gestures to a small corner that is shielded from any prying eyes by a row of potted citrus trees. I take out the package. He nods curtly. "They came?"

"They came, Papa." Opening the padded envelope, I withdraw two hardback novels in Russian and hand them to him.

His old hands run expertly over the inside of the covers. "*Da.* They are sewn inside." He looks at me shrewdly. "I think we leave them inside the books, *docha*, no? It's safer." Despite being slightly hesitant, his speech is almost back to normal.

"Yes. Do you have a safe place?"

"Of course. There's a loose tile in the bathroom, third from the left and four up from the bottom." Papa speaks with his head down, his mouth barely moving. "I will wait here."

I go into the bathroom. I'm almost certain there are surveillance cameras installed in the villa, but I doubt they're in the bathroom. I find the loose tile, put the package inside the wall, and carefully replace the tile. Flushing the toilet, I go back out onto the terrace and lean over the wall, as if admiring the city lights.

Papa touches my hand. "I don't think we will have to use

them. Your Roman . . . I think he will not want you running again."

There's a question behind his words, but right now, it isn't one I want to answer.

"I hope not, Papa." I give him a small smile. "But we can never be sure, can we?"

The old eyes narrow, scrutinizing me closely. "Is there something you need to tell me, Darya?"

I've never told him that Roman knows our real identities. I told myself it was because I didn't want to worry him.

But the truth is, I didn't want him to make me run again.

Today, though, perhaps because I feel surrounded by secrets, I don't want to keep them myself.

"Roman knows who we are, Papa. I didn't tell him," I add hastily. "He . . . found out."

He doesn't seem surprised. In fact, he smiles wryly. "When?"

I grimace. "Two months ago."

He nods. "This is why he avoids me, then."

"I didn't realize you . . ." Papa arches a subtle brow, cutting me off. "I don't know why he's avoiding you." I glance at him. "Do you?"

"Hm." His smile lessens, but doesn't fade completely. "I have some ideas." He pats my hand. "But you don't worry for this, *docha*. This is between your Roman and me."

53

LUCIA

It's past seven when I call Bryce to go home.

The apartment is dark and deserted, the children's discarded belongings exactly where they were when I left. I move around, picking things up and tidying them away, keeping mindlessly busy.

Take the test, Darya.

It's the first time in a while I've heard that steely voice inside me. But I guess it's Darya's strength I need right now, not Lucia's fudgy complacence.

"Time to face the gallows, girl," I say aloud. Just hearing my own voice helps, in some weird way. It almost makes me laugh, in a slightly hysterical kind of way.

I go across the corridor to my own apartment, smiling at Bryce. "If the kids come home," I say, "tell them I'll be in shortly." I lock the door behind me, get the test, and go to the bathroom.

It's the longest damned five minutes of my life.

Or it might have been, if the little pink plus sign didn't flash neon bright within about thirty fucking seconds.

"Holy shit." I stare at the white stick, completely unable to stand up. There's a dull roar in my ears, and the room swirls queerly about me.

None of it feels real.

Sitting on the closed toilet lid in this gleaming white bathroom.

The Borovsky safe in the room upstairs.

The passports stashed in Papa's villa.

Lance Ryder grabbing my arm.

Roman's face swirls just beyond my mental reach. I can't even conjure the sound of his voice.

How did I get here?

And I don't mean, physically, how did pregnancy occur. The only real miracle, given the manic rush of the past few months, is that it took so long to happen.

It's more that the road between the days when I served Roman his morning coffee to this moment of being served a pink plus sign on a white fucking stick seems incredibly short. As if I missed some important signpost on the way. One that says something like, *Hey, Darya? You're about to completely blow your fucking life up.*

A child isn't something I can run from. It isn't something I can lie about or keep secret.

A child is an inescapable reality.

A reality I have absolutely no idea how I'm going to face. Let alone how Roman will.

Or, God help me, the children. What are they going to make of this?

I put my burning face in my hands before I throw up.

How could I have been so damned stupid?

I don't know how long I sit on that closed toilet, head in

hands, staring at the white stick on the floor. It could be ten minutes, or an hour. All I know is that, at some point, I'm jolted out of my shocked stupor by a hard knock on my apartment door.

"Luce!" Ofelia's voice is high with tension. "Mama wants to meet you."

You have got to be fucking *kidding me.*

I wrap the offending stick in toilet paper and drop it into the shining silver bin.

Everything around here gleams, I think randomly. It's like a shiny, happy world where nothing is supposed to go wrong. I feel like a dark smudge on the pristine window, a carelessly spilled glass on the clean surface of their lives.

I glance at myself in the mirror, then quickly look away again. I'm a mess. Hair is falling out of my braid. My white shirt is crumpled, my linen trousers creased. I splash water on my burning face and take a few deep breaths to try to calm the hectic look in my eyes.

"Luce!" Ofelia knocks again.

"I'm coming." My voice at least sounds reasonably sane.

I guess that's one advantage of having spent the past six years faking sanity.

Ofelia is hovering anxiously outside my door. She's holding a new designer bag, the price of which would easily feed an entire family for a year, and she has twice as much makeup on as she did when she left the apartment.

"It's not good," she whispers in my ear. "Masha's been acting up all day, and Mickey disappeared with Luis in the middle of our meal. Mama's seriously pissed."

Great.

Trying to still my frantic pulse, I plaster on a smile and follow her through the door.

My first impression of Inger is, surprisingly, how beautiful she is in the flesh. It's not hard to see where Ofelia gets her amazing features from. If I'm being fair, the images in the tabloids don't remotely do Inger justice.

She has sloping cornflower-blue eyes, a few shades lighter than her eldest daughter's, fringed with long, dark lashes that look annoyingly natural. A perfectly diamond-shaped face with cut-glass Slavic cheekbones and sculptured lips. And her skin is completely, almost uncannily, flawless.

Add in endless tanned legs, subtle cleavage, and trim curves, and Inger Stevanovsky is one-hundred-percent pure Russian model knockout. Even dressed in a skintight pantsuit and dripping with far too much gold jewelry.

Unsurprisingly, she takes one look at me and curls her lip in contempt. "So *this* is the famous Lucia Lopez."

The moment she opens her mouth, the beautiful illusion is completely shattered. Her voice is petulant and shrill, her eyes flashing maliciously as she crosses the room toward me, holding out a pale hand topped with fierce red talons. It's limp and cold in my own.

"It's a pleasure to meet you, Mrs. Stevanovsky." I meet her eyes briefly when I smile, then lower them respectfully. If there's one thing I've learned over the past few years, it's how to be invisible.

"Is it." She injects the words with enough hostility to make her meaning more than clear.

I'm still trying to work out how to respond when Masha comes barreling out of her room and hurls herself at my legs.

"Luce!" She reaches up for the hug I would normally bestow.

Instead, I gently remove her arms and turn her around to face her mother. "I hope you had a lovely afternoon together."

"No." Masha turns back around and eyes me belligerently. "Shopping," she says, with such contempt I press my lips together to stop myself grinning. Masha *loathes* shopping.

"But you liked the toy store, Masha, remember?" Ofelia

says hurriedly, stepping over to remove her from me. "Why don't you get the Barbie Mama bought for you?"

"Don' like Barbie," says Masha mutinously. Fishing in the pocket of her jeans, she comes up holding a rock, which she flourishes triumphantly. "Look what I found, Luce! For Deda."

"I don't think Deda Yuri will want rocks, Masha." Inger's eyes glitter with annoyance.

"For Deda *Juan*." To my horror, Masha pokes her tongue out at her mother.

"Masha!" Ofelia has gone white.

"Well." Inger glares at me. "I can see that teaching manners is clearly not your forte, Miss *Lopez*."

There's something unsettling about the emphasis she puts on my name. The first time, I'd thought it was just my imagination. But this time, the calculating look in her eyes sends a shiver of unease through me.

"Do I dare ask who *Deda Juan* is?"

"Masha," I say quietly, trying to stay calm. "I'd love to see the Barbie your mama got for you. Have you said thank you?"

"Fank you," she mutters resentfully, but she goes out of the room obediently enough.

"Deda Juan is my father," I explain. "Masha took to calling him that. I have tried to correct her, I'm sorry. I'll make sure she isn't confused."

"I fail to understand why my children are spending time with your father. Does he have a working with children clearance?" Her distasteful insinuation is clear enough. I try to push down my sudden surge of anger.

"You know how strict Mr. Stevanovsky is about security." I meet her eyes steadily. "He would never allow the children to be in harm's way."

"Ha." Her eyes roam around the apartment. "You've certainly made yourself at home. The apartment looks nothing like it did when I decorated it."

Because nothing says "home" like a soulless white sea.

"Where is Roman?" She glares at me like his absence is my fault. "He assured me he'd be here when we got home."

Well, I'm glad he informed someone.

Increasingly unhinged, I'm still trying to work out what to say when the door opens behind me and, to my relief, Roman's voice intervenes.

"You said you'd be home at eight, Inger." I'm not sure I've ever heard him use this tone before. It's calm, courteous—and utterly chilling. "It's five minutes to the hour. I'm hardly late."

Holy shit.

If he ever used that tone with me, I'd be running a hundred miles in the opposite direction. Inger, however, seems completely unfazed.

"Romie!" Her icy expression transforms in an instant, to a girlish smile that matches the saccharine tone of her voice. I step out of the way to avoid being mowed down as she makes a beeline for Roman, throwing her arms around his neck and kissing him on the mouth. I try not to watch. Figuring the sooner I get out of here, the better, I start edging toward the door.

"Wait," Inger commands imperiously. Still clinging to Roman, she eyes me over his neck. "I bought Ofelia a dress for the ball today. I'm going to be busy all day tomorrow with the hairdresser and makeup. Can you make sure the dress is hung properly, and that she doesn't get makeup on it? I'll send my people over to get her ready after they're done with me. Mickey and Masha's outfits will be sent over in the morning."

Mickey and Masha's outfits? For a ball?

"Of course, Mrs. Stevanovsky." I don't dare look at Ofelia's agonized face. I can't see Roman's.

"Romie." Inger pulls back, though her arms are still locked around his neck. "You and the children will pick me up at the hotel at seven. Bring the limo, so we can all arrive together. It's just awkward with the paps if we're waiting for a second car to arrive."

Ha. So that's who he's attending the ball with.

It makes sense, I guess.

Show a united front to the press. Play happy family for the cameras.

It's not like I didn't spend several years playing that very same game.

I just didn't imagine that Roman would put the kids through that same kind of torture. To think that he will, even for Inger's sake, is disappointing.

Oh, sure, Darya. That's *why you're disappointed.*

That steely internal voice seems to be making a comeback. Clearly the logical part of me knows I'm in desperate need of a hard dose of reality.

"Is that all, Mrs. Stevanovsky?" Keeping my eyes down, I back toward the door.

"For now." Her eyes flare with triumph. "I'll let Romie know if there's anything else."

"Thank you," I mutter.

I open the door and flee, accompanied by the sound of her shrill, artificial laughter.

"Oh, Romie," I hear as the door closes. "Nikolai said she was *pretty.*"

———

I SHOWER in a numb state of confusion, then dress in the most comfortable pajamas I own. I'm in no mood for lingerie sets right now.

I have no idea what I'm in any mood for.

I curl up on my small two-seat sofa, nursing a cup of peppermint tea.

Is peppermint tea harmful to unborn babies?

I have no idea. I also have absolutely no appetite.

Now I'm starving it, too.

It?

What an awful thing to call a baby.

For some odd reason the nameplate on the safe pops into my mind.

"Borovsky," I mutter, holding my hand over my belly. "That's what I'll call you, since you're a secret that's in a safe place."

I find myself smiling, and that strikes me as the weirdest thing of all, in a day that has been chock-full of weird.

I sit in the same numb state for a good hour, until a tentative knock comes at my door. I wrap myself in my robe and cross the room, praying it isn't Roman. I'm not sure I have the strength for that encounter right now.

Instead, I open it to find three little faces staring at me. A tearstained Masha is standing between her siblings, clutching one each of their hands. Mickey and Ofelia look at me with mingled expressions of shame and tension that break my heart completely.

"Oh, darling." I kneel down, and Masha lets go of her siblings' hands, wrapping her arms and legs around me as I pick her up. "Come in," I say over her shoulder, and the kids file silently in behind her. Keeping hold of the taut little figure wrapped around me, I put chocolate on the stove and get the latest batch of *alfajores* out of the cupboard.

"Mama's gone," Ofelia says quietly. She and Mickey exchange a tense look. "She's out for dinner with Roman," she says nervously.

"Okay." I smile at her and stroke the hair back from her face, which has been washed clean of makeup. She's swapped the black dress and stilettos for sweatpants and a T-shirt, her hair in a loose ponytail. "You look exhausted." I hand her the cookies. "Want to watch *Dirty Dancing* again? I was just about to put it on."

Ofelia looks at me skeptically. "Aren't you angry?"

"Of course not, darling." My lying skills are seriously getting a workout today. "Roman and your mama have a lot of things they need to talk about in relation to you guys, and not a lot of time to do it. I'm glad they're catching up tonight."

"Yeah," Mickey mutters. "Sure." His jaw clenches, and the dark anger in his eyes is not at all unlike his godfather's.

"Don't be cross at Roman," I say. "He's got a lot going on right now."

"Ha." His laugh is entirely mirthless. He moves restlessly around the room. I watch him from the corner of my eye, wondering what's going on there.

"Ofelia said Dimitry came and got you this afternoon," I say to him, stroking Masha's back as I stir the chocolate. She hasn't said a word, but her breathing is still short and uneven, and she's as stiff as a board in my arms. "Is everything okay?"

"It's all fine," Mickey says shortly. "Just something at the lab Pavel wanted me to look at."

"Oh." I nod as if this is the most normal thing in the world, though why a fourteen-year-old has suddenly become indispensable to the lab is another mystery in a day of them. "And did you get it all finished?"

"Sort of." Mickey meets my eyes briefly, then his slide away.

Something is definitely off.

Ofelia pulls the pot off the stove and pours chocolate into mugs while I put cookies on the plate. We carry them over to the small coffee table. She sits beside me, while Mickey perches on one of the sofa arms. Masha stays right where she is, glued to me like a limpet on a rock. I notice she's sucking her thumb, which I don't ever recall her doing.

"The dress Inger bought for me is awful." It's Ofelia who

speaks first. "I can't wear it, Luce, honestly. I just can't." She turns pleading eyes to me. "Have you spoken to Roman about it yet?"

"Not yet," I say, smiling reassuringly at her. "But I will, as soon as I get a chance. Don't worry. I'm sure he'll support your decision to wear a dress of your choice." I have no idea if I'll get any such chance, or if Roman will do anything of the kind.

I also don't give a fuck.

Ofelia will wear what makes her comfortable, even if I have to hog-tie her bloody mother.

"By the time we go to pick your mama up, it will be too late for her to argue."

I should feel bad about so blatantly undermining Inger, but I don't.

I just don't.

"Seriously?" The tremulous hope in Ofelia's face is all the encouragement my inner demons need.

"Absolutely."

"Oh, thank goodness." She slumps back against the sofa in relief. "Inger will hit the roof," she says flatly.

It's not lost on me that she's dropped the "Mama."

Mickey snorts. "Not in front of the paparazzi, she won't." He shakes his head. "I don't know why she's making Masha and me go."

"Mickey!" Ofelia hisses warningly, but it's too late. Masha rears back, her face set in mutinous lines.

"Not gonna wear that dress," she says, rubbing her eyes. I suddenly realize the source of her earlier tears.

"Oh, I see." I stroke back the curls that are stuck to her damp forehead and make a face. "Did you get a dress today, too?"

Masha's thundercloud frown grows even blacker. "It *hurts*."

"Well, that's not good. Maybe I can have a look at it in the morning and see if I can fix it so it doesn't hurt?"

She shakes her head violently. "I don' *wanna!*" Her voice rises in pitch, and tears tremble in her eyes.

"Okay, sweetheart. It's okay." I hold her close, taking deep breaths to calm my internal fury. I'm actually glad Inger is nowhere close by. I'm not sure I would be able to restrain myself from actual violence for causing this degree of distress.

"Don' wanna," Masha says into my neck, between sobs. "Don' *wanna* go to a stupid ball."

"Inger's going to lose it if she's not there." Mickey looks grimly between Ofelia and me. "We've got to get her there, even if it's just for the photo op."

"Let's worry about that tomorrow," I say firmly, eyeballing them both. "Give me a chance to talk to Roman."

"Yeah." Mickey's hard tone is back. "I might have a little chat with Roman, too."

"That sounds like a good idea." I smile at him. Whatever is going on between him and Roman, it's best sorted out between the two of them. Preferably in the boxing ring, going by the look in Mickey's eyes.

"So." Patting Masha's shuddering back, I nod at the TV. "Are we going to watch nobody put Baby in a corner or what?"

That gets a reluctant laugh. Finally.

"That movie is *so* old." Mickey rolls his eyes.

"It's seriously uncool," adds Ofelia.

"Hey." I point a remonstrative finger at them both. "Don't you ever go knocking *Dirty Dancing*. It's my religion. And if you think that's old, wait until I make you watch *Gone with the Wind*."

"Gone with what?" Ofelia shakes her head. "No, don't tell me, I don't want to know. It's bad enough watching Baby carry a watermelon for the fiftieth time."

"It's a classic." I hit play. "Sit back and be educated, children."

"You're tragic." Ofelia snuggles into my side.

"I can't believe I'm watching this. *Again.*" Mickey settles himself on the floor, his long legs outstretched in front of him. After a moment, his head comes down to rest quietly on my leg. I touch it gently, like approaching a baby deer in the forest. He reaches up and covers my hand with his own, holding it there.

The movie starts rolling.

Too late, I remember the whole damn *Dirty Dancing* story-line revolves around an illicit pregnancy.

54

ROMAN

"So given the demands of my new contract, I can't possibly take the children until July." Inger rubs her lips together in the odd manner women do when they've pumped their mouths full of collagen. I've always wondered if they do it because their lips feel like an alien body on their face. For a procedure designed to increase a woman's sensuality, plumped lips have always struck me as mildly repulsive. Inger's might be a more subtle job, but I once had those lips wrapped around my cock, so I know exactly what they looked like in their prime.

They bored me back then.

Now they revolt me.

"And have you told the children that you won't be taking them back to the States with you?" I sip my water, eyeing her over the glass. I haven't touched the wine. Given the nightmarish day I've had, drinking is not a wise idea, particularly when I can't look at Inger without fantasizing about putting a bullet between her pretty little eyes.

Not a joke, unfortunately.

If she were a man she'd already be fucking dead, after the way she treated the children and Lucia today.

Lucia.

My fingers clench the glass convulsively. Given the way she tried to slip her security detail earlier, I'm not entirely sure I don't want to kill her, too. When it comes to Lucia—*Darya Petrovsky*—the line between love and danger is so blurred it's goddamn nonexistent.

Given that Bryce's news about Lucia's outing to the marina came on top of an early morning call from Pavel saying there's been another trojan attack on Mercura, I'm in absolutely no mood to deal with Inger.

"No, I haven't told the children they won't be joining me in the States. Not yet." She pushes the food around her plate without taking a bite. "I'll wait until after the ball. But that's enough about the children." She rests her chin on one hand and fixes me with what I'm sure she thinks is a seductive gaze. "Tell me about *you*, Romie. How is Hale Property going? What are you working on?"

I suppress a sardonic laugh with an effort. We've spoken for all of two minutes about the kids, which was ostensibly the reason for this dinner in the first place. I don't know why I should be surprised. Inger's never shown more than a superficial interest in any of her offspring.

"Hale's doing fine. We've just signed a multimillion deal to restore one of the white villages in the mountains outside Malaga." I'd normally never talk about this kind of bullshit outside of the office. But when it comes to Inger, mentioning large sums of money is the equivalent of giving a cocaine addict a little bump to get the party started.

"Oh, how fascinating!" She flutters her eyelashes. I'm

willing to bet her mental calculator is busy deducing how many of those millions she might be able to persuade me to part with.

I don't have time for this shit.

"Inger." I keep my tone measured with no small effort. "You asked me here to speak about the children, so let's do that. To start with, I don't think bringing all three children to the ball tomorrow night is a good idea."

Her eyes flash with annoyance. "I haven't seen my babies for months, Romie, and now you want me to give up a night with them?" She rubs those damned lips together again. "Aren't you always telling me I should spend more time with them?"

"Attending that ball isn't spending quality time with the kids, Inger."

It's using them for a pap walk, and you know it.

I suppress the second part with difficulty. My patience is paper-thin tonight.

I woke up to a call from Pavel saying that three new trojans appeared overnight. Mercura is under attack, and I need to get back to the lab and work out what the hell is going on, not sit here pretending to give a single fuck about Inger's woeful parenting.

Her eyes narrow dangerously. She's more than capable of creating a horrific scene in public, as I personally witnessed on multiple occasions during her marriage to Mikhail.

"I agreed to escort you to the ball," I say in a slightly softer tone, "and I'm allowing Ofelia to attend. Perhaps we could just stick to that arrangement?"

"Oh." Inger crosses her cutlery with a loud clatter and arches a perfect eyebrow at me. "So now you're *allowing* me to take my daughter out for an evening?"

Fucking seriously?

I'm dangerously close to blowing completely.

Correction: I'm *going* to fucking blow.

It's just a question of where, exactly, I allow the bomb to explode.

"I'm Ofelia's legal guardian," I say tersely. "Whether you like to admit it or not, Inger, you willingly signed over full custody to Mikhail—"

"And then I tried to take it back when he died!" Her voice is becoming shrill. Heads are starting to turn.

"You tried to take *Masha* when he died, and only because having a baby in your arms made your grieving widow schtick look better in the tabloids." I've lost patience. "We're leaving, Inger. We'll continue this discussion in private. No," I cut her protests off curtly. "We're not doing this here. You can leave with me now, or I can carry you out screaming. Believe me when I say I don't particularly care which option you fucking choose."

I push my chair back and stalk out, signing the check as I go. I don't need to look around to know that Inger will follow. She might love creating a scene, but only if she's the star of it. Being publicly humiliated in Malaga's finest restaurant isn't her type of role at all.

She pauses on the steps to pose for the waiting paps, smiling prettily, right up until the limo door closes, at which point her mask drops entirely.

"How dare you walk out on me," she hisses. "The *press* was there."

"Paps aren't fucking press, Inger. And they certainly weren't there for you, or did the distinct lack of clicking somehow evade you? Not that I could give a fuck." I shake my head impatiently. "That's not the point of this discussion."

She stares at me, her mouth slightly ajar. I've been very careful, over the years, to avoid triggering the nightmarish scenes I witnessed between Mikhail and Inger. I've always managed her with polite detachment and a carefully calculated mixture of flattery and financial inducement.

But I'm fucking done playing that game.

"Whether you like it or not, Inger, I'm the children's legal guardian. And unless you want a very ugly, extremely expensive legal battle—which, I assure you, I will fucking win—then it's long past time we got a few things very straight." I stare at her coldly. "I will always encourage you to spend time with Ofelia, Mickey, and Masha. What I will not do is allow you to use them as props in your photo opportunities. As for you 'taking' the children in July, until and unless I see a detailed schedule of your plans, and personally clear any and all individuals they will be spending time with, not to mention oversee their security detail, the only place you'll be taking them is to the Malaga boardwalk for ice cream. And even then, my security will be with them." I lean forward, pinning her with my death stare. "The days of you crashing in and out of their lives, upsetting them as you did today, are fucking done. You want to *spend time* with them? Then get on your hands and knees in the garden with Masha. Help Ofelia with her piano practice. Take some interest in the fucking amazing work Mickey is doing.

"And if I ever hear you speak to Lucia again like she's your goddamn servant"—my face is barely inches from hers—"the only place you'll ever be seeing the children is at your gravestone, when they show up to put fucking flowers on it. Is that clear enough for you, Inger?"

I realize with an odd detachment that I'm shaking with anger.

This isn't tearing an employee over a mistake. This is me genuinely losing my temper, something I've spent the past couple of decades making damn sure I never do.

It's oddly liberating.

I'll hand it to her, though. Inger doesn't look cowed. She doesn't even seem surprised.

Instead, she's got a calculating expression in her eyes that sets my teeth on edge.

"So this is about the nanny, then. I thought so." She lights a cigarette and blows the smoke directly at me. "Not exactly your normal type, is she? But then again, from what I hear, there's nothing normal about your little arrangement."

What the fuck?

I buy myself a minute by snatching the cigarette out of her hand and throwing it out the car window.

What does she know about Lucia?

"What do you think a family court judge would make of my children being left alone at night while their nanny goes upstairs to sleep in her boss's penthouse? Or being forced to amuse themselves on holiday while Uncle Roman spends siesta time getting his rocks off?"

Oh, thank Christ.

I almost sag with relief.

"I take it you had some enlightening conversations with Masha," I say dryly.

"If you mean that she didn't shut up about fucking *Luce* from the moment I picked her up, then yes. And since when have the children had the access code for your penthouse?"

"Since Lucia started spending her nights in it." I give her an evil smile.

"Well, then." Inger very deliberately lights another cigarette, a small, hard smile playing about her mouth. "Since we're clearly done with games, we can have a proper conversation." She lowers the window an inch and blows smoke out of it. "I want all three of my children at that benefit tomorrow night, Roman. My new cosmetics contract is for an all-natural line marketed at the traditional wife demographic. I'm still negotiating my rate, and I need to look the part. That means pap shots at the charity ball with all three children front and center."

I open my mouth to argue. She shakes her head impatiently. "Clearly the only way I'll get Masha to the ball without a screaming fit is if your darling *Luce* is there, so bring the nanny with you. Although I suggest you take her shopping first. It will be humiliating enough for her to be socially way out of her depth. The least you can do is buy her a decent dress."

"Wait." I stare at her. "You want me to bring Lucia to the ball?"

"I want my three children at that ball, Roman, which is the point. I need them there, and I need them to be perfect. If that means the nanny comes too, then so be it."

"And that's it?" I eye her warily. "What happens after the ball?"

Inger shrugs. "I go back to the US for my new contract. You bring the kids out for a few days over the summer, so I can get some pap shots. Your security detail, your schedule, just as you said." Her eyes narrow. "But I'll need a bigger allowance than what you've been paying me. *Much* bigger. And I'll expect your little nanny to make sure the kids are picture-perfect when I need them to be."

"No more surprise visits. And I approve every request from now on."

Inger scowls.

"I'll fall in with your rules, Roman. I won't fight you over the children. I'll even be nice to that damn nanny. Just make sure she gets all three kids there tomorrow night, dressed, smiling, and ready to cooperate." The limo glides to a halt in front of her hotel. "Do we have a deal?"

My phone vibrates in my lap. It's Dimitry. All I want to do is get the fuck back to Mercura.

Not to mention find out what the hell Lucia was playing at this afternoon.

"Fine," I say curtly.

Inger smiles like the cat that got the cream. "I'll see you tomorrow night, Roman."

"You need to get up here immediately." Dimitry doesn't even bother saying hello.

"I'm on my way." I end the call.

"To the lab," I order the driver. "Fast as you can." I sit back in the limo, eyeing the Scotch bottle. But booze isn't on the agenda tonight. Not with the amount of unanswered questions I have, about both Mercura and Lucia.

My phone lights up again, this time with Nikolai's name. I swear aloud. *Will this fucking day ever end?*

"Nikolai." I don't attempt to soften my tone. "Nice of you to bless us with your presence."

"Fuck off, Roman." He sounds unusually cheerful. "I needed a holiday. And besides, the publicity in Miami got Cádiz even more funding. We're making decent coin out of it now."

"Is that so." I couldn't give a shit. Nikolai's little games are the least of my problems right now.

"I'm calling to let you know that Inger's asked me to escort Lucia to that ball tomorrow night. I wanted to clear it with you first."

Fucking Inger.

I knew she wouldn't take the Lucia thing lying down. This is exactly the kind of shit I should have expected. She might tolerate Lucia's presence at the ball, but she's going to make damn sure Lucia knows her place.

Well, two can play at that game.

"Good of you to let me know, Nicky. Be at the kids' apartment by seven. We're all going together."

Except that it will be Inger who Nikolai escorts into that damn ball. I feel a return of my earlier evil smile.

Inger is about to pay in spades for that goddamn insult about Lucia's looks.

"Copy that. See you at seven." Nikolai is clearly full of piss and vinegar after his endless party in Miami. He's also obviously been spending too much time with Inger.

Given the paparazzi photographs taken of them both during the Miami summer, the two of them have been doing the horizontal tango for some time.

Inger's always liked having a backup plan.

She probably sees Nikolai as an opportunity to worm her way back into the family bank accounts, and Nikolai would no doubt think all his Christmases had come at once if she gave him so much as a sideways look.

He can fuck her on every available surface for all I care, so long as they both stay the fuck out of my business.

And besides, if Inger and Nikolai are together, they're unlikely to want the kids around. Which suits me fine.

And right now, I've got far more important things to worry about than who Inger is fucking.

I hit Pavel's number. "Where are we?"

"Well, it's not good." He sounds exhausted. I know how he feels.

After I'd been drinking until well after two that morning, Pavel called at five a.m. Dimitry and I were at the lab before six. I spent almost the entire day cloistered in my secure office, on a series of extremely awkward phone calls to the same people who had activated their invitations the previous day, doing damage control. I think I've managed to pull it off, but to say it was a day of high-level tension is a definite understatement.

"So you're saying it's under control for now?" I try to make sense of Pavel's fast-paced explanation. There's also nothing more frustrating than standing by in a room full of stressed tech heads, unable to do a fucking thing to help.

"I'm saying that something is fucking off." Pavel sounds uncharacteristically grim. "Are you bringing Mickey back up with you?"

I frown. "You'll need to work without him today. His mother's here, and she's almost as much trouble as the trojans. I don't want her asking him too many questions."

Not to mention that there's something up with Mickey. I caught him staring at me more than once today, with a wary look I can't quite make head or tails of. I need to find out what the problem is, but today hasn't allowed me time to scratch my balls, let alone have an in-depth conversation with an upset teenager.

"That's unfortunate." Pavel actually sounds pissed off with me. "He spent weeks turning that first trojan inside out, unraveling all the code. He's ahead of the rest of us, and we need all the help we can get."

"According to your own PR, Mercura had the best team in the world before Mickey ever turned up." I'm in no mood for pissed-off tech heads. "Manage it without him. I'll be there in fifteen." I end the call, grinding my teeth in frustration.

This whole day has been a clusterfuck.

I haven't even answered Lucia's message about Inger. At first I was just busy, but after Bryce called to say Lucia had tried to give him the slip, I was too fucking angry to trust myself to send a message.

I'm still angry.

I don't know what the fuck she's playing at, but the fact that her disappearance coincides with the trojans fills me with unease. I haven't had a chance yet to get Bryce's debrief. Thank Christ he wasn't stupid enough to take his eyes off her.

I walk into Mercura to find Pavel, Dimitry, and Bryce all waiting for me, faces longer than an airport runway. I point at Bryce. "You, in my office. I'll be there as soon as I can." I wait until he's gone then point at Pavel. "You first."

"The trojans are definitely coming from Andersson. But not from the *Guapa* this time. They're coming straight from his headquarters in Sweden. He's not even trying to hide it. In fact, there's something weirdly obvious about the viruses. It's like he *wants* us to find them." He takes off his glasses and pinches the bridge of his nose. His eyes are badly bloodshot. "And the weird thing is, they aren't trying to break our system. In fact, they're doing the fucking opposite."

"Explain."

"Every single one of the trojans has pointed out a hole in Mercura."

"How the hell is that not a problem?"

"Because it's like Andersson is doing our vulnerability testing for us. None of the trojans have actually tried to do anything other than flag the weaknesses in our own platform. And before you ask, yes, we've fixed the holes he's found. And no, I don't like the fact that he's found things we missed. But he's not trying to break in, boss. If I'm honest, it looks like he's trying to make the whole system stronger. Which makes no sense."

Unless he's planning to steal the whole fucking thing.

"And there's something else, which is why I wanted Mickey here."

I ignore that. "Just tell me."

"Mickey's been working on a theory about the first trojan. He thinks there's some kind of message embedded in the code. He's been working through it, and this afternoon, he found similar patterns in these ones. He was just starting to work on them when you made him leave."

"I told you, today isn't a good time for Mickey to be here. Surely your team can use his work?"

His face tightens. "To be honest, none of us are as fast as him. He just sees shit we don't." I have to hand it to Pavel—that must have cost him a lot to say.

And I'm not going to lie: I can't help but feel proud of Mickey. Even if he has got some bug up his ass about me.

A bug I'd clearly better sort out sooner rather than later, if he's going to be in the thick of this whole damn thing.

"I'll do what I can to get him up here tomorrow. In the meantime, there's only one question I need answering. Is there anything in what Andersson has done that will enable him to hijack Mercura?"

"No." Pavel's immediate answer is at least reassuring. "That would be impossible to do. He can't take control of Mercura. Nobody outside of here can, not even Andersson."

"So then we still don't know what he's actually trying to do."

"Nope." He looks as frustrated as I feel. "The annoying thing is that, right now, it seems that all he's doing is actually strengthening the whole platform. I have no idea why."

"Good enough." I glance through the window at the operations center, which is littered with pizza boxes, soda cans, and the inert figures of several exhausted techies. "If it's safe for now, then you all need to go and get some sleep. Leave a skeleton crew, take it in shifts. That's enough for one day."

Pavel looks like he's going to argue. I glare at him. "Go."

He nods reluctantly. "Boss."

Dimitry waits until he leaves. "There's something else, before you talk to Bryce." He moves a mouse, and a radar image comes up. "The fucking *Guapa* is currently cruising just off the Spanish shore. Like, ten nautical miles off."

"What?" I stare at the screen, feeling my blood pressure rising. "How did we not know it had left Miami?"

"Because technically, it didn't. The Miami marina is still showing it moored there. Except it isn't."

"*Khuy.*" This is getting worse by the minute. "Okay. There's fuck all I can do about that for now. I need to talk to Bryce." I hesitate. To be honest, I don't particularly like the idea of either Bryce or Dimitry knowing what Lucia has been up to. On the other hand, given all that's happening, I can hardly afford to keep them in the dark.

"Come with me," I say shortly. We go into my office, and Dimitry closes the door behind us. Bryce gives him an uneasy look.

"Whatever you have to say, Dimitry can hear." I give them both a hard look. "Nothing said here leaves these walls. Ever."

They nod. Bryce swallows nervously. "I got the tech boys to help me compile the footage," he says. "I'll talk you through it." He lifts a remote control, and the large screen on the wall flickers into life. He hits play.

"First we see Lucia leave the villa. She clearly waited until the coast was clear to go." I watch Lucia slip out of the gate and hurry down the street. "I followed her all the way to the marina. She met Abby there."

Dimitry folds his arms grimly, glaring at Abby's figure on the screen.

Bryce shoots him an uneasy look. "Abby gives her this package." He pauses the video, pointing it out and zooming in. "Books, apparently, from an online store."

Like hell.

"Lucia headed back up toward the main road. Which is where our friend Lance Ryder caught up with her."

He pauses the video and I tense, every nerve in my body screaming.

"I wasn't filming," Bryce adds. "I was out of the car, about to take the fucker down. But Lucia got away from him by herself, and I made the decision to stay on her. Pavel managed to pull CCTV footage from a camera in the alley afterward. It's not great quality, and it's a bit misleading." He hits play again.

It's grainy, and Lucia has her back to the camera, but Ryder's face is clear enough. He's leaning in close to Lucia, saying something to her.

I frown at the screen. "Play it again. Can we slow it down?"

"Yep." Bryce plays it in slow motion.

It takes about three replays for me to make out the words, and even then, only a few.

But they're enough.

Alexei is one of them. The others are *he's here.*

"She wasn't talking to Ryder willingly," Bryce says, seeing my face. "He grabbed her. She was trying to get away. She was fighting him—"

"Just tell me what happened next," I say through gritted teeth.

Lucia was definitely listening in the clip the camera caught. And it sure didn't look like she was fighting to me.

"She ran all the way back to the villa," he continues, "and called me shortly afterward to go home. But I thought you'd want the camera feed from the villa, so I got that, too."

He hits play again, and this time, I don't need anyone explaining shit to me.

I watch Lucia hand her father the package. Watch Sergei pull the books out of it, his hands running expertly over the inside covers. This footage is easy to zoom in on, since the cameras installed in the villa are ours, which of course means they're top of the range. I could get a clear shot of a goddamn hair fiber if I wanted to.

It's easy enough to see the passport shapes sewn into the books.

And if I had any doubt of what they might be, the

following shot of Lucia hiding the books behind a bathroom tile is clear enough.

The only part missing is the audio.

The two of them face away from the camera during the entire exchange, so while I can see the books in Sergei Petrovsky's hands, I can't see his face, and no matter how Bryce manipulates the view, I can't get a clear shot of their conversation. I'd bet that Sergei is aware of every camera in the place. Except, clearly, the one behind the bathroom mirror.

Lucia is planning to run again.

"Thank you for this, Bryce." I nod at him. "Well handled. You can leave it with us now."

Bryce doesn't move, though. He shifts uneasily from one foot to another. "I know the footage looks bad. But I saw how scared she was when Ryder approached her. Whatever it looks like onscreen, I promise you, boss, she wasn't happy to see him. Also she was—well, she was upset today. After she ran into Inger." He looks slightly defensive. "I just haven't seen her upset like that before."

"Noted." I'm only just restraining myself from punching him through the wall. "Good night, Bryce."

He's not dumb enough to hang around.

He shuts the door quietly, leaving Dimitry and me staring at the screen.

The Guapa *is sitting just off the Spanish coast.*

Lucia isn't just planning to run. She's planning to run with her brother—who, if I join some very obvious dots, seems to be working with Lars Andersson to try to hack Mercura.

Do I believe that Lucia knows what Alexei is up to?

No. I'm almost certain she has no idea about Mercura or what's at stake.

But do I believe she'll do anything to save her brother?

Yes.

Yes, that I'd believe.

Dimitry breaks the silence. "You think she's planning to run?"

"I think," I say slowly, "that Alexei Petrovsky might just be one very smart motherfucker."

He turns to me in surprise. "Where are you going with that?"

"Think about it." I've been doing nothing *but* thinking about it ever since the *Guapa* connection was turned up. Even when I was most of the way down a vodka bottle last night, I was still thinking, the cogs spinning in the back of my mind, trying to link the different moving parts.

"Alexei Petrovsky has spent years enduring humiliation and torture. All the while, he must have been waiting. Planning. Watching for an opportunity to regain everything he's lost."

Dimitry's eyes slide sideways. "Sounds like someone else I know."

I ignore that. "My point is, Mercura is one hell of an opportunity."

"Okay." He nods. "So in this scenario, what's Petrovsky's play?"

"Alexei's been playing the part of Orlov puppet for years now. They trust him enough to pick up their yacht or to represent the family at public events. He's won the Orlovs' trust by pretending to be their cowed dog. Which means they've forgotten he can be dangerous.

"When he brings them Mercura, my guess is he'll do it with just the right mix of fear and deference, like a servant giving a precious gift to his masters. He'll dangle Mercura as bait. He'll play just dumb enough to make it believable, but he'll also throw around Andersson's name and make himself the key to the Orlovs getting their hands on it.

"And when he's hooked them, he'll propose a trade: Mercura for his family's freedom. The Orlovs give up on whatever treasure they think the Petrovsky family can give them and take the one Alexei is offering instead."

"So we're back to the idea of him trading it for his family's freedom."

"Except he won't." The cogs click in place in my mind, and I'm suddenly sure I'm right. "He'll play the game long enough to be certain he's got his father and sister to safety. But a man doesn't endure what Petrovsky has, for as long as he has, without being determined to take his revenge. He's planning to take Mercura for himself—and he just happens to be best buddies with Lars Andersson, the one man in the world with the ability to make it happen for him.

"How they found out about Mercura," I add, "is a whole other question. One I'll work out, sooner rather than later. Although I'm willing to bet Lance fucking Ryder was involved. Gregor told me that prick hung around Pillars for days during the first trojan upload, asking all sorts of weird questions. I'll bet there's a connection there somehow."

"Okay." Dimitry nods slowly. "Let's say I agree that all this is plausible."

"Because it is," I interject.

"There's still no evidence to suggest that Lucia has any idea about Mercura or the trojans. Bryce is certain she was trying to get away from Ryder, not conspiring with him. There's no reason to believe she's going to run—"

I laugh hollowly. "Except for new fake passports that she's hiding, and the fact that she's barely spoken a word to me in days. Not to mention that come tomorrow night's ball, I'd bet my right ball the *Guapa* will be moored right offshore."

"I think you should ask her—"

"If I wanted fucking advice, Dimitry, I'd be asking. I'm not."

"Well, I'm giving it anyway." His tone is unusually harsh. "Lucia wouldn't betray you, Roman. Mickey knows it, and so do I. Talk to her. Ask her what's going on. At least give her a chance to explain."

I glare at him. "How is Mickey part of this discussion?"

"Because he's not an idiot. He tracked the whole Petrovsky/Andersson link in the first place, and he understands the connection to Lucia." He rolls his eyes when I frown. "Of course he's worked out who Lucia is, Roman. You honestly think he's this far into it with Pavel and hasn't joined the fucking dots?" Dimitry doesn't even pretend to be deferential. "Mickey's in it now. And Pavel seems to believe he's the best chance you've got of getting to the bottom of this."

"And I've already told you: *no*. If Lucia is planning to fuck us over in any capacity, then Mickey needs to stay away. Pavel's geeks were the best in the world before Mickey came on board, and so they still fucking should be. You can't tell me an untrained kid is better than the elite team Pavel personally fucking recruited."

"Well according to Pavel, Mickey really is that good." Dimitry stares me down. "And he's not a kid, Roman. Not really. He's also just as worried about Lucia as you are—"

"*I'm not fucking worried about Lucia.*"

There's a pause. Even I can hear the killing note in my voice. Dimitry's known me well enough to pick right about now to stop. Except the idiot doesn't.

"Mickey loves Lucia. The kids all do. He's afraid, with good reason, that you might decide to shoot her first and ask questions later."

"Oh, so you two are sharing fucking notes now?" The thought of Mickey confiding in Dimitry infuriates me almost as much as the fact that Lucia is planning to run.

"Well, he can't exactly talk to you about any of it, can he?" He sounds almost as angry as I do. "He knows you aren't telling him the full story. And for what it's worth—he's not the only one."

I stiffen.

Dimitry's eyes narrow. "And there it is," he says softly. "That, right there. The line you won't ever cross, beyond which lies whatever secret it is that's been festering all these years. Don't try to tell me there isn't more to this whole Petrovsky business than you're saying. I was there when you were running from the Orlovs, remember? You say Alexei Petrovsky has been watching and waiting. Well, I'd bet your fucking MTT that your file on the Orlovs is even thicker than his. And now you just happen to have his sister, which is the part that's starting to scare the hell out of Mickey."

There's a strange pressure on my chest, making it hard to breathe. I feel like I'm underwater, the room around me oddly indistinct. I inhale sharply through my nose, trying to regain control.

"Well, aren't you two quite the fucking investigation squad." My voice sounds rough even to my own ears. "I'd suggest you both give it a rest, Dimitry, and stay the fuck out of the way. I was handling business when Mickey wasn't even a spark in his daddy's eye and when you were still a skinny kid pissing your pants."

It's a low blow, and I know it. But I'm in no fucking mood for this shit. Not tonight.

"Have it your way," Dimitry mutters, shaking his head. "Fuck knows you always do."

IT'S past midnight when the limo drops me home.

I press the elevator button for the penthouse, then, halfway up, change my mind and hit the button for the floor below. When the doors slide open, I nod at the small army of security monitoring every screen and entrance and go into the children's apartment.

It takes all of one minute to realize it's empty.

I come roaring out of the apartment, ready to tear someone apart. One of the guards nods at the door to Lucia's apartment. "They're in there," he says, shifting uncomfortably.

I grimly punch in my master code, and the door opens with a soft click.

The television's blue light flickers on the walls, a logo bouncing around the dead screen. When my eyes adjust to the dim light, I make out Lucia sitting on the couch, Masha's arms and legs wrapped around her like a koala and Ofelia curled into her side. Mickey is sprawled on the floor, his head resting on Lucia's thigh.

They're all fast asleep.

I stare at the little tableau for a long time. Part of me aches to carry the sleeping kids into their bedrooms, then carry Lucia upstairs and lay her down in mine.

But I don't.

I cut myself off from this life the day I ran from my father's lifeless eyes. I've always known that one day the past would come to reclaim me, that my world would erupt in blood and violence.

And for months now, I've been trying to convince myself that I can somehow balance two impossible extremes. That I can have a family, a woman I love, and somehow still weather the storm of revenge that must be taken.

Because I do have to take that revenge.

Not just to avenge my parents, or as payback for the years I spent running.

Now I also have to take revenge to protect the family that adopted me. And the simple truth is that taking that revenge means killing anyone, or anything, that threatens the legacy Mikhail and I fought so hard to build.

That means Alexei Petrovsky will likely have to die.

And his sister?

I stare at her face, pale in the blue wash from the television. The long eyelashes, covering those liquid amber eyes that make my breath catch in my throat. The sweet bee-stung lips I can never look at without wanting to kiss. The elegant length of her neck, stray curls stuck to it where Masha's face has pressed them to her flesh.

Every part of my body aches with longing. Aches for her dancing figure in my kitchen, the scent of her cooking welcoming me home. Craves not just the touch of her skin on mine, but the way her heart seems to encompass my own, as if I fit inside her being as well as her body. Lucia isn't simply the woman I love. She's the missing part of my soul.

And now I have to let her go.

There isn't really any other option. I know I can't kill Lucia. I'm many things, and capable of darker deeds than most men will ever have to contemplate.

But killing Lucia?

Ordering someone else to kill her?

No.

I've known that, deep within myself, since the moment I learned her identity. There's not a chance in hell I can put Lucia in the ground.

But nor can I risk her falling into the Orlovs' hands.

And there's no way I can risk Mercura.

Which means that the only real thing I can do, the only *honorable* thing I can do, is stand by and watch her run. Guard her retreat. And make sure that nobody, not even her brother, can ever find her.

Maybe I'll win this fucking thing. Save Mercura. Bring the Orlovs down. Build an empire so fucking huge nobody can ever touch those I love again.

But I've lived this life for a long time. I know all too well that I might not survive what's coming.

I also know that if I do survive, Alexei Petrovsky will be dead.

And that alone will mean the end of any future Lucia and I might have had.

I stare at her for a long moment, resisting the urge to simply kiss her forehead, to get close enough just to inhale her vanilla-and-coconut scent. Lucia will wake the moment I touch her, a legacy of the long years she's spent running in fear.

Something she's about to have to do again.

Heartsick, I close the door softly and go up to the penthouse.

Mindlessly I walk down the corridor, tearing off my shirt and tie, longing for the numbing power of vodka, hoping there might be an inch left in the bottle Dimitry and I hit last night. I stop short in front of the partially open door to the secure room, then remember with a hard jolt of relief that I got the vodka bottle out of the safe last night when Dimitry was here and forgot to close the door when we were done.

It feels like a lifetime ago.

It's a measure of how unsettled I am that I forgot to close the safe and lock the door. That never happens.

I stare at the open safe. "I let you down, Papasha." The words rasp painfully from my chest. "But I won't let the children down." I feel a strange coolness on my cheeks and realize in detached surprise that its tears. I don't remember the last time I cried. Maybe when my mother left.

"I know you wanted a different life for me. I can't have that. But I can make sure the children do."

I kneel in front of the safe, my fingers touching the bronze nameplate.

"I'll save Mercura, and I'll win this war, Papasha. I swear to you that I will. I'll win it so thoroughly that when Mickey and his sisters grow up, there won't be anyone or anything left that can harm them." My voice cracks, but I force myself to finish. I may never be able to say this aloud to anyone else, but here, in this room, to my father's ghost.

"I'll fight this storm so they don't have to." I slowly close the safe door, letting my fingers slip the intricate locks into place.

"I'll end this thing, Papasha. Even if it ends me."

55

LUCIA

I wake on the couch at first light, the children's limbs entwined with my own.

I gently shake Ofelia and Mickey. "Time to go back to your beds," I whisper. Masha is still snoring against my shoulder. I carry her across the corridor, past an entire army of security, the older two kids blinking owlishly at the sudden bright light. They partially sleepwalk into their rooms. I lower Masha gently onto her bed and pull the covers over her, then stand for a moment, savoring her sleeping face.

I check on the other two. Ofelia stirs when I kiss her cheek. "Love you," she murmurs, before turning onto her belly and falling asleep.

Mickey is lying on his back, his eyelids drooping, but they widen when he sees me. "Will you be here when I wake up?"

My heart clenches so fiercely it hurts. "Yes, darling." I kiss his cheek. "I'll be here."

I hurry back past the guards, tears blurring my eyes.

In my own rooms, I sit on the couch, my knees tucked to my chest.

Yes, I'll be here when the kids wake.

But I might not be here tomorrow.

Tonight, after the ball, I'm going to talk to Roman. About everything.

Lance Ryder's accusations. Alexei. The passports that arrived yesterday.

About the vault, and why the Orlovs won't ever give up looking for me.

Most of all, I'm going to tell him about the baby growing inside me.

Whatever comes next, Roman has earned the right to be part of my decisions. And however much he's withdrawn from me, I can't live with all the secrets anymore.

But most of all, I'm going to talk to him because those three children deserve better than to go to sleep every night wondering what losses tomorrow might bring.

I go to the cupboard in my bedroom and pull out my old bag.

My go-bag, as I always think of it. It's a scuffed backpack, small enough to be a day bag, big enough to hold what I need.

It's the same one I carried when I left Miami.

I carried it with me every day after that, for six years. Right up until the day I moved into this apartment and told myself I was safe.

Lance Ryder's voice runs through my head again, on a disquieting loop:

"He's been buying up Borovsky safes anonymously for years, Darya. He knows who you are, and he knows why the Orlovs want you. Do you think it's a coincidence that he's got you in his home, under such close watch?"

Maybe tonight's conversation will go well. But maybe it won't.

Maybe I won't even get a chance to have it.

I've run long enough to sense when danger is close. And right now, I can taste it on the very air around me.

Waiting too long is dangerous. It's one of the first things my father taught me.

Which means that I need a plan. I need to be ready.

Slowly, my heart heavy as lead, I start to pack.

———

IT'S midmorning when there's a knock on my door. I open it smiling, expecting the kids.

Instead I'm met by an unsmiling Roman, holding a large bag over his arm. "Can I come in?"

His tone is close to the cold courtesy he used with Inger yesterday. It sends a chill of alarm through my body.

"Of course." I push open the door, trying to calm the sudden, panicked racing of my heart. My smile falters under his grim stare, which seems to rest anywhere but on me.

Something has happened. Something bad. Worse, I suspect it's something Roman has no intention of sharing.

The ominous sense of gathering darkness gains momentum in my soul, triggering my old flight instinct. It makes me feel physically sick.

"You're coming to the Russian Society ball tonight." Roman drapes the bag over a chair, and I realize there's a dress beneath a zipped cover. "I took the liberty of getting you a dress and shoes." He puts both down on the counter.

"The ball?" I frown in confusion. "Why would you want me to—"

"Inger requested that you attend. She wants the children there for the pap walk, and she thought your presence would make that easier." His eyes touch mine, then slide away. "I'm sorry to ask this of you, but I would very much appreciate your help. It should be over quickly enough."

I swallow nervously. After all the nights I've spent splayed under his hands, our limbs so entwined I can't tell where mine stop and his begin, everything about the detached formality of this conversation is utterly jarring. Normally I'd reach over and touch him. Catch his eye and smile. Breach the distance.

But this Roman isn't the man who has laid me out on any available surface and seduced my body, inch by sensual inch. He isn't the man who played with the children in his mountain pool, sunlight and water turning his dark eyes to fire.

It isn't the man who has sprawled next to me in the vast king-sized bed most nights for the past two months, one leg thrown possessively across my body.

I don't know who this Roman is. Only that he's a cold stranger, as remote from me as some two-dimensional character on a screen.

And, just like that, I'm fucking terrified.

"The makeup and hair people will be here in a few hours," he says calmly. "The girls will need your help to get ready. Mickey will be out with me for a while, but he'll be back in time to dress." He's still staring somewhere past me. "I'd appreciate it if you could make sure they all get a good lunch and a decent siesta. It will likely be a late night for them, especially Masha."

"Of course."

What else am I going to say?

"About the paparazzi," I start tentatively.

"Don't worry. I'll make sure you're kept out of camera range." He almost smiles. "I don't imagine Inger will want to share the spotlight anyway." He turns, heading for the door. "The makeup and hair people are here for you, too, not just the children. The car will be outside at seven. I'll come by the apartment five minutes before to collect you all."

"Roman." The name chokes in my throat. His hand pauses on the handle, but he doesn't turn around. "Can we . . . Tonight, after the ball, can we talk?"

His head drops slightly in what could be a nod, but he still doesn't turn. "Yes, Lucia." His voice is strangely thick. "We'll talk tonight. You have my word." He pulls the door open before I can answer and strides through it. The door swings closed, clicking into place with a chilling finality.

I stare at it for long minutes after he's gone.

I grew up around men who issued kill orders. I've seen the way they treat people once that order is given.

It's exactly the same way Roman just treated me.

As if I'm already fucking dead.

I PASS the day in a strange fugue state.

On one level, I go through the motions of getting the kids up, dressed, and fed. I let them all know I'll be attending the ball, which slightly mollifies Masha's indignation at having to attend herself. Mickey leaves early with Dimitry, who, notably, can't seem to meet my eyes. Nor does the increased security detail escape my notice.

They're making sure I don't go anywhere.

Once, a few years ago, I watched some paranormal show where the characters could switch off their humanity. They showed it onscreen as a slow blink. One moment, the feeling, emotional person was present in the eyes.

Then, *blink*, they were gone.

It's exactly the way I feel about running.

The time leading up to the moment of decision might be full of worry, second-guessing, and fear.

But when the time comes to leave, it happens in the blink of an eye.

It's time to blink, Darya.

With a tired, heart-wrenching sense of resignation, I flick the switch in my head and become Darya Petrovsky again.

AFTER LUNCH, when Ofelia and Masha go down for siesta, I call Abby.

"Hey, chica." She sounds exhausted.

"I'm so sorry. Did I wake you? I waited until I thought you'd be up."

"I'm up. It was just a hella busy night. Nikolai had the entire Cádiz FC in here, plus groupies. I had to watch a dozen of them drape themselves all over Miguel. Like I fucking care." She yawns. "I didn't get home until seven this morning, which pissed Dimitry off. I'm not sure he's too keen on me working here now that Nikolai's back."

"I can understand that." I'm surprised Dimitry didn't just knock Miguel flat.

"And you won't believe the skeezy fuck who was drinking with Miguel," she goes on.

"Oh, I'm pretty sure I can. Let me guess—Lance Ryder?"

She's silent for a moment. "Hang on. Did he track you down again, Luce?"

"Yeah." I shake my head. "But it doesn't matter. Hey, Abs, I've got a favor to ask."

"Anything." Abby's yawning insouciance is all gone. "But, Luce. Did you tell Roman about Lance Ryder? You should, if you haven't. I don't trust that fucker. He knows some bad people—"

"We're going to talk about it later." I brush over her question. "Listen. I have something I need to have delivered somewhere, but I'm going to be tied up with the kids all day before this ball, and I don't really want to bother the security guys. Is there any chance I could ask you to come and grab it for me?"

"Um. Yeah. I guess so." Abby sounds concerned. "Is it . . . something dangerous?"

"No, no, nothing like that," I reassure her. "I've just . . . There's a friend of mine who needs something, that's all. Can you do it?"

"Yup. I need a coffee anyhow. How about I come over now?"

"That would be amazing." I end the call, my heart thudding slowly. I know it's risky to involve Abby, but there isn't anyone else I trust.

When she knocks at the door half an hour later, I open it to find her joking with the guards, all of whom she seems to know by name. Her hair is piled up in a messy bun, and big dark sunglasses hide the shadows under her bloodshot eyes until she gets inside and takes them off.

"Wow." I give her a sympathetic look. "You really do look exhausted."

"Yeah, well. The price of a barmaid's life, you know." She gives me a half smile, but there's something lurking behind her eyes, a shadow of something I can't quite read.

"Maybe it's time to slow down a bit? I'm sure Dimitry could help—"

Her smile disappears completely. "Nope. I'm not signing up for gangster help, thanks. No offense." She gives me a slightly apologetic look.

"None taken. Besides." I force myself to smile. "I'm technically the au pair, remember?"

"Vaguely." Abby rolls her eyes, and I laugh along. The truth is, after tonight, I won't even be that. But I keep those feelings locked away inside. Darya knows better than to show anything out of the ordinary.

I need to give Abby the best performance of my life.

I hand her a coffee, proud that my hand doesn't shake at all. "So you know the lockers at the airport, where I used to stash my stuff when I was in between places?"

She watches me as she sips the coffee. "Sure."

"Well, I've got a friend who's in a . . . similar situation as the one I used to be in. As in, he needs to stay under the radar." I've thought this cover story through, trying to find any holes in it. "He needs my help, Abby. But I don't want to tip anyone off, and if I leave here, I'll have half of Roman's security team following me, which will freak him out. I wondered if you could drop a bag into one of the lockers for me, then text me which one, with the code?"

"Um. Yeah." Abby is frowning at me. "I can do that. But, Luce—"

"There's something else," I interrupt her hurriedly. "At Papa's villa. You know that package you got for me? With the books?"

Her frown darkens. "I fucking *knew* that parcel was dodgy."

"It belongs to my friend. And he needs it, Abby. It's—well, without it, he won't get far." I meet her eyes, focusing all my attention on remaining calm. "I know what this looks like. But I had to run once, and I had nobody to help me. My friend needs help even more than I did back then. The people after him won't stop coming."

"Wait." She stares at me, understanding dawning in her eyes. "This friend. He wouldn't happen to be a family member, would he?"

I allow uncertainty to enter my eyes. "I can't say, Abby. Please." I inject my voice with all the sincerity I can muster. "It took a lot of courage for him to reach out, and he trusts me. I can't let him down now just because Papa and I are safe."

Slowly I see the fear recede from Abby's eyes. I feel guilty as hell, allowing her to believe it's my brother I'm helping, and using Papa as my trump card. I've never told her in so many words that I left a younger brother behind, but she's come close to guessing more than once. And she knows I would never run without Papa. Using both of them gives my story credibility.

What she doesn't know is that, this time, I can't take Papa with me.

I hate lying to her.

"If you go now, Papa will be asleep. Take this." I hand her a small bag of Masha's rocks, all colored in decorative paint. "Tell Anna I asked you to plant them in the garden as a surprise for Masha, then go into the bathroom to wash your hands." Quickly I explain to her how to find the package. "Here's what I need you to put in the locker." I give her my old backpack, and Abby's eyes narrow worriedly.

"That's yours, Luce. I've seen you with it a thousand times—"

"And it brought me luck. Now I hope it brings my friend luck." I hold her hand tight. "Please do this for me, Abby. And please don't tell Dimitry. He'll jump to the same conclusion you did, that I'm running."

Her fingers pluck uneasily at the bag. "Are you?"

"My friend needs to be prepared for whatever comes," I say quietly.

That's what Darya Petrovsky learned, a long time ago.

Plan. Prepare. Think everything through a thousand times, then think it through again. Even if you don't end up running, the plan is in place.

I'd like to think there's a chance I won't have to run.

But Darya Petrovsky is literally itching to get on the road. She's replaying Lance Ryder's words, and images of that Borovsky safe.

She's remembering the way Roman couldn't meet her eyes.

She's thinking of kill orders and dead eyes.

Darya is in my head and my gut, telling me I might already have left it too late.

The airport is only ten minutes by taxi from the Russian Cultural Center, where tonight's ball is. A ballroom is a perfect opportunity. There's no better place to disappear than in a crowd.

"Lucia." Abby still has her hand in mine. "Are you certain this is the only option your . . . *friend* . . . has?"

Clearly, attempting to mislead her about who is running hasn't worked.

I just hope she doesn't say anything to Dimitry.

I think of the life growing inside me.

My little Borovsky.

I think of what it will do to the children, not to mention to Roman himself, if he decides to execute me or hand me over to the Orlovs.

It will kill any chance they have of being a family.

I won't have that on my conscience.

This is the best thing, for all of us.

"I don't have a choice, Abby." I blink back tears. "The children . . . I couldn't forgive myself if anything happened to them."

She wraps her arms around my neck, hugging me fiercely. "Then promise me you'll be safe, Luce."

But I can't promise that. It isn't a promise I can keep.

Instead I hug her tightly, trying to silently convey all I can't say.

Abby strokes my hair. "I know, Luce," she whispers in my ear. "I know."

ROMAN

The lab is humming, tech heads rattling away on their keyboards, staring intently at screens. Two of them have been throwing a ball one-handed back and forth for the past hour while simultaneously working with their other hand.

Mickey is hunched forward, his fingers moving lightning fast across the keyboard. Three other tech heads are standing around him, leaning over his shoulder.

"That's it," one of them is urging. "Yep. Yeah. Mick, you're close. Go, go, *go*—yeah!" They all punch the air, then just as quickly, tense again. "Oh."

I watch the drama in total confusion. "What the fuck is going on there, Pavel? Tell me Mickey isn't gaming on Mercura time."

Pavel gives me a look that's as close to contempt as he probably dares. "The trojans change shape when you try to unpick them and track their location. I told you Mickey took the first one apart, traced it back to Andersson in Sweden. Mickey's the fastest of us at decoding them, but Andersson is on the other end of the keyboard, and he's faster. But only just." He nods at the tense shoulders in the next room. "These guys are watching the equivalent of an Olympic race, with Mickey currently in second place."

"There's more at stake here than a fucking gold medal." I'm not in the mood for geek Olympics.

Pavel's eagerness slips a little at my tone. "If Mickey can make sense of the patterns he's finding, or track Andersson himself, we might understand what Andersson is trying to do here."

"Well, Mickey's going to have to pass the baton to the B team." I glance at the time on my phone. "Cinderella has to get ready for the ball, I'm afraid."

He squints at me. "Seriously? This is important, Roman. Er —boss."

That almost makes me smile. "Fine. I've got somewhere to be. I'll come back for him in a couple of hours. But no later." I glare at Pavel, who nods frantically. "When I come back, he needs to be ready to go, done or not."

"Copy that."

Mickey doesn't bother turning his head when I call a good-bye. Luis drove him up here this morning. I know I need to talk to the kid, explain everything about Darya's background, before things go much further.

Another part of me knows that the conversation we need to have isn't likely to end well. Besides, there's a visit I need to make, for which I'd rather not have an audience anyway.

I drive the Maybach down the mountain. It's midafternoon when I pull up in front of the villa. I have a quick word with the security team, which I've doubled, then send Anna home for the rest of the day. Bryce informed me of Abby's visit to

Lucia this morning, and I've been monitoring the villa footage all day. I watched Abby collect the package behind the tile barely half an hour ago.

Despite the decisions I came to last night, I'm not happy.

I'm not fucking happy at all.

I walk slowly up the stairs, the terrace gradually coming into view.

Sergei Petrovsky's wheelchair is by the wall, neatly folded up. He's sitting in a wicker chair in front of a low table with a chess board on it. He has his back to me, long legs stretched out before him. I know his mobility has been increasing.

Going by Abby's little expedition today, I can guess why he's been working at it so fucking hard.

I stand for a moment just staring at his straight, tall back. He blows a stream of smoke in front of him, then turns to the side, his long fingers crushing out the cigarette in a decisive gesture that gives me a cold jolt of recognition.

Suddenly I'm back on the landing, watching the tall visitor talk to my parents in the kitchen.

The long-buried memory blends with current reality like a projector overlay. Any doubt that the man now sitting in my villa is one and the same as the man who once sat in my father's kitchen is gone.

I watch him light another cigarette, cupping the flame with his hands, and wonder how I didn't immediately recognize who he was the first time I saw him.

Sergei Petrovsky, the man who failed both of my parents, is sitting only a few paces from where I stand, nonchalantly smoking as if he has nothing better in the world to do.

"If it is a bullet you wish to give me, you have hesitated too long, my friend." He speaks in Russian. Without looking around, he gestures to the wicker chair on the other side of the chess board. "Please, Roman. Sit."

He might as well be the *pakhan* welcoming one of his *vor*

who's come to pay tribute. I can't help but respect his air of calm.

My gait feels strangely stilted as I cross the terrace. I place a bottle of vodka on the table between us, with two small glasses.

"Ah." Sergei smiles, though his eyes have narrowed. "Graf vodka. Where did you find it? Lucia tells me it isn't sold here in Spain. Then again, she could be lying. She also tells me cigarettes are illegal, and yet." He waves the hand holding a cigarette. "As you see, she lies."

"Yes, she does." I pour us both a glass and push one toward him. "But then, so do you, Sergei, do you not?" I raise my glass. "*Za znakomstvo*, Mr. Petrovsky."

I use the toast for a new acquaintance.

"*Za znakomstvo* —Roman Aleksandervitch." His pale blue eyes watch me shrewdly as he tosses off the glass.

I refill them both. "How long have you known?"

"For certain? Not until now."

"But you suspected."

"Yes, Roman. I suspected." He leans back in his chair, hands folded loosely before him. "So. Ask your questions."

"Ha." It's a mirthless sound. I sit back and fold one leg over the other. "Today is not the day for questions."

"And yet you have not put a bullet in my head." One thumb rubs over the other hand, his eyes fixed on my face. "We do not know what tomorrow holds, Roman. Perhaps you should ask your questions now."

"Only one." I toss off the vodka. "What made you suspect my identity?"

"You have your mother's features, did you know that? No." His eyes dull, the lines suddenly deeper on his face. "You would not remember her, I think." He turns the vodka glass slowly in his hand. "But that is all you have of Rosa. Your eyes—these are Aleksander's. The way you move is his. But those, most of all." He nods at my hand on the vodka glass. "You have your father's hands, Roman," he says quietly. "Aleksander's hands were his greatest treasure. We wrapped them a hundred times over on our journey, to protect them from frostbite. 'Without my hands this is all for nothing, Sergei,' he would tell me. You see this?" He grasps my hand, splaying the fingers wide on the table. "Aleksander always said that people think a man needs slender, nimble hands to create jewelry or work on an intricate lock. The truth is that a man needs strong hands to work metal. I remember watching him in the workshop, his hands over yours, teaching you—"

His voice breaks off, and he looks away. "I saw the earrings you gave Darya," he says softly. "I would recognize Aleksander's work anywhere. But it was the way you fastened them in her ears. So fast, so sure. You—it was like watching Aleksander."

I'm not ready for this. I was sure his answer would just be lies and evasion. Perhaps involve Alexei. Or even Lance Ryder.

But not this. Not memories that cloud my brain and confuse past and present. Raw memories that remind me of who I lost—and of who was responsible for their loss.

"You failed them both." My voice is as harsh as the life Sergei forced me to live. "You promised to get my mother to safety, but you must have failed, because she never came back. You told my parents you'd protect me, but when the Orlovs came and killed my father, you were nowhere to be seen. You failed us all."

"Yes." He meets my eyes squarely. "Yes, I failed you, Roman. And for that you have every right to take my life."

"Then you admit it." I stand abruptly. My body is restless, unable to simply sit, and if I pour more vodka, I won't fucking stop. "You admit you betrayed them. I saw men with the Orlov tattoo drive through your gate, the same day my father died.

That was years before the coup. You were working with them, and you let them kill my father."

"No." Sergei's voice is almost as hard as my own. "I failed you all, that is true. I thought the Orlovs were allies, and I was wrong. It is a failure for which I will never forgive myself. But I never betrayed your parents, Roman. Or you."

"That makes no sense." I glare at him. My eyes fall on my phone, sitting on the chess board. It's five p.m.

I don't have time for this.

I pocket my phone and take a step toward the doors.

"Wait." Sergei grips my arm with surprising strength. His eyes are no longer pale, but a fierce, hawkish blue, filled with a story I'm not sure I want to hear. "There is so much you don't know." He meets my eyes. To his credit, he doesn't flinch at the killing fury in mine. "Kill me after I speak, if you must. But first, you need to know the truth, Roman. Your mother—"

"No." I unpeel his hand and toss it aside, striding for the doors. "Not today, old man. I got what I came for. I only came to make sure you can't fucking leave."

You'll only slow her down.

"Wait!" He's reaching for his wheelchair, but it's too far. He tries futilely to pull himself out of the wicker seat, his head twisting toward me. "Wait, Roman," he gasps, his eyes widening as I start to close the doors. "Your mother. She—"

"No, you old bastard." I slam the doors on him, leaving him mouthing silently behind the glass.

Whatever you've got to say, I'll hear it when I'm damn well ready.

"You SHOULD HAVE LEFT me at the lab." Mickey's voice is hard and tense. "I don't need to go to the damned ball. I've got work to do—"

"And it will have to wait," I say curtly. "Your mother asked that you all attend tonight."

"Since when do you give a shit about what Inger wants?"

"Don't speak about your mother like that." I glance sideways at him. His hands are clenched in tight fists, his face set and pale. "Whatever you're working on isn't anything Pavel and the team can't manage. I know you're incredibly good at this stuff, Mickey, and I admire that. But Mercura isn't your responsibility. Trust me when I say I'll manage this."

"Trust you." His mouth curls. "Sure, Roman."

I wrench the car onto the side of the road and turn to face him. "Right. That's enough. What's going on? You've been giving me side eye for days now. And Dimitry tells me you're worried about Lucia."

"Don't you mean Darya?" Mickey turns hard eyes to me. "I think we're past pretending I don't know who she is, Roman. And, yes, I'm worried about her. You should be, too." His eyes narrow, studying me with a disquieting intensity. "Unless you've been playing her all this time for your own reasons."

"I'd be very careful about what you say next," I say grimly. "You might be family, but that doesn't mean I won't put you on your ass if you piss me off."

"Right." His eyes gleam with a rather dangerous light. I can't help but admire the kid. It takes some balls to face me down. "Because you're the only one who makes the decisions around here, huh? Even if it means using Lucia to get what you want."

"Jesus, Mickey." I'm not sure whether to be exasperated or impressed. "What exactly do you think I'm planning to do?"

"I think you've been planning to use her from the beginning." He doesn't back down at all. "And I think you've been lying to her. Just like you've been lying to us."

"*Lying* to you?" I frown, confused. "About what?"

"About who you are."

My heart temporarily stops, then starts again, with an oddly irregular beat.

"Yeah." Mickey looks at me narrowly. "That made you stop talking, didn't it?"

I run through half a dozen scenarios in my mind, but the only one that makes sense is Sergei Petrovsky.

I'll kill that bastard for talking to the kids.

It's frightening how much I want to hurt that treacherous old prick. Lucky I saw Sergei before this particular discussion, or he'd be bleeding by now.

"Mickey." I clench my fists in my effort to keep my voice even. There's been way too many surprises today. And the side of the road is no place for this conversation. "Whatever you think you know, I doubt it's the full story. Either way, I'm happy to sit down and answer any questions you have tomorrow. But right now, we're already running late, and I've had a hell of a day. The last thing I want is to have a run-in with your mother—"

"Really." His eyebrows arch skeptically. "You haven't minded running into Inger in the past, though, have you? Is that the reason she and Papa split up?"

"*What?*" Now I'm genuinely confused. "Where the hell is all this coming from?"

He studies me closely for a moment, then his eyes cloud over, and he looks away. "Nothing," he mutters. "Forget it."

It clearly isn't nothing. But again, there's no goddamn time for this conversation. "Look," I begin, trying to think how best to head this all off at the pass. "Whatever you think of me right now, Mickey, I would never do anything to hurt Lucia."

Liar.

There's a more than even chance I'm about to send her running for her life. But I don't have time to explain to him why that's a good thing.

"She's part of this family," I say quietly. "And I told you once before: we protect our family."

Even if they betray us.

"Then you're not planning to kill her?" Mickey asks the question so directly I'm almost lost for words.

I stare at him in absolute shock. "Of course I'm not going to kill her!"

What the fuck? I really need to start teaching him how we do and don't operate in this family.

"And you're not going to use her, in any way, that could hurt her?" He's watching every minute shift of expression in my face.

"No!" My patience is running out. "Mickey, look. Tonight we have to attend this ridiculous ball as a family, including Lucia—Darya," I correct myself, when he frowns. "We're attending because doing so means that you kids won't have to spend the entire summer being pushed from nanny to grandparent while Inger works. It's the deal I made with her, a deal that means I can keep you here, safe with me. It's one night, a few hours. Then it will be over, and you and I can go upstairs to my apartment, sit down, and talk this through properly. Will you at least trust me to do that?"

Not that I know what the fuck I'm going to say. This is a Mickey I don't know, and given his clearly exceptional investigative skills, one I might need to treat with a little more respect than I have thus far.

"You need to know that right now I don't actually trust you at all." There's nothing remotely childish about his hard return. Fourteen years old or not, the Mickey talking to me now is no boy. And the glare he's giving me isn't at all unlike those I delivered at his age. "I'll give you tonight. But the minute this ball is over, you and I are talking. And if I don't like the answers I get, Roman, I'm leaving. And I'm taking my sisters with me."

"Jesus Christ, Mickey." I shake my head. "Remind me of this conversation the next time we're training in the ring. It will help me not go soft on you."

I pull the car back onto the road. We drive the rest of the way back down the mountain in a tense, stiff silence.

Tonight is shaping up to be a real fucking treat.

ROMAN

God, she's beautiful.

Lucia is wearing the mulberry silk slip dress I bought for her yesterday. It clings to every curve, the luscious breasts I've loved a thousand times swelling temptingly over the lace neckline, the line of her legs elegant above the strappy stilettos. The lush fall of her hair is swept into a complex chignon behind her head. Her eyes are smoky caverns, lips glistening deep plum. A set of diamond-and-pearl earrings made by my father's hands drip down her neck. I included them in the bag I left on the counter earlier, before my conversation with Sergei.

She's never looked so desirable—or so dangerous.

There's a strange gleam in her eyes, a hard, brilliant edge that seems to absorb the light and throw it back into the apartment. The almond-shaped eyes that have always seemed liquid soft are changed, turned inward, become a mirror for the room instead of a pool in which I can lose myself.

I can't look at her.

"Ofelia, you're stunning." I turn my smile to a safer target. "That dress is perfect."

She returns my smile shyly. "Do you really like it? Luce chose it." She touches her earrings. "These are hers." It takes me a moment to remember where I've seen the earrings before: the first night I took Lucia out to dinner.

The night she signed the contract.

I look at them more closely and choke back a laugh. That night, I dismissed them as cheap knockoffs. Now I wonder how I could have been so blind. Me, who was handling House of Fabergé jewelry before I could walk.

We see what we want to see.

It's one of the first rules of hiding in plain sight; I know that better than anyone. It never occurred to me, back then, that a poverty-stricken waitress would be wearing priceless antiques in her ears.

"They're lovely, *umnyashka*." And they'll make every damned Russian snob in the room sit up and take notice. I couldn't have chosen better myself.

"Mama bought me a different dress." Ofelia gives me a worried look. "She won't be happy I'm not wearing it."

"It's too late for her to make you change."

Which Lucia knows damn well.

I almost grin. "I'll manage Inger, don't worry."

"What 'bout me?" Masha, looking distinctly unimpressed, does an unsteady turn in front me.

"Well, *myshka*, you look beautiful too." Except I hate everything about seeing Masha in a prim, tight-fitting dress, with a rigid sash around her waist and patent leather shoes. I prefer her tearing around in leggings and a T-shirt, covered in dirt.

"Dwess hurt." She scowls. "Luce fix-ed it."

"I'm glad." I bend down and smile at her. "You won't have to wear it for long, sweetheart, I promise."

"We should go." An unsmiling Mickey, looking a decade older than his years in his tux, stalks to the door without looking at me. "Didn't you say Nikolai is already waiting for us in the limo?"

Khuy.

He's not going to make this easy for me.

"Sure." I smile around at the room, my eyes skimming past Lucia's face. "Let's go."

"OFELIA!" Inger settles herself in the limo next to Nikolai and glares at her daughter. "What are you wearing? I thought I told you—" She turns to Lucia, but whatever temper storm she was about to unleash dies in her throat. Her mouth forms a perfect O of shock.

"Well. *You* certainly pulled out all the stops." Inger gives Lucia a look with enough daggers to kill ten men.

The sheer satisfaction I feel at her blatant dismay almost makes up for everything else that is currently going to shit in my world.

Almost.

"It's a pity we couldn't shop together." Lucia smiles coldly. "My dressmaker would have made you something that fit properly."

I bite my lips together to hide my grin. Mickey hastily turns his bark of surprised laughter into a cough. Ofelia is looking at Lucia with something like awe.

Only Nikolai, pressed into the corner opposite mine, doesn't seem amused. "You look stunning, Inger." He scowls around her at Lucia, who simply arches her eyebrows and stares right back at him.

Holy fuck.

I wasn't wrong about her being different tonight. I've never seen Lucia do anything but seek the peace. Tonight is like watching another person. Someone born to this life, who knows exactly how to occupy her place in it.

Because she was born to it, I realize with a discomforting jolt. *And the place she grew up occupying is one Inger can only dream about.*

It's not Lucia Lopez, waitress and au pair, who got into this limo tonight.

It's Darya fucking Petrovsky.

And I've never wanted her more.

Inger, not in the least mollified by Nikolai's compliment, picks an imaginary piece of fluff from her skintight, sequined sheath, which shows far too much of her ample chest. "This is a custom-made Versace."

Darya stares out of the window with supreme disinterest. "Is it."

"Romie." Inger reverts to the petulant whine that sets my teeth on edge. "When we arrive, you and I need to go ahead with the children. Nikolai and Lucia will follow us."

"Leave the arrangements to me, Inger." I give her a look hard enough to make her clamp her lips together sullenly.

We fall into an uncomfortable silence. I try not to look at Darya as the limo speeds through the darkness. She's sitting diagonally opposite me, curled into the door. Masha, next to her, is sitting bolt upright and gripping her hand tightly, sitting as far away from Inger as possible.

Mickey, opposite Darya, is watching her warily, but she avoids his eyes, just as she does mine.

She's staring out of the window as if she's already gone.

I have an almost compulsive urge to lean over and grasp her arm, force her to look at me. I can't shake the strange feeling that the speeding limo is catapulting us all toward some dangerous future, a place I'm not ready to meet yet.

The kids, clearly sensing the tension, sit ramrod straight, all looking anywhere but at their mother. Inger's expression is growing darker by the second.

"Ofelia." Her sharp tone makes me grind my teeth. "You could at least have worn the Gucci earrings I bought for you, instead of those department store knockoffs."

"Those earrings are original pieces from the House of Fabergé, Inger, and they're over a century old." Her confused expression triggers an oddly reckless desire I haven't felt in a long time. "They once belonged to Czar Nicholas's daughter. And they aren't just expensive—they're fucking priceless."

Ofelia gives a horrified little gasp. Darya stiffens but doesn't move, still staring out of the window.

"But you said—" Ofelia begins, frowning at Darya.

"Roman gave them to her." Mickey interrupts his sister before she can complete her sentence, glaring at me. "For your sixteenth birthday, Ofelia, didn't he?"

"Oh." Looking utterly bewildered, Ofelia nods hesitantly. "Yes, he did."

Inger looks between us all, her eyes narrowing spitefully. But all she says is, "Please don't swear around my children, Roman."

My lips curl. I reach for the Scotch bottle and pour myself a glass, then one for Nikolai. "Take this," I growl at him. "You're going to need it."

The limo speeds on into the night.

Luis opens the door and stands aside. I step out and extend my hand to Ofelia, drawing her out with me.

The paparazzi go predictably nuts, bulbs flashing from every direction.

"Roman! Who's your date?"

"She's not my date." I give them the Hale Property CEO fucking smile. "This is my daughter, Ofelia Stevanovsky." Ofelia smiles at me nervously and presses close to my side. I'm aware of Nikolai helping a glowering Inger out just behind me, but I blatantly ignore them both. A moment later, Mickey comes to stand nearby, Darya's arm tucked through his own, Masha still clinging to her hand. The clicking intensifies.

"My son," I say, turning to indicate Mickey. "And my youngest, Masha."

I gently extricate Darya's arm from Mickey's and place her on my other arm. Mickey takes Masha and walks around us to stand beside Ofelia, placing himself protectively on the outside of his sisters.

"And this," I say, drawing Darya forward, "is my date. Miss Lucia Lopez."

I don't wait for their questions, and I completely ignore a furious Inger, who is currently standing two paces behind us. Turning my family toward the red-velvet-covered stairs, I walk them slowly up toward the entrance to the ballroom, cameras tracking every step.

"What are you doing," hisses Darya through gritted teeth. "You promised no paparazzi."

"I changed my mind."

"This is insanity," she mutters.

"Then call me crazy." I turn my little group at the top of the stairs to face the cameras. I keep my CEO smile firmly in place, and despite her glittering eyes and feverish color, Darya gives poised smiles at exactly the right time.

Inger and Nikolai, mounting the stairs with twin expressions of resentment, are entirely ignored by the snapping paps.

I turn us all back around as they get close and put my lips close to Darya's ear. "But I don't think I'm the only one feeling a little reckless tonight, Darya. Am I?"

I hold her eyes just long enough to see the uncertainty creep into hers.

Then we walk through the entrance.

I know what I decided. I know I have to let her run.

But that doesn't mean I'm fucking happy about it. And it sure as hell doesn't mean I'm going to let up, not for one second, until the minute she's actually gone.

DIMITRY FINDS me the minute we're in the door. "You were right." His eyes scan the room grimly. "The *Guapa* is anchored directly offshore, within easy tender distance. Looks like Alexei is planning to make his move."

"Of course he is." I've hit the weird, calm plateau that always takes over before the storm erupts, the place where time slows down and every sense is heightened. The opulent ballroom glitters like the fake replica of a more elegant time that it is. I nod at the passing faces and return greetings, introducing the children while all the time scanning the marble floor and balcony tiers for the faces that don't belong.

Searching for one particular face: a man with a missing eye.

Alexei Petrovsky.

The fucker's here, I'd bet Hale on it.

"Check every damn corner of the place. Including the kitchens."

Dimitry nods and disappears into the crowd.

"Sure." I nod permission to a nervous-faced boy who's just asked Ofelia to dance. I know his grandfather, met the kid more than once at the school events I've attended the past few months. Ofelia gives me a grateful smile and takes his hand, moving onto the dance floor.

"I'm going to ask the waiter for a drink for Masha." Mickey stalks off without waiting for my permission, his sister's hand in his.

Great. So he's still not over whatever this is, then.

Mickey's no sooner gone than Inger's furious face appears in front of mine.

Awesome.

"What the *fuck* was that shit you pulled at the entrance, Roman?"

"Keep your voice down, Inger. You don't want people staring, now do you?" I'm still scanning the room, not looking at either Inger in front of me or Darya beside me. "Nikolai." I rest my eyes briefly on my pain-in-the-ass adopted brother. "Maybe you should get your date a drink."

"*You're* supposed to be my date," says Inger through a clenched-teeth smile. "That was our deal."

"I told you I'd attend the ball with you, Inger." I finally meet her eyes, not even attempting to hide my contempt. "Which I have. But since the paparazzi has photographed you and Nikolai falling out of every Z-list bar in Miami for the past two months, not to mention entwined in varying states of nudity on half a dozen hotel balconies, you'll forgive me for not wanting to play the part of doting family man. Given the very public display you've put on, I think you can rest assured that your trad wife image has already been fucked up beyond all recognition. And if you think I'm going to allow the children to suffer the public humiliation of being associated with your indiscretions, you can fucking think again."

I turn away, leaving Inger mouthing furiously behind me.

Let her be furious.

I've got more important concerns tonight.

I greet Boris Obolensky, the grandfather of the boy Ofelia

is dancing with and one of the wealthier benefactors of the Russian Cultural Center. He and I've done quite a bit of business. He's in his seventies, and his wife, Katerina, is the daughter of an exiled Russian princess. Their grandchildren were all in the Holy Week parade with the kids.

"Boris." I shake his hand. "May I present—" I turn to introduce the couple to Darya, but Katerina is already moving toward Inger, wearing a rather pained smile.

"Hello, dear," she says in heavily accented Spanish, eyeing the sequined Versace with barely disguised distaste. "My daughter tells me you did a wonderful job at the Holy Week parade. The children are very lucky to have a nanny like you."

I find Inger's look of abject horror even more satisfying than I did her outrage when she caught sight of Darya in the limo.

Katerina is still standing with her hand out and a rather haughty look of surprise at Inger's lack of a response when Darya steps between the two.

"Princessa Katerina Petrovna," she says smoothly in Russian. "I'm Lucia, the children's au pair." Katerina's eyes widen as they run over Darya from head to toe. Her face creases into an approving smile as Darya takes her hand and drops a perfectly subtle curtsy. "Your grandson, Matvei Olyavitch, is dancing with Ofelia," Darya goes on, smiling. "It's very sweet of him. She's been practicing for weeks."

"Oh!" Katerina's hand flutters to her mouth. "But you are perfect, *rypka!*" she says in Russian, beaming at Darya. "Now I understand why my daughter said you were such a treasure. Roman, where *have* you been hiding this one?" She taps me playfully on the arm. "Come with me, dear." She casts Inger a dismissive glance. "Do excuse us, won't you?"

Tucking Darya's arm through her own, she steers her toward a group of austere-looking matrons, who are eyeing the milling crowd with extremely critical eyes. I watch long enough to see their faces soften into approving smiles as soon as Darya greets them.

Turning my back firmly on Inger's outrage and Nikolai's sullen resentment, I take Boris by the elbow. "Come and meet my son, Mikhail. He's a bloody genius on computers."

Hopefully flattery will help whatever is bugging the kid.

"Computers!" Boris chuckles. "I can barely operate my iPhone."

I roll my eyes. "Tell me about it. Let's get a Scotch, shall we?"

LUCIA

"But then you must know Irina Ketzinyovna!" One of the matrons pinches my cheek affectionately.

"I do have that honor." I smile at her. "Her granddaughter takes Russian classes with Ofelia."

"Then it is settled." Katerina beams around at the table. "You will come to tea with us next week, Lucia."

I laugh and agree, falling into a discussion with one of the women about what books the girls will be studying in Russian class next term. This entire night has been like walking on a knife edge, with a precipice drop at either side.

Deflect questions about my past.

Evade, rather than lie.

Drop enough hints to reassure the women that I am from their world, but for complicated reasons, can't speak of my own origins.

We're all Russian. Hidden tragedy and family secrets are our lifeblood. To be an enigma, particularly a tragic one, is an intrinsically Russian archetype. Add my entrance on Roman's arm, and I've easily become the most fascinating project the matrons will have for some time.

Or I could be, if I was staying.

That thought sends a prickle of awareness down my spine, the uncanny sense I have whenever Roman is watching me. And he *has* been watching me. Roman's eyes have followed my every move from the moment he laid eyes on me earlier this evening.

I'd be lying if I said I don't enjoy him watching me.

I forgot how devastating he is in a tuxedo. Everything about him, from his dark, dangerous eyes to the hard muscularity beneath the tailor-made suit, makes every other man in the room seem utterly insignificant. They all jostle to shake his hand. Their wives watch him with openly covetous eyes. Even the stately matrons try to flirt with him, and he, in turn, handles them with a suave charm that melts even the frostiest demeanor.

I want to walk across the room and wrap my arms around his neck. I want him to claim me in front of the room, then take me somewhere quiet and fuck me with my dress around my hips.

I want to be his. And I want to mark him as fucking *mine*.

There's something about becoming Darya again that has made me feel like living dangerously. Part of me knows that tonight might be the last time I have this, a taste of the world that was once mine, and which has lately, no matter how briefly, been mine again. From confronting Inger in the limo to embracing my Russian heritage, I've felt more empowered tonight than I have in years. Tonight I don't feel like the beaten, cowed Darya Petrovsky who ran from the Orlovs. Brave as she was, that Darya was also desperate. Even though she'd been raised to the finest of all things, somehow she always shied away from the spotlight, from owning her place and her heritage. By the time the Orlovs beat and scarred me, Darya had almost become resigned to being a victim.

Darya had never been forced to fight for her survival. When the Orlovs came, she had no arsenal with which to fight back.

Darya had been raised to glide elegantly through rooms like this one. But she wasn't equipped to survive the world beyond them. I'll never know who Darya might have grown into, had she stayed in her gilt-and-marble palace forever.

Because instead, Darya had to become Lucia Lopez.

A survivor. Sometimes a warrior. Someone who had to stand up for both herself and her father. I didn't get from Miami to Morocco without learning how to stand my ground under threat or take what I need, instead of waiting patiently for someone to offer it.

But tonight, I feel like something not entirely Darya or Lucia.

Darya knows these rooms, these people. She understands the rules and precisely how to behave.

But Darya would also have quietly absorbed Inger's taunts with a pained smile and diplomatic silence.

Lucia, on the other hand, knows how it feels to be the waitress standing behind the counter, struggling for a share of the tips and the next shift. Lucia knows how to confront a threat from those who would take what is hers. She understands that, sometimes, pretty manners and diplomatic silence aren't enough.

Darya knows how to run.

But Lucia knows how to stand and fight.

Ever since I slipped the mulberry silk dress on tonight, I've felt as if my two personalities have merged. The past few months with Roman have forged me into something new again. A woman who knows her own worth and who isn't afraid to fight for it.

My hand slips to my belly. *Who isn't afraid of anything, if it means taking care of the life inside me.*

"Miss Lopez." A handsome face swims into focus before me. It's the son of one of the women at the table, a slender, well-dressed man in his midthirties. "Can I tempt you to dance?"

"Oh, yes, *rypka*, you must!" Katerina pushes me toward the man, giving me the standard Russian grandmother sales pitch in my ear as she does. Her hissed fact sheet tells me that the man in question is a highly eligible bachelor, has a more than adequate income, and very respectable bedroom skills.

Russian women are nothing if not thorough when it comes to their research.

"So, Lucia." He waltzes me skillfully into the center of the dance floor. "You've created quite the sensation this evening. There's nothing the *dvoryanstvo* like better than seeing old Russia triumph over the new. You're quite the modern Russian fairy tale, Miss Lopez."

"I do my best," I say, laughing as he expertly turns me beneath his arm. "And I imagine that dancing with the fairy tale will do wonders for your standing with the old dragons watching us?"

"You really do know the game." He chuckles.

"Oh, I grew up playing it, believe me." Oddly enough, there's a definite pleasure to be found in exercising those old skills. It's like a professional baseball player going back to slum it in the minors. I have nothing to lose in this room, and thus, ironically, I'm the most celebrated thing in it.

Isn't that always the way?

"Excuse me." Roman's low growl sends a shiver through me. "I'm reclaiming my date."

My dance partner's face falls into respectful lines, and he

drops me like I'm a hot coal, taking a wary step backward. "Of course, Mr. Stevanovsky." He nods courteously in my direction. "Miss Lopez."

"Good lord," I say lightly as Roman's arms close around me and I feel the familiar, delicious thrill race through my veins. "You didn't have to terrify him."

Roman's mouth curls, sending a bolt of lust straight between my thighs. "And you didn't have to seduce him." He puts his mouth close to my ear. "But we both enjoy the game, don't we, Darya?"

I shiver, pressing myself closer to him. His arms tighten about me, his thigh slipping between mine as he guides me across the floor. He moves my body like he owns it, like we're one being. I know that this will be the dance the *principessas* bawdily speculate on during tea tomorrow morning.

"They're watching us," I murmur, feeling him hard against me.

"Let them watch." Roman spins me out and pulls me back in, his hand roaming to the base of my spine. "In fact, let's give them something to really feast on." He dips me low over his arm, running his hand down my throat, between my breasts, and down my abdomen as he pulls me slowly back up. As my head comes up, his lips claim mine, briefly, but enough to let everyone in the room know to whom I belong. My arms slip around his neck, and he pulls my hips into his. "Now," he murmurs, "they're really watching."

He's right. And I don't particularly care.

My lips touch Roman's ear. "I'm sorry for what I said to Inger in the car."

He spins me out and brings me back, grinning darkly. "No, you're not."

"No." I laugh as he half dips me again. "You're right. I'm not."

"She had it coming."

"I wish the kids hadn't seen it."

"They needed to." His smile fades. "She's terrorized them for years. And I've let it happen for too long. She needs to know she can't treat the kids like accessories, and they need to know I've got their back."

I've got their back, I note sadly. *Not we.*

I wrap my arms about his neck and bury my head in his shoulder, savoring the feel of his bulk against me, the muscular heat of him through my thin silk dress. Over his shoulder I can see Ofelia blushing and smiling as a very proud-looking Matvei guides her across the dance floor. Mickey is in a corner by the bar, deep in animated conversation with a business acquaintance of Roman's who builds some kind of computer stuff. Masha is sprawled across Katerina's lap, beaming as the doting group of matrons alternately pinch her cheek and feed her treats, paying her exorbitant compliments in Russian. Seeing me watching her, she gives me a crumb-smeared grin and waves energetically. I wave back, blowing her a kiss over Roman's shoulder, and the matrons all sigh and clap their hands appreciatively.

I catch a glimpse of Inger across the room, staring balefully at us, Nikolai obediently holding her glass as well as his own. She's beckoning to Ofelia, who is pointedly ignoring her, and frowning at Masha, who seems oblivious. Mickey is too absorbed by his conversation to notice her.

I should feel guilty, but I don't. I really don't. I've seen the damage Inger has inflicted on her children. I hope that whatever comes, Roman continues to care for them as he has until now.

"The kids need you," I whisper against his ear. "They love you, Roman. Don't forget that."

"What about you?" He pulls back and stares at me, something dark and fierce in his eyes. "No," he says roughly when I don't immediately answer. "Don't answer that. Come with me for a moment." He leads me off the dance floor without waiting for me to answer, taking me through one of the exits and into a private office that is dark. The door shuts behind us with an audible click, and he turns the lock. Neon light streams through the slatted blinds over the window, falling across a wide leather desk.

"What—"

But Roman's mouth stops my question. He takes my clutch out of my hands, then slips his hands under my ass and me onto the desk, pulling my dress up as he does. His mouth is hard and hungry, and after the long days of separation, his touch fires me like a lit match to a pile of fuel.

He slips fingers between my legs before I have time to object, manipulating me with such mastery I'm whimpering in seconds.

"You're the most beautiful goddamn woman in that room," he growls, his lips and fingers driving me so fast toward orgasm I can barely catch my breath. "And I have to fuck you."

He doesn't need to ask if I'm ready. And I have not even the remotest thought of refusing. When his cock leaps free, I'm already gasping with need.

He fucks me hard and deep, my legs wrapped around his back, his arms holding me from falling back on the desk. In the shifting neon lights his face is dark and set, his eyes boring into mine as he thrusts into me, hitting every place he needs to drive me into insanity.

Part of me wants to make him slow down, to savor this, to try to talk.

Another part of me just wants to take what he is offering. To lose myself in the bliss that binds us when we do this, the place where our bodies meet and there is no need for words or anything else.

He doesn't hold back, doesn't try to tease me. He drives me straight to the orgasm I need, pushing me ruthlessly over the edge, and for once, he doesn't put his hand over my mouth when I scream. He explodes as my first spasm hits, pumping into me with a hot urgency utterly unlike his customary control.

For a long moment we stay there, his arms wrapped around me, my legs holding him inside me. Then gradually he withdraws, handing me the tissue box on the side of the desk, turning away as I clean myself.

His eyes no longer meet mine, and I feel cold unease stealing through me again.

I can't help but feel this was a goodbye fuck.

When I turn around to face him, he tugs my dress down and smooths it with a half smile that I seize like a starving man would food. I twine my fingers with his. "The matrons in there will certainly be talking when they see us walk back in there together, looking like this."

"Every one of them knows you belong to me. Now every man does, too." There's a certain savagery in his voice, an unsmiling menace, that sends another surge of unease through me. He withdraws his hand from mine.

"Roman." I put my hand on his face, trying to make him look at me. "Tonight, after the ball—can we talk?"

His eyes meet mine properly, and for a moment the pain in them takes my breath away. I'm about to ask what's wrong, but a knock at the door interrupts us.

"Lucia!" Ofelia's voice is muffled. "Are you in there? I need you."

Roman hands me my clutch and nods at the door. "Duty calls, Miss Lopez." His sardonic drawl is back, eyes the same glittering mask he's worn all night.

I walk ahead of him to the door, horribly aware that he didn't agree to talking with me after the ball.

"MATVEI'S *SO* NICE!" Ofelia's eyes shine as she leans over the powder room sink, reapplying her lip gloss. "I've never really talked to him that much, you know? But he picks his sister up from the same Russian class I go to, and guess what? He said he's been watching me for ages! He even hangs around sometimes to listen to me practice piano afterward. He said he wanted to ask me out after the Holy Week parade, but he was too nervous. Can you believe that? *He* was too nervous to ask *me* out!"

She shakes her head, beaming, as she washes her hands. There are several private powder rooms adjacent to the restrooms, each fully stocked with all manner of cosmetics. We're taking a breather in this one, which, given my little encounter with Roman, is a welcome chance to fix my makeup and gather myself.

"Of course he was nervous." I tilt her chin up and rest my own on her shoulder, meeting her eyes in the mirror. "I very much doubt he's ever met anyone so elegant, intelligent, and beautiful in his life. Not to mention kind, talented, and caring."

"Oh, Luce." She leans her head against mine. "Not really, but thank you for saying that. You always see the best in me."

"That's because it's all true." I kiss her on the cheek and tuck a stray bit of hair into her coiffure, then fix my own.

I wonder if Ofelia has any idea how stunning she really is. Somehow I suspect that a lifetime of Inger's harsh criticisms have left her with a very skewed perception of her own beauty and gifts. And privately, I imagine that Matvei's reluctance to ask her out has a lot more to do with his fear of Roman than of Ofelia rejecting him.

I make a note to remind Roman to go softly on the boy when he comes asking, then feel a painful clench of my heart when I realize it's unlikely I'll be around long enough to have that conversation.

"Are you okay, Luce?" Ofelia frowns concernedly at me in the mirror. "Is it Inger? Is that why you disappeared with Roman? Did she say something else awful to you?"

"No, no, darling." I hasten to reassure her, trying not to blush. "And I'm sorry about what I said in the limo. I shouldn't have said those things to your mother at all, especially not while you were in the car with us. It was poor behavior on my part."

"No." Her face clouds over. She lowers her head, shaking it slowly. "She deserved it. Inger always does that. Always says horrible things, to me or Mickey. And Nikolai . . ." She looks away, biting her lip.

It's my turn to frown. The children's antipathy toward their uncle hasn't escaped me, particularly tonight, when not one of them so much as kissed him hello. "What is it about Nikolai?" I ask, smoothing her hair back. "Did he do something to you, Ofelia?"

"No. Not to me." She shakes her head again. "I mean, he doesn't like me much, but I don't really care about that. The only person he cares about is Inger. But last summer, when we were on the yacht, he was really weird with Masha. Like, at first, it was kind of sweet—he'd jump in the pool when she had her floaties on and help her swim, or put her on his shoulders when we were onshore in town. But he always had his phone out when she was around. Like, *always*. It was weird. Mickey and I were pretty sure he was trying to film Masha, or take pictures of her. In the end, Mickey confronted him about it." She winces. "It didn't go well. Nikolai completely lost it, and Inger totally blew her top at us both, like how dare we imply such horrible things, blah blah. In the end we came home early."

"Wait." I try not to let my fury and disgust show. "Do you mean what I think you mean, Ofelia? Because if so, that's a very serious allegation—and one Roman should know about."

"Well, that's the thing. Mickey and I were going to tell him. But before we did, Mickey hacked Nikolai's phone to see if we were right. There were photos and videos of Masha on there, but honestly, there was nothing off about them. She was always clothed. Most of the shots were just of her face. And he wasn't sharing them to anyone. We stayed glued to Masha's side for the rest of the holiday, but we never caught him trying to do anything. And Masha didn't seem at all worried about him. She doesn't like him, just like we don't, but that's mainly because he's all over Inger like, *all* the time." She makes a face. "It's gross. *He's* gross." She shoots me a sideways glance. "And did you know they were basically together all summer? It was all over the tabloids."

I hoped she might not have seen those reports.

"You should probably talk to your mother about her private life, not me. But I do think you should tell Roman about Masha." I don't like anything she's just said about that. At all. "He needs to know. Promise me you'll talk to him about it?"

Ofelia pulls a face in the mirror. "Can't you talk to him? He always listens to you." She gives me a rather sly smile. "Especially when you look like you do tonight. He can't take his eyes off you, which is probably why he pulled you into that office."

It's my turn to pull a face. "Ew. Gross."

"No." She gives me a small smile. "Actually, it isn't. Not with you guys." She dries her hands. "Hey. Did you know there's, like, an actual towel guy outside the powder room? Like, he hands you a hot towel from a tray before you go back out to the floor."

"Fancy." I wink at her.

"Soooo fancy." She rolls her eyes. "I'm going back to Matvei. Have fun!" She gives me a little wave. The door closes behind her, leaving me in the powder room, staring at the mirror, my heart thudding.

What the hell is Nikolai playing at? I don't care whether the photographs are innocent or not. There's absolutely no reason for him to be taking pictures of Masha, to be filming her. Something is off. And damn right I'll be talking to Roman about it. Whatever else I'm planning to do, I need to make sure he knows about this first.

I open the door onto the wide, carpeted corridor, and the white-gloved doorman proffers his tray, lifting the silver lid. I'm about to decline when I see the writing on the card sitting on the towels.

Take one. Pretend to wipe your hands.

I look up and then, seeing the eye patch, hastily drop my eyes. Hands shaking, I take one of the towels.

"Alexei?" My voice is barely a whisper.

"You have to run. Right now."

I'm shaking so badly I drop the towel on the floor. I bend down to pick it up, using the moment to try to collect myself. "Is it really you?" I whisper as he bends down beside me, taking the towel from my hands.

"Yes. Stand up, take another towel."

I slowly do as he asks.

"Listen." My brother's voice is low, tense, and full of urgency. "Roman's real name is Roman Borovsky. He's the son of Aleksander Borovsky, and he holds the missing key to the vault."

"*What?*" I barely manage to get the word out. "No—"

"I don't have time to explain. The Orlovs know who he is. They know about his fingerprints being the third set on the lock, and they suspect he has the missing key. And now they have all of you in one place. They're coming for you all. Here, Darya. Tonight."

"Roman won't let them—"

"All it takes is one of the children. Do you understand? The Orlovs will take the children. How long do you think Roman will hold out when they start carving up those kids? How long will *you*? You know what they do to little girls." He grips my hand. "If you're not here, they've got nothing, just like before. You must go *now*, Darya. And forget about taking Papa. They're watching him." He takes an envelope out of his pocket. "I've explained it all in here. There's a ticket inside. Can you get your passport?"

I nod weakly.

"Follow the instructions in the envelope. I'll find you. Trust me, Darya."

Two of Roman's security men begin to approach us. They're staring at Alexei's bent head, frowning as they speak into their earpieces, making a beeline for us. "Go," I whisper to him, slipping the envelope into my clutch. "I'll handle them."

"Promise me," he mutters. For a moment his lone eye meets mine. It's dark, and so full of shadows it makes me want to cry. Worse, his face is lined in white scars, the remnants of torture I can imagine all too well.

But Alexei is still in there. He's still my brother.

And I believe him.

I promise, I mouth silently.

Aloud, I say, "Yes, I know who you mean. She's in the room at the end, just down there." I force myself to smile and laugh. "No, she won't think you're forward. Go on, ask her out." I turn toward the guards, still smiling, as Alexei moves off down the corridor. "So cute. He really likes one of the cocktail waitresses, but he was too scared to ask her out." I let my brow crease in concern. "Is everything okay? You guys look worried."

"Sure, everything's fine." One of the guys gives me a hard look. He nods at the other one, who moves down the corridor after Alexei.

I'm pretty sure he'll be too late. The powder room at the end has an exit onto the fire escape.

I walk back to the ballroom, so unbalanced I feel like I might bounce off the walls on either side.

ROMAN

I *promised myself I'd let her run.*

But that was before I saw her in that damn gown.

Before I felt her hot, silk-clad curves under my hands, and the need to take her one last time took my breath away.

Darya Petrovsky is the star of the ball.

It gave me a savage pride to face the press with her on my arm. To watch her confront Inger and hold her own with the Russian elite. To hold her on the dance floor, knowing that every man in the room wished he was me.

It's a wonder I made it into that office before I ripped her dress off.

Seeing Inger glaring at me, I give her an evil smile. I probably shouldn't take so much satisfaction in knowing that Darya and I were fucking loudly enough to leave Inger in no doubt of what we're doing. To leave *anyone* in any doubt. Then again, it's hardly like anybody in this room can afford to get offended by anything I do.

I own every single one of them, one way or another.

Ofelia comes out of the powder room and heads over to Matvei, smiling shyly. The kid just spent five minutes almost pissing his pants as he stuttered out a request for Ofelia to come to tea with his mother tomorrow. It was a very proper invitation, and despite his red-faced nerves, he looked me in the eye and shook my hand when he asked. I had a moment where I genuinely considered scaring the shit out of him just for the hell of it. I'm clearly losing the killer edge, however. In the end, I just gave my permission and told him to send a car for her at ten.

That means Darya is alone in that powder room.

Telling myself I'm just concerned for her safety, I head across the dance floor, smirking at Inger's thunderous expression as I pass her.

Oh, just wait. The show hasn't even begun yet.

I catch Darya just as she's coming out of the corridor. One look at her face wipes the smile off my own. She's holding her clutch with both hands, so tightly her knuckles are white.

"What happened?" I ask tersely, my eyes traveling all over the corridor.

"Listen, Roman." Her eyes dart away from mine, and her lips are entirely bloodless. "You need to ask Nikolai why he was taking photographs of Masha last summer. Ofelia and Mickey said he was filming her, and when Mickey hacked his phone, there was a stack of photographs and footage of her on there."

"*What?*" Completely blindsided, I stare at her, feeling a slow, deadly rage build inside me. "Nikolai did fucking *what?*"

"You need to know." Darya glances over her shoulder, then around the room. "Roman, I think I need to lie down. I—don't feel very well. I think I've had too much champagne."

"Bullshit." I stare at her narrowly, whatever momentary peace I've found utterly stripped away. "You've been drinking soda water all night."

It's here. I can feel it. In her warning about Nikolai. In her pale face and shaking hands gripping the clutch. That dumb excuse about needing to lie down.

Alexei found her.

And now she wants to run.

And despite all of my logical decision-making, despite knowing that it's safer, for her and for all of us, if she's gone—despite all of those things, I suddenly know I can't bear to let Darya go.

I didn't expect this to happen. To hesitate.

I've been waiting for this moment. Planning for it, even. I have an envelope inside one jacket pocket containing a letter, ticket, passport, and a thick stack of cash. I've known all night that it was going to come to this. With the *Guapa* moored right offshore, Alexei was always going to come for his sister tonight.

It's what I would do.

I thought I could tell her to go. I even planned a speech, which I almost gave to her back in that office. I was pathetically relieved when Ofelia interrupted us. And now that I'm here again, I can't do it. The words are stuck fast in my throat. All I can see is her wide, terrified eyes, the body I still crave beyond all reason, vulnerable beneath that thin layer of silk.

How can she run anywhere, dressed like that?

Every man will want her. Any of them could try to take her against her will.

My fists clench involuntarily. Even the thought of someone putting a hand on that beautiful body makes me physically sick. Imagining her trying to fight someone off, sobbing as she tries to get free, terrifies the absolute hell out of me.

"Darya." I choke on the name as my hand clasps her arm. "Don't do this. Don't run."

"Why not?" Her eyes flare with a sudden, fierce anger. "Why, Roman? Because you can't bear to let me go? Because you would be bereft without me?" She twists from my grasp. I'm so surprised by her anger that I let her.

"Darya—"

"Or is it," she says in a low, furious voice, her face close to mine, "that you don't want me to run because you know that without me, you can't get into my family's vault?"

Cold, brutal shock washes through me, momentarily robbing me of both breath and words.

"All this time, you've talked to me about trust." Her face is deathly pale, with not even the faintest hint of color, her eyes glittering with hard anger. "But when were *you* going to trust *me*, Roman? When were you going to tell me that you're Roman Borovsky?"

The air dances and swirls around me, the noise of the ball suddenly muffled behind a queer, dizzy wall. I stare at Darya, her words reaching me as if from a long distance.

"I saw that Borovsky safe you keep behind a locked door in your penthouse. I told myself it was just a coincidence. But it isn't, is it, Roman?"

I shiver involuntarily. "How—" My voice cracks. "How did you get into that room?"

"*That's* your question? Seriously?" Her laugh is strangled. "You got drunk with Dimitry and left the damned door open, that's how. Your maid wanted to know why the safe inside that room was empty. She was worried you'd think she robbed you. But you don't keep valuables in that safe, do you, Roman? The safe *is* the valuable thing. You keep it locked up in that room because your father made it. Well, I hope it warms your bed after I'm gone." Her chest is heaving, her voice rasping in her throat. I want to interrupt her, to explain, but I'm tongue-tied, my mouth thick and clumsy.

"My mother." Her voice catches. "She died because the Orlovs couldn't get into our vault without your fingerprints, or the key your father hid. They didn't believe us when we said we didn't know where the key was. They *hurt* me, Roman!" Her voice cracks painfully. "They hurt my brother. They're *still* hurting him. My father nearly died. And all that time, you were what?" She flings out an arm toward the ballroom. "In places like this, drinking champagne and planning for the day when you'd find me? When you'd reclaim your legacy? Is that all this has been to you, Roman?"

"No!" I roar, loudly enough to make those closest to us turn around curiously. "Come with me." I take her by the elbow and steer her toward the end powder room, where someone is just coming out. "You need to understand—"

But my words never leave my mouth.

There's an earth-shattering explosion.

I throw myself onto Darya and hit the floor, and then everything turns to darkness.

I WAKE to Darya saying my name, trying to wriggle out from beneath me. "Roman!" She's shaking my shoulders. "Roman, you have to wake up."

I lurch to my feet with her clutch in my hand, my fists balled and knees bent, swaying as I try to regain my senses. I wipe my hand across my face, and it comes away covered in blood.

I turn away from her, trying to breathe, fumbling in my pockets.

She's going to run now. I know that.

I need to get it together.

I slip the envelope containing the passport, ticket, and cash into her purse.

"The children." Darya grasps my arm, reaching for her clutch. I let her take it and turn back to find her anger of a moment ago gone, replaced by white terror. "You have to find the children, Roman. The Orlovs are going to take them—"

"*What?*" I stare at her, first in utter shock, then, as the meaning of her words dawn on me, in disbelief.

A millisecond later, both are eradicated by overwhelming, all-consuming, fucking *fury*.

"You *knew?*" My voice shakes with rage. "You knew the Orlovs were coming for the *children*, and you did nothing?"

The guilty slide of her eyes away from mine is all the confirmation I need.

Darya knew this was coming. She knew, and she simply let those bastards walk in and unleash hell.

Charming everyone was a lie. Fucking me was a lie. Everything she's done from the moment she walked out in that dress tonight has been one big, horrible lie.

And I loved her so much, I fell for it.

I can't deal with this. With her.

I need to find my children. I need to make them safe.

Men are coming toward us through the smoke.

My men.

Warriors who need me to lead them. Who can help me save my children.

Darya backs away from me, her eyes darting this way and that, seeking an escape route. I do nothing to stop her. I look at the torn silk dress I paid for, the clutch held tightly to her belly, and my father's jewels in her ears, and I wonder how the fuck I could ever have been so stupid as to believe in her innocence.

Dimitry puts his mouth against my ear. "Ofelia and Masha are gone. The Orlovs have them both."

White-hot rage races through me, hardening immediately into something far darker. Into the single-minded focus I honed long ago, on the streets.

Into the savage killer the fucking Orlov family made me become.

I take one last look at Darya. "You said once you'd never run again unless I told you to."

She stares at me, white-faced and trembling, and I know she's as guilty as hell.

My lips curl in contempt. "So go on, then, Darya Petrovsky. Run. Run fast.

"Because if any harm has come to my children, I swear I'll hunt you down and fucking kill you myself."

I turn around and walk away from her.

It's time to forget Darya Petrovsky.

My children are gone—and the Orlovs just bought themselves a fucking war.

Lethal Alliance is out now on Amazon.

DARYA
Roman and I are an impossible dream.
Divided by a past we didn't choose, and promises we can't betray.
But now the Orlovs have taken Roman's children. There's nothing he won't do to get them back.
Even if that means killing my brother.
Nothing is what it seems. Nobody can be trusted.
Not even me.

ROMAN
I thought I knew my enemy.

But the darkness is worse than I ever knew. And now it's come for those I love.
Saving them means uncovering the secrets that hold us all hostage.
Secrets bound by blood. By death. And by loyalty and honor.
Secrets that threaten to destroy Darya and I forever.

LETHAL ALLIANCE IS OUT NOW ON AMAZON

LETHAL LEGACY AND LETHAL ALLIANCE
are the first two books in the Lethal Legacy bratva romance series. To get sample chapters and ARC's sign up to my newsletter at www.fehupress.com.

www.ingramcontent.com/pod-product-compliance
Lightning Source LLC
Chambersburg PA
CBHW011922190726
48283CB00009BA/2842